LINCOLNWOOD PUBLIC LIBRARY

P9-CMB-616

Praise for the n

"Skillfully nuanced characterization."
— *Chicago Tribune*

"Heartrending, funny, honest, and true."
— Eloisa James, *New York Times* bestselling author

"Exceptional storytelling." — Fresh Fiction

"Ashley excels at creating multilayered, realistically complex characters." — *Booklist*

"Smart, skilled writing." — *Publishers Weekly*

Titles by Jennifer Ashley

Below Stairs Mysteries

A SOUPÇON OF POISON
(an eBook)

DEATH BELOW STAIRS

Shifters Unbound Novels

PRIDE MATES

PRIMAL BONDS

BODYGUARD

WILD CAT

HARD MATED

MATE CLAIMED

PERFECT MATE
(an eBook)

LONE WOLF
(an eBook)

TIGER MAGIC

FERAL HEAT
(an eBook)

WILD WOLF

BEAR ATTRACTION
(an eBook)

SHIFTER MATES
(anthology)

MATE BOND

LION EYES

BAD WOLF

WILD THINGS

WHITE TIGER

GUARDIAN'S MATE

RED WOLF

The Mackenzies Series

THE MADNESS OF LORD IAN MACKENZIE

LADY ISABELLA'S SCANDALOUS MARRIAGE

THE MANY SINS OF LORD CAMERON

THE DUKE'S PERFECT WIFE

A MACKENZIE FAMILY CHRISTMAS

THE SEDUCTION OF ELLIOT MCBRIDE

THE UNTAMED MACKENZIE
(an eBook)

THE WICKED DEEDS OF DANIEL MACKENZIE

SCANDAL AND THE DUCHESS
(an eBook)

RULES FOR A PROPER GOVERNESS

THE SCANDALOUS MACKENZIES
(anthology)

THE STOLEN MACKENZIE BRIDE

A MACKENZIE CLAN GATHERING
(an eBook)

DEATH
BELOW
STAIRS

Jennifer Ashley

Berkley Prime Crime
New York

BERKLEY PRIME CRIME
Published by Berkley
An imprint of Penguin Random House LLC
375 Hudson Street, New York, New York 10014

Copyright © 2018 by Jennifer Ashley
Excerpt from *Scandal Above Stairs* copyright © 2018 by Jennifer Ashley
Penguin Random House supports copyright. Copyright fuels creativity, encourages diverse voices, promotes free speech, and creates a vibrant culture. Thank you for buying an authorized edition of this book and for complying with copyright laws by not reproducing, scanning, or distributing any part of it in any form without permission. You are supporting writers and allowing Penguin Random House to continue to publish books for every reader.

BERKLEY is a registered trademark and BERKLEY PRIME CRIME and the B colophon are trademarks of Penguin Random House LLC.

Library of Congress Cataloging-in-Publication Data

Names: Ashley, Jennifer, author.
Title: Death below stairs / Jennifer Ashley.
Description: First edition. | New York : Berkeley Prime Crime, 2018. |
Identifiers: LCCN 2017012873 (print) | LCCN 2017018380 (eBook) | ISBN
9780399585524 (eBook) | ISBN 9780399585517 (trade paperback)
Subjects: | GSAFD: Mystery fiction.
Classification: LCC PS3601.S547 (ebook) | LCC PS3601.S547 D43 2018 (print) |
DDC 813/.6—dc23
LC record available at https://lccn.loc.gov/2017012873

First Edition: January 2018

Printed in the United States of America
1 3 5 7 9 10 8 6 4 2

Cover art: *Woman on stairs* by Elisabeth Ansley/Trevillion;
Wallpaper by Reinhold Leitner/Shutterstock
Cover design by Emily Osborne
Book design by Laura K. Corless

This is a work of fiction. Names, characters, places, and incidents either are the product of the author's imagination or are used fictitiously, and any resemblance to actual persons, living or dead, business establishments, events, or locales is entirely coincidental.

1

❦————❦

London, March 1881

I had not been long at my post in Mount Street, Mayfair, when my employer's sister came to some calamity.

I must say I was not shocked that such a thing happened, because when a woman takes on the dress and bad habits of a man, she cannot be surprised at the disapprobation of others when she is found out. Lady Cynthia's difficulties, however, turned out to be only the beginning of a vast tangle and a long, dangerous business.

But I am ahead of myself. I am a cook, one of the finest in London if I do say it, and also one of the youngest to be made head cook in a lavish household. I worked some time in the winter at a house in Richmond, and it was a good position, but the family desired to sell up and move to the Lake District, and I was loath to leave the environs of London for my own rather private reasons.

Back went my name on the books, and the agency at last wrote to my new lodgings in Tottenham Court Road to say they had found a place that might suit. Taking their letter with me, I went along to the house of one Lord Rankin in Mount Street, descending from the omnibus at South Audley Street and walking the rest of the way.

I expected to speak to the housekeeper, but upon arrival, the butler, a tall, handsome specimen who rather preened himself, took me up the stairs to meet the lady of the house in her small study.

She was Lady Rankin, wife of the prodigiously wealthy baron who owned this abode. The baron's wealth came not from the fact that he was an aristocrat, the butler, Mr. Davis, had already confided in me—the estate had been nearly bankrupt when Lord Rankin had inherited it. Rather, Lord Rankin was a deft dabbler in the City and had earned money by wise investment long before the cousin who'd held the title had died, conveniently childless.

When I first beheld Lady Rankin, I was surprised she'd asked for me, because she seemed too frail to hold up her head, let alone conduct an interview with a new cook.

"Mrs. Holloway, ma'am," Mr. Davis said. He ushered me in, bowed, and withdrew.

The study in which I found myself was small and overtly feminine. The walls were covered in yellow moiré; the curtains at the windows were white lace. Framed mirrors and paintings of gardens and picturesque country lanes adorned the walls. A delicate, gilt-legged table from the last century reposed in the middle of the room, with an equally graceful chair behind it. A scroll-backed chaise covered with shawls sat near the desk.

Lady Rankin was in the act of rising from the chaise as we entered, as though she had grown weary waiting for me and retired to it. She moved listlessly to the chair behind her desk, sat upon it, and pulled a paper in front of her with a languid hand.

"Mrs. Holloway?" she asked.

Mr. Davis had just announced me, so there was no doubt who I was, but I nodded. Lady Rankin looked me over. I remained standing in the exact center of the carpet in my second-best frock, a brown wool jacket buttoned to my throat, and my second-best hat of light brown straw perching on my thick coil of dark hair.

Lady Rankin's garment was white, filmy, and high necked, its bodice lined with seed pearls. Her hair was pale gold, her cheeks thin and bloodless. She could hardly be thirty summers, but rather than being childlike, she was ethereal, as though a gust of wind could puff her away.

She glanced at whatever paper was in front of her—presumably a letter from my agency—and then over the desk at me. Her eyes were a very light blue and, in contrast to her angel-like appearance, were rather hard.

"You are very young," she observed. Her voice was light, as thin as her bones.

"I am nearly thirty," I answered stiffly.

When a person thought of a cook, they pictured an older woman who was either a shrew in the kitchen or kindhearted and a bit slow. The truth was that cooks came in all ages, shapes, and temperaments. I happened to be nine and twenty, plump and brown haired, and kind enough, I hoped, but I brooked no nonsense.

"I meant for a cook," Lady Rankin said. "Our last cook was nearly eighty. She is . . . gone. Living with her daughter." She added the last quickly, as though fearing I'd take *gone* to mean to heaven.

I had no idea how Lady Rankin wished me to answer this

information, so I said, "I assure you, my lady, I have been quite well trained."

"Yes." Lady Rankin lifted the letter. The single page seemed too heavy for her, so she let it fall. "The agency sings your praises, as do your references. Well, you will find this an easy place. Charles—Lord Rankin—wishes his supper on the table when he arrives home from the City at eight. Davis will tell you his lordship's favorite dishes. There will be three at table this evening, Lord Rankin, myself, and my . . . sister."

Her thin lip curled the slightest bit as she pronounced this last. I thought nothing of it at the time and only gave her another nod.

Lady Rankin slumped back into her chair as though the speech had taken the last of her strength. She waved a limp hand at me. "Go on, then. Davis and Mrs. Bowen will explain things to you."

I curtsied politely and took my leave. I wondered if I shouldn't summon Lady Rankin's maid to assist her to bed but left the room before I did anything so presumptuous.

The kitchen below was to my liking. It was nowhere near as modern and large as the one I'd left in Richmond, but I found it comfortable and what I was used to.

This house was a double town house—that is, instead of having a staircase hall on one side and all the rooms on the other, it had rooms on both sides of a middle hall. Possibly two houses had been purchased and knocked into one at some time and the second staircase walled off for use by the staff.

Below stairs, we had a large servants' hall, which lay across a passage from the kitchen. In the servants' hall was a long table where the staff could take meals as well as a row of bells that would ring when someone above stairs pulled a cord to summon the servant he or she wished. Along the passage from the kitchen and servants' hall was a larder, and beyond that a laundry room, and then a room for folding clean linens, the housekeeper's parlor, and the butler's pantry, which included the wine cellar. Mr. Davis showed me over each, as proud as though he owned the house himself.

The kitchen was a wide, square room with windows that gave onto the street above. Two dressers full of dishes lined the white-painted walls, and a hanging rack of gleaming copper pans dangled above the stove. A thick-legged table squatted in the middle of the floor, one long enough on which to prepare several dishes at once, with space at the end for an assistant to sit and shell peas or do whatever I needed done.

The kitchen's range was neatly fitted into what had been a large fireplace, the stove high enough that I wouldn't have to stoop or kneel to cook. I'd had to kneel on hard stones at one house—where I hadn't stayed long—and it had taken some time for my knees and back to recover.

Here I could stand and use the hot plates, which were able to accommodate five pots at once, with the fire below behind a thick metal door. The fire could be stoked without disturbing the ovens to either side of it—one oven had racks that could be moved so several things could be baked at the same time, and the other spacious oven could have air pumped though it to aid roasting.

I was pleased with the stove, which was quite new, likely requested by the wealthy lordship who liked his meal served precisely when he arrived home. I could bake bread in one oven while roasting a large joint of meat in the other, with all my pots going above. The greatest challenge to a cook is to have every dish ready and hot at the same time so none come to the table colder than any other. To aid this, a shelf above the stove that ran the length of it could keep finished food in warmth while the rest of the meal was completed.

Beyond the kitchen was a scullery with a door that led to the outside stairs, which ran up to the street. The sink was in the scullery so that dirty water and entrails from fish and fowl could be kept well away from the rest of my food. The larder, a long room lined with shelves and with a flagstone floor, looked well stocked, though I'd determine that for myself. From a cursory glance, I saw bags of flour, jars of barley and other grains, dried herbs hanging from the beams, spices in tinned copper jars with labels on them, and crates of vegetables and fruit pushed back against the coolest walls.

The kitchen itself was fairly dark, as most kitchens were, despite the high windows, so we would have to burn lamps all the time, but otherwise, I was satisfied.

The staff to run this lofty house in Mayfair wasn't as large as I'd expect, but they seemed a diligent lot. I had an assistant, a rather pretty girl of about seventeen who seemed genial enough—she reminded me of myself at that age. Whether her assistance would be useful remained to be seen. Four footmen appeared and disappeared from the servants' hall, as did half a dozen maids.

Mrs. Bowen, the housekeeper, was thin and birdlike, and I did not know her. This surprised me, because when you are in service in London, you come to know those in the great houses, or at least *of* them. However, I'd never heard of Mrs. Bowen, which either meant she'd not been in London long or hadn't long been a housekeeper.

I was disturbed a bit by her very thin figure, because I preferred to work with those who enjoyed eating. Mrs. Bowen looked as though she took no more than a biscuit every day, and then only a digestive. On the other hand, I'd known a spindly man who could eat an entire platter of pork and potatoes followed by a hearty dose of steak and kidney pie and never had to loosen his clothing.

Mr. Davis, whom I soon put down as a friendly old gossip, gave me a book with notes from the last cook on what the master preferred for his dinners. I was pleased to find the dishes uncomplicated but not so dull that any chophouse could have provided them. I could do well here.

I carefully unpacked my knives, including a brand-new, sharp carver, took my apron from my valise, and started right in.

The young assistant, a bit unhappy that I wanted her help immediately, was soon chatting freely with me while she measured out flour and butter for my brioche. She gave her name as Sinead.

She pronounced it *Shin-aide* and gave me a hopeful look. I thought it a beautiful name, conjuring mists over the green Irish land—a place I'd never been—but this was London, and a cook's kitchen was no place for an Irish nymph.

"It's quite lovely," I said as I cut butter into the flour. "But I'm sorry, my girl, we can't be having *Sinead*. People get wrong ideas. You must have a plain English name. What did the last cook call you?"

Sinead let out a sigh, her dreams of romance dashed. "Ellen," she said, resigned. I saw by her expression that she disliked the name immensely.

I studied her dark brown hair, blue eyes, and pale skin in some sympathy. Again, she reminded me of myself—poised on the edge of life and believing wonderful things would happen to her. Alas, I'd found out only too soon the bitter truth. Sinead's prettiness would likely bring her trouble, well I knew, and life was apt to dash her hopes again and again.

"Ellen," I repeated, trying to sound cheerful. "A nice, solid name, but not too dull. Now, then, Ellen, I'll need eggs. Large and whole, nothing cracked."

Sinead gave me a long-suffering curtsy and scuttled for the larder.

"She's got her head in the clouds," Mrs. Bowen said as she passed by the kitchen door. "Last cook took a strap to her." She sounded vastly disapproving of the last cook, which made me begin to warm to Mrs. Bowen.

"Is that why the cook was dismissed?" I already didn't think much of this elderly cook, free with a strap, whoever she was. Sinead's only crime, I could see so far, was having dreams.

"No." Mrs. Bowen's answer was short, clipped. She ducked away before she could tell me anything more interesting.

I continued with my bread. Brioche was a favorite of mine— a bread dough made rich with eggs and butter, subtly sweet. It was a fine accompaniment to any meal but also could be served as pudding in a pinch. A little cinnamon and stiff cream or a berry sauce poured over it was as grand as anything served in a posh hotel.

It was as I began beating the flour and eggs into the milk and sugar that I met Lady Rankin's sister. I heard a loud banging and scrabbling noise from the scullery, as though someone had fallen into it down the stairs. Pans clattered to the floor, and then a personage in a black suit burst through the scullery door into the kitchen, boot heels scraping on the flagstones, and collapsed onto a chair at the kitchen table.

I caught up my bowl of dough before it could be upset, looked at the intruder, and then looked again.

This person wore black trousers; a waistcoat of watered

silk in a dark shade of green, with a shining watch fob dangling from its pocket; a smooth frock coat and loose cravat; a long and rather dusty greatcoat; a pair of thick leather gloves; and boots that poked muddy toes from under the trousers. The low-crowned hat that went with the ensemble had been tossed onto the table.

Above this male attire was the head and face of a woman, a rather pretty woman at that. She'd done her fair hair in a low bun at the base of her neck, slicking it straight back from a fine-boned face. The light color of her hair, her high cheekbones, and light blue, almost colorless eyes were so like Lady Rankin's, that for a moment, I stared, dumbfounded, believing I was seeing my mistress transformed. This lady was a bit older though, with the beginnings of lines about her eyes, and a manner far more robust than Lady Rankin's.

"Oh Lord," the woman announced, throwing her body back in the chair and letting her arms dangle to the floor. "I think I've killed someone."

2

As I stared in alarm at the young woman, she looked up at me, fixed me with a gaze that was as surprised as mine, and demanded, "Who the devil are *you*?"

"I am Mrs. Holloway." I curtsied as best I could with my hands around my dough bowl. "The new cook."

"New? What happened to the last one? Nasty old Mrs. Cowles. Why did they give her the boot?"

Since I had no idea, I could not answer. "Has something happened?"

The lady shoved the chair from the table and banged to her feet, her color rising. "Good God, yes. Where the devil is everyone? What if I've killed him?"

"Killed whom?" I asked, holding on to my patience. I'd already decided that the ladies of this family were prone to drama—one played the delicate creature, the other something from a music hall stage.

"Chap outside. I was driving a rig, a new one, and he jumped out in front of me. Come and see."

I looked at my dough, which could become lumpy if I left it at this stage, but the young lady was genuinely agitated, and the entirety of the staff seemed to have disappeared. I shook out my hands, wiped them with a thick towel, laid the towel over the dough bowl, and nodded at her to lead me to the scene of the problem.

Fog shrouded the street onto which we emerged from the scullery stairs, Lady Cynthia—for that was Lady Rankin's sister's name—insisting we exit the house through the servants' entrance, the way she'd come in.

The fog did nothing to slow the carriages, carts, delivery wagons, small conveyances, and people who scurried about on whatever business took them through Mount Street, which was situated between Grosvenor Square and Berkeley Square. London was always a town on the move. Mud flew as carriage wheels and horses churned it up, droplets becoming dark rain to meld with the fog.

Lady Cynthia led me rapidly through the traffic, ducking and dodging, moving easily in her trousers while I held my skirts out of the dirt and dung on the cobbles and hastened after her. People stared at Lady Cynthia in her odd attire, but no one pointed or said a word—those in the neighborhood were probably used to her.

"There." Lady Cynthia halted at the corner of Park Street, a respectable enough place, one where a cook should not be lurking, and waved her hand in a grand gesture.

A leather-topped four-wheeled phaeton had been halted against the railings of a house on the corner. A burly man held the two horses hitched to the phaeton, trying to keep them calm. Inside the vehicle, a man slumped against the seat—whether dead or alive, I could not tell.

"Him," Lady Cynthia said, jabbing her finger at the figure inside the phaeton. "He popped out of nowhere and ran in front of me. Didn't see the bloody man until he was right under the horses' hooves."

I was already moving toward the phaeton, pressing myself out of the way of carts and carriages rumbling through, lest I end up as the man inside. "Did you summon a doctor?" I asked Lady Cynthia when we reached the phaeton, raising my voice to be heard over the clatter of hooves and wheels.

"Why?" Lady Cynthia gave me a blank stare with her pale eyes. "He's dead."

I opened the phaeton's door to study the man slumped in the seat, and let out a breath of relief—he was quite alive. I'd unfortunately been witness to those brutally and suddenly killed, but one thing I'd observed about the dead was that they did not raise their heads or open eyes to stare at me in bewilderment and pain.

The burly man holding the horses called to Lady Cynthia. "Not dead, m'lady. Just a bit bashed about."

"Good," I said to him. "Send someone for a doctor, if you please. Perhaps, my lady, we should get him into the house."

Lady Cynthia might wear the clothes of a man, but she hesitated in the fluttery way young ladies are taught to adopt these days. Cooks, I am pleased to say, are expected to be a bit more formidable. While several passersby raced away at my command to summon a physician, I had no compunction about climbing into the phaeton and looking the fellow over myself.

He was an ordinary person, the sort one would find driving a cart and making deliveries to Mayfair households, though I saw no van nearby, nothing to say who his employer was. He wore a plain but thick coat and a linen shirt, working trousers, and stout boots. The lack of rents or stains in his clothing told me he was well looked after, perhaps by a wife, or maybe he could afford to hire out his mending. Or perhaps he even took up a needle himself. But the point was he had enough self-respect to present a clean and neat appearance. That meant he had work and was no ruffian of the street.

I touched his hand, finding it warm, and he groaned piteously.

Lady Cynthia, hearing him, looked much relieved and regained some of her vigor. "Yes, inside. Excellent idea, Mrs. . . . Mrs. . . ."

"Holloway," I reminded her.

"Holloway. *You.*" She pointed a long, aristocratic finger at a sturdy youth who'd paused to take in the drama. "Help us carry him into the house. Where have *you* been?" She snapped at a gangly man in knee breeches and heavy boots who came running around the corner. "Take the rig to the mews. *Wait* until we heave this man out of it."

The thin man, who appeared to be a groom—indeed, he would prove to be the head groomsman for Lord Rankin's town stables—climbed onto the box and took the reins, sending Lady Cynthia a dark look. His back quivered as he waited for the youth and the burly man to help me pry the hurt man out of the phaeton.

I looked into the youth's face and nearly hit my head on the phaeton's leather top. "Good heavens," I said. "James!"

James, a lad of about fifteen or so years with dark eyes, a round, rather handsome freckled face, and red-brown hair sticking out from under his cap, shot a grin at me. I hadn't seen him for weeks, and only a few times since I'd taken the post in Richmond. James didn't move much beyond the middle of London, as he made his living doing odd jobs here and there around the metropolis. I'd seen him only when I'd had cause to come into London and our paths happened to cross.

James, with his father, Daniel, had helped me avoid much trouble at the place I'd been before Richmond, and I'd come to count the lad as a friend.

As for his father . . .

I could not decide these days how I regarded his father. Daniel McAdam, a jack-of-all-trades if ever there was one, had been my friend since the day he'd begun deliveries in a household I'd worked in a year or so ago. He was charming, flirtatious, and ever ready with a joke or an encouraging word. He'd helped me in a time of great need last autumn, but then I'd learned more about Daniel than perhaps I'd wanted to. I was still hurt about it, and uncertain.

After James and the burly man worked the injured man from the carriage, I pulled myself upright on the phaeton's step and scanned the street. I have sharp eyes, and I did not have to look far before I saw Daniel.

He was just ducking around a corner up Park Street, glancing behind him as though expecting me to be seeking him. He wore the brown homespun suit he donned when making deliveries to kitchens all over Mayfair and north of Oxford Street and the shapeless gloves that hid his strong hands. I recognized his sharp face, the blue eyes over a well-formed nose, the dark hair he never could tame under his cloth cap.

He saw me. Did he look abashed? No, indeed. Mr. McAdam only sent me a merry look, touched his cap in salute, and disappeared.

I did not know all Daniel McAdam's secrets, and I knew he had many. He'd helped me when none other would, it was true, but at the same time he'd angered and confused me. I was grateful and could admire his resolve, but I refused to let myself fall under his spell. I had even allowed him to kiss me on the lips once or twice, but that had been as far as *that* went.

"Drat the man," I said.

"Ma'am?" the groom asked over his shoulder.

"Never mind." I hopped to the ground, the cobbles hard under my shoes. "When you're done in the stables, come 'round to the kitchen for a strong cup of tea. I have the inkling we will all need one."

A doctor came and looked over the man Lady Cynthia had run down. He'd been put into one of the rooms in the large attic and pronounced to have a broken arm and many bruises. The doctor, who was not at all happy to be called out to look at a mere laborer, sent for a surgeon to set the arm. The surgeon departed when he was finished, after dosing the man with laudanum and giving Mrs. Bowen instructions not to let him move for at least a day.

The man, now able to speak, or at least to mumble, said his name was Timmons and begged us to send word to his wife in their rooms near Euston Station.

At least this is what Mr. Davis related to me. I had scrubbed my hands and returned to my brioche when the hurt man had been carried upstairs. I needed to carry on with my duties if I was to have a meal on the table when the master came home. Lady Rankin had said he returned on the dot of eight and expected to dine right away, and it was after six now. Sinead, though curious, obediently resumed her kitchen duties.

As Sinead and I worked, Mr. Davis told us all about the doctor's arrival and his sour expression when he'd learned he'd come to see to a working-class man, and the fact that this Timmons would have to spend the night. One of the footmen had gone in search of his wife.

By that time, I had shaped my rich bread and was letting it rise in its round fluted pan while I turned to sorting out the vegetables I'd chosen from the larder—plump mushrooms that were fresh smelling, asparagus nice and green, a firm onion, ripe tomatoes.

"Lady Cynthia is beside herself," Mr. Davis said. He sat down at the kitchen table, propping his elbows on it, doing nothing useful. My chopping board was near him, and I thumped the blade menacingly as I cut through the onions Sinead had peeled for me. Mr. Davis took notice. "She's a flibbertigibbet but has a kind heart, does our Lady Cynthia," he went on. "She promised Timmons a sum of money for his trouble—which Lord Rankin will have to furnish, of course. *She* hasn't got any money. That's why she lives here. Sort of a poor relation, but never say so."

"I would not dream of it, Mr. Davis." I held a hothouse tomato to my nose, rewarded by a bright scent, the tomato an excellent color. I longed to bite into it and taste its juices, but I returned it to the board with its fellows and picked over the asparagus. Whoever had chosen the produce had a good eye.

Mr. Davis chuckled. I'd already seen, when he'd led me through the house, that he could be haughty as anything above stairs, but down here in the kitchen, he loosened his coat and his tongue. Mr. Davis's hair was dark though gray at the temples, parted severely in the middle and held in place with pomade. He had a pleasant sort of face, blue eyes, and a thin line of mouth that was usually moving in speech.

"Lady Cynthia and Lady Emily are the Earl of Clifford's daughters," Mr. Davis said, sending me a significant look.

Interesting. I left the vegetables and uncovered the fowl I was to roast. I'd cook potatoes and onions in its juices and throw in the mushrooms at the end, along with the tomatoes for tang. For fish, I had skate waiting to be poached in milk, which I'd finish with parsley and walnuts. Early March could be a difficult time—the winter fruits and vegetables were fading and spring's bounty barely beginning. I enjoyed cooking in spring the most, when everything was fresh and new. Biting into early greens tasted of blue skies and the end of winter's grip.

I had heard of the Earl of Clifford, who was famous for being a bankrupt. The title was an old one, from what I understood, one of those that kings had been bestowing for centuries—reverting to the crown when the particular family line died out but given to another family when that family pleased royalty enough to be so rewarded.

I did not have my finger on every title in Britain, but I had heard that Clifford was the eighth of this earldom, given to a family called Shires. The present Lord Clifford had, in his youth, been renowned for bravery—deeds done in Crimea and that sort of thing. He'd come home to England to race horses, tangle himself in scandals, and have notorious affairs with famous beauties. He'd finally married one of these beauties, proceeded to sire two daughters and a son, and then gambled himself into ruinous debt.

His son and heir, as wild as the father, had died tragically at the young age of twenty, going slightly mad and shooting himself. Lady Clifford, devastated by the death of her favorite child, had gone into a decline. She was still alive, I believe, but living in poor health, shutting herself away on her husband's estate in Hertfordshire.

The daughters, Lady Cynthia and Lady Emily, had debuted and caught the eyes of many a gentlemen, but they'd not fared well, as their father's debts were common knowledge, as were their mother's nerves and their brother's suicide. Lady Emily, the younger, had married Lord Rankin before he was Lord Rankin, when he was but a wealthy gentleman who'd made much in the City. Lord and Lady Clifford must have breathed a sigh of relief when he'd put a ring on Lady Emily's finger.

I had known some of the Clifford story from gossip and newspapers. Now Mr. Davis filled in the gaps as I plunged a tomato into hot water, showing Sinead how this loosened the skin so it could be easily peeled.

"Lady Cynthia was not so fortunate." Mr. Davis stretched out his long legs, making himself as comfortable as possible in the hard wooden chair. "She is the older sister, and so it is a scandal that the younger married and she did not. And, of course, Lady Cynthia has no fortune. She is agreeable enough, but when she found herself in danger of being on the shelf, she chose to become an eccentric."

While I left Sinead to finish peeling, seeding, and chopping the tomatoes, I warmed butter and basted the hen, which was a plump, well-juiced specimen. Lord Rankin, it seemed, spared no expense on his victuals. Happily for me, as a cook's job is made ten times easier with decent ingredients.

"Poor thing," I said, shoving the fowl into the roasting oven and licking melted butter from my thumb. I closed the door and fastened it, and snapped my fingers at the lad whose task it was to keep the stove stoked. He leapt from playing with pebbles in the corner and grabbed a few pieces of wood from the box under the window. He opened the grate and tossed in the wood quickly, but I was alarmed how close his little hands came to the flames. I warned him to be more care-

ful. I'd have to make up the balm I liked of chamomile, lavender, and goose fat for burned fingers if he wasn't.

The boy returned to his game, and I wiped my hands and
looked over Sinead's shoulder as she moved on to tearing lettuce for the salads. I liked to have my greens washed, dried,
and kept chilled well before serving the meal.

"Lady Cynthia took at first to riding horses in breakneck
races," Mr. Davis continued. "Amateur ones of course, on the
estates, racing young men fool enough to take her on. She has
a light touch with a horse, does Lady Cynthia. She rode in
breeches and won most of her gallops, along with the wagers.
When our master married Lady Emily, he put a stop to Lady
Cynthia's riding, but I suppose she enjoyed wearing men's attire so much she didn't want to give it up. Our lordship don't
like it, but he's said that as long as Lady Cynthia stays quiet
and behaves herself she can wear trousers if she likes."

Mrs. Bowen chose that moment to walk into the kitchen.
She sniffed. "Speaking of your betters again, Mr. Davis?"
She studied me getting on with the meal, then with head
held high, departed for the servants' hall, disapproval oozing
from her.

Mr. Davis chuckled. "Mrs. Bowen puts on airs, but most of
what I know about the family I learned from her. She worked
for Lady Clifford before she came here."

I pretended to absorb myself in my cooking, but I was curious. I have a healthy interest in my fellow beings, more than
is good for me, unfortunately.

As Mr. Davis went momentarily silent, my thoughts strayed
again to Daniel. He popped up here and there throughout
London, always where something interesting was happening,
and I wondered why he'd chosen the moment when Lady
Cynthia had run down a cart driver.

"If Lady Cynthia hurt this man for life with her recklessness," I observed, "it could go badly for her."

Mr. Davis shook his head. "Not for the daughter of an earl decorated for bravery and the sister-in-law of one of the wealthiest men in London. Lord Rankin will pay to keep our Lady Cynthia out of the newspapers and out of the courts, you mark my words."

I believed him. Wealthy men could hide an embarrassment to the family, and Lady Cynthia viewed herself as an embarrassment—I had noted that in her eyes. I myself saw no shame in her running about in gentlemen's attire—didn't we enjoy the courageous heroines who dressed as men in plays of the Bard? Cheer for them in the Christmas pantomimes?

I saw no more of Lady Cynthia that evening, or indeed of anyone, as I turned to the business of getting the supper done. Once I gave my attention solely to cooking, 'ware any who stepped in my way.

Sinead proved to be capable if not as well trained as I would have liked, but we got on, and she burst into tears only once. She ceased her sobbing after she cleaned up the salt she had spilled all over the lettuce and helped me pull the roasted fowl out of the oven, bubbling and sizzling, the aroma splendid. I cut off a tiny piece of meat and a speared a square of potato and shared them with her.

Sinead's face changed to rapture. "Oh, ma'am, it's the best I ever tasted."

She exaggerated, I knew, although I suppose her comment was a testament to the previous cook's abilities. I thought the fowl's taste could have been richer, but I would not be ashamed to serve this dish.

Mr. Davis and the footmen were already in the dining room above. I rounded up the maids to help me load a tureen of steaming asparagus soup into the lift, followed by the lightly poached skate, and then when it was time, the covered plate of the carved fowl with roasted vegetables and the greens. I hadn't had time to fix more than the brioche for pudding, and so I sent up fruit with a bite of cheese alongside the rich bread.

It was my habit never to rest until I heard from the dining room that all was well. Tonight, I heard nothing, not a word of praise—but not a word of complaint either. The majority of the plates returned scraped clean, although one of the three in each course was always only lightly touched.

Such a shame to waste good food. I shook my head over it and told the kitchen maids to pack away the uneaten portions to give to the beggars.

I'd learned long ago that not every person on earth appreciates good food—some don't even know how to taste it. Instead of growing incensed as I'd done when I'd begun, I now felt sorry for that person and distributed the food to the cold and hungry who better deserved it.

"Who is the faint appetite?" I asked Mr. Davis when he, Mrs. Bowen, and I at last took our supper in the housekeeper's parlor, with Sinead to wait on us.

"Tonight, Lady Cynthia," Mr. Davis said between shoveling in bites of the pieces of roasted hen and potatoes I'd held back for us. "She is still most upset about the accident. She even wore a frock to dinner."

Apparently, this was significant. Mrs. Bowen and Sinead gave Mr. Davis amazed looks.

One of the footmen—I thought his name was Paul—tapped hesitantly on the door of Mrs. Bowen's parlor and entered when invited.

"I beg your pardon, ma'am," he said nervously. "But his

lordship is asking for his evening cup of coffee." He swallowed, his young face rather spotty, his Adam's apple prominent. He darted Mrs. Bowen a worried look. "He's asking for Sinead—I mean Ellen—to deliver it."

An awful hush descended over the room. I was struck by the paling faces of Mrs. Bowen and Mr. Davis and the unhappiness in the footman's eyes, but mostly by the look of dread that came over Sinead.

She set down the teapot she'd lifted to refill Mrs. Bowen's cup and turned to that lady pleadingly, distress in every line of her body.

Mrs. Bowen gave her a sorrowful nod. "You'd best be going on up, girl."

Sinead's eyes filled with tears, every bit of cheerfulness dying. She wiped her hands on her apron, curtsied, and said, "Yes, ma'am," before she made for the door.

She found me blocking her way out. "Why?" I asked the room, not excluding the footman. "What is the matter with Ellen taking the master his coffee? Mrs. Bowen, Mr. Davis, you tell me this minute."

Mr. Davis and Mrs. Bowen exchanged a long glance. Sinead would not look at me, her cheeks stark white and blotched with red.

It was Mrs. Bowen who answered. "I am afraid that his lordship occasionally believes in the idea of . . . I suppose we could call it droit du seigneur. Not often, fortunately."

"Fortunately?" The word snapped out of me, my anger, which had touched me when I'd seen Daniel in the street, finally finding a vent.

I was well aware that a hazard for young women in service, no matter how grand the household, was that the master, and sometimes his guests, saw no reason not to help themselves to a maid, or a cook's assistant, or, indeed, even a cook, when they fancied her. The young woman in question was powerless—all she could do was either give in or find herself another place. If she fled the house without reference, gaining new employment could be difficult. If she gave in to the master's lusts, she risked being cast out with a stain on her character. If her own family would not let her come home or if she had no family, she had no choice but to take to the streets.

I had learned as a very young cook's assistant to keep myself buried in the kitchen and rarely cross paths with the gentlemen of the household. As cooks seldom went above stairs, I had been able to keep out of sight. My ruin had been entirely my own fault and nothing to do with any house in which I'd worked.

"It does not happen often, does it?" I asked testily.

I was pleased that at least Mr. Davis and Mrs. Bowen looked ashamed, Mrs. Bowen bordering on wretched. "Only when his lordship has been made unhappy," Mr. Davis said.

And he'd been made unhappy today by Lady Cynthia running down a man in the street, a story everyone in Mayfair likely knew by now. "Good heavens—why on earth do you stay here?" I demanded of all present. "There are masters respectable enough in other houses, and wives who will not put up with that sort of thing."

Mr. Davis regarded me in some surprise. "We stay because it's a good place. His lordship is generous to the staff. Always has been."

"I see. And sending a young woman as sacrifice every once in a while is a small price to pay?" My mounting anger made my blood fire in my veins. "Well, I will not have it. Not in my kitchen."

"Mrs. Holloway, I understand your unhappiness," Mrs.

Bowen said. "I share it. But what can we do? I try to keep the maids occupied away from his lordship, but it is not *my* house. Her ladyship ought to keep him under her eye, but she cannot."

I full well knew Mrs. Bowen was right. Some gentlemen are high-handed enough to believe *everything* they do is justified. Those who have power and wealth behind them are only encouraged in their prideful thinking. The frail Lady Rankin likely knew what her husband got up to but hadn't the strength to confront him about it.

My heart sank at the thought of having to look for another place when I'd only just found this one. The kitchen was well stocked, the house efficiently run, and the street near to an omnibus that would take me easily to the place in London where my heart was. Why, oh why, did Lord Rankin and his base needs have to ruin a perfectly good situation?

My fury made me reckless. "I won't have it," I repeated. "Ellen, sit down and calm yourself. *I* will take the master his coffee."

3

They tried to stop me. I'd expected they would. I knew Mrs. Bowen, Mr. Davis, and the rest of the staff feared I'd stride into Lord Rankin's private rooms and punch him in the nose like a champion boxer, or perhaps pour the steaming coffee into his lap.

I intended to do no such thing. I returned to the kitchen, prepared a tray with a porcelain cup, saucer, and coffeepot, arranged sugar and cream on the tray, and added a tiny, elegant spoon and a plate of cream biscuits I'd found in the larder.

I smoothed my hair, put on a fresh cap and apron, took the heavy tray in my own hands, and marched upstairs.

The entirety of the servants gathered at the bottom of the back stairs to watch me go, their eyes wide. The nervous footman Paul, who'd been sent to fetch Sinead, ran ahead of me and opened the door at the top of the stairs, and then took me to the master's study on the second floor above the ground floor, in the back of the house.

Paul explained in a whisper that the study had a connecting door on one side that led to his lordship's bedroom and a door on the other side to his wife's bedchamber. I observed tartly that he must worry about getting them mixed up. Paul nearly choked on a laugh, and then he fled me, rushing back downstairs as though fearing he'd be blamed for my boldness.

I set the tray, which was growing heavy, on a table in the hall outside Lord Rankin's study and knocked on the door. When I heard the master say an abrupt, "Come," I opened the door, lifted the tray, carried it inside, and set it on an empty table in the middle of the room.

Lord Rankin rose from behind a desk. He wasn't very tall—he had perhaps an inch or so on me—but he was imposing. He had a commanding air that was focused on all in his path, which made one forget his height not many seconds after he fixed you with his stare. I imagined the gentlemen of both the Stock Exchange and the House of Lords quaked in their boots when he stood up to speak.

Lord Rankin's build was trim but not thin, that of a man who prided himself on not being slovenly but who would not disdain a good meal. He had all his hair, which was very black, and sharp brown eyes that appeared to rapidly assess all he beheld.

Those all-seeing eyes rested on me as I closed the door and returned to the coffee. I did not fancy being shut in with this man, but I did not want to distress his wife or Lady Cynthia in case my voice carried down the hall, nor did I want the staff to creep up here behind me to listen.

"Who the devil are *you*?" Lord Rankin began his acquaintance with me by stating. "I sent for Ellen."

"Ellen is very busy," I said. "Cooks' assistants have much to do, and I could hardly spare her. I am Mrs. Holloway, your cook. As I was the only person finished with her duties, I took it upon myself to carry up your coffee."

Lord Rankin continued to drill his steely stare into me, his seeming calm like a layer of ice on an otherwise roiling lake. He looked me up and down, taking in my dark hair that was coming unraveled and the cuffs of my frock stained from cooking. I hadn't had time to change more than my apron, and my attempt to look morally superior was having no impression on him.

"Mrs. Holloway," Lord Rankin said coolly. "Please fetch a second cup from the cupboard behind you."

Not at all what I expected him to say. I started visibly, and his expression grew sour. "At once, if you please," he snapped.

Good heavens, did he mean for *me* to take the coffee with him? Before I could explain that oh no, sir, I was a servant and didn't have meals or even coffee with the master of the house, he came around the desk, took me by the elbows, and bodily turned me in the direction of the cupboard.

It was then that I saw the second man. He wore a gentleman's suit and stood by the window, gazing out into the darkness, his back to me.

I had no more than a glimpse before Lord Rankin gave me a little shove in the small of my back, sending me stumbling toward the cupboard. I bit back a cutting reply, yanked open the gilt and glass doors of said cupboard, and extracted a cup and saucer from the coffee and tea set there.

I closed the door, resisting the urge to slam it—my employer's rudeness wasn't the door's fault. In the reflection of its glass, I saw that the master's guest had turned from the window, every line of him taut with anger.

I nearly dropped the crockery. The gentleman at the window was Daniel McAdam.

A far cry from the roughly dressed man I'd seen on the street, he wore a black broadcloth coat that fitted over his shoulders with a smoothness that spoke of expense. His charcoal gray waistcoat complemented his coat, and a discreet watch chain led to a narrow pocket—nothing flashy or showy for Mr. McAdam. His hair had been brushed back from his forehead and tamed flat, which was one reason I hadn't recognized him at once. Daniel's unruly dark hair was usually a tangle rumpled by wind and work.

He appeared to be, in sum, a highly respectable gentleman of the City. He even had the haughty stance of a man who dealt with other people's money all day long while making a hefty profit for himself at the same time.

Though I fumbled with the cup and saucer and my face must have been brilliant red, Daniel made no indication, neither with expression nor twitch of his face, that he knew me at all. He remained motionless, unflappable, simply watching while one of Lord Rankin's staff got above herself.

I knew, however, that Daniel hadn't needed to turn from the window. He could have kept himself hidden from me, and I'd never have been the wiser. But his eyes bore a deep sparkle of rage—not at me, but at Lord Rankin. He'd turned around because Lord Rankin had pushed me.

I longed to give Daniel a nod to let him know I was all right—the likes of Lord Rankin did not frighten me—but I didn't dare. Whatever game Daniel was playing, he'd not thank me for blundering in and spoiling it.

I managed to carry the cup and its saucer to the table, deposit it, curtsy, and wait to be dismissed.

Lord Rankin waved his hand. "Go. I am not to be disturbed the remainder of the night. Tell Davis."

I curtsied again, suddenly the most respectful servant alive. "Yes, my lord."

I swung around, resisting the urge to glance at Daniel again, and scuttled out of the room. I made it onto the landing and hung on to the banisters to catch my breath.

But my ordeal was not over. Lord Rankin came out behind me and seized me by the elbow. I cut off my yelp of surprise, not wanting Lady Rankin or Lady Cynthia to hear and rush out to discover Lord Rankin in a half embrace with me.

"Say nothing at all about my guest," Lord Rankin said rapidly into my ear. "Not a word to any of the staff, or my wife, or anyone in this household. Do you understand?"

He punctuated his question with shakes of my arm. Because Lord Rankin, as I said, was not much taller than me, I could look into his eyes, close to my own. I saw in them vast rage and also terrible fear. The fear surprised me. What on earth could worry him so?

I was not to find out tonight. Lord Rankin shoved me toward the top step and so abruptly released me that I nearly toppled down the stairs. I caught myself on the newel post, took one step down, and turned back.

"I would never betray a confidence," I told him coldly. "Good night, my lord."

I turned and walked down the stairs with all the dignity I could find in myself. I felt Lord Rankin watching me go, but when I reached the bottom of that flight and glanced up again, he had gone.

The staff, of course, surrounded me when I returned to the kitchen, demanding to know what had happened.

"Nothing at all," I said, trying to keep the nervousness

from my voice. I took off my clean apron and hung it on a peg, fresh for tomorrow. "I left the coffee things for his lordship, and he dismissed me."

The maids, footmen, and Mr. Davis drew back, disappointed, as did Mrs. Bowen, though she feigned to be uninterested. I would say no more, but folded my lips and finished what I would need to before I retired for the night.

Going about my usual routine did not calm my mind as much as I would have liked. Seeing Daniel in Lord Rankin's study had given me quite a shock. Knowing Daniel even now was a few floors above made my nerves jump and my atrocious curiosity flare.

This was not the first time I'd seen Daniel in a gentleman's guise. I'd only known him before that as a cheerful delivery-man bustling about London, with a ready smile for everyone he encountered, until one evening last autumn when I'd spied him, unbeknownst to him, in Oxford Street. Daniel had been dressed in an elegant suit, similar to the one he wore tonight, and had been handing an equally elegant lady into a carriage. He'd only half explained the deceit when I taxed him with it, telling me he'd been watching people who needed to be watched.

Whether he was one of the police, a detective in plain clothes, perhaps, I had no idea. I did not think so, because Daniel came and went as he pleased and never spoke of reporting to anyone above him—not that I imagined he'd impart such information to me. He seemed to switch his personas at will, following no pattern, appearing and disappearing with no warning.

I knew that letting a man like Daniel into my life, more than I already had, would be the height of foolishness. I was still angry with him for his deception, not that my disapprobation had dampened his enthusiasm or his smiles. His smiles made him all the more dangerous.

I thought of the fear in Lord Rankin's eyes, and wondered what had made Daniel come to him. Was Lord Rankin a man who needed watching? Or was he afraid of something and had asked for Daniel's help? I had no idea, which frustrated me greatly.

At least my activities in the kitchen, done with briskness and a stern countenance, kept the others from questioning me. I performed the same tasks I did in every house, the continuity of them giving me a sense of command of my world. I measured a small quantity of yeast into a bowl, put in a splash of milk and sugar to proof it, then made notes about the dinner I'd prepared tonight in my little notebook in case I wanted to put together the same or similar dishes again. My hand trembled more than necessary, my penciled lines wobbling.

Once I finished writing, I added flour to the yeast and mixed up a fat dough, which I set in a cool place in the larder to rise for tomorrow's bread.

I was undisturbed in all this. The other servants—aside from the scullery maid who, oblivious and singing, washed crockery at the sink in the next room—moved hurriedly past the kitchen if they neared it at all and let me be.

Only Mr. Davis did not fear to put his head in. "You might have got us all the sack," he said, his eyes sparkling. "But good for you, Mrs. H. He needed his comeuppance."

Before I could reply, he disappeared, but his praise comforted me somewhat. At least someone believed I had done right.

When I put out the lamps, lit a candle in a chamber stick, and headed for the back stairs, all the others, including the scullery maid, had already gone up, the hall dark and quiet. I drew a breath of relief as I walked through the echoing passage, the flagstones solid under my feet.

"Mrs. Holloway."

I stifled a shriek and swung around to see Sinead emerging from the linen room. She looked somewhat downcast but not sorry she'd nearly frightened the life out of me.

"Good heavens, girl, what are you still doing down here?" I demanded.

"Mrs. Bowen set me to folding the linens," she said, then she went pink and flicked her gaze from mine. "Thank you, ma'am, for what you did. It was brave of you."

I swallowed and tried to find my breath. "Not at all." My action had been foolish and presumptuous, but I had no regrets, even if the encounter had not turned out as I'd imagined. I cleared my throat and spoke as staunchly as I could. "You'll not have to worry about that while I am here, my dear."

Sinead did look worried, and I softened my brisk tone. "You remind me of myself, when I was cook's assistant." I put a gentle hand on her arm. "Don't worry. I'll look after you and see you're trained proper. You'll be able to have any post you ask for once I'm finished with you."

Sinead dissolved into a smile. With her dark brown hair and large blue eyes, she really was a very pretty girl. She reminded me as well of another young lady who was very close to my heart.

"That sounds ever so nice." Sinead beamed at me and then curtsied. "Good night, ma'am. I'll try my best for ye."

I started off again, but she made no move to follow me. "Are you not coming up?" I asked.

Sinead gestured into the room behind her. "Have to finish here, or Mrs. Bowen will scold something awful."

"Well, don't be too long about it," I said. "There will be plenty to do tomorrow."

"Not to worry, Mrs. Holloway," Sinead said. "I won't be a tick. Good night."

"Good night," I said, feeling better, and I left her. I should have offered to help her, I knew, but I was bone weary and still bewildered by my encounter in Lord Rankin's study.

Sinead said another cheerful good night and skimmed into the linen room. I started up the back stairs, and then up, up, up, through the house to the servants' quarters in the quiet attic.

My heart was pounding by the time I reached my bedchamber and not only from the arduous climb from the very bottom of the house to its top. Now that I was not focusing on my duties, troubled thoughts flooded me. Daniel had been so different in manner and dress tonight from the man I usually knew that I could have passed him in the street and not been aware.

No, that was nonsense. I would always recognize Daniel.

Lord Rankin had certainly been furtive about his visit—he'd been very angry that I'd come with the coffee and not Sinead.

Perhaps he'd sent for Sinead because she'd be so relieved that Lord Rankin had truly wanted only coffee that she'd likely not pay any attention to the second gentleman in the room. Daniel would have remained looking out the window, and the most Sinead would have been able to say was that Lord Rankin had a visitor. Lord Rankin had not worried about me knowing another man was there until Daniel had turned around and showed me his face.

Or, had Daniel come here because of *me*? In the post I'd

taken before I'd gone to Richmond, Daniel had watched that house to ensure that I was well, or so he'd said. Perhaps he'd come here to find out what sort of employer I'd found myself with this time.

No, I was not vain enough to believe that everything Daniel did involved me. He'd visited me several times while I'd been a cook at Richmond, but he'd respected my impatience with him and did not press his attentions. He'd stayed in London most of that time, showing no interest at all in the inhabitants of the Richmond house that I knew of.

I set down the chamber stick and by its feeble light shakily unbuttoned my frock, made myself clean its cuffs, and hung the dress and my petticoats up on their peg. In my corset and chemise, I washed myself, studying my startled pink face in the mirror as I raised it from the basin. My hair hung in dark tendrils around my cheeks, and my blue eyes were fixed.

I was still shaky as I finished undressing, slid into my nightgown, climbed into bed, and pinched out the candle, the spark stinging my fingers. I had to wonder whether Daniel was still in the house with Lord Rankin. Or had he gone, lingering to look up at the windows and wonder which was mine?

Again, nonsense. Daniel would never be so romantic, and besides, one could not see the windows of the top story of this house from the street.

I huffed and settled myself, forcibly burying my agitation. Daniel must certainly cease popping up in front of me in different guises when I was unprepared for it, or he'd give me apoplexy. I would have to scold him long and loud when I saw him again.

* * *

A cook's day begins very early, and I was up and back downstairs well before sunrise. I wore a clean frock, my face and hands scrubbed, my cap pinned over the braided coil of my hair.

I walked briskly into the kitchen as the lad who tended the fires was stirring the flames to life in my stove. This house was efficiently run by the dragon Mrs. Bowen, and so the lad had already blacked the stove and raked out the ashes and disposed of them. All I had to do was fill a kettle and put it on a ring on top of the stove as soon as the boy had the fire going strong.

I went to retrieve the bowl of dough I'd put in the larder before retiring, intending to set it on the table in the warm kitchen for its final rise.

While Mrs. Beeton might advocate purchasing bread at a bakery or even from a bread-baking factory to save oneself work, I believe nothing is better than home baked. When bread is made en masse in a vat then divided up and sold all over the city, who knows what chemicals might have infiltrated it, or what vermin had taken up home in it? I believed, as did the cook who'd trained me, that fresh-baked bread every day is the key to good health and good spirits. I was never afraid to bite into a piece of bread I'd wrought with my two hands.

I entered the larder, which was cool and dark to keep food from spoiling. I reached for the bowl I'd covered with a plate—better than a cloth, because if the plate were moved or broken, I'd know that mice had been there to have a go.

I clasped the bowl between my hands, turned, and made for the door of the dim room. I hadn't gone two steps when I tripped over something on the floor.

I glanced down, saw a foot in a black worsted stocking and stiff-laced shoe sticking out from the corner beyond the cupboard in which my dough had rested. The light was faint, but I could follow the shoe and stocking to a petticoat and a gray broadcloth skirt. The owner of the skirt was too far into the dark corner for me to see, but she was unmoving. I took a step toward her, crouching down to peer into the shadows.

What I saw made me rise and back away hastily, my breath coming in broken gasps. I stood transfixed, odd sensations pouring over me, while I clutched my bowl of dough and tried to continue breathing.

I'd read nonsensical tales in popular magazines in which maids, when stumbling upon an inert member of mankind, dropped entire trays full of the household's best porcelain. I'd always considered the maids in these stories to be fools—a dead body is no reason to destroy so much crockery.

But as I looked down at the young woman whose face had been rendered a bloody pulp, I felt my fingers going numb and the bowl of dough in danger of sliding out of my hands.

Quickly I set the bowl on a table then returned to poor Sinead and knelt beside her. For indeed, it was Sinead, my young assistant who'd bade me a cheery good night only hours ago. Though I could not see her face, I recognized her work dress, starched apron, and sturdy but work-roughened hands. Her cap lay beside her on the floor, and blood soaked the cap, her white collar, every bit of her hair, and what was left of her face.

My throat worked in horror, but I put a hand on hers. "Oh, my poor dear Sinead," I whispered, deciding that, in death, she deserved to have the name she longed for. "Oh, my dear. I should have been looking after you. Forgive me." And tears overcame me.

4

I am not certain how long I knelt in the dark of the larder, holding the hand of the young woman whose only fault had been to want to be called by the name she wished. My heart burned in pity and then rage, both at whoever had hurt this harmless, helpless girl, and at myself. I'd stood next to her only the night before and vowed that I'd look after her, guide her. Then I'd gone upstairs, too tired to carry out my promise. I'd failed her before I'd even begun.

Time meant nothing as I stroked her hand, my anger and grief swelling my chest and making breathing a chore. My fingers were all pins and needles, but I didn't want to let go of Sinead's hand. I felt an obligation to comfort her in death, to care about a young woman I barely knew, as I hadn't had time to in her life.

Gradually my senses returned to me, and I realized things had to happen. Mr. Davis and Mrs. Bowen might come looking for me here upon finding an empty kitchen, or the footmen or maids would blunder in, and there would be alarm and chaos.

The police would have to be summoned. Sinead had obviously been attacked. At the angle in which she lay—on her back, arms at her sides—she could not have simply tripped and hit her head in falling. No blood on the edges of tables and the large dresser next to her confirmed this, plus there was not much blood on the flagstones, though I could not see well in the dim room. Someone had hit her and then dragged her into the corner, as though trying to hide his crime. Whether the culprit meant to kill her or not was hardly the issue.

The thought of some thick-fingered constable touching her, or a sergeant declaring she'd probably fought with her lover and paid the price, made me shudder, but I knew there was nothing for it. Her death would have to be investigated.

My blood cold, I stepped from larder to the linen room, snatched up a tablecloth, and returned to lay it reverently over Sinead's body.

I remembered her telling me she must finish folding things for Mrs. Bowen before she went to bed. Even now, the linen room was neat and tidy—presumably Sinead had completed her task. Or had Sinead been using it as an excuse to linger, to see this lover the police would suspect in secret? Had they met here below stairs when everyone in the house was abed?

Fury at the man who'd killed her worked its way through my shock. I thought it must be a man by the way her face had been beaten. A woman's face could be bruised and bloodied by the man who swore on his life to be in love with her—I knew this because it had happened to me, before my so-called husband had disappeared and gone to his grave.

There was one person I wanted to have come and look at

this crime, who would know what to do better than most. The trouble was, finding the bloody man would be a daunting task.

Before I left the larder again I looked it over in case the culprit had left any hint of his identity, but I found nothing. Sinead's hand when I'd held it had been cold. The larder itself was cool, but if she had been killed this morning, she'd have still been warm. I'd helped lay out enough of the deceased— my own mother included—to know this.

I concluded that she'd died somewhere in the middle of the night, probably shortly after I'd left her to go to bed, which renewed my unhappiness at myself. I would be repeating *If only I'd stayed; if only I'd ordered her to come upstairs with me* for the rest of my life. The killer had likely fled to one of the far corners of London by now, perhaps even leapt on a train and was now on the Continent, out of our reach.

I straightened the tablecloth I'd draped over Sinead's body, picked up my bowl of dough, and left the larder. I closed its door and locked it with my key—Mrs. Bowen had already given me keys to the rooms I'd use most. The larder and Sinead must not be disturbed until Daniel could have a look.

No one was in the kitchen yet, and I wondered where on earth the staff had got to. Households were always busy in the early morning, and I could not imagine that Mrs. Bowen let the maids and footmen slacken their duties for any reason. The boy had tended the stove, yes, but even he had disappeared.

I walked heavily down the passage in search of Mrs. Bowen. She was responsible for the staff, even more than I, and she would need to hear of Sinead's death right away. I'd tell her then to go hunt up Daniel, or at least try to send word to him.

Mrs. Bowen was not in her parlor, however, nor in the servants' hall. I made my way up the back stairs and through the door covered with green baize that divided the servants' domain from the master's to see if Mrs. Bowen was attending her duties there.

When I entered the ground floor, I discovered why no one was below stairs. Mrs. Bowen indeed had them all working, and working hard. Footmen hurried about with coal scuttles, one maid was dusting every inch of the hallway, while another moved a mop made of rags back and forth on the stairs. Another maid was busy dusting the front parlor, while yet another laid the fire in the empty dining room. No one seemed to realize anything was unusual about this morning; no one seemed to have missed Sinead.

The maid on the stairs gaped at me as I approached her, obviously surprised to see me outside the fortress of my kitchen. "Where is Mrs. Bowen?" I asked her.

She continued to gape, mouth open in a round face under a white cap. "Don't know," she said breathily. "I'm sure."

"Of course you must know," I began sharply, then relented. I'd frightened her by popping up in front of her, and she had no idea how to respond.

I lifted my skirts and went past her to the first floor and then up to the second. "You there," I said to a straight-backed maid who walked through the second-floor hall with a gown over her arms and her nose in the air. "Mary," I hazarded a guess.

She turned around and stared at me much as the downstairs maid had but kept her lips firm. "Sara," she said primly. "I am upstairs maid and also wait on Lady Rankin and Lady Cynthia. Is something the matter, Mrs. Holloway?"

"Do you know where Mrs. Bowen is?" I asked her.

Sara raised her brows, still haughty. "Not upstairs, ma'am." As I continued to glare at her, my impatience and agitation mounting, she took a step toward me and lowered her voice. "Mrs. Bowen might have stepped out. She has a beau and sometimes goes to see him at night. No one's to know below stairs. Just Mr. Davis."

Mrs. Bowen with a lover. Interesting. I might be curious about that any other time, but I was far too agitated at the moment. "Well, send her to speak to me at once if you see her."

"Yes, Mrs. Holloway." Sara stepped back, a confidante no longer, and hurried toward Lady Rankin's chamber.

I hesitated on the landing, debating what to do next. I ought to search for Mr. Davis if I couldn't find Mrs. Bowen; however, I wanted to confirm one thing. There had been a murder last night in this house, and yesterday, we'd brought in a stranger.

The man Lady Cynthia had run down had been put into an attic room that was more a storage space than anything else. There was a cot in the chamber, where maids or footmen who were sick stayed, I'd been told, so they wouldn't infect the other maids or footmen whose beds they shared. Sometimes, in houses with a large staff and too few rooms, three or four might sleep in a bed. I considered myself fortunate to have a chamber and a bed all to myself in this house.

Mrs. Bowen apparently had *not* stepped out with her gentleman friend—at least, if she had, she'd already returned, because I found her coming out of the very room where the hurt man lay. She started when she saw me, nearly dropping her jangling ring of keys.

"Mrs. Holloway," she said when she recovered, closing the door behind her and making her voice crisp. "Whatever are you doing?"

The question I ought to have been asking her. "Looking for our accidental lodger. Is he better this morning?"

"I wouldn't know." Mrs. Bowen stood squarely in the middle of the passage and gazed at me coolly. Before I could ask a question, she said in a burst, "He's gone."

"Gone?" I pushed past her, having to turn sideways and nearly shove her out of my way to do so. "Where has he gone?"

I opened the door to the makeshift bedchamber and peered inside. The bed was turned back, the sheets rumpled, but there was no sign of our guest—Mr. Timmons, I remembered his name was.

"Perhaps he felt better and returned home," Mrs. Bowen said, but she sounded uncertain.

"He had a broken arm," I pointed out. "And a dose of laudanum. I doubt I'd be early to rise and rush out if it were me." Of course, a man with a broken arm and a belly full of laudanum likely couldn't have bashed a young girl to death either.

And why had Mrs. Bowen come to check on him? Compassion? Curiosity? Or had she simply given the other staff so many tasks there'd been no one left to look after Mr. Timmons? She'd not come up here to offer him food or drink—her hands were empty now that she'd let go of her keys, which swung gently from their chain against her skirts.

As Mrs. Bowen stood watching me, worry in her eyes, I made up my mind how to proceed.

"Mrs. Bowen," I said. "I have something upsetting to tell you. But you must promise me to keep it quiet. At least for now."

Mrs. Bowen did not take the news well. She went gray as I conveyed the fact of Sinead's death, and her hands went to her face, her fingers white streaks on her paling cheeks. When she at last spoke, her careful English accent fell away, and her voice was pure, broad Welsh.

"Oh, dear God, no. Oh, the poor, motherless girl."

She gazed at me pleadingly, her brisk efficiency gone, as though begging me to say I was mistaken or playing a joke. When I reached out to put a comforting hand on her arm, Mrs. Bowen started violently, gazing at me with unfocused eyes.

I led her downstairs as quickly as I could. We did not pass any of the other staff, mercifully, as they were still madly cleaning the master's part of the house.

We entered the passage to the kitchen and servants' hall to see Mr. Davis in front of the larder door, ready to unlock it with his key.

Mrs. Bowen shrieked, tearing herself from me and rushing at him in panic. I said swiftly, "Mr. Davis—no! We mustn't touch anything."

Mr. Davis turned to us, his handsome face bewildered. He was washed and shaved, his hair freshly pomaded with a new part in the middle. He blinked at me then at Mrs. Bowen, who'd halted a foot from the door and hugged her arms around herself, as though fearing to touch the brass doorknob.

"Let me in," she said to me in a near whisper, though she too had a key to this room. "We must lay her out, must do right by her."

"Not yet," I said firmly. I wanted Daniel to look at Sinead, the larder, and the rest of the rooms below stairs if necessary, before we brought in the constable. If we went inside and mucked about, I feared we'd ruin vital information.

Mrs. Bowen's cheeks were wet with tears, but her voice became steadier, the Welsh fading again. "We must do so at once, Mrs. Holloway. Ellen—Sinead—was one of us. We must put her somewhere and not let her lie in the larder. It isn't dignified."

"Someone killed her, Mrs. Bowen," I returned, my tone harsh. "We must wait so that we can discover who."

Mr. Davis's eyes widened in shock. "Killed? What are you saying? That Ellen was *killed*?" He looked back and forth between me and Mrs. Bowen, his mouth falling open as he took in our anxious and upset countenances. His cultured accent deserted him as well, and his common London upbringing shone through. "What the devil are you on about, Mrs. H.? Ellen was never killed."

"She was indeed." A lump swelled in my throat, making speech difficult. "She was struck down, and she is dead."

Mrs. Bowen fumbled with her keys, her hands trembling mightily, hence why she'd begged me to open the door for her. "I must go to her. I must . . ." She continued to clank the keys, as though she could not remember which fit the door.

I put a stilling hand on her arm. "Leave her be. Please."

Mr. Davis looked at me in agitation. "If anyone killed her it were a passing housebreaker." He pressed one hand over his other fist, as though scrubbing it. "Stands to reason. He tried his hand at robbing the place; Ellen caught him. Poor little thing. No need to keep her locked away."

"Would a cracksman come to the larder?" I asked, waving vaguely at the house around us. "There are plenty of valuables upstairs—silver, statuary, paintings. Why bother with the kitchen?"

"The wine cellar," Mr. Davis said with conviction. "And much of the silver is stored down here. Ellen heard him, came to investigate, and he killed her and dragged her into the larder to hide her. Nothing more to it than that."

Mrs. Bowen bit back another sob and rubbed her hands over her arms as though terribly chilled.

"Has anything gone from the butler's pantry?" I asked, trying to remain practical. "Or the wine cellar?"

Mr. Davis shook his head. "Not that I've seen. Though I've not done an inventory this morning."

Perhaps Mr. Davis was right, and this was a simple burglary gone wrong. The would-be thief had struck out and then run off once he realized Sinead was dead. The explanation was uncomplicated and likely the right one—perhaps I was seeing intrigue where none existed.

Mr. Timmons in the attic probably had nothing to do with this unless he'd been the burglar's accomplice and let the man into the house. However, getting himself run down and breaking his arm would be a severe price to pay to find a way inside. I couldn't imagine he'd done that on purpose. No, Mr. Timmons had merely gone home in the night, once the laudanum had worn off, wanting to be in his own home with his wife to tend him.

The burglar was an easy solution, one that I could see Mr. Davis and even Mrs. Bowen wanted to accept. One that I knew in my bones was completely wrong.

I at last relented and opened the door for Mrs. Bowen, admonishing her not to touch anything. I needn't have worried, however, because when I peeled back the tablecloth and Mrs. Bowen saw Sinead, she only stood in place, her hands together, shaking her head, crying silently.

"Shut the door," Mr. Davis said curtly once he'd taken a look. "Mrs. Bowen, you need a cup of tea. Mrs. Holloway, the family will be wanting their breakfast. You tend to that. I'll break the news to the master and send for a constable."

The gossipy Mr. Davis was now ready to take charge, at last behaving like the head of staff he was. I let out a breath and nodded, knowing we could not keep the death quiet any longer. Even so, I vowed to bring Daniel here before the constables saw Sinead and drew their conclusions.

I covered her body again, locked the larder door, and returned to the kitchen. Mr. Davis took Mrs. Bowen off to her parlor, speaking soothingly to her all the way. It was true that Lord Rankin and his family would want their meal on time—the death of a kitchen maid, who was nobody in their world, could not be allowed to disrupt the routine of the house upstairs.

The kettle I'd put on was boiling now, and I poured the water into a teapot into which I'd scooped tea, automatically measuring out exactly one teaspoon per cup plus one for the pot. After that, I threw on a shawl and went out through the scullery and up the outside stairs to the street, frantically looking for any sign of James—the one person I knew would be able to find Daniel.

I hurried from Mount Street around the corner to Park Street and thence to the mews that ran between Mount Street and Upper Grosvenor Street, where I'd seen Daniel disappear the day before, but I never saw him or James. I continued through the mews, where grooms brushed horses and stared hard at me, wondering what a cook was doing hastening through their world. I emerged onto South Audley Street at its end and went back around to Mount Street, realizing my errand was futile.

I hurried, wanting to be there when the larder was opened for the constables so I could tell all later to Daniel—if I ever saw the blasted man again. I had no idea where Daniel lived, and so I could not send for him. He only turned up when it pleased him to shock the life out of me, then he'd vanish for weeks at a time.

Lord Rankin might know how to find him, as Daniel had been a visitor in his own house, but I knew Daniel did not want me to betray my association with him. Otherwise, he'd have greeted me last night or made some sign that he knew me. There was no shame in recognizing another man's cook. No, Daniel was playing some sort of game with Lord Rankin, and he'd not thank me for rushing to the master and demanding he summon his previous night's visitor.

I returned to the house and the kitchen, ready to throw together a meal with the ingredients I had in the cupboards there, but I found myself trembling so hard I had to stop to support myself on the kitchen table's sturdy top.

Sinead was dead—the cheerful, pretty young woman at the brink of her life. Gone forever, her life taken by some person who'd thought so little of her he'd simply struck her down because she was in the way. I'd told her she reminded me of myself— I could imagine such a terrible thing happening to me at that age, and I could imagine it happening to the much younger girl in my life, the one for whose sake I'd taken this post at all.

For a time I held on to the table, my eyes blurring, my breath burning my lungs. I was angry at the house for going on as though nothing happened, for expecting to go on. Sinead was nothing to those upstairs, less even than a mouse behind the skirting board. Meanwhile, Mrs. Bowen went to pieces, while Mr. Davis did his best to comfort her—I could still hear his voice down the passage.

When I could stand upright again, I poured the tea. Mr. Davis returned to the kitchen to splash a dollop of the master's best brandy, fetched from the wine cellar, into each of our cups. He told me he'd carry Mrs. Bowen's back to her parlor and then go up and tell Lord Rankin. I watched Mr. Davis straighten into his butler's persona as he went down the passage, and imagined he'd convey the news of Sinead's death in a cool, apologetic tone, never mind how real his own distress had been.

The brandy-laced tea revived me somewhat, enough to sort out a makeshift breakfast for the family—sausage and eggs with toast made from yesterday's bread—and a quick hash of these with potatoes for the staff.

Once I put the breakfast on the dumbwaiter to be cranked up to the dining room, Mr. Davis sought me out again. "He wants to see you," he said, rather nervously. "His nibs. His lordship, that is."

"See me?" I asked in surprise. "Why?"

Davis only shrugged, letting his butler's persona slide away. "Couldn't tell ya. He weren't too happy his kitchen maid got herself killed, though I would like to have seen him be a little more upset. Maybe he wants to hear from you how you found her."

Lord Rankin was that sort of man, I decided, liking to have his finger on everything that went on in his household. "And the police?" I asked. I wanted to run out again and look for James or Daniel, and having to rush upstairs at Lord Rankin's bidding first vexed me.

"Footman went to fetch a constable. I imagine he'll be back soon."

Best I got it over with, then. I put aside my apron, smoothed my hair, and climbed the stairs, my heart heavy.

When I reached the dining room, however, Lord Rankin did not have any interest in my tale of Sinead. Instead, he tried to sack me.

5

Lord Rankin was seated at the head of the table in the dining room, a luxurious chamber with soaring ceilings, white-painted panels, and light blue silk wallpaper. A pretty room, preserved in the classical style of the last century, frozen in time before the ostentation of this century had all but obliterated such elegance.

The breakfast I'd prepared along with coffee and tea reposed on the table, a steaming cup at Lord Rankin's elbow. Most of the rest of him was hidden by the open spread of the *Times*.

Lady Cynthia sat on one long side of the table, far from Lord Rankin. She'd resumed her man's dress, today a frock coat and gray and white checked waistcoat, with a gold watch fob dangling from her pocket. The clothes sat well on her figure, and I wondered if she'd been fitted for them, and if so, what the tailor who'd made them thought. I suppose if she paid well enough, he kept his thoughts to himself.

She, like Rankin, had a newspaper in front of her face, this one the *Telegraph*. Cynthia lowered it when I came in, folding it neatly to give me her attention.

Lord Rankin, on the other hand, continued reading, letting me remain halfway between door and table until he deigned to notice me. He was lord and master here and made certain with every passing second that I knew it.

At last Lord Rankin closed the newspaper, flapped it once to straighten its pages, and folded it in half to lay on the table. No doubt a footman would retrieve it for his valet to press in case Lord Rankin wished to read more later.

"Mrs. Holloway." Lord Rankin fixed me with his sharp stare. "I dislike my household to be disrupted. You arrived yesterday and have disrupted it several times already, once by bringing up the coffee when you had no business to, and second by racing through the house causing all sorts of fuss this morning. My wife was awakened by you and her maid having a discussion outside her door, and her maid had to give her a tonic. Likewise I hear it was your idea to bring a person inside my house yesterday after Lady Cynthia's ap-palling accident, one who has vanished into the mist, taking God knows what with him. Therefore, you will return to your agency and look for another position."

I froze in place, shock rendering me immobile. While I thoroughly disapproved of Lord Rankin's behavior toward the female staff and knew Daniel's presence in his study could mean nothing good, I did not yet want to leave. Not only was this house well situated, where I could easily reach the part of London I needed to, I wanted to make certain Sinead was done well by, that Mrs. Bowen was all right, that whoever had killed Sinead was caught. There was far too much going on here for me to simply depart.

Also, Lord Rankin had no business dismissing me. The domestic tasks were the purveyance of the lady of the house or, in her absence, the housekeeper. I assumed Lady Rankin was still in bed if she'd taken a tonic—likely laudanum—but a genteel lady would not be awake and up this early in any case. Any other day I would send a tray up to the mistress via her maid when she called for it. I wondered if Lady Rankin knew at all that her husband was sending me off.

"I promise you, your lordship, there will be no more trouble," I said quickly.

Lord Rankin's gaze became icy. "No, there shall not be, because you will not be here. When I give an order to one of my staff, I do not expect it to be countermanded by another, nor do I expect that member of staff to decide who comes into my house without consulting me or my wife." Lady Cynthia had been beside me when I'd recommended we bring Mr. Timmons inside, but presumably, she did not count in Lord Rankin's eyes. "Please pack your things and go. You will be paid for your one day."

I remained rooted in place, both chilled and outraged, but I had no room to argue, and I knew it. This was Lord Rankin's house—he owned it outright; it wasn't part of the entail, according to Mr. Davis. He was at perfect liberty to decide what persons did and did not live in it or work in it. My home was a lodging in the Tottenham Court Road, at least when a room was available there. I had no power here except over my lord's and lady's digestions.

If Lord Rankin dismissed me, the agency might decide to take me from their register—their reputation was at stake as much as mine every time I took a position or was dismissed from such.

I was working my way around to telling him I'd give notice instead—a less risky way to depart—when Lady Cynthia drawled, "I say, Rankin, it's too bad of you. She's a dashed decent cook, and it's not her fault someone tried to rob the place and clouted the maid over the head. More the fault of your doors and windows than anything else."

Lady Cynthia hadn't eaten much of my food last night, and what I'd cooked this morning had been very plain, so she hadn't actually tasted much of what I could do, but I had no intention of arguing with her. I simply stood and looked virtuous.

Lord Rankin turned an interesting shade of red. He could hardly explain to Lady Cynthia that he didn't trust me because I'd seen Daniel in his study—at least, I assumed this was what his anger was about. He only moved the freezing gaze from me to her.

"*You* caused that intruder to be brought inside when you ran him down, Cynthia," he said. "If you'd have killed him, you'd be in Newgate this very hour. I posit that *you* are responsible for the girl's murder."

Instead of being cowed, Lady Cynthia snorted. "You think *Timmons* killed her? The man was bashed up—couldn't have hurt a fly. Hardly my fault he stepped in front of me, was it? We did the charitable thing by bringing him home and fixing him up."

She seemed to have recovered her remorse about hurting Timmons. Lord Rankin was nearly purple now, but his voice remained cold. "You will no longer be allowed near the rig or the horses," he managed to say.

Cynthia shot me a cheerful look. "That's all right. I'll take the omnibus. And anyway, you can't dismiss Mrs. Holloway. Not behind Em's back—Emily told me she liked her. Said she was a damned fine cook, served better food last night than Em's had in years. I refuse to explain to my sister why you sacked a perfectly good cook and Em has to begin the search all over again."

Lord Rankin obviously hadn't thought of this. From his look, the idea of telling his frail wife he'd turned me out was not a happy one. Perhaps delicate Lady Rankin had more power than I realized.

Lord Rankin jerked his paper from the table, crumpling it irreparably in the process. "Go back to your duties, Mrs. Holloway, and we'll say no more about it."

Relief washed through me. I would not have to return to the agency to try to explain what had happened, to beg them to keep me on. I *would* have to make certain that Lord Rankin did not ask for any more maids to visit him after supper, but I could take steps to prevent that.

I curtsied the best I could, and Lord Rankin lifted the newspaper as a barrier between himself and the world. Cynthia gave me a wink, but I made myself keep my face neutral as I skimmed out of the room, still a cook and still employed.

By the time I made my hasty way below stairs again, the constable had arrived, with him a policeman in plain clothes, a serviceable suit. Mr. Davis was with the two men in the servants' hall, giving the constable and suited gentleman the frosty gaze of a butler of a fine household, put out because his duties had been interrupted. Policemen, the look said, were a necessary evil and to be barely tolerated.

Beyond, through the kitchen to the scullery, I saw a man in a long coat—Mr. Davis whispered to me as I rushed in that he was the coroner. A violent death meant the body was examined as soon as possible, and Lord Rankin had the influence to make certain it was done immediately.

"What was she doing down here?" the constable, a thin man with thinner hair slicked back from a high forehead, was asking Davis. He had a notebook and pencil, and held the pencil's tip to the page, peering suspiciously over it at Davis before switching his gaze to me. "She worked for you, eh? What were you doing that you'd find her so quick?"

I looked straight back at him, lifting my chin as I strove to catch my breath. "I was coming to prepare breakfast for the family and the servants. As I do every day."

The man in the suit, whoever he was, only watched me with unnerving light brown eyes while the constable scribbled my answer into his notebook.

"Next of kin?" the constable went on, pencil poised once more.

I had to admit I had no idea. Mrs. Bowen had said she was "motherless," but as Mrs. Bowen was still shut in her parlor I could not ask her at the moment. Mr. Davis did not know either.

"She was Irish," I said. "That is hardly helpful, I'm certain. You cannot run the length and breadth of that country asking who has a daughter or sister called Sinead. There are plenty of Irish in England as well."

"But I can ask the police in Ireland," the suited man said, giving me another sharp look. "You have not been cook here long, have you?"

"One entire day," I answered, refusing to be cowed. "Before that, I was in the home of Mr. Langford in Richmond. Mrs. Langford gave me excellent references, and I am on the books at the Weller Agency on the Strand, who are quite reputable."

"I have no doubt you're a paragon, Mrs. Holloway," the man in the suit said in a dry voice. "The coroner will take the body, but when he's done, he'll give it back to the family if he can find them. If not . . . well, it's up to Lord Rankin."

Meaning Lord Rankin might be kind and pay for Sinead to have a proper burial or he might decide to turn her out to the parish and consign her to a pauper's grave, shared with vagrants and the like who'd died around the same time.

It was hardly Sinead's fault someone killed her, I thought indignantly. She deserved to be laid to rest with care. I would simply have to find her family or persuade Lord Rankin to be charitable.

The suited man asked me about Mr. Timmons—Mr. Davis must have mentioned him. I explained how Mr. Timmons had been tucked into the attic but now had gone home. The constable made note of the direction Timmons had given us, no doubt ready to rush around and question him.

"May I see Sinead before you take her?" I asked as the suited man started to turn away, finished with us.

He looked me up and down but flicked his fingers toward the scullery, where they'd carried Sinead for the coroner's examination. Taking the gesture for approval, I strode from the servants' hall and through the kitchen to the scullery.

The coroner had laid Sinead out on the flagstone floor and rested her hands on her chest. Much of the blood on her face had been wiped away, presumably so the coroner could see the wound. I gazed down at the large gash that ran from her forehead to her cheek, and swallowed, bile rising in my throat.

The coroner, a plump, cheerful-looking personage, was just washing his hands in the large sink in the corner.

"Poor little thing," he said. "He didn't have to hit her that hard, now, did he? An innocent lass like her. A crying shame." He wiped his hands on a thick towel, leaving streaks of blood behind.

I knelt down to touch Sinead's face. "I'm so sorry, my dear," I whispered. Again I admonished myself for not being with her, too preoccupied with my own life to notice troubles in hers.

I remained kneeling there while the coroner clinked instruments back into his bag. I tried to ignore the metallic clanking, refusing to speculate on what sort of instruments he'd been using.

As I bowed my head over Sinead, I glimpsed a shadow on her throat. Leaning closer, I saw a black mark across her neck, which would have been hidden by the high collar of her dress, now opened by the coroner's examination.

"What is that?" I asked, pointing.

The coroner came to me, leaning down and resting his hand on his knees. "Ah yes. Must have been a necklace there. Someone's wrenched it off. Nothing to do with her death though. She was killed with that." He waved his hand at a heavy marble bowl that rested on a towel, ready for the police to take. "Found it stashed away on the back of a shelf."

The bowl was a mortar, small and deep—a cook or cook's assistant would grind spices or seeds in it with a pestle. The side of the bowl bore a dried rivulet of blood.

The mortar and pestle had been sitting on a table in the larder—I'd seen it when I examined the room upon my arrival yesterday. Sinead's attacker must have reached for the nearest thing he could find and struck her with it, then hidden it once Sinead was dead. He'd also pulled her into a corner, but that hadn't concealed her for long.

The murderer must have been in a hurry—too rushed to take Sinead's body and the mortar away with him, perhaps to drop both into the river. That must mean he hadn't come here deliberately to kill her. They'd quarreled, as I'd been speculating, he'd hit her, then panicked when he realized what he'd done. He'd hastily tried to hide what had happened and then fled.

I creaked to my feet, my vision blurring with inconvenient tears. "What will you do with her?" I had only a vague notion of what happened to victims of murder.

"She'll come with me to the morgue." The coroner wiped his hands again, dropped the towel on the edge of the sink, and reached for a frock coat he'd left dangling from a hook meant for hanging up clean pots. "I'll take good care of her, don't you worry. The dead do no harm to anyone, poor things. I'll finish my examination in my morgue, though in this case the cause of her death is fairly obvious. You pack up her things and find a nice frock to lay her out in. Now, you might want to go, missus, while my assistants take her away."

I could not leave, I found, could not turn my back on Sinead and flee. I waited while two men came in with a litter, bundled Sinead onto it, covered her with a sheet, and carried her up the back stairs.

A crowd had gathered in the street to watch while the coroner and his men slid Sinead into a van with open back doors, the horses twitching nervously in their harness. The doors closed with a final snap, the horses started, and the cart clopped away, the wheels rumbling hollowly on the pavement.

B ack inside, the scullery maid, weeping, was already scrubbing, scrubbing, scrubbing the floor of the scullery, no doubt set to the task by Mr. Davis. Mrs. Bowen was nowhere in sight.

I snatched up the bloody towel the coroner had left and carried it to the laundry room, dropping it into the tub where other towels from yesterday were soaking. I rinsed my hands there and went back to the kitchen with a heavy step.

I needed to go on with the cooking for the day. I was firmly acquainted with upper-class households—the routine was so well established it ceased for nothing, not even death. We servants might be given a few hours to attend Sinead's funeral on the day it happened, but likely not much more than that.

I would need another assistant. Mrs. Bowen should help me procure one, but as she did not appear, I chose one of the downstairs maids, who'd come in for her bite of breakfast. *Her* name indeed was Mary, and she seemed eager to shuck dusting for shelling peas. I had her wash her hands after eating and set her down at the table with said bowl of peas, then I walked up the outside stairs and into the street, once more in search of James.

The road was crowded with wheeled vehicles pulled by brisk horses, early risers heading out to their clubs or offices in the City, or wherever gentlemen in Mount Street took themselves to during the day. Drovers, carters, peddlers, and errand boys also swarmed the street.

I did not see James at first, but lads like him, who hung about looking for odd jobs, began to approach me. They'd seen me emerge from a posh house in cook's garb and knew I'd have the power to employ them on the spot, plus a master who likely had the means to pay. I started to dismiss the lads with a wave of my hand then thought better of it, dispensing farthings to them as I asked if they'd seen the boy I looked for.

James was hardly a boy anymore. He'd grown at least a foot since the day I'd met him, and his voice was deepening. I worried for what he'd do once he became a man—a youth can get away with much, but a man must find true employment or starve. I did not think his father would let him go hungry and homeless, but I also knew nothing about Daniel's plans for him.

"You're looking for me, Mrs. Holloway?" James sang out as

he strode toward me, his wrists sticking out from his coat sleeves at least an inch.

I drew James aside, not wanting to announce my business to the entire street. "It is your father I would like to speak to." I handed him the rest of my farthings. "*If* he can possibly spare me the time."

James grinned. "He might do." He touched his cap, and then grabbed my hand, dropped the farthings back into it, and closed my fist around them. "Don't need your coin, Mrs. H. Be back soon." Another touch of his cap, another grin, and he was gone.

The smile, the gesture, the amusement at my generosity—all reflected his father. The pair of them were charmers, that was for certain, and charm like that could lead a woman less careful than I straight into trouble.

I knew little about Daniel, but I was certain of one thing—he came and went on his own time. I took myself back to my kitchen, knowing I needed to continue meals for the family.

There was no midday dinner—Lord Rankin had left for the Exchange while I'd searched for James, and Lady Rankin was still in her bedchamber. That left Lady Cynthia, but she too departed before noon—to see friends, Mr. Davis said. He opined that she gathered with other ladies who liked to dress in trousers to smoke cigars. *Appalling*, he finished, rolling his eyes, though it was clear he found Lady Cynthia very interesting.

I made a simple repast of chops, potatoes, and greens for the staff's dinner, and at the same time I cooked down the bones and any meat clinging to the carcass of last night's hen. Leaving that to simmer, I turned my efforts to tea, a meal that, Mr. Davis assured me, the ladies of the house *would* take. I mixed up a special seedcake, putting in extra nutmeg and caraway seeds, and I had Mr. Davis fetch me a little brandy to add to the batter.

I made this seedcake with Lady Cynthia in mind, as gratitude for her speaking up for me with Lord Rankin. I might not have riches with which to reward those good to me, but I could cook—my largesse came through my fingers and my knowledge of what ingredients to put with what. I thanked her as I knew how.

As I removed the cake from the oven, the aroma heavenly, Mr. Davis's voice floated into the room as he spoke in stentorian tones to someone behind him.

"Cook might have some tasks for you from time to time, but for most of your day you will stay *out* from underfoot, especially in the kitchen, understand? Mrs. Holloway has a great deal of work to do, and so far she does it beautifully, so we do not want to get in her way, eh?"

"Don't you worry, guv," came the answer. "None will even know I'm 'ere."

The words were tinged with the cant of London streets—South London, if I were any judge—but I knew the voice. He might be speaking like a lowborn deliveryman, but I would always recognize the smooth tone behind the words, the timbre that never failed to catch my attention.

Daniel McAdam stood deferentially in the kitchen doorway, twisting his cloth cap in his hands. He glanced about in reverence, as though conscious of his privilege in being indoors in a house such as this.

As I halted, dumbfounded, the cloths with which I held the cake pan slipped, and my beautiful seedcake went down, down, down, heading for the slates where it would be smashed into a heap of crumbs and crockery.

6

The cake pan halted two feet above the floor, caught on an outstretched towel spread taut in Daniel's broad hands. He lifted the towel, cake pan and all, carefully, carefully, and deposited it safely on the table.

"Whew." Daniel released the ends of the towel, retrieved his cap from where he'd dropped it on the floor, and wiped his brow with the back of his hand. "Smells too good to be ruined, that does. Will you save a slice for old Danny?" He lifted his brows, mirth in his dark blue eyes, but nothing in his stance or voice let slip that we had ever met before.

"The cake is for the mistress's tea," Mr. Davis said scornfully. "But if we're kind to Mrs. Holloway, she might make one almost as nice for us." He sent me an exasperated look behind Daniel's back.

"Beg yer pardon, missus," Daniel said to me. "I meant no offense." He tilted the corners of his mouth, the smile of a man who tried to get away with as much as he could in this world.

I started to speak, but words lodged in my throat. I should either dismiss him with a shake of my head, or tell him not to worry himself and thank him for saving the cake, but nothing would emerge from my mouth but a strange sort of breathless sound.

Daniel touched his hand to his forehead, half saluting me, and followed Mr. Davis out of the kitchen.

I stood for a long time, watching the door through which Daniel and Mr. Davis had disappeared. Not until Paul the footman burst in with a load of clean crockery from the scullery and asked me what was the matter did I jerk myself from my immobile stance and turn back to the table. There, I stared at the cake Daniel had rescued, in a daze.

He'd come. James had found him, and he'd answered my summons. But why he'd chosen to blatantly walk into the house itself, when he'd been seen upstairs as the master's visitor the night before, I had no idea. I only knew that frustration would soon surge through my numbness, and when it did, I'd seize Daniel by the ear, and demand to know what he thought he was doing.

As Daniel's and Mr. Davis's voices faded up the outside steps, I forced myself through the motions of preparing tea. I had done it often enough that I could finish like an automaton—slicing and toasting the bread I'd baked before dinner and cutting the seedcake, loading plates with pieces of fruit, adding to the tray a good-sized dish of clotted cream.

I sent the entire repast up in the dumbwaiter and turned to take an inventory of the kitchen and larder, necessary if I were to plan more meals today. I went through this in sort of a fog, my feet and hands doing things, my eyes seeing without my mind registering much at all.

The larder and spice drawers were well stocked, but I'd

need fresh produce, another sack of flour, meat from the butcher for tomorrow, and fresh fish for tonight. I made up a list and gave it to Mary, telling her to take a footman with her to the market to help her carry the heavy items. Then I set the joint of beef that was the last bit of meat in the house to braising in its juices with onions and the stock I'd made from the hen. Only once that could be left simmering did I wipe my hands and go in search of Daniel.

I found Mrs. Bowen instead. As I moved past the servants' hall, the door to the housekeeper's parlor opened, and Mrs. Bowen stood on the threshold. I had not spoken to her since I'd given her the news of Sinead's death, and she'd not turned up for meals, but the household was so well-oiled that the footmen and maids had carried on without her.

Mrs. Bowen's eyes were red from weeping, and wisps of graying hair straggled from her cap to her wan face. I took her by the elbow, steered her firmly back inside the parlor, and shut the door.

"Now, then, Mrs. Bowen." I guided her toward the seat she favored, a velvet-upholstered Belter chair with a curved back, possibly a castoff from the floors above, and pushed her gently into it. "It is a horrible thing that's happened, but there's no use in giving way."

I said this to convince myself more than anything. My numbness was fading, and anger began to spread through my veins in slow heat.

I took a seat on a plainer chair of dark walnut, its back decorated with metal studs to hold the upholstery in place. "You said she was 'motherless,'" I went on as Mrs. Bowen sat motionlessly, staring straight in front of her. "What did you mean? Did you know Sinead's family?"

"Her name wasn't Sinead." Mrs. Bowen remained gazing

into empty space. "Or Ellen either. It was Katie. Katie Doyle. Her mother was my dearest friend."

I started—I hadn't realized Mrs. Bowen's connection to Sinead was so close. "What happened to her mother?" I asked, softening my tone.

"She died, didn't she?" Mrs. Bowen looked at me at last, her eyes filled with rage and grief. "She was shot and killed on the street like an animal."

I started again, harder this time. I hadn't expected *that*. I'd assumed the lady dead of a disease, taken too young, as consumption and other too-common maladies will do. "Shot?" I repeated in shock.

"Fenians." Mrs. Bowen spat the word. "Katie was only a girl when she and her mum were caught in a crowd near Waterloo Station, when a Fenian explosive went off. Not content with blowing up people, the bloody men started shooting as well. Katie's mother was struck, though Katie was able to run away. Poor child. She was raised by her aunt, then I helped her get a place in a house where I worked, and we came together to this one. And now Katie has died by violence too. There are those who want to give the Irish home rule, but those people are not to be trusted—ever."

Sinead herself was Irish, as was her mother, I assumed. I said nothing of this, however. When violence grips a mob, they do not stop and take the particulars of the passersby before they massacre them. That such things could still happen in this day and age was monstrous.

"Mrs. Bowen, I do not believe a stray Fenian wandered into the house and killed Sinead," I said briskly, keeping to the name the lass had wanted to use. "She must have interrupted a burglar, as Mr. Davis speculates." I knew that explanation was the wrong one, but I hoped to calm Mrs. Bowen's stunned grief.

Mrs. Bowen only gave me a dark look. "Not to be trusted," she repeated. "The sooner we heave every Irishman out of England and pen them on their island home, the better every Englishman will be." She rose, the frosty chill of the professional housekeeper returning. "Thank you for speaking with me, Mrs. Holloway. I have been most upset, as you can imagine. I will be better directly, and resume my duties."

"I think no one will mind if you rest awhile longer." I stood up with her and laid a soothing hand on her shoulder. "Seeing what a good friend you were to Sinead, and to her mum."

Mrs. Bowen turned away, dislodging my hand, then brushed off her skirts and stepped to a mirror to smooth her hair. "No indeed, Mrs. Holloway," she said. "As you stated, there is no use giving way. The police will find who did this dreadful deed, and then I shall visit him and tell him exactly what I think."

"I will go with you," I said. We shared a look, two women who understood how to do the most with what limited power we had in this world. She gave me a terse nod, and we departed.

I next tackled Mr. Davis; metaphorically, of course. I cornered him in the butler's pantry, where he was decanting the wines for supper—a robust red to go with the beef and in its sauce and a sweet wine for pudding. The white wine for the fish would stay in its bottle until needed.

"That man you brought in," I said, choosing my words carefully. "What do you know of him?"

Mr. Davis glanced up, his elbows out as he let the wine trickle from the bottle into the decanter poised to catch the red stream. He quickly focused his attention on the wine again, slowing the flow as the bottle began to empty.

"You mean McAdam?" Mr. Davis asked. He peered at the bottle and the sediment collecting in the remaining liquid, raised the bottle's neck so only the last clear drops would trickle out to the decanter, and then upended both vessels and set them on the table. "He's harmless, he is. Makes deliveries up and down this street, but he's having hard times and wouldn't mind the extra odd job. He won't give you trouble, Mrs. H." Mr. Davis's lips twitched. "From what I've seen, the ladies don't much mind him coming around."

"Oh yes, I've observed him about," I said coolly. It would be odd to claim I hadn't as Daniel delivered all over London, including to the last London house I'd worked in. Anyone could easily discover that fact.

Mr. Davis gave me a shrug. "He comes and goes. Just watch that the maids don't succumb to foolishness around him. Though he seems honorable, for his sort."

I could say nothing about this—what kind of honor did a man have who pretended to be such different people?

I wondered though—if Mr. Davis knew Daniel from the streets, and presumably others in the household did as well, would they not have recognized him when he arrived to visit Lord Rankin last night?

"Who was on the door after supper last night?" I asked abruptly. "Letting people in and out, I mean. Visitors and such."

Mr. Davis looked perplexed. "Rufus, I believe. There were no visitors last evening though. The master or mistress would have told me who was expected. Ah—" He gave me an enlightened glance. "Are you of a mind that a visitor was let in but hid instead of leaving again, and so killed Ellen?"

Far from what I'd been thinking, but I shrugged. "I am wondering, that is all."

"Hmm. Well, it's a terrible thing." Mr. Davis swirled the

dregs of the wine bottle, peered at the cloud inside, then poured the gritty sediment into a small bucket on the table beside him. "I hope the police find the fellow soon and hang him high. Now, Mrs. Holloway, shall we have a taste?" He held up the decanter invitingly.

I stared. "Of the master's wine?" I kept my voice down but put all my disapproval into it.

"Not to worry, Mrs. H. I mean just a nip. I always taste it, in case it's off. It would never do for the master to have befouled wine now, would it?"

Without waiting for an answer, Davis took two plain glasses from a cupboard and poured about a finger's width of wine from the decanter into each. He slid a glass to me and lifted his. "To your good health, Mrs. H."

I could have refused, saying I'd have no truck with stealing the master's supplies, but it was such a small amount, and Davis was right. I always tasted my food before I sent it up in case a mistake had been made in the seasoning, or some disaster such as fish sauce having been used in the dessert cream. Likewise, I tasted the wine before I put it into my food—I'd certainly never do otherwise.

I lifted the glass, tipped it to Mr. Davis, and drank. The wine was good, rich, and full. "An excellent vintage," I pronounced.

"It ought to be," Mr. Davis said. "He brings it in from France. But he can afford to, can the master. The previous Lord Rankin was a parsimonious miser. The food and drink have much improved in this house since the present Lord Rankin took over, I can tell you."

Another reason Mr. Davis put up with Lord Rankin's eccentricities, I surmised.

As I left Mr. Davis to more decanting, it occurred to me to

wonder—Lord Rankin had sent for Sinead last night to bring up the tea. The staff, and indeed I, had assumed it was for his usual reason of the master having his bit of recreation with one of the maids, but Daniel had already been with Lord Rankin when I'd entered his study.

Lord Rankin had been furious to see me, because he'd expected Sinead. Had asked for her specifically. At the time I'd thought it because she'd be so relieved that the master *didn't* want to have his way with her that she'd never notice Daniel in the room, but Lord Rankin could not necessarily count on that fact.

There was nothing for it but that I must find Daniel forthwith and shake some answers out of him.

D aniel had apparently left the house to run errands. I had too much to do to look for James again to find him for me, so I sent the footman called Rufus—a thin lad with a shock of blond hair—scurrying out to look for James instead.

I started to describe James but it turned out that most servants around here knew him, as they knew Daniel. For explanation, I told Rufus I wanted James to run an errand for me. I could see that he wondered what errand, but one look at my stormy face made him close his mouth and not ask me.

James clattered down the scullery stairs with Rufus not long later, and I abandoned rolling out the pastry for my lemon tart to beckon James upstairs and outside with me.

"I need to speak to your father," I said when we reached the street.

James looked perplexed. "I told him already. He works here now, don't he?"

"I mean in private. I can't very well ask him questions in the kitchen. There's always someone about."

"Right you are." James gave me his sunny look and prepared to dash off.

I grabbed his jacket and tugged him back. "Bring me some item so that it looks as though I needed you for a true errand." I pressed tuppence into his hand. "Think of something. Oh, and if you can just ask about for a Mr. Timmons and discover whether he went home, and—well, anything you can find out about him."

James blinked, but his swift mind filed my questions away, and off he went, giving me a wave behind him.

Supper was a difficult meal tonight, as I had no true assistant. Mary, whom I'd recruited, had brought back all the correct things from the market and was eager enough but dreadfully inexperienced at cookery. She handed me salt to put into the sweet custard instead of sugar, spilled a good measure of flour, and dropped the peeled bits from the carrots into the soup instead of the chopped carrots themselves.

Mrs. Bowen emerged to resume her duties, if tiredly. She admonished poor Mary until she had the girl in tears, which did not make matters better. In the end, I put Mary in the scullery to help with the washing up, and had Paul, who was a bright boy, assist me. He did well, though he complained bitterly about doing "women's work."

"Chefs are men," I pointed out as I directed him to take the heavy roasting pan out of the oven. The pan contained the beef I'd already braised and then set to roast, and now I scattered chopped potatoes around the beef and ladled the pan's juices over all. "Famous ones at that. See how far you might rise?"

"But they're French," Paul said glumly.

"Not all of them." I waved for him to shove the pan back into the roasting oven, and I worked the lever for the bellows to bring the fire up high. "Many chefs are as English as you or me, but they give themselves French names so they'll be hired on. Paul is a perfectly good French name. You should do well."

Paul only scoffed, not believing me.

Now to prepare the rest of the vegetables. The stove had a water pipe that rose up from the oven, with a little valve I could turn to let out steam. I put greens in a pot and slid it beneath the pipe, turning on the steam, which cooked the vegetables but left their bright color. The carrot soup, rescued, was simmering, waiting for me to finish it with cream and perhaps a bit of grated nutmeg. For pudding, I had my tart made with custard and the last of the winter's lemons—the tart was smooth on the tongue and had an exquisite mixture of sweet and savory. It was cooling in the larder, away from the heat of kitchen. I perspired freely over the great, hot stove, a towel in my apron pocket with which to wipe my face.

I was somewhat distressed to see that Sinead wasn't much missed, except by Mrs. Bowen. The maids and footmen were shocked, there was no doubt, and whispered among themselves, but they took up her duties and filled the hole her absence made without saying a great deal about it. But then, we had no choice, did we? We performed our tasks or we'd be sacked. A lordship was not going to pay his staff to sit about and weep.

During all the scurrying, chopping, basting, kneading, and stirring in the kitchen, James returned carrying a loaf of white sugar that I knew had cost more than the tuppence I'd given him. He whispered into my ear as he handed it to me, along with the tuppence, "Dog and Bell, Edgware Road."

I gave James a nod, wondering how Daniel expected me to meet him so far from the house. I turned away to rescue the greens from over wilting, and when I looked around again, James had gone.

At last the meal was ready to go up, the cream of carrot soup resting in its tureen; the fish pale in its butter sauce; the beef proudly browned and crackling with heat, its sauce of wine, demi-glace, and shallots poured around its base; the potatoes crisp; the greens resting in a bowl with a light sprinkling of a wine and lemon sauce; the lemon tart to be set on the sideboard for after. Mr. Davis departed with his decanters of red and bottles of white, and I and the maids shoved the dishes onto the dumbwaiter.

Instead of waiting to see what came back tonight, I set Paul and Mary to watch and tell me what dishes were eaten and what not, shucked my apron, and told Mrs. Bowen I was going out to take some air. The servants' meal was already prepared, waiting to be warmed and served, and she and Mary could do that.

Mrs. Bowen only gave me a stony glance and belatedly told me to take care. I donned my hat, coat, and gloves, and set off.

London after dark is a different place than in daylight. There is as much hustle-bustle as always, but now the gentry are out and about as well as less salubrious members of society— the inebriated, the ruffians, and the ladies looking to entice a man from the straight and narrow.

Lord Rankin didn't go much to the theatre, opera, and homes of his neighbors, Mr. Davis had told me. Our master preferred to work every day, eat a good meal every night, and then retire. Drove his wife spare, Mr. Davis said, though Lady Rankin often went out with friends after supper and left her husband at home.

I moved past carriages loaded with ladies and gentlemen in finery, past shops blazing with light as they catered to the final customers of the evening, past young women in false finery looking for their *first* customers. I was able to climb onto an omnibus heading north past Oxford Street, tucking in my skirts so they wouldn't be sat upon by the passengers to either side of me, all of us packed in tightly. The omnibus bumped its slow way along the street, pulled by a team of hardworking horses.

I pushed my way out in the middle of Edgware Road, twitching my skirt from the grasp of a gentleman who for some reason was trying to finger it. I gave him an admonishing look as I descended—he ought to know better.

The Dog and Bell was a public house in a lane off the Edgware Road. I paused outside its lighted windows, the thick glass distorting my view of the interior, the door firmly closed against the cold air. As a respectable woman, I would hardly go into a taproom, but I was not certain how I was to find Daniel if I did not go inside. I could enter the snug, but I'd never been to this particular pub and had no idea where that was.

Daniel solved the problem by coming outside for me. He tipped his cap, bent his elbow to invite me to grasp his arm, and led me inside, like a man taking his young lady for an outing on a fine London night.

7

The snug in the back of the pub was a cozy room with benches lining its walls under high windows. A door cut off the noise from the taproom, and the windows to the outside world were set high enough in the wall to lend a modicum of privacy.

Only three other patrons were using the snug—a couple quite involved with each other and an older man wearing a frown that creased his face. The elderly man looked disapproving of the noise and singing coming from the other parts of the pub as well as of the spooning lady and gent at the next table.

The couple and the man looked up when we entered and gave Daniel nods of greeting. "McAdam," said the young man, who had a round, rather sweating face. His sweetheart flashed Daniel a smile, but it was clear her interest was for her beau.

"Now, then, McAdam," the older man said, before he went back to nursing his pint.

The couple, after sending me a curious glance, began to

mind their business again. I strove to look innocuous as Daniel led me to the very back of the room, where the benches bent in with the narrowing walls, rather like the bow of a ship.

The barmaid who scooted in to take up empties from the other tables had a plump bosom, a few missing teeth, and sleek blond hair. She gave Daniel a wide grin but departed again without asking if he wanted anything.

Daniel left me at the table while he stepped to the tap-room, returning after a few minutes with a pint for himself and a half for me. I sipped politely from the glass he put in front of me, but I hadn't much use for ale.

"Is this your local?" I asked him.

Daniel shrugged. "One of them."

Likely he had one in every neighborhood in London. What guise did he use in those? Or was the Daniel I sat across the table from the true one?

"How are you, Mrs. Holloway?" he asked me comfortably. "We've not had a proper chat since you left Richmond."

No, we hadn't, but I considered that scarcely my fault. "I did not flee my kitchen to meet you here for inane chatter," I said. I kept my voice low, though the others in the room seemed to have no intention of listening. "What are you up to?"

Daniel leaned back, resting his shoulders against the smooth wall. The light here was dim, only a few kerosene lamps to give us illumination. Under them, Daniel's hair was very dark, his eyes midnight blue, and I noticed a few lines about his mouth I hadn't seen before.

"If you mean why did I traipse through the servants' hall with your butler this afternoon—I sent word to Lord Rankin asking if I could be there," Daniel said, copying my quiet tone. "He's letting me look into the death of the kitchen maid."

"Is he?" I asked in surprise. "So he has some concern for it after all." My outrage returned. "He tried to give me the sack, the wretched man."

Daniel frowned as he lifted his glass and took a noisy sip. "That might be a good thing, actually."

I sent him an indignant look. "Me on the streets begging for a position? Hardly good, Mr. McAdam."

"I mean *good* because Rankin's behavior shows he does not suspect that you and I are allied. I do not want him to know. Also, it would be safer for you if you were gone from that house."

I deliberately ignored his last statement "Allied?" I turned my glass around the table. "Are we allied?"

"I hope we are friends." Daniel studied me in that way he had—watching, and calculating the effect of every one of his words.

"Do not try to turn me up sweet," I admonished. "We are not like *them*." I motioned with my eyes at the couple who had their heads together. They were not kissing—I hoped they had the sense to refrain from *that* in a public place—but they were quite taken with each other.

Daniel had kissed me before. More than once. I'd allowed it, but I was no longer certain it had been wise. The glint in his eyes told me he remembered the kisses, and remembered them well.

"I did not say so. *Friends*, I meant, Mrs. H."

"Mrs. *Holloway*," I said. "I do not know why my name has degenerated to a single letter."

"A sign of affection." Daniel took another sip of ale. As he did, I saw him . . . change.

Outwardly, he remained exactly the same—a working man in a coat of a thick weave somewhat threadbare at the elbows and frayed at the collar. A black kerchief tied around his neck exposed a bit of brown throat above his heavy cotton shirt. His hat lay crumpled on the bench next to him, and his square-toed booted feet rested near my bench.

Daniel's appearance remained the same, but his eyes quieted and grew more thoughtful, his countenance smoothing into that of the man I'd seen upstairs in Lord Rankin's study. Gone was the roguish twinkle in his eyes and his lopsided smile. The man across from me now was one who gazed out at life in all its ugliness and vowed to use the power he had to do something about it.

I no longer wondered that the inhabitants of Lord Rankin's household hadn't recognized Daniel when he'd visited in a polished suit and greatcoat. I'd never have known who he was in Lord Rankin's study if he hadn't turned around. Even then, I might not have recognized him had I not already seen him in both guises.

I slid my ale aside and leaned across the table. "By the bye, who *did* let you into the house last night? It could not have been Mr. Davis—he'd have known you straight off when you came 'round this morning."

Daniel continued to look somber. "The girl you call Sinead—she let me in herself."

My eyes widened in astonishment. "She did no such thing. Mr. Davis would never let a kitchen maid answer the front door. No maid, in fact. *Footmen* answer the doors, guide guests about, and serve meals—Mr. Davis might be chatty, but he does know how to instruct a household."

Daniel shrugged. "Perhaps she was commanded to by Lord Rankin. I know only that it was she who admitted me and showed me upstairs to the study."

"And Sinead he requested to bring the refreshment." I sat back and rested my fingers on my glass in contemplation. "Why would he want no one but Sinead to know you were there? He was certainly enraged when I arrived with the coffee instead."

A ghost of Daniel's smile flitted across his face. "I was surprised to see you march in there myself. Though I should not have been, I suppose." He lifted his glass. "It was a masterful performance. Thank you for your discretion."

"Humph. Did you expect me to throw open my arms and shout, *Daniel, whatever are you doing here?* I knew you were up to some intrigue. Of course, I expect you to tell me all about it now."

"I would like to." Daniel reached out and covered my hand where it rested on the table, his bare fingers warm on my gloved ones. "But I can't. Not everything. It is for your own well-being, Kat."

I gave him a narrow look. "You let me worry about my well-being. I've grown quite good at taking care of myself." Had ever since I'd learned that the man I thought I'd married had never been my husband at all, and I was left alone in the world, ruined and needing to make my own living. A lady learns what she is made of then. Fortunately for me, it turned out to be stern stuff.

Daniel squeezed my hand, his rough and work worn. "No doubt you have. But this concerns bad people, and I don't want them to have any idea you exist. I can tell you that I was there to speak to your master on grave matters, and I will warn you he is not the paragon he pretends to be. Me visiting him and my present employment in the house were my idea, not his. He dislikes the thought of me being there at all, in either guise, but he will not fight me."

I listened in some surprise. Lord Rankin was as a god in his own home, the very picture of a lord and master. The ladies of the house were quite under his thumb from what Mr. Davis had said, despite Lady Cynthia's rousing defense of me this morning. But then, she hadn't had much to lose telling Rankin to keep me on, and Rankin had seemed loath to upset his wife. Perhaps he was not as much a god as he would like to be.

"I already know he is no paragon," I said. "He likes to have his way with the maids. That is why I came up—I feared he meant to do so with Sinead."

"Does he?" Daniel didn't look very astonished. "Well, that will stop."

"Indeed, it will. I'll not have such goings-on in a house I'm in."

Daniel's grin returned. "I'm sure you won't, Mrs. H. I beg your pardon—Mrs. *Holloway*."

I gave him a severe look. Daniel never left off teasing me.

His hand rested comfortably on mine, very warm it was. I gently withdrew, lifting my glass of ale as an excuse. I took a quick sip, made a face, and set it down. "I don't suppose they do a nice cup of tea here?"

Daniel—my Daniel—laughed. "I'm certain they would if *you* showed them how it was done, Kat."

"Do cease," I said sternly. "Sinead has been killed, and I am very upset."

His smile vanished. "I know. I know, and I'm so sorry. She did not deserve that. But don't you see—I don't want such a thing to happen to *you*. I didn't think Rankin's house would be dangerous, but I was wrong, and I will have to live with that mistake." His gaze dropped to his ale but not before I glimpsed a dark flash of guilt in his eyes. Sinead's death distressed Daniel greatly, I saw, a fact he was striving to hide.

"You are not to blame," I said in surprise.

Daniel drew a breath as he looked at me again. "You are kind, but I might be. Which is another reason I wish you *would* give Rankin your notice."

I drew myself up. "I refuse to flee because a madman struck down an innocent young woman. I'd rather stay and run him to ground. He deserves to be caught, tried, and hanged."

Daniel studied me for a time, looking for I knew not what.

Finally, he gave a satisfied nod. "Very well. Truth to be told, I will welcome your help."

"Would you?" I started to lift my glass again then thought better of it. "I did plan to help whether you welcomed it or not. But you have taken a position in the household, which means you will be on the spot if anything happens. I'll hardly need to make a report."

"Not necessarily," Daniel said. "You are in the middle of things, ensconced in your kitchen like a goddess on her throne. You see all, hear all, speak to everyone. People bring their troubles to you. I will have to come and go—I must make a show of doing *some* labor or your butler will complain that I am slacking."

I gave him a long look. *Goddess on her throne* indeed. He had a silver tongue, this one.

"Very well," I said. "I will tell you if whoever committed this dreadful deed rushes to me and confesses. That is, if I do not thump him soundly first."

"Best you don't." Daniel grew serious again. "Dangerous men fill London, Kat. I don't like the fact that one penetrated a house in which you are living. That is one reason I will be living there too."

"Living there?" I asked abruptly. I'd come to accept that he'd be underfoot, but I hadn't thought Lord Rankin would provide his room and board.

"Not in the house. I'm not a refined servant, so I'll be in the mews with the groom and other stable lads—I'm a dab hand at looking after horses. *And* I can do a bit of carpentry or plumbing if need be."

I nodded, pretending I was unworried that Daniel and I would be essentially under the same roof. "Very capable. I must wonder where you discovered all these skills."

"On the streets, my dear friend." His cheeky look returned. "One learns so much by simply surviving."

"Oh, of course." Men trained for years to be carpenters or understand drains, just as a cook took a long time to master her craft. Daniel was adept at evading questions. I cleared my throat. "I will tell you right now, Mr. McAdam, that if you are late to meals, you will have to find for yourself. I am too busy to prepare special plates for you."

Daniel gave me a smile, amusement in his blue eyes. "Kat, you break my heart. But I will endeavor to remember."

"And for heaven's sake, don't slip and call me *Kat*. As the cook I will far outrank you." Why did that thought make me feel just a little smug?

Daniel lifted his pint to me. "I will accord you all respect," he said, and grinned. "Mrs. H."

I went home on my own, not wishing for those at the house to see me arriving chummily with the new man-of-all-work.

The March night had turned blustery by the time I left the pub, whipping my coat about as I moved down the street in search of an omnibus. One clattered toward me, but it was overly full, and I preferred to walk rather than be squashed too heavily against fellow members of humanity. As a girl, I'd heard about Mr. Darwin and his scandalous suggestion that men and women were in fact descended from the apes, but I tonight could not help but see a resemblance to our hairy cousins as the human beings in the crowded omnibus grappled to hang on to straps or one another.

I followed in the omnibus's wake to Oxford Street, where the crush of traffic, both foot and wheeled, threatened to swallow me. I kept my hands firmly on my pockets, as I knew cutpurses and thieves would take advantage of the crowd and try to steal my coins, my handkerchief, even the gloves off my hands if they could. They'd get a clout about the ears if I caught them, but often these thieves were slippery and silent, robbing a person blind without the victim even realizing.

I would have thought the citizens of London happy to remain comfortably at home on such a cold night, wind barreling down the streets like a gale through caverns, but no. They hurried to and fro, rushing to their amusements no matter what the weather.

They sought lower forms of entertainment on the streets themselves, ladies of the evening now even more obvious on the corners at Oxford Street. Disgraceful, though I couldn't help feeling somewhat sorry for the ladies. Once a woman was ruined, there was little she could do, no one she could turn to. But for luck and the grace of God, it might be *me* sa-shaying to the coach that slowed to a stop ahead of me, smiling hopefully at the gentlemen inside.

The lady I watched in her wind-tossed finery—velvet gown and fur stole, if you please—peered into the coach, and then abruptly lost her smile and swung away, hurrying back into the shadows.

As I passed the conveyance I glanced inside to see the silhouettes of two gentlemen in high hats, their garb no different from what Lord Rankin might wear. I wondered what had caused the lady to turn away so hastily.

"Evening, Mrs. H."

A voice, one I knew, sang out from the carriage window. I halted, peering more closely, and then I understood the courtesan's abrupt departure. I dropped a brief curtsy. "Good evening, your ladyship."

The door swung open, assisted by a foot in a well-made man's boot under striped cashmere trousers. "Climb in, Mrs. H.," Lady Cynthia said. "We'll take you home."

8

The booted foot belonged not to Lady Cynthia but to another young woman, who regarded me languidly from where she lounged next to her. The coach was dimly lighted by a lamp on the floor, illuminating dark gold velvet cushions, shadowed luxury.

I hesitated. "You are kind, my lady, but it is hardly proper for me to ride in his lordship's coach."

"Not a bit of it," Lady Cynthia said cheerfully. "This hack ain't Rankin's; it's hired. *I* don't mind a cook in my carriage. Give her your hand, Bobby."

Bobby's fingers stretching toward me, covered by fine kid leather, were as slender and well formed as her foot.

I wasn't certain I wanted to be shut up in a coach with Lady Cynthia and this Bobby, whoever she was, but nor did I relish walking home in wind growing colder and damper by the moment. A deluge would soon follow, I was certain.

I relented, took Bobby's hand, which turned out to be surprisingly strong, and let her pull me up into the coach.

Much better than the omnibus, I decided when I dropped onto the seat opposite the two ladies. The cushions were soft, the bench well sprung, the walls of the coach upholstered in the same gold velvet as the seats. Once the door was shut, the lantern glowed on the lush fabrics, suffusing the interior with warmth.

"Thank you," I said sincerely. "It is a hideous night for a walk."

"Just so," Lady Cynthia returned. "No reason for you to trudge about in the chill. Bobby, this is Mrs. Holloway, our cook."

I nodded my head at Bobby, noting Lady Cynthia had given me no other name for her. I wondered if her Christian name was Roberta—I'd known a girl in my youth with that name who'd been nicknamed Bobby—or if the lady only took the moniker while she wore the clothes of a man.

Both Lady Cynthia and Bobby were dressed so, from the hats I'd seen through the glass to well-tied cravats, to waistcoats—Bobby's dark green, Lady Cynthia's ivory this evening—with watch chains and fobs, trousers, and polished boots of supple leather.

"Are your underclothes gentlemen's too?" I asked before I could control my tongue. Then I flushed. My curiosity causes me no end of trouble.

Bobby dissolved into peals of laughter. She was a little older than Cynthia, though not by much, and had cut her hair short rather than wear it pinned it up as Cynthia did. I wondered if she wore switches when she dressed as a woman—if she ever did, that is. Bobby seemed quite comfortable in her male attire. She had brown eyes under thick brows and a narrow mouth in a squarish face. She resembled a gentleman more than Cynthia did, whose blond hair was coiled into a feminine braid at the back of her neck.

"The answer is, yes, they are," Lady Cynthia said as my face heated. "Quite comfortable things are gentlemen's undergarments. You ought to try them, Mrs. H. You'd not go back to a corset soon, I'll wager."

"Thank you, no." How silly I should look cooking in my kitchen in a gentleman's frock coat and trousers. Without a corset I should certainly come to some disgrace, as I was rather ample in the chest. The ladies before me were both slim in the torso, so likely they could tuck themselves into their straight shirts without difficulty. "Gentlemen wear corsets," I remarked. "Those who wish to tame their unruly stomachs anyway, though less port and Yorkshire pudding would achieve a better result, I think."

Bobby was off in laughter again. She apparently found me quite entertaining.

"Why were you wandering the streets, Mrs. Holloway?" Lady Cynthia asked. "After a choice bit of beef for tomorrow?"

"An errand," I said, trying to sound offhand. "Nothing important."

Bobby, recovering from her fit of laughter, leaned into Lady Cynthia and put her feet up on the seat beside me, her boots an inch from my skirt. "Are you a good cook?" she asked me.

"She is indeed," Cynthia replied before I could. "Wise of my sister to hire her. Best food I've eaten in an age. Mrs. H. is an artist."

Hardly. I used recipes I'd tested time and again, and I had enough experience to know which ingredients work best with what, that was all. However, I did not want to seem churlish, so I nodded. "Thank you, your ladyship. You are kind."

"Old Rankin tried to throw her out this morning," Cynthia

said. "All because the cook's assistant managed to get herself killed. Rankin's a fool—always has been. I tried to warn Em about marrying him, but he is disgustingly rich and rather bullied her into it. As long as you listen to my sister, Mrs. Holloway, and not the old bore, you'll do well."

I scarcely had an answer for this, so I said nothing and tried to look unruffled.

Bobby continued to lean into Cynthia, removing her hat to rest her head on Cynthia's shoulder. Bobby pulled out a cheroot, and Cynthia obligingly lit it with a match she struck against the sole of her boot.

Bobby puffed the cheroot gently, the tip glowing orange in the dim light. The coach began to fill with acrid smoke, and I suppressed a cough.

Most gentlemen were polite about smoking in close quarters with ladies, even ladies who were servants, but I had the feeling these two young women played hard at being gentlemen, copying what they perceived to be their mannerisms without knowing the reasoning behind them. I was not certain what appeal their charade held—they might dress as men and try to behave like them, but when all was said and done, they were still women, with the same restrictions as the rest of the female sex.

"Did you enjoy your outing?" I asked, endeavoring to be polite. In truth, I was avidly curious about what they'd been getting up to.

"It was splendid," Bobby said. "We went to a very illegal casino and lost our little all. Then we went to a club for gentlemen only and it was dark enough that we sailed right in."

"Not a club like White's, you understand," Lady Cynthia said. "We'd have to be members to darken *that* door, and our clothes only do so much for us."

Bobby went off in laughter again, finding everything hilarious tonight. I recognized that she was drunk, though she didn't slur her words or fumble with her cigar. But she'd imbibed *something* to make her merry.

Cynthia smelled of brandy, and now we all stank of cheroot. Lady Cynthia sent me a sympathetic look, as though knowing Bobby took a bit of getting used to.

"It was a dank place in the Haymarket," Cynthia explained. "This club, that is. Quite disreputable."

She seemed to want a reaction from me, so I nodded, and Cynthia looked pleased. Bobby continued to lounge against her, blowing smoke at the ceiling.

We passed out of Grosvenor Square and south down Park Street. When we reached the corner of Mount Street, I said, "I think you ought to let me out here. It would never do for me to arrive at Lord Rankin's house in your coach."

Cynthia chuckled, and Bobby continued her laughter, nearly lying in Cynthia's lap now. "Why not give old Rankin a turn?" Cynthia suggested. "Be good for him."

"Because," I said, "if I may speak frankly, my lady, I need this post."

"Good Lord, Cyns," Bobby said, opening her eyes wide. "Don't make the poor thing risk her job. She's a respectable, hardworking woman, not the idle rich, like us."

This gave rise to more paroxysms of mirth, this time from both of them. Cynthia studied my disapproving face and said, "We're laughing because neither of us have bean, Mrs. H. We'll be touching *you* for money soon."

I could scarce imagine what she meant by that—and perhaps I did not want to know—but the next moment, Cynthia rapped on the coach's roof and bellowed for the coachman to stop.

Bobby bestirred herself to open the door for me, pushing down the latch and then kicking the door until it banged against the side of the coach. The horses moved restlessly in their traces, and I had to descend without assistance. I went carefully, trying to hold my skirts so they would not fly up and give Park Street a glimpse of my legs in their sensible black worsted stockings.

The coachman scowled down at me, no doubt incensed that a mere cook should ride inside his carriage, but he at least waited until I was safely on my feet before he started the horses. I seized the door and slammed it shut, and the coach headed down Mount Street, lamplight gleaming on its now-wet roof.

Rain was indeed falling, though in gentle droplets for now. I hurried along to Lord Rankin's, slipping and sliding on the wet cobbles. When I reached the house, I plunged down the outside stairs and in through the scullery, stripping off my gloves and coat as I entered the kitchen.

"Stepping out, are you, Mrs. H.?" Mr. Davis crossed into the kitchen from the servants' hall, a bottle of wine dangling from each hand. "Have a bloke, do you? Or is it *Mr.* Holloway?" He gave me a curious look, as though hoping I'd tell him all about my inglorious past.

"Indeed no, Mr. Davis," I said, pretending I hadn't suppressed a guilty start. "An errand."

"You missed your own supper," he went on. "Excellent it was too."

"Thank you, Mr. Davis," I said. "I am not hungry."

I was, truth to tell, but I'd saved myself a heel of bread, a bit of cheese, and a chunk of the seedcake, which I'd hidden in the larder, and I'd make do with that. I was sad to see the teapot I'd used empty, and so I set a kettle on the still-warm stove to remedy that.

The master's valet, Simms was his name, came gliding in, a shirt over one arm, a polishing box and pair of shoes in his other hand. He fixed me with a haughty eye. "Any tea, Mrs. Holloway?"

"I've only just put the kettle on, Mr. Simms. It will be ready directly."

Mr. Simms gave me a sniff. "There's a row going on upstairs, and no mistake. Lady Cynthia's just come in with a very drunken lady friend, both of them dressed up in gents' clothing–deplorable." He disappeared into the servants' hall, where I heard him drop the polishing box and shoes onto the table there.

I heaved a sigh. Mr. Davis winked at me, deposited the wine bottles on my table–they'd be for my dishes tomorrow–and returned to the servants' hall.

By the time the water was in the teapot, the tea steeping, Mr. Davis had spread newspaper on the table in the servants' hall and was carefully rubbing polish onto the shoes with a circular motion, the cloth wrapped around one finger. Simms sat at the table across from him, mending a tear in the master's shirt.

I set teacups before both men and poured tea into them, then into a cup for myself. I sat down, warming my hands on my teacup. The footmen and maids were still engaged in various duties–scrubbing the night's dishes and cleaning the servants' area, or they were upstairs banking fires or readying the bedrooms for the family.

Of Mrs. Bowen, there was no sign. Mr. Davis volunteered, before I could ask, that she'd gone upstairs early, claiming a headache. Still upset about Sinead, he opined.

I was as well, but I'd learned that the best way to get through grief and sudden shock was to carry on working–there is a soothing element in routine. I believe that is why so many cling to religion—they know that, whatever horrors the world throws at them, they can say the words of ancient prayers or light candles or count beads as the papists do, and be comforted.

I was C of E and unlikely to become anything else, but I admitted that the rituals of our Sunday service were mired in tradition, so that one knew exactly what would happen every time. Old-fashioned and staid, some said. Refreshing, I always thought. A refuge from a mad world.

Not that I was an avid churchgoer. I went on Easter and Christmas, of course, and any other time I could get away, but a cook is expected to labor even on Sundays.

I took a welcome sip of tea, trying to banish the bite of ale and tang of cheroot smoke from my throat. Simms dipped his needle with skill into the master's cuff, frowning as he did so.

"Did you see any of the master's visitors yesterday, Mr. Simms?" I asked. Simms would be the closest of us to Lord Rankin—surely he'd known of Daniel's arrival. I wanted to discover whether Simms was in on the secret.

Mr. Simms gave me an impatient look as he pulled the thread through the cloth—he'd already decided I was far beneath him, I could see.

Mr. Davis huffed a laugh. "Mrs. H. is convinced the murdering bastard came in through the front door, raced downstairs, found Ellen, and did her in."

I shot Mr. Davis a look of disapproval at his language, but he only went on polishing the shoe.

Simms paused thoughtfully. "His lordship didn't have no visitors last night, but I did see a man lurking, I thought."

"Did you?" I asked in eagerness. "Where? Did you tell the police?"

Simms became haughty again. "I hardly speak to police-men, Mrs. Holloway. The fellow was outside anyway, not skulking about the house. He was sort of lingering by the railings, as though waiting for something. Or someone."

"Well, there you are," Mr. Davis said. "A murderer would be fleeing, wouldn't he? Not hanging about waiting to be caught. Stands to reason."

I said nothing, but the two of them had missed the point. Any person lurking about a house where there'd been a murder was interesting, whether they'd done the murder or not. They might have seen something, or been a lookout or some other sort of accomplice.

"Did you see what this man looked like?" I persisted.

Simms pursed his lips in annoyance. "I'm not in the habit of staring at people out of the window. He was an ordinary gentleman. He was there and then he was gone."

I hid a sigh, sipped tea, and let the matter drop. Mr. Davis sent me a sympathetic look, one that acknowledged that Simms was full of himself.

I was hungry, so I left them to their chores and made for the larder and the food I'd stashed there. The floor had been scrubbed, all traces of Sinead and her blood long gone.

I couldn't help raising the candle I'd lit to look into the corner where I'd found her, a lump forming in my throat when I gazed down at the clean slates. I'd barely known the young woman, but I grieved for the senseless waste of her life. She ought to have been given the chance to do more in the world, learn a trade, fall in love, bear a child.

Swallowing, I turned from the sight and lifted the cloth on the plate with the small meal I'd set aside.

I let out a very unladylike word. I found nothing on the

plate but crumbs—no bread, no cheese, and only a few stray pieces of caraway to indicate seedcake had ever been there.

I growled, snatched up the plate, and carried it to the scullery. The scullery maid had already finished and gone up, so I sloshed water and soap over the plate, reminding myself that I thought rote work to be soothing. My frustration and annoyance soon put paid to such lofty ideas.

I had no idea who'd eaten my dinner—I fixed on Simms, with his superior airs, but only because I already did not like him. It might have been the scullery maid herself, hungry after her day of hard labor. I'd be less irritated at *her*, but even so, she should not have taken the food without asking.

I finished and put the plate away, assured myself that the kitchen door was firmly bolted, and then climbed all the way to the top of the house and my dark, cold bedchamber. I stripped my gown from my body, washed my ruddy face, and went to bed hungry.

In the morning I was sore all over and had no idea why. I pulled myself out of bed, washed with a sponge and hot water carried to me by an early-rising maid, and put on a clean frock, apron, and cap.

I moved stiffly down the stairs, realizing I was sore because I'd been holding myself rigidly since finding Sinead dead. Bracing myself against my own anger and grief, perhaps, or perhaps waiting for another terrible thing to happen.

Downstairs the oven's fire was stoked high, the boy—Charlie, his name was—having already attended to it, the kitchen waiting for me to create meals. It was chilly this morning, but once I began cooking, I knew I'd not notice.

I approached the larder for my supplies and found as I drew near that my heart began to pound, and my throat went dry. At the doorway I halted, my feet refusing to obey my command to move forward.

I told myself not to be so silly. The odds of finding yet another member of the household dead were very slim. Sinead had been taken away, and soon would be given a decent Christian burial.

However, I could not make myself walk into the larder.

How long I stood in the doorway I did not know. I chastised myself—how could I be a cook if I was afraid to enter the room that held all my supplies? Would I have to give notice and take another post? And what reason would I give? That I was terrified of a pantry?

Yesterday, I'd been in and out of this larder, both before it had been cleaned of Sinead's blood and after. I'd tried to hide supper for myself in here and hadn't flinched when I'd gone in looking for it.

There should be no reason I hesitated this morning. Except, perhaps, that I had bounced down here yesterday morning, full of ambition in my first full day of cooking, and had stumbled across Sinead quite unexpectedly. Perhaps my body expected such a thing to happen again and was bracing for it, like a horse who has fallen at the exact same spot in a road once before.

Well, this state of affairs could not continue. Either I forced myself into the room or I walked away and commanded one of the maids to fetch what I needed. I could not simply stand in the doorway all morning.

A large, work-worn hand landed on my shoulder. "Everything all right, Kat?"

I shrieked and spun around, my heart beating wildly.

When my feet landed back on the earth, I spluttered, "Daniel McAdam, what the devil are you doing?"

Daniel lowered his hand and stepped away from me, his dark hair mussed, his coat misbuttoned, his eyes holding consternation rather than his usual good humor. "What is it?" he asked in a gentle voice.

I dragged in a breath. I wanted to fling myself at him and sob my troubles onto his shoulder, wanted him to hold and comfort me. Daniel had strong arms and was quite good at holding, as I had learned.

A fine thing that would look when any of the servants happened into the passage. Simms in particular would be scathing. I curled my hands to fists and lifted my chin.

"Nothing," I said with difficulty. "I am quite all right. But as long as you are here, please be useful and fetch me a rasher of bacon and the butter from that cupboard." I pointed into the larder at a tall chest. "Oh, and the loaf of sugar—it's on the top shelf. But don't you dare tread your muddy boots into my kitchen. Make sure you've scraped them clean first."

I caught a twinkle in Daniel's eye as I sailed past him and back to the kitchen, trying to ignore the rumbling chuckle behind me.

Daniel's presence in the house that day both made me feel better and unnerved me. On the one hand, I started every time I heard his voice, but on the other, I looked over my shoulder when I didn't hear him to see whether he was about.

His presence distracted me so much that I found myself reaching for washing soda instead of arrowroot to put into frothing eggs that I beat for a sponge cake; mistaking thyme for dill; and plunging a runner bean instead of a vanilla bean into a bowl of sugar. Only the diligence of Mary, who'd learned something from her mistakes yesterday, stopped me.

Daniel was no sham at being a man-of-all-work. He had the knack for turning up the moment he was needed, producing exactly the right tool to fix a leaking drain or to stop a creaking window or locating the correct copper pots I needed for my sauces. Notwithstanding how well Daniel could assume the mannerisms of a middle-class gentleman, he obviously knew how to take care of a house. This Daniel *had* to be the real one, I argued to myself.

Mr. Davis was appreciative of Daniel's help. He showed this appreciation by sitting at the kitchen table in his shirtsleeves, reading a newspaper while Daniel did the work of footmen, maids, grooms, and errand boys.

"These Fenians are becoming a handful," Mr. Davis said from behind the long page. "Imagine laying dynamite in railway stations to blast into innocent people, children and all. Happened in the north just yesterday." He made a noise of disgust as he turned the page. "We should put the lot of them in boats and shove them back to Ireland." Mrs. Bowen had expressed a similar sentiment, I recalled, when she'd told me of Sinead's mother killed in such an event.

"You would depopulate a large portion of this country," I remarked as I pounded butter into puff pastry dough. "Including many of the servants in this house. *You* would have to do extra work." I folded the dough over and rolled it hard with my rolling pin.

Mr. Davis lifted his paper out of the way of the scattering flour. "We'd hire Welshmen and good English girls," he said decidedly. "You Irish, Daniel?"

Daniel, who was crossing the room bearing a coal scuttle in each hand, shook his head. "Scots," he said, without a trace of any accent but London, and went into the scullery.

"Mmm." Mr. Davis continued to read. "Ah, this might be more agreeable to relate. A chap with a telescope reckons he's spied the planet that wanders about on the other side of the sun and pulls other planets out of their rightful paths."

I stopped rolling and blinked at him. "What on earth are you talking about?"

Davis chortled. "It's not *on earth* at all. According to gentlemen from Cambridge, there is a planet on the other side of our sun, which is why Mercury doesn't go around right. And now a chap reckons he's spied it."

I had my rolling pin poised in the air as I stared at him. Mr. Davis turned the page, moving on to the next story, and I slammed the pin back to the dough. If the butter melts while puff pastry is being rolled, the layered effect is ruined, and one has to begin again.

"I've never heard such utter nonsense," I proclaimed, putting an end to the matter.

Mr. Davis continued to read silently, offering no more argument, as I folded and rolled my dough several more times before I set it aside to rest and chill. Then I went to the scullery to wash my floury, buttery hands. Daniel was there, now scraping a patch of mold from the wall in the corner.

"You there," I said imperiously. "I'm off to the market. You will come with me and carry things. Is that all right, Mr. Davis?" I called back into the kitchen. "May I take him?"

Mr. Davis didn't move from behind his paper. "We're ahead of things because of him. Don't keep him away too long though."

"No, indeed." I removed my cap and tied on my bonnet—my everyday one of dark blue with lighter blue lining, then put on my coat and picked up the basket I used for my shopping. "Come along, Mr. McAdam."

Daniel shuffled along behind me without complaint, and we left Mr. Davis to his paper.

"I'm not only going to the market," I confided to Daniel once we reached the street. "I wish to visit Lady Cynthia's casualty, Mr. Timmons."

Daniel nodded. "An excellent idea, Mrs. Holloway. Well done. It's this way." He set off at a brisk pace east toward Davies Street, and I had to jog to catch up with him.

9

Daniel led me to Oxford Street and then up the Edgware Road, retracing my steps of the night before. Then along to Great Marylebone Road, where he convinced me to go down a flight of steps to the underground Metropolitan train that would take us east toward our destination.

I disliked the underground trains—too much smoke, noise, and danger. Who knew what would befall us in the dark tunnels? Or how the smoke escaped—if it did—instead of choking us all to death? But I would not let Daniel guess how nervous I was, and so simply followed him below the earth.

Daniel paid for my ticket like a gentleman. If he'd truly been helping me with the shopping as a menial, I'd have bought our tickets with some of my household money. Daniel, however, had approached the ticket man and procured our passage before I could say a word. I merely said my thanks and let him help me into the train.

We chugged through tunnels past Baker Street and Great

Portland Road, Daniel and I sitting side by side, me with my basket perched on my lap. We said little, since we were surrounded by fellow passengers, and rode in silence, his shoulder pressing mine as the train jerked and rumbled through the tunnels.

We emerged into daylight at Gower Street. I spent time brushing down my skirt from the soot it had acquired, and then Daniel took me northward behind Euston Station with its many rails and yards full of trains. Unused cars rested forlornly on side tracks, patiently waiting to be called for.

Daniel led me to a narrow street lined with a row of tall houses, each built of monotonous gray brick. The colorlessness was relieved every once in a while where one of the inhabitants had decided to paint their door a bright color. This effect was ruined by long exposure to London grime, however, and these lively red, blue, or green doors were now blackened, their paint cracking.

Mr. Timmons lived in a house in the middle of the row. The four-story dwelling had once been a single home, but the owner had turned it into rooms—the Timmonses lived together in two chambers on the top floor. Daniel gave the landlady his warmest smile, but either she was immune to his smile or shortsighted, as she only grunted and pointed the way up the stairs.

I'd learned as we'd walked that Daniel had been here yesterday, looking in on Mr. Timmons. I reflected that Daniel had been very quick to rush here and then to Lord Rankin's, but I held my tongue for now.

"I'm glad you've come," Mrs. Timmons said as she opened the door to us. She was a tired-looking woman with gray in her brown hair and a lined face. Her reddened hands told me she washed more dishes than only her own. "He's taken a turn."

I was sorry to hear that. Mrs. Timmons ushered us from the front room to the back one, a tiny space under the eaves. We barely fit into this small room, and the fire that burned fitfully on the hearth hardly kept it warm. Mr. Timmons lay on his back in bed, covers over his chest, his splinted arm resting on the quilts.

Timmons looked much as he had the day before yesterday, his face pale and drawn, his brown eyes holding pain. The fringe of hair on his head was going to gray.

Seeing the man now confirmed my belief that he'd never rushed down to the kitchen, bashed Sinead over the head, and sprinted out the door. He could barely move. He recognized me, I could tell, but whether or not the memory was a pleasant one, I could not say.

"Why did you leave Lord Rankin's house?" I asked him after Mrs. Timmons had informed her husband brightly that he had visitors. I stood at the foot of his bed and viewed him critically. "You were hardly fit to go anywhere at all."

Timmons glanced at Daniel then back to me and wet his lips. "Didn't want to be a burden," he said, then he shook his head. "Truth to tell, missus, I didn't like staying there. You were kind to me, but the others made it clear I weren't wanted. I were afraid the master would have me thrown to the pavement if I stayed too long, so when I felt a bit more myself, I legged it."

"But *how* did you?" I imagined Daniel had asked him all this yesterday, but I could not hold my tongue. "How did you manage to reach home in such a state?"

"I know blokes what drive carts around Mayfair," Timmons answered readily. "I persuaded one of them to take me as far as Regent's Park, and I asked for rides after that. A carter was kind enough to drop me at the end of my road."

He wet his lips again, his gaze darting to Daniel. Daniel, imperceptibly, nodded at him.

I caught the nod, to my irritation. It informed me that Daniel had rehearsed with Timmons what the man would tell me and perhaps anyone who asked him. I turned a frown on Daniel, but he didn't seem to note my disapprobation.

Mr. Timmons was clearly ill and not feigning. His wife looked anxious, and Timmons was obviously well tended by her. I had observed when we'd found him that he must have someone to look after his clothing, and indeed she appeared to be a most solicitous wife.

I stepped to the outer room when it was clear Timmons was fading to sleep, and gave Mrs. Timmons a remedy I had for pain—chamomile steeped in boiling water with a scraping of fresh ginger. It was good for aches and also settled the digestion.

After a few more sympathetic words to Mrs. Timmons, Daniel and I left them alone.

"A waste of an outing," I declared as we walked along the lane, back toward Drummond Street. "I might have saved a journey if you'd told me what you told *him* to say."

Daniel's expression wasn't as guilt-ridden as I'd hoped. He expressed no surprise I'd tumbled to his subterfuge and no shame either. "I ought to have known I couldn't deceive you. But I wanted you to see Timmons, to put your mind at rest that he was home, cared for, and could not possibly have lifted a marble bowl and struck a young, robust girl with it. You would not have taken my word for it, would you?"

Very likely not. "No," I conceded, but stiffly.

"Come on, then. I'll buy you a coffee before we journey back."

"Stopping at a market along the way," I reminded him as I fell into step with him. "I truly do need things for supper."

He laughed at that. He was always laughing, was Daniel. At one time in my life I had loved laughter.

Vendors lined the roads near Euston Station, the station itself with its Greek pediment and Doric columns proclaiming it an edifice as important as an ancient temple. Daniel led me to a vendor and asked for two cups of tea—I explained to him that I didn't much care for coffee. The tea, served in chipped mugs, was strong and rather fierce, but in the cold wind, after the chill of Mr. Timmons's rooms, I welcomed it.

The wind held, very faintly, a gentler note, a promise of spring to come. That was still a way off though, it warned. I stepped to the lee side of the vendor's cart to avoid it, and Daniel followed me. In the relative privacy we sipped tea.

"My apologies for not escorting you to a more agreeable place," Daniel said. "I don't believe I'd be let into a tea shop, not one you would approve of anyway, not in my present attire."

He indicated his work clothes with his thick gloves, his boots muddy and splotched from muck on the roads. His cap was pulled down over his eyes, anchored against the wind.

"I do not mind," I said. "I have no inclination to linger over tea and cakes today."

Truth to tell, I enjoyed tea shops, where I could sit still while someone else brought me refreshment, and gossip with a companion without worry. I hadn't had much time for such things lately.

"One day, I'll dress up fine and take you to a restaurant," Daniel proclaimed before he took a long slurp of tea.

I raised my brows. "Oh, you will, will you?" I had a brief vision of myself sailing into an elegant dining room on Daniel's arm, he in his well-tailored suit, me in . . . Hmm, I'd have to find a new frock for the occasion. "Absurd," I said. "If you walked into a restaurant with a cook on your arm, they'd likely send me to the kitchens to help with the meals."

"We wouldn't mention that you were a cook, of course. We would be Daniel and Kat—Mr. McAdam and Mrs. Holloway—enjoying a supper."

I sent him a pitying look. "My dear Daniel, no matter what fine feathers I put on, everyone would know me for a domestic. That is what we *are*."

Daniel swept his gaze from the top of my prim bonnet to the toes of my sensible shoes. He lifted his cup to his lips again. "That depends on the feathers."

His scrutiny over the rim of his mug made my cheeks heat. "Now you are becoming unseemly," I said hastily, trying to retain my dignity. "One cup of tea does not mean you can take liberties, Mr. McAdam."

Daniel's grin flashed. "I'd never dream of taking liberties with *you*, Kat. You'd send me off with your rolling pin fast enough. Or one of your very sharp knives."

"And *that* is a joke in poor taste." The tea rested heavily in my stomach. I'd once had to fend off a gentleman in my kitchen with a carving knife, with dire consequences for both of us. Daniel knew it, drat him.

Daniel lost his smile. "My apologies. You are right—I should not make fun of horrible things. Enjoy your tea, my dear, and I shall leave you alone."

"No, indeed, you'll not get off that easily." I took another sip of the awful tea. "Why did you instruct Mr. Timmons to say what he did? Why was he in Mayfair that day anyway? Surely it is a bit far for him to make his deliveries, or whatever he was doing."

"Not necessarily. Carters go all over London, up and down, to every corner, wherever they're sent. They know London like no others, unless it's the cabbies."

"Is that why you are a deliveryman most of the time?" I asked. "So you can go up and down London and see every corner?"

Daniel acknowledged this with a nod. "I find jobs for a day, or a week, whatever I need, and leave when I'm finished."

"An itinerant deliveryman. How interesting." I knew he'd never tell me his real purpose for flitting all over London, so I didn't bother asking. "We are straying from the topic. Why should Timmons come to Mayfair? Why should he be so far from home at the precise moment Lady Cynthia ran him down?"

"Unless Lady Cynthia meant to." Daniel took a long draught of tea. "And then she grew remorseful and ran to you for help."

I stared at him. "Why on earth should Lady Cynthia run down Mr. Timmons? She didn't even know him." I watched Daniel's unchanging expression and sighed. "A moment—you are saying she knew exactly who he was and deliberately struck him."

"Possibly," Daniel said, something dark flickering in his eyes. "Once again, I am blaming myself for another taking hurt, and I'm not wrong. Timmons was at Mount Street because I asked him to be there." He leaned to me, his breath warm from the tea. "I've been watching Rankin's house, as I told you. Mr. Timmons was handy and needed extra work, so I asked him to help me keep an eye out."

My temper mounted but thoughts clicked into place. "I see. That is why you and your son were so conveniently about that morning. You came to confer with Mr. Timmons, or some such thing. Please, tell me, Daniel, if Lord Rankin is a man to attract your suspicions, why did you not warn me off taking the post?"

Daniel gave me an exasperated look. "Because I could not find you, bothersome woman. You had left your post in Richmond by the time I was— By the time I began observing

Rankin, and I had no idea where you were. You changed your boardinghouse from the last one I knew of. Your agency turned me away with a flea in my ear when I went to ask after you."

"As they should," I returned. "They're a very good agency, and likely they guessed you had no intention of employing me. I moved to a boardinghouse in Tottenham Court Road because the landlady in King Street closed her house to stay with her sister, who'd become very ill."

I wondered what Daniel had stopped himself from saying. *By the time I was*– What? Keeping an eye on Lord Rankin? Back from wherever he'd disappeared to before that?

"The agency refused even to send a message to you," Daniel said, frowning. "Which was maddening, because I knew Lady Rankin was seeking a cook and would pay for the best. So by the time I *could* warn you, you were already ensconced in Rankin's household. I did encourage you to leave the post last night, if you recall."

"And I ignored you," I reminded him. "I need the wages, plain and simple. You offered to find me another post once, a long time ago."

"Which you refused point-blank." Amusement crept back into Daniel's expression. "I vividly recall you doing so. That post is filled, but I'm certain I can find another for you."

I readily believed that Daniel could do anything he wanted, so I remained silent. No doubt he'd find a position for me in a house tucked away in a dull corner of London where nothing ever happened. I'd knead, stir, chop, and baste with tiresome repetition until I crawled off to weary retirement.

"I will weather Lord Rankin for the moment," I said. "As long as you assure me he did not kill Sinead."

"I don't *believe* he did. Certainty is elusive. He is dangerous, Kat, I will tell you that." Daniel let out a breath. "Though he would be most dangerous to you if you had large amounts of money invested through his firm."

I blinked at him. "Good heavens, are you saying he is a swindler? Oh dear, his poor wife. And Lady Cynthia."

If Lord Rankin used his position to swindle from gentlemen, he would ruin not only himself but his entire family. Lady Rankin and Lady Cynthia would never be able to hold up their heads among their society friends—many of whom might be investors with him. If Lord Rankin lost all the money, Lady Cynthia and her sister would be destitute. From what Mr. Davis had told me, their own family had no money, in spite of its lofty title, so it wasn't likely a dowry or widow's portion would help Lady Rankin. Lady Cynthia would have nothing at all and be left to the charity of her parents.

"I often pity the upper classes," I reflected, cradling my mug of cooling tea. "*I* have the option to take a job to keep myself fed, no matter how menial that position might be. Lady Cynthia has no prospects unless she marries and no inheritance unless some benefactor provides it for her. She must beg for room and board from her friends and family, be the poor relation, the spinster no one wants. No wonder she puts on trousers and behaves boorishly. I might do the same."

"Your philosophy is sometimes frightening, Kat." Daniel gave me a fond look, pried the teacup out of my hand, and returned it to the vendor.

He took my arm and led me away, hopefully to find a cab—I did not wish to ride the train through tunnels again.

As Daniel helped me cross a noisome puddle in front of the grand portico of Euston Station, he bumped into a well-dressed young man with a tall hat, who was hurrying from a coach, probably running for a train. Several young men in similar dress followed him, upper-class gents off on some journey.

As the young man snarled at Daniel, Daniel touched his hat and took on his South London accent. "Beg pardon, sir."

The young man gave him a glare. "Watch where you're going, you lout."

Daniel doffed his cap as the young man fell into step with his friends and they strode toward the station, backs covered with black cashmere greatcoats of well-tailored expense.

"And a fine good morning to you, sir," Daniel called after them cheerfully.

The first man turned back, and his friends did as well once they'd realized he'd stopped. They were all young—in their twenties it looked like, wearing the latest in waistcoats, trousers creased as smartly as their valets could make them, boots polished with care. The valets in question continued to the station where they would settle the tickets and wait for their masters to finish their business.

Their business at the moment was to surround Daniel. I was shoved aside, not rudely—they barely noticed I was there.

"What did you say?" the first young man demanded in such a highbred voice I could barely make out the words.

Daniel now had his cap in his hands. "I wished you good day, sir." He gave the men surrounding him his most personable smile. "Wherever you are destined. Good day for it. Traveling."

For the first time since I'd met him, I did not observe Daniel's overt friendliness melting those it was directed to. Perhaps the young men were drunk, or hungover, or simply coldhearted and very taken with themselves.

"How dare you even speak to me," the first man said. He

had a pale face, hair just as colorless, a thin body, and blue eyes that were red-rimmed—*hungover, yes*. For all his frail appearance, his expression held the belligerence of a pugilist in his final match.

Daniel retained his smile, though his eyes had cooled. "Beg pardon, sir," he repeated.

He was doing this all wrong, I could have told him. A day laborer should bow his head, shuffle away, and say nothing more, satisfying himself by muttering his anger to the next laborer he passed.

I tried to save Daniel by starting forward. "Come along, you," I commanded in ringing tones. "I have many more errands today."

I pretended to not notice the toffs, since I should never think to speak to them if they did not address me first. I conveyed with my words, voice, and demeanor that I was impatient with my hired help and would take him out of their way as soon as I was able.

Ignoring me, the first young man swung out a kid-gloved fist and cuffed Daniel on the side of the head.

Daniel rocked back, then he snapped his neck straight again, a hard look in his eyes.

All would have been well if the young gentleman had satisfied himself that he'd taught Daniel a lesson and moved on, but his blue eyes grew colder still, and he struck Daniel again.

"Insolence," he spat. "Go tell your master to beat you."

Daniel at last took a step back, realizing he needed to end this encounter, but apparently he didn't move deferentially enough. The young man came for Daniel again, backhanding him. Then, his eyes narrowing, he began striking Daniel again and again, his face red, his lips pulled back into a snarl.

His friends only watched, nonplussed, until Daniel brought

his own fists up to defend himself. Then, gleefully, they pounced on him.

Four men against one, they surrounded Daniel and began pounding him until he fell to the pavement. They planted their polished boots into his ribs, thighs, and back, over and over again. Daniel could only shield his face with his arms and roll into a ball to avoid the worst of the blows.

This had gone beyond gentlemen berating an impudent workman. These young lads who'd spent the previous night drunk and had nothing better to do today were taking out their pique on Daniel. Large fists in expensive gloves rose and fell, boots of best calf leather slammed into Daniel's ribs and hips.

"Help!" I shouted at the passersby. They were happy to stop and gape, but no one moved to assist. "Useless pillocks!" I shrieked at them, then flung myself at Daniel's assailants.

10

I seized the elbow of one of the gentlemen with both hands and yanked him backward. I was not as tall as he was, but laboring in a kitchen–lifting roasting pans, cleaving meat, wrestling with iron stoves–had made me strong. The young man lost his balance and stumbled into me.

"For shame!" I yelled into his face. "Shame on you!" I pushed him away with my empty basket.

The young man gazed down at me blearily, then to my surprise, he straightened up, looking like a chastised schoolboy. In his hazy state, he must have confused me with his nanny.

He shook free of me but grabbed his nearest friend. "Leave off," he growled. "We have a train to catch."

The next man straightened up, wiping his nose, which was dripping, though not with blood. "Come on," he said to the others. "That's taught him a lesson," he went on, running his gloved hand under his nose again. "Leave it, Minty," he called to the gentleman who'd begun the beating and who was still kicking Daniel. "Someone will shout for the police, and if you get yourself banged up again, your dad will cut off your balls."

Minty, whoever he was, reached down and punched Daniel three more times, then straightened up, snatched a handkerchief from his pocket, and wiped his face of blood.

"I'll have *him* up before a magistrate," he snarled, dabbing at his cut forehead. "See him hanged."

The one I'd scolded rolled his eyes. "We don't have time. We'll barely make the train as it is, because you're such a layabout. He's not worth it."

"He *hit* me, the bastard," Minty returned. His hands were shaking, a strange light of hatred in his eyes. "He's a dead man."

"Minty." The word from the man I'd scolded was stern, and Minty jerked around. His friend pointed a stiff finger to the columns of the station. "Go. You can whinge about it on the way."

He must be the leader of this tribe, not Minty, because Minty, after shooting a glare at me, obediently turned and made for the station. He shoved people out of the way, but they only sidestepped him and drifted over to enjoy the entertainment of me falling to my knees at Daniel's side.

I put my hand under Daniel's head, and as I did so, he uncurled himself and sat up, blood all over his face.

The passersby suddenly became solicitous. A woman with a basket filled with greens crouched down beside us. "All right, love?"

Daniel started to touch his face, but I grabbed his wrist to prevent him from brushing his wounds with his dirty gloves. The entire left side of his face was swollen, cuts slicing both cheeks and forehead, and blood ran from under his hair.

"Ee, that's nasty," the woman said, studying him. She shook out a large handkerchief and handed it to me. "Use this, love."

An older man bent down, hands on his knees, as I touched

the offered handkerchief to the gash on Daniel's forehead. "You need help?" the old man asked. "You shouldn't have provoked them, lad."

Daniel spit blood onto the pavement. He shot a glare at the young men disappearing into the station and said a few words ladies should never hear.

The woman next to me grinned. "Aye, they should stay in their posh houses where they belong. But he could have you, lad, for hitting him back."

"Pure accident," Daniel mumbled. He sent me a glance. "Take me home, missus?"

I climbed to my feet, accepting the assistance of the man and woman, and together we hauled Daniel upright. He was a bit unsteady, but his legs worked—at least the toffs hadn't broken his bones.

"Best get him indoors," the old man advised me. "Give him some gin for the pain."

"Water and lavender to wash the cuts," the woman put in. "Can you take him all right, love?"

"Yes, indeed." I gave them a nod that was as dignified as I could make it, but my heart was racing, my worry high.

My fear made me sharp as I helped Daniel limp away, the kind woman telling me to keep the handkerchief. "We'll have to walk all the way back now," I snapped. "No one will let you on a train or omnibus looking like *that*."

Daniel, damn the man, had the impudence to grin. "We'll take a hansom. Don't worry, Kat. I'll be fine."

"Fine?" I said in a near-shout. "Die of infection, I would say. We need to get you home and cleaned up before Mr. Davis sees you. He'll sack you, and I need you there."

Daniel's look softened. "Aw, Mrs. H.—you're sweet." He sounded as drunken as the toffs.

"Don't talk nonsense," I said in a tight voice.

Daniel did not in any way look remorseful. He lifted his hand at a passing hansom, letting out a whistle that released a spattering of blood.

The hansom, to my surprise, slowed for us. Cabbies were tough men, for the most part, who had no compunction about refusing to let ruffians or other undesirables into their carriages. This one, however, leaned from his perch on the back to peer at us, and his eyes widened.

"McAdam? God's balls, what the devil happened to you?"

"Hoping it would be you, Lewis," Daniel called up to him. "Give us a ride home, eh?"

"If you can heave yourself in." The man called Lewis stopped his horse, then tipped his hat to me. "Ma'am."

He had to keep hold of the horse, so Daniel actually handed *me* in, seeming plenty steady enough to do so, before he hauled himself up behind me.

The hansom was a typical one—two wheels and a seat with doors that closed in front of us, the driver in the back to guide the one horse. As soon as Daniel sat down and snapped the door shut, Lewis tapped the horse and clicked his tongue. The horse started forward at a smart trot, the cab jerking as it began.

I took the already bloody handkerchief and resumed dabbing at Daniel's wounds. I was still shaking, fear and anger swirling together.

"Do you know every cabbie in London?" I demanded.

"Only some of them." Daniel let me wipe blood from the corner of his mouth. "I drive a cab occasionally myself."

"Of course you do. Friend of yours, is he?"

"Colleague." Daniel's voice gentled. "I am well; don't worry yourself. I've taken far worse beatings from far worse ruffians. Those lads were half drunk and unpracticed."

"That is a speech to make me feel better, is it?" I glared at him. "Do you often seek beatings?"

Daniel winced as I touched an open cut. "In my younger days, when I was foolish, I am afraid I did. In this case, there was not much I could do but tuck myself up and wait for them to grow tired of their fun. If I'd fought back, they—or some passing copper—would have dragged me to a magistrate, who would have me up for assault before I could get things sorted out, and I don't have time for that. I never expected you to join in."

I gave him an incredulous look. "Was I to stand aside and wring my hands? Screech *oh, oh,* like a wet heroine in a silly melodrama?"

Daniel tried to laugh, then grimaced when it pulled at his mouth. "I believe I adore you, Kat."

"Enough of that. Stay quiet until we reach Mount Street. We can try to get you in through the mews and hope the head groom holds his tongue."

"He would. He's a decent sort."

I had paid no attention to where we were, bent on cleaning as much blood as I could from Daniel's face, but when I looked around, we seemed to be on Southampton Row, heading no-where near the direction of Mayfair. We turned east then south again not long later, moving along Drury Lane toward Long Acre, then Covent Garden, skirting that busy area but continuing south.

"Wherever are we going?" I asked Daniel. "Did you plan to ride back through St. James's, perhaps taunt a few more toffs?" I was nervous, fearing Daniel might do just that.

Daniel shook his head. "When I said *home,* I did not mean Mount Street." He pressed aside my hand with the scarlet-blotched handkerchief. "I meant *my* home. At least, my lodgings—the ones I'm keeping for the moment."

"Oh." I lowered the handkerchief to my lap, curiosity seeping through my anger. Daniel was going to let me see where he lived, wonder of wonders.

The hansom stopped south of Covent Garden in Southampton Street, near the Strand. The house we halted before looked no different from its fellows—a brown-red brick building with white trim on the windows, shops on the ground floors and rooms above.

Mr. Lewis calmed the horse that shifted in the traces, the two-wheeled cab moving a little as we descended. Daniel climbed stiffly out first and insisted on handing me down. He also insisted on passing Lewis up a coin, though Lewis tried to refuse.

"You answer to another," Daniel told him. "I'd not see you lose your post for giving us a ride for nothing."

Lewis ceased his arguing, pocketed the coin, touched his hat, and tapped the horse with his long whip. The horse clopped away, the wheels of the hansom rumbling on the cobbles as Lewis headed for the Strand.

The shop in the bottom of the house where Daniel lived was a pawnbrokers. Three small gold-painted balls hung from the sign above its door, and its narrow window showed a number of disparate wares—a nicely painted black box, a pair of silver-plated tongs with some of the silver flaked off, and a copper colander. A black-painted door next to the shop opened to reveal a plain staircase, narrow wooden steps leading upward between two white walls.

Daniel trundled up this staircase, taking sharp breaths now and again as pain caught at him. I shook my head and came behind.

"Good heavens." A woman's voice rang down from the upper floors, followed by the woman herself stepping onto the landing. She had gray hair pulled into a severe bun under her white cap, a frock as equally gray as her hair, and a pinafore with so many ruffles I had no idea how it served as an apron. Perhaps she sought to enhance the plainness of her gown and hair with a frivolous pinny.

"Whatever have you done to yourself, Mr. McAdam?" the woman asked as she started down the stairs. She looked past him at me, her gaze full of curiosity. "Is this your cook?"

I had no idea who the woman was, or why she ought to be staring at me so impertinently. Daniel only clung to the wooden railing and pulled himself to the landing on the first floor.

"She is indeed," he said. "Mrs. Williams, this is Mrs. Holloway, the finest cook in London."

Mrs. Williams gave me another assessing look. "Tell me what happened to him, dear. What did he do to earn such a thumping this time?"

I pressed my lips together as Daniel unlocked a door on the first floor and opened it into a sunny room. He ushered me inside as though we entered an elegant parlor.

I answered Mrs. Williams as we went in. "He said too much to the wrong person."

Mrs. Williams gave me a look of understanding. "Aye, he has a silver tongue on him, does our Mr. McAdam. Gets him into trouble sometimes, the foolish lad." Her lilt, now that she relaxed her rather rigid English, sounded Scottish. "Good of you to bring him home, dear."

I did not correct her and say that Daniel had brought *me* here. He'd disappeared into the back room, presumably his bedchamber. Mrs. Williams heaved a sigh. "I'll fetch some water."

She stalked out, leaving the door open, and I looked about with interest.

The sitting room was bright because the day had turned

so, sunshine not yet blocked by the buildings across the road. The floor was covered by a colorful carpet—a floral design bordered in black—that was old but clean and not threadbare.

None of the furniture matched. A desk stood in the corner, and several chairs were put about, one an old-fashioned Belter chair with a carved back, another from even longer ago—Chippendale style with claw and ball feet. A third chair was newer, in a plainer mode that was becoming more fashionable nowadays.

Daniel had a sofa, a small thing that two people could barely fit onto, and only one table, not even large enough for a spread of tea. Perhaps Mrs. Williams had a parlor where lodgers could invite their guests, or perhaps she reasoned they'd find their sustenance elsewhere—in taverns or tea shops, Covent Garden being just up the road.

I saw no evidence of personal things belonging to Daniel. No photographic portraits of family, no souvenirs from various places around London—or anywhere else for that matter—no small knickknacks we all pick up from time to time.

In short, nothing of Daniel McAdam rested in this room. I wondered how long he'd lived here, and if he had rooms elsewhere in London that housed his true belongings.

Mrs. Williams bustled back in with a bowl and an ewer. She looked about for somewhere to set it down, and I cleared a lamp off the small round table, allowing her to rest the bowl there.

Daniel walked out from the inner room as Mrs. Williams poured the steaming water from the ewer into the bowl. He'd rid himself of his coat and bloodstained shirt but pulled on another shirt, which he'd modestly buttoned to the throat. He wore a resigned look, knowing we women were going to fuss over him.

"Thank you, Mrs. Williams," I said. "I will make sure Mr. McAdam is well."

Mrs. Williams was obviously curious about Daniel's battle, but she only nodded politely and moved to the door.

"Mrs. Holloway will give you her recipe for her lemon sponge cake before she goes," Daniel told her. "Light as down it is."

"Of course," I said, not bothering to give Daniel an annoyed glance.

Mrs. Williams looked delighted with this, smiled at me, and departed. She left the door open once again.

I pointed to the plain chair, and Daniel sat without argument. I dipped a cloth Mrs. Williams had left into the hot water and began to clean his wounds.

He had a cut in the shape of a cross next to his eye, a deeper gash on his forehead, a lump on his jaw, a cut on the side of his lip, and skin scraped off his left cheek, though the swelling had subsided there a bit. Those were only the injuries I could see. Who knew what bruises he had on his ribs and chest? Daniel's shirt was closed up to his chin, hiding his torso.

"I cannot help remarking," I said as I worked, "that these rooms are suspiciously close to my old boardinghouse. A brief walk through Covent Garden, and there it is."

"Not so curious." Daniel flinched as my cloth dug a bit of pavement out of his cut. "When I was looking for you a few weeks ago, I wandered the streets in this area to see whether you had moved somewhere close by. I saw that Mrs. Williams had rooms to let, and I thought they would suit me."

"For a time," I muttered.

"Pardon?"

I cleared my throat. "You seem to move about. Here, there, never long in one place."

"True." Daniel sucked in a breath again as I pulled out a small piece of glass he must have rolled onto. "Those lads truly worked me over, didn't they?"

"Why did you provoke them?" I asked, my fears surging. The cloth hovered, dribbling dark blotches onto my skirt. "If you are going to playact, Mr. McAdam, you ought to remember which part you are taking at the moment."

Daniel flushed, which made his bruises still more purple. "Right as always, Mrs. H." Coolness entered his eyes. "The young man who rammed into me—Minty, they called him?—made me lose my temper. You are right that I should have let him go, but I could not resist."

"And got beaten down for your trouble." My fingers continued to shake, water dripping everywhere.

Daniel closed his hand over mine, his warm and steady. "I beg your pardon, Kat. I never meant to upset you. I am arrogant and forget not to be."

He squeezed my hand, his strength undimmed, and his blue eyes met mine.

Daniel had eyes a woman could look into for long stretches of time. Dark, clear, unfaltering. A dangerous thing was Daniel's gaze.

I worked my hand free and pressed the cloth to the cut beside his eye. He let out a hiss of pain.

"All that over a young man you don't know and never are likely to," I said, my voice not quite as firm as I would have liked.

"Not quite." Daniel reached into the pocket of his trousers and withdrew a card case.

The card case was gold and shining, decorated with an inlay of blue and red stones in an oval across its top. Daniel opened it and extracted a thick, ivory-colored card.

"Lord Frederick Piedmont," he read. "A stretch to call him Minty, isn't it? But perhaps it refers to something other than his name."

I stood up, aghast. "Good heavens, you picked his *pocket*?"

Daniel nodded as though the fact was of no moment. "While he was bashing me about. I thought I'd like to know my assailant, in case I wish to bring him to court. Or other things."

"*Daniel.*"

Daniel looked up at me, took in my shock, and his expression softened. "He'll never miss it, Kat. I expect he has dozens."

"That is hardly the point. What will you do with it? Take it downstairs to the pawnbrokers? Then this Minty truly *will* have you up before the magistrate. I do not believe your connections—whoever they are—will help you then."

Daniel rose to his feet a bit unsteadily, dropped the card case and card to the table, and took hold of my hands. "You're a wonderful woman, Kat Holloway. Don't worry. I will return it anonymously to his father, and our Minty will conclude he dropped it."

I let out a breath. Daniel held the wet cloth as well as my

hands, but this time I did not pull away. "How do you know who his father is?"

"Lord Freddy Piedmont—Minty—is the youngest son of the Marquis of Chalminster." He chuckled. "Chalminster is always in a bother about his sons."

I didn't answer, not quite knowing how to. As a cook working in prominent households, I did know about aristocrats and other well-heeled ladies and gentlemen—you came to remember who was whom, and besides, the newspapers are full of their exploits. But Daniel could pick names out of the air and put them together like no one I had ever known. No matter how many calluses Daniel had on his hands, he understood the genteel world as no deliveryman should.

But I couldn't believe Daniel himself was one of them. No highborn gentleman stooped to the manual labor Daniel did, not even for a lark. Daniel performed his tasks well too, uncomplaining, unflagging. I couldn't imagine Minty, a spoiled, rather cruel young man, lasting all day on a delivery cart, toting things down into the kitchens of his highborn neighbors.

Daniel seemed to be no one from nowhere. And yet he moved among high classes and low, changing from one to another like a chameleon. Lord Rankin certainly seemed intimidated by him. Daniel lived here, in small, cheap rooms like a working-class man, with a working-class landlady who regarded him with fondness.

"You told me you had your eye on Lord Rankin," I said slowly, "and that he was a swindler, but that it was too dangerous for me to know more. But I think I ought to know, if I'm to help you."

Daniel raised one of my damp hands, kissed the heel of it, and released me. "I believe I am changing my mind about asking for your assistance. About this part of it, anyway."

I made a noise of exasperation. "Well, of course you need

me to help. Else you would have found some way by now to remove me from the house, no matter how much I protested. You know this." I pointed a wet finger at him. "Please tell me, very specifically, why you are watching Lord Rankin."

Daniel sighed. The sigh came from the depths of him, a man realizing the woman before him was not the capitulating, malleable creature she was supposed to be. The many articles and books postulating that women are inferior beings and have not evolved as far as men are, in my opinion, written by rather ignorant males. I have concluded that either the writers are unmarried or they have carefully chosen their wives from females of deficient intellect, who will never contradict them.

Daniel moved past me, closed the door so softly the latch did not click, came to me, and led me to the very center of the room. Away from the windows, chimney, and registers, I realized.

When he spoke, his voice was very quiet, and I had to step close to hear him.

"You speculated that Lord Rankin would be ruined for being caught committing fraud," Daniel began. "But he won't." His look turned annoyed. "He's very clever, is our Lord Rankin. A genius with figures, and we are having great difficulty unraveling his, though I have my best man working on it. But what he *has* done is make certain some very bad gentlemen have made a great deal of money through him, money they use to commit even more terrible acts. Including ones against Britain."

My eyes widened. Not only a swindler—a traitor? Was Rankin that much of a fool?

I did not consider myself robustly devoted to crown and country, other than to feel relief that I'd been born a British subject and did not have to grub for my living in some squalid backstreet on the Continent. But a man had to be idiotic to finance a plot against the Queen or Parliament—if caught, he'd be reviled in all corners of the kingdom and executed in shame. Traitors used to be drawn and quartered. I was not certain what the penalty was these days, but it was certain to be dire. Lord Rankin's family wouldn't live it down for generations to come.

Daniel continued. "Rankin defends himself by saying he had no idea what these gentlemen were doing with the money he made for them. He might be telling the truth." Daniel's look said his opinion was divided. "To prove his loyalty, Lord Rankin is continuing his tasks for these clients but reporting to me everything they say and do, and showing his ledgers every night to one of my colleagues. I don't have much of a head for finance."

I wasn't certain what shocked me more—Lord Rankin's perfidy or discovering something at which Daniel wasn't skilled.

But how had Daniel convinced Lord Rankin to cooperate? And who were these colleagues he spoke of? Was Daniel truly of the police, as I'd speculated?

My mouth was dry. "That's why you visited Lord Rankin in your guise as City gent."

"And why he was not pleased at your intrusion." Daniel's eyes sparkled with amusement. "He did not know what to make of you. Rankin fears—ever he fears—that a person will discover he is helping men who blow up railways and other horrific acts and make him pay."

"You mean he thought I'd blackmail him?" I asked, astounded. "The very idea. I'd never stoop to anything so sordid."

Daniel's look turned grim but he put a soothing hand on my arm. "I persuaded him he had nothing to fear from you."

I imagined the conversation—Lord Rankin with his piercing stare, Daniel facing him with the chilly hardness I'd seen him assume. Lord Rankin had obviously been the loser of the argument.

I wet my lips and stepped back, which broke Daniel's hold. "Thank you for telling me."

He let me go without comment. "I considered what you said to me in the pub last night and decided it was better you knew. I also know you are not a fool or a talkative woman. I only hope my telling you does not put you in danger."

"I *am* a talkative woman," I told him. "But I can also keep tales like this to myself."

"I realize that." He gave me a grateful look. "James doesn't know, however. I want to keep him out of this as much as I can." He shook his head, long-suffering. "Persuading him is sometimes more difficult than persuading you."

I forbore from comment. "James already knows you're in some sort of intrigue. You have him roaming Mount Street for you."

Daniel's expression turned pained. "Actually, I told him to stay well away. But as I say, the boy has a will that won't be stopped."

"Rather like you." I gave him a pointed glance. "James isn't a boy anymore, is he? He's sprung up a good foot since last year. He'll be a man soon. What then? Shall you help him find a trade? At least let him live in rooms with you?"

He did not admonish me for delving into his private life, but he did not answer either. "You do ask the most difficult questions," he said. "I wish you *were* a featherhead sometimes. I'd win more arguments."

"If I were a featherhead, you never would have spoken to me twice," I told him. "And we would not be here, musing over difficult questions."

"Again, she is wise," Daniel said to the room. "You are a wonderful woman, Mrs. Holloway."

My face heated. "Don't be daft," I said, and waved him to

the chair again, where I made him sit still while I finished ministering to his wounds.

Because we were so near Covent Garden, I insisted we walk to its markets before we found another hansom that would take us to Mayfair.

The afternoon was getting on, so most of the best produce would be gone, but I'd shopped in this market for ages, and I knew who would hold things back for me, and who procured the things I liked especially. In this area, I was the expert, and Daniel only followed along.

I bought a plump, shiny sole just brought in from the coast, which the fishmonger wrapped in paper for me. Daniel carried that while I piled my basket full of vegetables I'd picked over—brussels sprouts, endive, parsnip, potatoes, and fresh rosemary and parsley. James had brought me sugar when I'd sent him on his faux errand, so I did not need that, but I chose some peppercorns I particularly liked from a spice merchant. Last, I bought some bright oranges I'd use in a pastry cream for my sponge cake, and then was ready to return home.

Daniel told the cabbie he flagged down to let us out on South Audley Street so no one would see us driving up in style in a hansom. We walked home from there, Daniel carrying both the large fish and my heavy basket.

It was late afternoon, the shadows deep, the streets dim canyons where gaslight had not yet been lit. I had a few hours left in which to prepare supper, so I was not worried, but when Daniel and I entered the kitchen, Mr. Davis came charging in from the servants' hall, glaring at me in fury.

"Mrs. Holloway," he snapped, his usually neat hair pushed awry. This gave me the chance to see he wore a switch of false hair on the crown of his head—it had fallen askew to reveal a bald patch. "I thought you'd gone as well. What the devil have you been playing at, woman? Good Lord." Mr. Davis stopped as he caught sight of Daniel's bruises, and his mouth sagged open. "What happened to you?"

"Nothing to worry you," Daniel said cheerfully. He set the basket of the vegetables and fruit on the table, and after I stripped off my gloves, hung up my coat, and rinsed my hands in the scullery, I moved to sort through them.

"What did you mean you thought I'd gone as well?" I asked Mr. Davis as I chose the largest of the sprouts, the crispest endive, and most unblemished of the small white potatoes.

Davis touched his hair, realized his hairpiece was askew, and pushed it right. He did it perfectly, which told me he'd worn the false hair for some time now.

"Mrs. Bowen has given notice. We're at sixes and sevens, you disappeared, and Mary ran to her room in hysterics thinking she'd have to do the cookery. The master is due home in *two hours*. Bloody hell."

"*Mr.* Davis!" I said through his rising voice. "I can certainly turn out a meal to satisfy even the master in such a time. It took quite a while to find the best produce, and your new man was slow." I gave Daniel an admonishing look that slid easily from him as he carried the fish into the larder. "Send someone to fetch Mary. She will have to dry her tears and come down and help me. Then you can tell me about Mrs. Bowen."

A pity, I thought as Davis, galvanized, dashed into the servants' hall and commanded a maid to run up to Mary. Mrs. Bowen had run this house very well, which made my job much easier. Plus, I'd liked her, despite my misgivings about her when I'd first met her. I knew she was grieving over Sinead and could only hope that when she felt better, she'd return.

Two hours is a very short time to prepare even a simple meal, so I had to do everything correctly from the start. Fortunately, I had prepared well that morning, so I had buns baking in a trice, Mary had competently trussed the fowl as I'd showed her—though I rubbed it with herbs to be certain it would have good flavor—and I washed and chopped the vegetables to be strewn into the pan when it was time. My puff pastry made the base of a plum tart, and I whipped up an orange-flavored pastry cream to spread between layers of sponge cake.

I had learned long ago that one does not need to prepare elaborately bizarre meals with strange ingredients from foreign lands to make a good meal. Most people, even aristocrats, appreciate good wholesome cooking without dishes of long names no one can pronounce. A good taste is what they truly wish for.

While I worked, Daniel vanished, to do whatever jobs Mr. Davis set him to. He'd take his meals with the men in the mews, not in the servants' hall with the other staff. I tried to forget about him and concentrate on the meal, but all he'd said today danced in the back of my mind. I'd need time to sit still and think things over.

I seemed to have recovered from my reluctance to go into the larder, for which I thanked Daniel. Though my heart fluttered the first time I approached it, I remembered his strong voice behind me, the comfort of his presence. He'd taken me out of myself today, renewed my strength with his confidence in me, though I would never tell him so.

Having much to do and little time to do it in also helped a great deal. Such a thing tends to push fears aside, I have found, and one focuses on one's task. That is why they say idle hands are the devil's workshop.

I grew more certain as I worked that it was Mr. Simms who

had taken the dinner I'd put aside for myself last night. A valet should have no cause to go into the larder, less still to linger there, but I discovered him in its doorway twice in an hour.

"If you need something from the larder, Mr. Simms, ask Mary or Paul," I told him severely the second time. "Or me. Now, please excuse me. I need to get on."

Mr. Simms had given a guilty start when I'd come up behind him, but he resumed his arrogance as he moved out of my way. "I am only making certain all is well, Mrs. Holloway," he said in his stuffy tones. "Since Mrs. Bowen has gone off."

"Leave the larder to me, Mr. Simms, if you please. I am well trained to look after it."

I gave him a stern look, which only made his nose rise higher into the air as he stalked off. He *had* been inside, I saw, because a crock of butter had been moved, and the bowl of grapes looked considerably emptier. Bloody man. A pompous valet stooping to steal food from his employer was a sad thing indeed. Worse, the blame for missing food would be laid at the cook's door, and so I needed to keep a careful eye on him.

Mary and I finished the meal and sent it up; then I prepared a repast of pork and potatoes to serve the staff when the family was finished. Mr. Davis, Mr. Simms, and I sat in Mrs. Bowen's parlor, with the young footman, Paul, to wait on us. Mr. Simms carefully did not look at me, as he shoveled his meal into his mouth.

"You should be housekeeper, Mrs. H.," Mr. Davis told me as I set my feet on a footstool and sighed in weariness. "You'd take care of us right well."

"No, indeed," I said in true horror. I couldn't think of anything more dreadful. "I'd never be able to stay out of the kitchen, and I'd drive the new cook mad. No, I am happy where I am."

Mr. Davis shrugged. "Fair enough. We've been eating well the past few days, haven't we, Simms? Mrs. Cowles—that was our old cook, Mrs. Holloway—she was a good body but absentminded. Apt to forget to put butter in the sauce or sugar in the cake."

Simms nodded without looking up. His fork screeched as it scraped across his plate.

"All were as meek as you please at table tonight," Mr. Davis went on. He paused to snuffle into a handkerchief then tucked the handkerchief into his coat pocket and cleared his throat. "Lady Rankin asked his lordship about his day, as per usual. He talked all about it and, as per usual, her ladyship and Lady Cynthia were sublimely uninterested."

Simms huffed a laugh and took another helping of plum tart.

"His lordship *did* begin with the opinion that young ladies needed husbands," Mr. Davis continued. "He told them he'd avoided a near disaster today when a young woman wanted to play the markets with money she'd inherited from a benefactor. She wished to invest heavily in African mines—ones proved to not exist, apparently. The young lady was most angry with his lordship when his lordship pointed this out, but he saved her some blunt, didn't he? Lord Rankin declared that what this lady needed was a husband to tend to her money, and he looked most keenly at Lady Cynthia when he said it."

Simms swallowed a large bite of tart and tried to look superior. "Should take the back of his hand to Lady Cynthia, I'd say. His lordship has the right of it. No husband will tolerate a wife who likes to wear trousers. There'd be no more of that, no mistake."

True, a husband would likely put his foot down about the trousers, and Lady Cynthia wouldn't have much choice but to obey.

I grew indignant on her behalf. Lady Cynthia and her friend Bobby were a bit silly, but harmless, in my opinion. They simply longed for the freedom gentlemen had, to go where they wanted and do what they liked. I would also like that freedom, but at least, as I'd observed to Daniel, I could walk about town on my own and work at a job I enjoyed without it being scandalous. I didn't have to be flattering, entertaining, and beautiful while pretending, like Lady Rankin, that I hadn't the strength to lift my hand.

Lady Cynthia, unfortunately, would have to marry or depend the rest of her life on Lord Rankin's generosity. And if Lord Rankin were arrested for helping the horrible men Daniel had told me of, the entire family would be in dire straits. So would we, his staff, of course. We'd all be out a post.

After supper the maids did the washing up, and I brought out my knives to sharpen. I laid them across the table in the servants' hall, where I'd be out of the maids' way—filet, cleaver, parers, two chef's knives, and a brand-new carver I'd scraped the money together to purchase this winter. I'd lost the old carver in an unfortunate manner.

These were my very own knives, which came and went with me, my property. The cook who'd trained me had taught me that I should never trust a household to have good ones. If the house's mistress made economies in the kitchen, she'd very likely scrimp on the knives, which were expensive, not understanding how important they are. Good knives can make the difference between an easily prepared meal and endless labor.

I allowed no one else to sharpen my knives but myself. I laid out my whetstone, dripped a bit of water onto it, and began.

The rest of the staff faded away as I worked—perhaps the sight of all the blades made them nervous, especially as I barked a *No!* at Paul, who tried to pick one up. The maids doused lights in the outer rooms until I was left in the darkness with one small lamp I'd set on the table.

I barely noticed them go, so absorbed I was. Sharpening could be soothing, no noise but the scratch of blade on stone, my gaze on the knife's edge as it moved precisely across the whetstone, no hurrying.

The even routine let my thoughts calm. The events of that day and the day before flowed through my head, all that I had learned, all that I had observed, my thoughts unwinding from their jumble. We had not heard back about Sinead and when we could have her funeral. If her mother was dead and Mrs. Bowen gone, it might fall to me to make the arrangements. No matter. I could do that for her at least.

I thought about Mr. Timmons and why Daniel had set him to watching the house, as well as all Daniel had told me about Lord Rankin. Daniel had not seemed very surprised about the identity of the young man who'd struck him, and I wondered if Daniel had recognized him at the station, and his provocation had been deliberate. Perhaps he had his eye on this Minty fellow as well on Rankin. I would have to shake Daniel until he told me everything.

Not until I raised my head to slide the carver back into its leather sheath did I realize how alone I was. The shadows pressed from the corners of the room, and all was black without.

I had one more knife to sharpen, my cleaver, a large square knife with which I hacked apart chicken carcasses, cut up tough joints of meat, and chopped up beef bones.

I was drawing it quietly across the stone when I heard a noise in the larder. At that same moment, the lamp flickered with the last of its kerosene and died, leaving me in darkness.

12

I went very still. The noise could have been made by Simms returning to have a go at more food, but I was alone in a house where death had walked, with no light and no help. Simms or indeed any of the servants would have brought a light with them if they were going to raid the larder. It was quite solidly dark down here.

A modicum of light must have filtered down from the street, however, because I saw, across the hall, a silhouette show briefly in the larder's doorway before it disappeared.

I rose as quietly as I could, laying the cleaver on the table. It would be foolish for me to go blundering about in the dark with a blade—I might hit an innocent who'd come down to the kitchen for a perfectly good reason, or I might trip and hurt myself.

I could hear nothing for a moment, then there came a clinking noise from the larder followed by the sound of something being dragged across the flagstones.

Then came a cry. So muffled it was, I could not tell if it

came from a man or woman, but I became aware there were two people down here with me. The cry was not repeated, but I heard scuffling, fists on flesh.

As I stepped into the passage, a body collided with mine, the breath leaving me as I folded in half. Footsteps pounded on the floor of the kitchen toward the scullery, and at the same time, hands caught my shoulders and pressed me smoothly aside.

I stifled a shriek, recognizing the touch, but Daniel was gone a second later. He said nothing, made no noise, but he sprinted after the person who'd knocked me aside. Next I heard the bang of the scullery door and running feet on the stairs outside—the intruder's, then Daniel's.

I straightened up, resting my hand on the wall to steady myself while I drew deep breaths. When my lungs eased, I tottered into the kitchen, lit a candle in a candlestick kept on a shelf near the door, and carried it with me to the larder.

All was quiet, no one there. Whoever had rushed out of the house had left no accomplice behind.

Nothing looked out of place. The drawers were closed, cupboards shut, copper pots and baskets that hung from the beams undisturbed. Even the items Mr. Simms had moved remained where I'd replaced them.

As I moved farther into the room, toward the corner where Sinead had been found, I discovered what had made the scraping sound. A wooden crate, empty of the produce it had once held, had been moved from the wall and now sat at an angle that would trip the unwary. As I began to push it back where it belonged, my candlelight fell on a scrap of paper behind it. I set down the candlestick, bent to fetch the paper, shoved the crate safely against the wall, and left for the servants' hall.

There, I relit the kerosene lamp, which would give me better light, and sat down at the table, blowing out the candle. As a thin finger of smoke curled from the candle's still-glowing wick, I smoothed out the paper and examined it.

It had been torn jaggedly, about two thirds of the page missing, if it had begun as a common-sized sheet of paper. There was writing on it, but I could make no sense of anything. I knew my letters—I'd attended grammar school as a tot then learned more about writing and numbers from the first cook who'd apprenticed me. She'd told me it was a good thing for a cook to be able to read cookery books, as the lady of the house might not understand the nuances of recipes or read them out correctly.

The paper held the remains of two lines, but the letters spelled out no words I knew, and they were interspersed with numbers. Here and there a vertical line had been carefully drawn on the page between the numbers.

As I puzzled over this, Daniel came down the outside stairs far more loudly than he'd gone up. He entered the scullery, closed and bolted the back door, thudded across the kitchen and into the servants' hall, and dropped into the chair across from me, breathing heavily.

"Lost the bugger," he said. "Ran faster than I could." He drew a few more ragged breaths and fixed his gaze on the paper in front of me. "What is that?"

"It was in the larder," I said calmly. "Under a crate—whoever was the person you chased moved the crate to find it. Or, he might have been tucking it underneath, but I can't imagine why anyone would do so."

"Or it was dropped there long ago and has nothing to do with this person." Daniel sounded discouraged.

"Who was he? Did you get a look at him?

Daniel rested his arms on the table. His face held the cuts and bruises from his fight today, his skin mottled red, black, and blue.

"Blast if I know," he growled. "Slippery, moved fast, but I couldn't tell you if it were a man or a woman. Man, I think."

"I agree," I said. "He was quite strong, and I felt no flutter of skirts when he ran into me."

I did not finish the sentence with the conviction with which I'd begun it. I had met two women now who didn't like to bother with skirts, and I'd felt Bobby's strength when she'd pulled me into the coach.

Still, a man did feel different from a woman—the way a man carried his weight was not the same. A man led with his chest and shoulders, where a woman's balance was solidly in her hips and legs. I'd shared a bed with a man and learned a bit about males, though that was something I didn't like to think about too much. At the time I hadn't minded, hussy that I'd been, but thinking of my naïve happiness always brought hollow pain.

I pushed my contemplations aside to concentrate on the paper. "I prefer to think this was put there deliberately. But it says nothing but nonsense."

"Let me see." Daniel reached out his hand.

I did not rush to give it to him. "In stories I read in magazines, writing like this means a secret message." I studied the letters one more time then finally slid the paper to him. "Which sounds rather daft in real life. More likely it's something perfectly ordinary."

Daniel moved the lamp closer to the page as he ran his fingertips over the writing. "Curious," he said. He lifted his head, his eyes alight with interest, and folded the paper in half. "I'll take it with me and see if I can make sense of it."

I slapped my hand to the paper before he could pick it up. "Not until I copy it out, thank you. *I* might make some sense of it."

Another man might have growled and told me to leave it,

but Daniel only lifted his fingers away without argument. I took my notebook and pencil from my apron pocket and opened the notebook to a blank page.

The book was full of my jottings about cookery—what had worked or gone wrong in a recipe, what I'd tasted at a restaurant and wished to replicate, and other notes about ingredients and seasons, along with the responses of those who'd eaten a particular dish. A cook can't be expected to remember everything she does with a meal—I often varied recipes and rarely cooked a dish the same way twice. My notebook was very helpful to me.

I kept my pencil sharp so I could make a note whenever the fit took me. Now I unfolded the paper I'd found and began to copy it.

I went slowly and carefully, not wishing to make a mistake. If it *was* a secret code, one error might render the whole thing useless.

I was about halfway finished when I noticed Daniel had gone very still. His fingers remained in the same place on the table, and his body did not move. The only motion came from the flame of the lamp on the rare occasion that it flickered, sending abrupt shadows across the folds of his coat.

I glanced up without lifting my head to find Daniel watching me. Not what I did, but *me*. His hands lay unmoving before him, and his gaze was on my bowed head.

He was studying me with a look I'd caught on my own face during a visit to someone I was deeply fond of. There was caring in that look, and worry, and gentle wonder.

For a brief moment, the trappings of our stations fell away. Daniel, the good-natured man-of-all-work, and even Daniel the City gentleman vanished. I was no longer Mrs. Holloway, the cook, who'd seen a long and tiring evening in the kitchen and would face another equally long day in the morning.

We were simply Daniel and Kat, or even more basically, a man and a woman. Nothing about where we were, or who we were, or how we came to be there seemed to matter. Just for that moment.

Daniel caught my glance. He remained motionless for a few seconds longer, and then a slow flush stained his cheekbones around the bruises.

I looked back at him, my gaze quiet, before I lowered my head again to my task. Out of the corner of my eye, I saw Daniel swallow, his Adam's apple moving.

I made myself finish writing, willing my fingers not to tremble.

"There," I said, laying down my pencil and closing the book.

Daniel took up the paper without a word and concentrated on folding the page and tucking it into his pocket. His silence unnerved me. He said nothing; his ready smile didn't come, nor did his unending stock of banter.

"Well," I said briskly. I set aside my notebook and began to pull the whetstone to me, taking up the cleaver I hadn't finished sharpening. "You ought to return to the mews before someone misses you. Nothing is a hotter place for gossip than below stairs in a Mayfair household."

Daniel shook his head, making no move to rise. "You go up. I want to stay in case the villain returns."

I had a momentary vision of coming downstairs the next morning and finding *Daniel* dead in the larder with blood all over his face.

"No," I said in a hard voice. "You shouldn't stay here alone."

A ghost of Daniel's grin returned. "I will not be alone. I'll be here with the very sharp knives of Kat Holloway. I'll finish the cleaver for you. I know how to grind a blade."

Humph. I ought to have guessed sharpening knives would be among Daniel's vast store of knowledge.

I did not lift my hand on the whetstone. "I will stay with you."

Daniel's tone became stern. "No, you will not. I can more easily fend off a villain if I am not trying to protect you at the same time. And you are right about gossip. I shouldn't like slanderous things said about you, Kat."

For the first time since he'd taken the paper, he looked directly at me. His eyes held a severity of purpose, a strength that lay behind both the deliveryman with the winning smile and the coolness of the middle-class gentleman.

Which one was he? I knew he was neither. The true Daniel McAdam eluded me—eluded everyone. He was somewhere inside the man across from me, with his stern eyes and will of iron, his purpose a mystery. Only with James had I seen any softness in him, and in the moment just now when I'd caught him looking at me. But the walls between us had risen once more, Daniel shutting me out.

He was correct about one thing—Mr. Davis would have a fine time discussing the fact that Mrs. Holloway and that McAdam were up all night together in the kitchen, this after they'd spent the entire afternoon traipsing about London and coming home late. I doubted the villain would return tonight in any case. He'd been chased away, very surprised at being caught.

I thought of how noiselessly Daniel had moved, and how quickly, in an experienced, precise manner. I knew that if those young men this afternoon had faced the true Daniel, they'd have limped home licking their wounds. Daniel had been defeated because he'd chosen to be. Which made me wonder again whether he'd provoked the fight deliberately, and why.

"Very well," I said, pretending to be pragmatic. "Mind you don't put an uneven edge on the cleaver, and make jolly certain you lock the knives into the drawer over there. Knives are expensive, and if you ruin one or lose me the lot, I expect you to give me the price of them."

Daniel's lazy grin flashed. "I'll not fail you, Mrs. H. You can count on old Daniel."

I wasn't certain how to respond to that, and he knew it. Bloody man. "See that you *don't* fail," I managed.

I gathered up my notebook and pencil, returned his impudent stare, and then stamped into the hall and toward the back stairs. I heard his chuckle float out behind me, which both irritated me and comforted me at the same time.

I n the morning, I found my knives locked securely in their drawer in the kitchen, the cleaver as sharp as could be. I held its edge up to my eyes to study it and was a bit annoyed that it looked perfect. No man should be good at all the things Daniel claimed he was.

But, no—he'd told me he couldn't make much headway with accounts. He had to ask for help on that measure.

This did not give me much satisfaction, nor did the fact that the kitchen was completely free of any indication Daniel had been there last night. The whetstone was in its proper place, the knives locked up, the key to their drawer in the pocket of the apron hung where I always kept it.

Mary had brought out my bowl of dough for the day's bread without being told. I was pleased—after her first awkwardness she was showing the makings of a good assistant, once I could be certain she knew one ingredient from another. But we all need to be trained—none of us are born with the knowledge of our profession, no matter what some scientists claim. What they get up to in the Royal Society, I have no idea, but they turn out some daft ideas.

I set the dough into pans to rise, instructing Mary to put them in the oven in two hours exactly and to take them out in one hour more. For breakfast, I sliced leftover bread from the day before, set Mary to toasting it, and then put the slices, slathered with butter, on a rack and sent them upstairs. Ham and boiled eggs in their shells went with them, as well as a serving of breakfast cakes made with bicarbonate of soda, flour, and milk.

For the servants, I pounded together scraps of leftover ham and chicken with butter, a pinch of nutmeg, mace, and salt, as well as a smidgen of cayenne pepper. This I spread on the remainder of the toasted bread and set it before them, along with a hash of leftover potatoes and vegetables, and the rest of the eggs in the house. Mary would have to buy more eggs—I liked them to be as fresh as possible.

The remains of the pounded meat I put into jars and covered them with melted lard to keep them fresh, instructing Mary to put them in the coolest part of the larder. I then prepared everything I knew I would need for tonight's supper for Lord Rankin, with Mary at my elbow so she'd understand what I needed her to do.

I did not see Daniel. I sent a tray over to the stables for the groom and his lads with Paul the footman, and assumed Daniel would be among them, taking a morning meal before beginning his chores.

I ate a few spoonfuls of hash, then I put aside my apron and fetched my coat and bonnet from the coatrack in the housekeeper's parlor.

"Going out again, Mrs. H.?" Mr. Davis asked me in surprise. He leaned on the parlor's doorframe, completely ruining his butler's dignity in a common man's slouch. "You were out all afternoon yesterday. Send Mary to the markets if you need comestibles."

"She *is* going," I answered without heat as I set my most prized hat on my head—cream straw with black feathers and pink ribbon. I wanted to appear at my best today. "It is Thursday, which is the cook's day out in this household."

For once, the cheerful light in Mr. Davis's eyes deserted him. "Yes, but we have no housekeeper. Mary ain't quite up to her duties yet, and who will have to keep things running smoothly all by himself? *Me,* Mrs. H. You can't desert me." He sent me an anguished look.

"Good heavens, I am not deserting you, Mr. Davis. I left plenty of food to be warmed up for the family and for you lot during the day, and I will be back to cook the master's meal tonight. I *never* miss my day out. That you must learn."

"Days out don't mean nothing to the upstairs," Mr. Davis said darkly. "If terrible things happen because we're short-handed, it's me what gets the blame."

"Then you must not let terrible things happen." I pulled on my gloves and settled them around my fingers. "I took this post because it came with one full day and one half day out a week. Now I will enjoy them. Good morning, Mr. Davis."

I lifted my reticule and shooed him out of my way. Mr. Davis straightened and moved aside so I wouldn't actually brush against him as I went past him out of the parlor.

My heart beat quickly as I hurried through the hall to the scullery and up the stairs. Not until I was well out into the street did I release my breath in relief.

My days out were special to me for a very important reason, and for that reason I would fight to keep them, even if I had to beat my way past Mr. Davis every time I wanted to leave the house.

I had fare for the omnibuses, but those that passed me once I went out to busier roads were crushed full, so I had to walk a long way before I found any transport. I at last came upon a horse-drawn tram that had space for me, and I climbed aboard, settling myself as it clacked on rails ever eastward.

The family who cared for my daughter, Grace, who was now ten years old, had a small house in a lane off Cheapside, near St. Paul's Cathedral. I left the tram at Ludgate Hill and walked the remainder of the way.

My heart always soared when I beheld the majestic dome of St. Paul's against the smoky sky. As I say, I was not much of a churchgoer, but I never failed to be moved by the graceful building and its elegant architecture—it signaled that I was near my daughter. St. Paul's will always have that meaning for me.

The girlhood friend who looked after Grace was called Joanna Millburn, and she was married to one Samuel Millburn. Joanna had found in life what I had hoped to find—a happy marriage to a good, warmhearted man. While Mr. Millburn did not possess much in the way of ambition, cleverness, or studied handsomeness, he was good-natured and kind, and had no difficulty looking after the daughter of his wife's friend as well as his and Joanna's own four children.

When my daughter greeted me with her usual exuberance, clinging to me in Joanna's scrupulously clean front sitting room, everything small and mean in the world fell away. I inhaled the scent of her hair and experienced again the wonder that this little girl was mine.

Grace, never timid, pushed away from me, already speaking. "How are you, Mama? I woke up so excited you'd come today. How is your new place? What is the housekeeper like? I made a cake today, all by myself—well, almost by myself. It's in the oven now. Mrs. Millburn will say when it's done."

"Land, child." I set her next to me on the sofa, smoothing her skirts and looking her over with greedy eyes. Grace's face and hands had been scrubbed pink, her pinafore was starched to crackling, and crisp pink bows secured the two braids of her dark hair. "What a chatterer you are," I said. "I'll tell you all about my new place if you'll let me get in two words."

Grace did not look abashed. "The lady next door says children should be seen and not heard, but Mr. Millburn says that's rot. Is that a bad word? Rot?"

I'd heard far worse, but I let my tone become admonishing. "Do not say it in front of your next-door neighbor, then. To me, of course, you may say anything you like."

This prompted an impetuous hug. "I love you, Mum."

My heart ached. "I love you too, sweetheart."

We went out—I always took Grace for an outing. Today we walked to St. Paul's Churchyard and the park there. Vagrants lounged about, pathetic things, often men from far-off lands, struggling to stay fed a long way from home. I gave them pennies, as usual. I believe in charity for those who can't help themselves.

We went to a tea shop full of ladies who wore clothes much like mine—respectable, understated, and not expensive—and had tea and cakes, Grace's baked treat for me notwithstanding. It was always special to have tea and cakes in a shop.

I told Grace about Mr. Davis and his penchant for gossip, the piece of false hair on his bald spot, which made her laugh, and how he liked to read things out from the newspaper. I also told her about Lady Cynthia and her friend Bobby dressing up like gentlemen, and about riding in the coach with them. I said nothing at all about Sinead and her death, seeing no reason to upset Grace with this news.

My spirits were high when we returned to the Millburns. The cake Grace made had come out of the oven in our absence, and if a little lopsided, it was quite tasty. We shared it with Joanna and her husband and children, the oldest two of whom were a boy and a girl about Grace's age. All in all, it was a merry little meal.

Grace was tearful when it was time for me to depart, but she went upstairs with the Millburns' children to do more studies. I heard them laughing and exclaiming as Grace told them about my funny stories, their boisterousness pleasant to hear.

The sky was darkening, and I needed to return to Mount Street and prepare another repast for the Rankin household. As much as I wanted to linger, I had to say farewell until my half day out on Monday.

As I began to gather my things in the foyer, Joanna came to me. "May we speak to you a moment, Kat?" she asked in a subdued voice.

I felt a qualm but hung my coat and hat back on hooks on the hall tree, the hat's feathers fluttering. My chest tightened with worry as I followed Joanna into the sitting room, which had been cleared of our tea by Joanna's maid-of-all-work. Samuel Millburn was already there, standing up when we entered and giving his wife a grave glance.

I fully expected them to tell me something had happened to Grace—she'd been hurt or ill—although she'd seemed quite healthy. Or that they could no longer keep her. I did not at all like the seriousness on their faces.

"Gracious," I said, my throat dry. "You both look as cheerful as a churchyard."

Joanna flushed, and Samuel's expression held guilt. "Do

not worry," Joanna said quickly. "This is good news. At least—we hope so."

"What?" I folded my hands to keep them from fluttering. "Are you expecting again?" I moved my gaze to Joanna's belly, but it seemed flat enough under her plain green frock and white pinafore.

"Good heavens, no." Joanna's usual verve returned. "I'm far too old for that now. No—Kat—dear . . ."

She bade me sit down on the sofa, then she sank next to me and took my hands. Samuel lowered himself into a nearby chair and watched us closely, a concerned look on his plain face.

"What we wanted to say to you, Kat," Joanna said, "is that we wish to adopt Grace." She finished in a rush. "To take her in as ours. To have her become our daughter in truth."

13

They gazed at me, did my friends, their faces set with hope, eagerness, and anxiousness about my response—Joanna with her faded brown hair in a tight bun, the prettiness of her girlhood still on her face and in her brown eyes; Sam with his black hair combed flat and a thick mustache that couldn't hide the gentle lines about his mouth.

I sat so still I believe my heart ceased beating. I couldn't draw a breath, my lungs not understanding how to work.

I said nothing for so long that Joanna cast a worried glance at Samuel.

"We already think of Grace as our own," Sam said into the silence. "She is like a sister to our brood. She and our oldest, Jane, have become quite close."

"The little ones adore her," Joanna put in. "Sam tells me that adoption will not be much of a problem in the legal sense. Your husband died penniless with no provision for her, no will stating his wishes for her, no one in his family willing to take her in, so you have said."

I made myself nod to her question. There was no will. My false husband had taken ship from Gravesend ten years ago, when I'd been carrying Grace, and never returned. The ship in question had gone down with all hands, no survivors. When I'd begun inquiring about a will, it came to light that he'd had another wife in Bristol, a woman he'd married before he'd met me, with whom he'd sired two children. Thus I learned that his perfidy had made me a fallen woman and my daughter illegitimate. I desperately hid this fact from the world, but my actions did not erase the truth.

I knew nothing about my husband's family, and in any case, I'd never tried to find them. Grace was mine. That was all.

Now my friends smiled at me and offered to relieve me of my burden.

I cleared my throat, but when I spoke, my voice was choked and unlike my own. "The expense," I managed. "I must provide…"

Joanna's hopeful smile widened. "That is more good news. Sam has been given a rise in wages and a better position. That is why we waited to approach you. We would have done so long ago, but we've been poor as church mice, as you know."

I did know. I sent a good part of my wages to Joanna and Sam to buy my daughter clothing, food, and fuel to warm her.

"Now you will not have to provide for her," Sam went on.

Joanna at last seemed to sense some of my distress. She put a comforting arm around me. "Goodness, we sprang this on you too quickly. Of course, you must think it over. But do let us help you, dearest Kat. You have endured enough."

My neck hurt as I bent it in a nod. "Yes. I will think on it." I drew in a long breath, looking both of them over. "You are good, good people," I said, meaning the words. "But I must…"

I shook off Joanna's hold and rose to my feet, my hands so numb I dropped my reticule. Sam quickly fetched it as he sprang up and gave it back to me.

He was a kind man. I saw it in his eyes. He was a fine husband to Joanna and loved his children. He'd care for Grace as much as he did his own daughters—he was that sort of person.

I took myself out of the parlor, fetched my coat and hat from the foyer, and managed to don them unassisted, although I have no idea how. I pulled on my gloves as Joanna came to see me off, my face so fixed I thought it would crack.

"Good-bye, dear Kat." Joanna kissed my cheek and held the door open for me. She whispered, "We want what's best for Grace. Please believe that."

I did believe it. I'd known they'd care for Grace, which was why I'd left her here weeks after she was born while I went out and found a post that would pay me as well as I could expect.

The door closed behind me. I moved my feet from doorstep to road, automatically pointing myself to Cheapside, with St. Paul's looming above the rooftops.

After that, I have no idea where I went. Cheapside becomes Newgate Street, which leads alongside the gray, forbidding bulk of the prison. I'd once spent a terrible day inside that prison, certain I'd never leave it, but at the same time relieved my daughter had been safe with the Millburns not far away.

I had vowed never to pass that place again, but here I was walking by. The walls did not reach out to engulf me; indeed, I barely noticed the miasma of fear and despair as I passed.

The road became the Holborn Viaduct, taking me up and over the railway and other roads, and dropping down again into a circus, from which several streets radiated.

I should have continued on the wide lane of High Holborn, but it was so choked with carriages and carts, horses and people, that I automatically turned aside, seeking a less-crowded path. I came to myself in a little court in a maze of tiny streets, with no idea how I'd come there or which little passageway would take me out again. I wandered about lanes that contained what I supposed were law offices—the houses were uniform, respectable, faceless, uncaring.

At last a kindly black-gowned pupil took pity on me and escorted me through the warren until we came out on Fleet Street. He chattered at me in the way of the young, though I had no idea of one word he said. He lifted his hat to me when we emerged, and I believe I thanked him for his assistance.

At Temple Bar I realized my feet ached, and that I had a long way to go before I reached Mayfair. Ahead of me was the bulk of St. Clement Danes, the curve of street around it packed with vehicles and people.

I ought to have found an omnibus or a hansom, but I pushed my way through, mindlessly walking, though I wasn't certain where anymore. I passed the slender elegance of St. Mary le Strand without stopping to admire it as I usually did. The only significance it held for me was that it told me I was near Somerset House and Waterloo Bridge.

At Southampton Street I came out of my daze. I stood at the corner and looked up its length toward Covent Garden and the chaos of its market at the end.

People bumped me as they hastened by, men in dark suits that would hide the grime of London's coal smoke. Women with baskets moved briskly past, some shooting me irritated and disapproving looks. Whatever was my business, I'd best get about it, their gazes told me.

I turned and walked up Southampton Street, but I halted long before I neared Covent Garden. I stood in front of the house that held Daniel's lodgings, though I knew he would not be there. He was at the house on Mount Street, running errands for Mr. Davis, trying to investigate Sinead's death, and keeping a close eye on Lord Rankin.

It was not the thing for a lady to stop uninvited at a gentleman's lodgings, but my thoughts were anything but clear at the moment. Perhaps Mrs. Williams would let me into her parlor and give me a cup of tea, which might fortify me long enough to get home.

If I ever went back to Lord Rankin's, that was.

The house's front door, next to the pawnbrokers, was unlocked, but no one was about. I heard a swishing noise in the back of the hall when I went inside, where another door led out into a tiny yard, but it was only a maid on her hands and knees, scrubbing the floor. She didn't look up, never noticing me.

I took the empty stairs to Daniel's floor—no sound came from Mrs. Williams's rooms as I passed them. I was not certain why I wanted to go stand at Daniel's door, but something drew me there.

I rested my hand on the door handle, an old-fashioned thing shaped like a bird's wing. To my surprise, the handle turned and the door opened.

I stepped quickly into the front room and shut myself inside. As I did, my strength rushed out of me, and I found myself sitting down on the nearest chair, the plainest one, my legs no longer able to hold me. My corset cut into my side and up under my arms, but I could not move to make myself more comfortable.

I sat, unable to think, unable to do anything but struggle to breathe, struggle to understand what I was feeling.

The entire reason I rose in the small hours of the morning and dragged myself into a kitchen to cook for people who mostly didn't notice what they ate was because of Grace. Everything I did, everything I endured was to make sure Grace was well, healthy, fed, clothed, cared for.

I was an arrogant woman, telling others about the moral virtue of hard work, when I only performed it for one end—the well-being of my daughter. Without that to drive me, what I did was empty. Drudgery. The pride I took in creating praiseworthy meals was meaningless.

My friends were offering me a way to see that Grace was kept well for life. Mr. Millburn was a respectable man in a respectable position—he could ensure that Grace moved in such circles herself, which would enable her to marry well when the time came. Also, she would have a father, Sam, the only man she'd ever known as such.

I should want that for her. I loved Grace—I should want her to have a happy home, a good future, people who would care for her. After all, that was why I had asked my friend Joanna to take her in while I worked.

They could give her what I couldn't—what I was struggling to work toward. A home, a name, a comfortable life.

And yet, the selfish soul in me couldn't bear to let her go. I found my arms closing around myself, hugging tightly, as though I held Grace in my embrace. I closed my eyes, rocking back and forth, images of the night the midwife had put her into my arms taking over my thoughts. The midwife had advised me to give Grace to a foundling hospital, since my husband was gone and I had nothing. The woman had stood over me, hands outstretched, and told me to give her the babe—she'd take her away quickly, best thing.

I'd held Grace and defied the midwife, sending her off with harsh words. Grace was *mine*. My daughter, my only love, my life.

People adopted children all the time, I tried to reason with myself. Nephews, nieces, grandchildren, children of friends. It was common for families to raise not only their immediate offspring but those who'd found their way into their homes for whatever reason. The Millburns were offering nothing people hadn't been doing for hundreds of years. Could I deny Grace that?

And yet . . .

The door banged open. I jerked up my head and opened my eyes, but I knew even before I saw the man who'd entered that he wasn't Daniel. Daniel charged the air in a room, sent the very dust motes crackling.

The man who peered at me, squinting a little and stooping forward as though nearsighted, had thick dark hair that swept back from his forehead and a young face, though I could see he was past his first youth, perhaps in his early thirties. His clothes were well tailored, his watch chain gold, and he held a hat and walking stick that had likely come from expensive shops. In short, he wore the same sort of clothing as Daniel did when he dressed as the City gent, and I wondered dimly if Daniel didn't copy this man's ensemble.

"I beg your pardon," the man said to me in a cultured baritone. "The door was open."

I rose slowly to my feet with a creak of corset, my usual robustness absent. "If you are seeking Mr. McAdam, he is not here," I said, my voice tired.

The gentleman looked me up and down, the squint deepening, as though he had no idea what to make of me. A woman being found alone in a man's lodgings could mean she was a harlot, but I saw him puzzling that I didn't appear to be so. I might therefore be some sort of relation, but if this man knew Daniel even slightly, he would know that Daniel never, ever spoke of family other than his son, James.

"Oh," the man answered at last. "I am not seeking him." He gave me another look up and down then flushed as though realizing how rudely he was assessing me. "I am seeking a parcel, possibly in that desk over there." He pointed to the small table with a drawer in the shadowy corner.

"Possibly?" I repeated. Some of my daze receded as I realized I ought to be more on my guard. This was a stranger, invading Daniel's rooms, looking for something in Daniel's absence. "May I ask who you are, sir?"

He looked taken aback at my tone, no doubt wondering why *I* had invaded Daniel's empty rooms.

"I am Thanos," he announced. When I blinked at this declaration, delivered in stentorian tones, his flush deepened. "That is to say, my name is Mr. Elgin Thanos . . . Hang on, I have a card here somewhere." He began patting his pockets, looking more puzzled as his hands tapped his chest, sides, thighs. "Blast it, I'm always losing the dratted things. Oh, beg pardon for my language, Miss . . . Er."

"Mrs.," I said crisply. "Mrs. Holloway."

Mr. Thanos's face lit, and he stopped beating his coat. "Ah, Mrs. Holloway. You're the *cook*. So delighted to meet you, so very delighted." He came at me, hand extended.

Bewildered, I took it and was rewarded by a warm, firm grip in a smooth kid glove. "Thank you," I said neutrally, not certain whether to curtsy. I decided to keep my knees straight and greet him as a mutual acquaintance rather than a potential employer.

Mr. Thanos wrung my hand once more then released me. "He has not said one word about me to you, has he?" The man shook his head. "That is our Mr. McAdam. Secretive man—but he raves on about you and your cleverness. And the wonderful meals you cook. Cruel of him—most nights I manage to

survive on a biscuit and tea, and in he comes waxing elo-
quent about your leek and mushroom soup, beef so tender it
makes you weep, and vanilla soufflé light as a cloud, the
bloody man. Oh, beg pardon again. My tongue, it speaks long
before I have thought out what it is supposed to say."

I listened in fascination, but I still had no idea who he was.
Thanos was a foreign-sounding name, Greek perhaps, but he
looked and sounded perfectly English—though I supposed
his hair was a shade blacker than most Englishmen's. With
his squint, I could not tell what color his eyes were, but he had
a pale face, the wan complexion of a man who rarely went out
into the sun.

Mr. Thanos regarded me genially a moment longer before
he walked quickly to the desk, opened the drawer, and extracted a bulky brown envelope, the sort a solicitor might use.
Without worry, he untied the strings that held it closed and
pulled out a sheaf of paper.

Curiosity trickling through my confusion, I moved to
where I could see the precise black writing on the very white
paper.

It meant nothing at all to me. Columns of numbers divided by thin red lines marched across the page, notes in spi-
dery handwriting filling the margins. I was familiar with
accounts, as I had to keep record of what I bought for the
kitchen, but there were so many lines of numbers on this
page that they began to whirl before my eyes.

Mr. Thanos peered at the figures in the same disconcer-
tion, then he sighed and pulled a silk pouch from his pocket,
from which he extracted a pair of spectacles.

He put these on, looping them around his ears, and
blinked once, twice, as though adjusting to them. His squint
went away, and he turned upon me a pair of eyes that were

very wide and black behind a set of thick lenses. "Excellent," he said. "Now I have something to work with."

My miasma of emotion cleared a bit, and I understood finally who he was. "You are the man helping Daniel—Mr. McAdam, I mean—understand the finances."

Mr. Thanos started from his rapt concentration on the numbers. "Eh? Oh yes. I am indeed." He gave me a pleased bow. "Didn't I tell you? I know I have a card somewhere." He absently patted his pocket again before his eyes swiveled back to the pages. "I say, these are beautifully done."

He turned the papers around to me as though showing me a prize painting.

"I am afraid I don't know anything about figures," I answered. To me, Mr. Thanos with his odd name and cheerful mannerisms was far more interesting than a pile of ledger sheets.

Mr. Thanos looked surprised, but he nodded. "I suppose I would be as thoroughly lost if you put bags of produce in front of me and told me to combine them into a meal. I'm certain I would turn out something disgusting. We all have our strengths, eh? My father liked to say that, rest his soul." He beamed at me, holding up the pages again. "These, dear lady, will lead us to dire criminals who fund those who like to blow things up." He shook his head, sorrow quickly entering his expression. "Nasty bastards. But we'll get them."

There—I saw it. The look Daniel sometimes had. Determination, anger, the dedication to putting things right.

Mr. Thanos's attention moved back to the papers and became fixed. He drifted toward the desk, sitting down without another word. He bent his head over a page as though the figures on it pulled him toward them and blotted out the rest of the world.

I removed a handkerchief from my reticule and dabbed at my eyes, still shaky. I waited a moment, but Mr. Thanos's back did not move—he'd become so wholly absorbed in the task that I wagered he had no idea I was still in the room.

The shadows had grown long. I must return to Mount Street and become the cook again, to grub for my living, working for the day my daughter and I could be together at last.

Swallowing a sob that jumped to my throat, I gathered up my reticule and stuffed the handkerchief back inside.

"Good day, Mr. Thanos," I said.

He never heard me. He lowered his head, trying to read the papers in the fading light. I set my reticule down again, lit a lamp on the table with matches from the match safe on the wall, and carried the small light to the desk.

Mr. Thanos glanced up, said, "Oh, thank you," and went back to it, his finger marking where he'd left off.

I didn't bother saying good day again, or good-bye—he'd never have heard me. I let myself out of the flat and went down the stairs, steadying myself on the railing.

My encounter with Mr. Thanos had at least cleared my head somewhat. As I made my way along Southampton Street to Covent Garden, I had the presence of mind to seek an omnibus that wasn't overfull, and had a corner to myself as we bumped from Covent Garden to Long Acre through Leicester Square and so to Piccadilly. I decided to descend near Berkeley Street and walk the rest of the way, as I'd already grown restless, and wanted time to regain my equilibrium before I entered the kitchen, where the staff would be.

My thoughts were troubled, however, and would not leave me alone. Mr. Thanos had provided a brief diversion, but the ride in the omnibus and the suffocating London air had done little to relieve me.

The Millburns were good, kind people. Why should I be so reluctant to let them do as they proposed?

It made me feel mean and small. Hurt and confused. And terrified. What did I have to live for if not Grace? She'd changed my life the moment she'd been put into my arms.

I knew London well enough to walk up Berkeley Street without paying attention to it, and to go around the park in the middle of Berkeley Square toward the corner of Mount Street. It was strange, I reflected in the very back of my mind, how well I knew the roads of Mayfair, a place a person like me could never hope to live in my own right. I'd dwelled most of my adult life in this corner of London and nearby it, even though I'd never truly belong there.

A wagon rattled past me as I started down Mount Street. Out of the corner of my eye, I saw its sturdy wheels slow and then halt next to me.

"All right, Mrs. H.?" Daniel's voice rang down at me. "You look all in. Climb up—I'll take you home."

Home. It wasn't *my* home. Never would be.

I studied the seat on the wagon—two hard boards, which would entail me being squashed next to him, my backside bruised on the uncomfortable seat. Would set tongues to wagging all over Mayfair.

I was tired, however, and a ride would rest my feet. I walked to the back of the wagon, its bed piled with sacks of whatever Daniel was delivering, and prepared to scramble on. A youth darted out of nowhere, grabbed a box from the bed of the wagon, set it down for me to use as a step, and held out a hand to steady me aboard.

"Thank you, James," I told him graciously. James nodded at me, the warmhearted courtesy of his father shining through.

I settled myself, if awkwardly, on the sacks. James lifted

the box into the bed and waved at me as Daniel clucked to the horse to drive on.

As we rolled along Mount Street we passed the bulk of a building that had long been the workhouse for the parish of St. George's, Hanover Square. The workhouse had been shut down a few years ago when the parish became reorganized with several others, but the brick building remained, windows empty, some broken, a reminder of the sad souls who'd existed there. A churchyard had surrounded it as well, but that was also no longer used, the bones of the dead lying undisturbed.

The edifice both haunted me and made me feel better at the same time. Had I not worked as hard as I had, hiding my daughter with my friends and pouring my entire life into my craft of cooking, I would have lived in that workhouse or a similar one, my child perhaps taken from me long ago, or perhaps living there alongside me.

Instead, Grace had grown up in a house of love, well-fed, clothed, cared for, never knowing the misery of the workhouse. *I* had done that. If nothing else, I could comfort myself with that knowledge.

Daniel halted the wagon precisely at the stairs that led down to the kitchen at the Rankin house. He set the brake, leapt from the seat, and came to help me alight. The horse, used to the routine, simply stood, using the excuse to cant a hind leg and take a rest.

As Daniel's firm hand came under my arm to assist me to the ground, he looked into my face, his ready smile departing. "Kat, what is it?" he asked in a quiet voice.

I shook my head. My trouble was too new, too raw, and too private to share with Daniel in the middle of the street.

He released me, watching me, but let me go.

I scurried down the stairs and into the kitchen. Mary was bustling about preparing things for dinner, the scullery maid had her arms up to her elbows in soapy water in the deep sink, and Davis chivied the footmen with both good-natured banter and rather cutting remarks—"Wipe them smudges off that silver—I could have a fishmonger do what you're doing with your greasy fingers and pay him half."

Daniel did not follow me in. He began unloading the wagon, with the help of James, who'd jogged behind us with his usual energy.

I pretended to sharply look over what Mary had done while I took off my hat, but my mind was not in the present. Mary could have made a sweet pudding with offal and sugar, and I'd never have noticed.

I gave her a nod and unbuttoned my coat as I made for the housekeeper's parlor to hang up both coat and hat.

"Oh, I say, Mrs. H.—" Mr. Davis called behind me.

I opened the door to the parlor, and stopped. Inside, Mrs. Bowen was just rising from the Belter chair, while Lady Cynthia, in her man's dress, lounged in a chair at the table, her booted feet propped on its polished surface. Lady Cynthia brought her boots down with a thump as I walked in, and both women regarded me with expressions of furtive guilt.

14

"Mrs. Bowen," I said in stunned surprise.

"Mrs. Holloway," Mrs. Bowen said in return, her voice stiff.

Lady Cynthia remained seated, though her feet were on the floor now, and smoothed her sleek hair with shaking fingers.

"I thought you'd given notice," I went on to Mrs. Bowen, as she, standing with her hands clasped over her black bombazine gown, remained in rigid silence.

As I stared at her, she at last gave me a slow nod. "I changed my mind. I need to stay."

"I see." I didn't really. Lady Rankin must be very understanding of servants who came and went as they pleased to not sack Mrs. Bowen for her vacillations. Or perhaps Lady Rankin had simply been glad she did not have to bother searching for another housekeeper and had welcomed Mrs. Bowen back.

I looked past Mrs. Bowen at Lady Cynthia, wondering why

she was lounging in the housekeeper's parlor. She seemed to realize my curiosity, because she rose with a sniff.

"I came looking for a Bradshaw," she said. "Blasted Sara was supposed to bring me one, but I suppose she has forgotten. I wager my sister needed her hair crimped again, or some such."

A reasonable explanation, but I noticed Mrs. Bowen and Lady Cynthia exchange a conspiratorial glance as I stepped into the room and draped my coat over the hook on the stand.

"Are you traveling, my lady?" I asked Lady Cynthia as I turned away from the coatrack. A Bradshaw, as *Bradshaw's Railway Handbook* was fondly called, was a paper-covered book that listed the timetables for every line in Britain. Bradshaws also contained a plethora of advertisements and information on hotels, sights to see, towns to stroll through, and so forth on the railway lines, for Britain, the Continent, and even India. Though I'd leafed through them from time to time, I'd never perused a Bradshaw completely, as my travels rarely took me far from London.

Lady Cynthia gave another sniff then jerked a large handkerchief from her pocket and wiped her nose with it. "I'm off to Brighton in a few days. With Bobby. London's dull as a post." Her face lit. "I say, come with us, Mrs. H."

I regarded her in astonishment. "You mean to cook for you?"

"Of course. What do you say? Cook for two women in a seaside cottage who don't eat much? You'd have plenty of time to walk about on the shingle."

I had a vision of myself hurrying down the rocky seashore in my cap and apron after the two young women in frock coats and suits, and wanted to sink into hysterical laughter. My imagination put my daughter there, running barefoot in the waves, and then I wanted to burst into tears.

I cleared my throat. "Thank you, Lady Cynthia, but no. I have a position here."

"For that stick, Rankin, and my sister who can't be bothered to lift her head from her pillow?"

Her disgust was clear. I said gently, "Perhaps her ladyship is unwell."

"Her ladyship is a lazy cow," Cynthia declared. "Rankin married her because he knew she'd never bother to contradict him. He knew *I* wouldn't bow to him, so he jumped over me and lighted on Emily. Lucky dodge for me, I'd say."

Her words were robust, but I saw a flash of pain in her eyes, one so brief it wouldn't have been noticed had I not been looking in particular.

Had Cynthia fallen in love with Rankin when he'd come calling on her sister? Or was Cynthia simply chagrined at having been dismissed in favor of the far more feminine and pliable Lady Emily?

Cynthia looked away and strode out of the room, and any insight to her was lost. "Bring up that Bradshaw when you find one, Mrs. B.," she called behind her.

"Of course, my lady," Mrs. Bowen answered.

Cynthia began to whistle, the sound dying as she clumped up the back stairs to the main house.

I stood looking down the passage until Mrs. Bowen gave a little cough. "I am sure you have cooking to do, Mrs. Holloway."

I certainly did. I departed for the kitchen, knowing my curiosity about the true reason Mrs. Bowen returned would have to wait until later.

I'd learned long ago the benefit of good preparation, and before I'd gone this morning I'd measured out and set aside ingredients that wouldn't spoil for the night's dishes, showing Mary so she could ready things for me in future. I thanked heaven I had done all this, because tonight I could barely remember what was what. But because I had my *mise en place*, I easily put together turbot in a butter sauce and an almond soup made from mutton I'd left to boil with spices, pulverized almonds, and leftover chopped boiled eggs from breakfast. No food need be wasted when it can be turned into a tasty soup.

For meat I gave the family pork cutlets that had been boiled then fried quickly with breadcrumbs and butter and a little onion Mary had chopped. Then greens—dandelion, chervil, and lettuce—served warm with butter and a sprinkling of new cheese, peas with a bit of ham, all accompanied by my crusty bread that Mary had baked at the correct time. She was learning quickly, I was happy to see.

For pudding I sent up fruit and cheese as I'd had no time to prepare a tart or cake. I could only do so much.

A bell went off as I finished putting together the staff's meal—the bell was for Simms, the valet. He cursed, grabbed a roll from the platter, and stuffed it into his mouth as he ran out.

The servants drifted in as their duties above stairs let them come down for their supper. I served everything in the servants' hall, too unsure of Mrs. Bowen's temperament tonight to presume to set up a meal for the senior staff in her parlor. Mary and I carried serving platters to the servants' hall and I also readied a tray for the coachman and his lads in the mews.

Mary sent me a sly smile as we piled dishes on the tray. She'd been darting me such smiles all evening, and now I had time to ask what was the matter with her.

"Coachman says they want *you* to carry the supper out to the stables, Mrs. Holloway," Mary said, her lips curving as though she found this funny.

I took in her pleased look, and her blue eyes, freckled face, and light brown curls massed above her forehead that made her look a bit like a sheep. "Coachman says that, does he?" I asked tartly. "I've cooked the food; why should I tote it about?"

Mary's smile deepened to show two fetching dimples. "It's not so much *him*, but that Daniel McAdam. *He* thinks it would be nice to have you bring it."

A chuckle behind me startled me, but it was only Mr. Davis, strolling into the servants' hall and seating himself to open his newspaper. "Have a care, Mrs. H. I think he's sweet on you."

"Nonsense." I carried the last bowl, the greens, into the servants' hall and plunked it on the table. "He likes to tease."

"Be careful he don't convince you to marry him," Mr. Davis went on. "He's a long way beneath you. Best to keep to your class."

"Which is what, a butler?" I asked, more sharply than I intended. I had no idea what class Daniel was, drat him.

"You could do worse than a butler," Mr. Davis said without offense as he spread his newspaper wide and began to scan the columns. "I see the Queen is off to hide herself in the country again. She ought to stay put and do some ruling, I think. Calls herself Countess of Balmoral when she wants to go incognito—and then takes her own special train. I ask you."

"She lost her husband," I said. "Have some sympathy." Queen Victoria had had a decent husband at least, as much as many aristocrats had never liked poor Albert. Or so I'd heard. I'd been a girl of about Grace's age when the Prince Consort had died.

"Twenty years ago." Davis flapped the newspaper. "Now she's devoted to that Scotsman, Mr. Brown. Another case of a woman marrying beneath herself—although she hasn't actually *married* him. Though rumor pops up now and again that she has."

"Mr. Davis!" Mrs. Bowen's freezing tones cut through his genial ones as she marched into the servants' hall and took her place at the head of the table. "Do keep your remarks respectful. Her Majesty has had a difficult time, as any woman does in the world of men." She bent a glare on Mr. Davis, who only looked amused, but he folded up the paper and set it aside to dig into his meal.

"Heed my warning, Mrs. H.," Mr. Davis said as I turned to leave for the kitchen.

"I have no intention of marrying anyone," I told him firmly from the doorway. "And neither does the Queen."

I did not mention my errand to the stables, knowing Mrs. Bowen would not approve, so I said nothing more. To Mr. Davis's continued laughter, I hung up my cap and apron in the kitchen, swung a shawl around my shoulders to keep off the damp, covered the tray, and headed for the mews.

The stables for Lord Rankin's house lay in a passage called Reeves Mews, a narrow lane that cut behind the gardens of the large homes on Mount Street. Each carriage house had room for horses and a town coach on its ground floor, with small chambers above for the coachman, head groom, stable hands, and any other servant who didn't have a place to sleep in the main house.

When I reached Lord Rankin's stable, a lad of about twelve summers opened the door to admit me into a large space of warmth and horsey scents. He led me up the stairs in the back of the carriage house to the common room above, where four men, including Daniel, and a half dozen young lads waited to eat.

Daniel, ever gallant, met me before I'd taken more than

two steps up, took the tray from my hands, and carried it the rest of the way upstairs.

By the time I'd made it to the common room—to make sure all was well with the food—Daniel had already begun placing the platters on the table. Hands shot out and grabbed things in genial chaos.

I knew precisely why Daniel had told the groom to ask for me to bring over the tray. It had nothing to do with courtship, as much as Mr. Davis wished to make it seem so, and everything to do with finding out what had upset me today.

My guess was confirmed when Daniel lifted the now empty tray and carried it back downstairs for me, as though worried the thing would be too heavy for me. The stablemen, busy raking in food, didn't notice us go.

On the ground floor, with only the horses to hear us, Daniel set the tray on the bottom step, tugged me from the stairs, and stood me near the high wheel of Lord Rankin's landau.

"Tell me what happened," he said, his eyes holding quiet concern.

I knew he meant me to explain why I had looked so desolate when he'd stopped his wagon for me on the street. I didn't much want to speak about it, fearing I'd break down and become a sobbing wretch, not good for anything.

"Nothing at all," I said, trying to keep to my usual crisp tones. "Nothing to do with Sinead, or Lord Rankin, or people blowing things up." My nose itched, and I thrust my hand into my pocket for a handkerchief. I envied Lady Cynthia and her large man's hankie. Mine was sturdy linen but small and dainty, meant to dab away delicate female tears.

"What is it about, then?" Again he spoke in a gentle but persuasive tone.

I had the feeling that if I did not tell him, Daniel would

take it upon himself to find out. He knew many of my secrets already—had known them before I'd revealed them to him one day last autumn. He knew all about my daughter and where she lived, as well as my sham marriage, and how hard I'd worked to make certain Grace was taken care of.

I cleared my throat and decided to simply tell him. "The friends who look after my daughter wish to adopt her. Is that not good news?"

Daniel said nothing. I looked up from wiping my nose, and I saw in his eyes complete understanding of every bit of turmoil in my heart.

"Oh, Kat."

"Don't," I said savagely. "Do not make me cry or moan. I am a selfish, selfish woman. I must do what is best for Grace. She is far more important than I am. Or my sentimentality."

These words should have been brisk and decisive. Instead, every one came out of me with supreme effort, and my voice broke on the last.

My vision blurred. The coach wheel became a wash of black and gold, the stables around us dissolving, Daniel a dark smudge in the shadows.

I was falling, but no, Daniel caught me. He was strong—his arms held me as my legs weakened.

"She is yours," Daniel said into my ear. I heard more the rumble of his voice than his individual words. "A part of you. Never let anyone take that away."

Daniel's coat smelled of wool, horses, and London smoke, the coarsely woven fabric holding the scents.

"They've been so good to her," I said, using the argument with which I'd been berating myself. "I can't let her starve. Or go to a workhouse." The brick walls of the shut-down workhouse on Mount Street, its windows bleak eyes into nothing, haunted me.

"*Is* she starving?" Daniel asked me in a reasonable tone. "Scrubbing floors in a workhouse? Of course not, because you have made certain of it. Will your friends throw her out if you refuse them? I doubt that. If they were that sort of people, you would not have sent her to them in the first place."

I recognized that he spoke the truth. Joanna and Sam would be disappointed, hurt, if I turned down their kind offer. But I doubted they'd take their regret out on Grace.

"It would be a good thing for her," I continued. "Not only now, but later, when she goes out to find work, when she wishes to marry. Being part of a decent family will help her. Shall she be the daughter of Mr. Millburn, a respectable solicitor's clerk? Or the fatherless child of a cook who is hiding her disgrace?"

Daniel said gently, "She will be the daughter of a good woman who looks out for her."

I wanted to believe him, to cling to his words, but I could not convince myself Daniel was right. "What chances will she have if she remains with me? I do not want Grace to go into service—I want her to have a family of her own, with a large-hearted husband who has more than two coins to rub together."

I felt the vibration of his chuckle. "She'll be able to do what she pleases, I'll wager. The world is changing, with new jobs for young women in shops and businesses, new machines like the telegraph that ladies seem to take to more readily than gentlemen."

I drew back from his embrace, but my hands remained limply on his chest. "I know you are trying to comfort me,

Daniel, but—forgive me—you know nothing about it. You are obviously *not* a deliveryman or man-of-all-work, but a toff who has decided to dress up and play among us, the same way Lady Cynthia dresses up like a gentleman and sneaks into their clubs. *You* grew up without fear for your future. Those rooms you have near Covent Garden are not where you truly live. There is nothing of you there. You use the boardinghouse as part of your play."

"Partly true." Daniel didn't sound worried I'd concluded all this. "But you are wrong that I grew up without fear. I grew up as James did, on the streets, always searching for my next meal, not knowing who or what I was. One day, I will tell you all about it, I promise you. When I found James in the same situation, when I discovered he was my son . . ." Daniel stopped and took a long breath, all amusement gone. "I held on to him. I wrapped my arms around him and didn't want to let go."

His hands tightened on my arms. I stared up at him, startled from my grief and uncertainty.

"You've had to face the same decisions about James, haven't you?" I said, realizing.

"Oh yes," Daniel answered. "Should I send him away for his own sake? Keep him near me? Be his father in truth? Leave him be and make sure he is well from afar?"

Curiosity momentarily overcame my own troubles. "What did you decide?"

"I claimed him as my own, had it legally declared. Then I found a place for him to stay where he would be safe. Living with *me* would not be safe." Daniel looked exasperated. "I had to drag him back from running away three times before I convinced him to *stay*. He did not trust me, but I did not blame him too much. He'd been deceived by men before who'd vowed to take care of him—one took every penny he earned and gave him nothing, another tried to have his way with him. I made James tell me who they were, and I had a few . . . chats . . . with these fellows."

From the coolness in his voice, I imagined the villains had come out much the worse for these "chats." I had often wondered about James's mother, but Daniel had never mentioned her, and James had once told me he did not remember her. He'd been living with a charwoman when Daniel arrived in his life. One day I would pry the story from Daniel, but not this moment.

Daniel rubbed my arms, his confident expression returning. "Don't worry, Kat. We'll look after Grace. She'll grow up safe and happy—we'll make sure of it."

I felt a small measure of relief. If Daniel would help me, I might not feel obligated to hand Grace over to my friends completely while I became only a marginal part of her life.

I'd feel more relief if I trusted Daniel without reservation. That is, I did trust him—mostly—but I did not understand him. Daniel came and went without warning, whenever he pleased. Trustworthy, possibly. Reliable, no.

I wiped tears from my eyes. "Thank you," I said, my gratitude sincere. "I will think on it."

Daniel's hands were heavy on my arms, his eyes dark in the shadows. Instead of releasing me, he leaned down and brushed a kiss to my lips.

His mouth was warm against mine, and for a moment, I simply gave in to the enjoyment of it.

I knew that if I let myself, I could have more from Daniel than brief kisses. He would give me all I asked for; of that I was certain. He was handsome, strong, and could be kind.

But I had already brought one child into the world—hence my present difficulty. I would not risk bringing in another.

I let myself indulge in the kiss for now, closing my eyes to savor the warmth easing through my heart. I would hold this moment to me like a treasure, to be taken out and remembered when I was cold and alone in the night.

Daniel eased the kiss to its end. He said nothing, but the question was in his eyes. Perhaps not for the immediate moment, or even tonight, but someday.

I shook my head the slightest bit, slid from his embrace, picked up the tray from the stairs, and left the stables. The mews were cold, rain and wind beginning, and I huddled into my shawl as I hurried home.

I was not very hungry, but I understood the need to keep up my strength, no matter the state of my emotions. When I returned to the kitchen, it was to find that the servants had finished every drop of soup as well as all the pork cutlets, so I ate greens and buns, saving a bit of the vegetables for soup tomorrow.

The staff went about their various chores for cleaning the kitchen and servants' hall and shutting down the house upstairs for the night. Lady Rankin was actually going out, and so was Lord Rankin, though to different places—Lady Rankin to the opera, Lord Rankin to a lecture by members of the Royal Society. I was surprised he was interested in science, but some men became patrons of the Royal Society to make themselves appear to be clever.

I wanted to corner Mrs. Bowen and find out more about why she'd left and then returned so quickly, but she eluded me, going upstairs to see that Lady Rankin set off without hindrance. Simms departed with Lord Rankin, Mr. Davis shut himself in the butler's pantry to see to the silver, and I sent Mary to bed early, as she'd done much work for me today.

Alone, I made up my lists for what I'd need from the markets in the morning. Mary had not had time to get the eggs, so I would have to, as well as fresh produce, fish, and meat. The kitchen grew quiet as I puttered about, and though my heart still quickened every time I went into the larder, I seemed to be able to do so now without the numbing panic I'd experienced the morning after Sinead's death.

As I worked, I wanted to let Daniel's words reassure me. *Don't worry, Kat. We'll look after Grace. She'll grow up safe and happy.*

He was so confident, so certain. I envied him that surety.

Someone banged through the green bias door and hurried down the stairs. I hadn't lived here long enough to distinguish footsteps, though I'd already learned the difference between Davis and Simms—the first quick and quiet with buoyancy, the second lugubrious and slow, as though Simms resented the fact that he had to come below stairs at all. These footsteps were rapid but clattering, and I experienced a moment of fear when I couldn't place them.

I saw a person in a man's frock coat and trousers in the dim passage, and I came to my feet, thinking for a startled instant it was the master. I relaxed in relief when Lady Cynthia dashed into the kitchen, her restless hands already moving as she spoke.

"What's happened to my Bradshaw, Mrs. H.? Old Bowen's let me down. Sara's useless—if Rankin wasn't too mean to pay for a proper lady's maid for my sister, there would be someone to wait on the rest of us. Simms won't even speak to me."

I saw frustration in Lady Cynthia's eyes, and behind it,

hurt. An unmarried woman in her world, a spinster, was a rather useless thing. Even the staff in this house treated her as an appendage to the main family, a hanger-on until she managed to marry, if she ever did. I felt pity for her.

"I beg your pardon, my lady," I said in a kind voice. "There was much to do in the kitchen tonight, and Mrs. Bowen had to catch up with things after her few days out. I'll hunt up a Bradshaw for you."

I took my keys from my pocket and ushered Cynthia from the kitchen. I didn't have as many keys as Mrs. Bowen, who could unlock every door and every cupboard in the house, but I could open the larder, the housekeeper's parlor, and the servants' hall, in addition to the kitchen. The butler's pantry, where the silver was kept, and the small wine cellar would be off-limits until I proved I could be trusted.

Lady Cynthia followed me down the passage. "I say, you're a good sort, Mrs. H. Not like *some*."

I wasn't certain which *some* she referred to, and I did not ask. I unlocked the housekeeper's parlor and we went into the small room.

It was a simple chamber with a narrow sofa and Mrs. Bowen's favorite upholstered chair, a small dining table where the senior staff took meals, a desk that was shut and locked, and an open bookcase.

I did not have the key to the desk, so I scanned the bookshelves, hoping to find what Lady Cynthia needed. I could always pop 'round to a newsagents to fetch a Bradshaw, but I did not fancy going out into the dark and rain until I found a newsagents still open for business.

The bookshelf held several cookbooks, two of which belonged to me, and various books belonging to members of the staff—a collection of Mr. Dickens's stories, books about foreign lands, works on housekeeping and gardening, and one book on the philosophy of science. I was interested in the ones about foreign lands, places I'd likely never go, but I wondered about the one on the philosophy of science. Probably it was Mr. Davis's; he was interested in odd bits of information.

"Ah," I said. Among the travel books rested a brownish yellow paper copy of *Bradshaw's Railway Handbook*. I thumbed the pages, which were worn with use. "Brighton. Let me see."

I flipped through until I came upon timetables for the London, Brighton, and South Coast Railway. Most trains to Brighton began at London Bridge Station—though the fast trains originated at Victoria Station—then made their way south.

"There's a train at nine twenty in the morning on weekdays," I read, "which reaches Brighton about an hour and a half later. Another at eleven, twelve, and two . . . all the way to ten o'clock at night. A fast train leaves from Victoria Station at eight in the morning. If you are an early riser, you can reach Brighton with plenty of time to enjoy that city for the rest of the day."

"*I* am an early riser," Lady Cynthia said with a scornful laugh. "I can't say the same for Bobby."

I barely heard her. My gaze became fixed as I stared at the columns of numbers and letters. The columns were ruled, the times marching horizontally across the page, the names of the stations listed vertically.

A spark of excitement struck me. The scrap of paper I'd found in the larder had similar columns, though no actual names of stations, but it might be the jottings of someone noting what trains arrived where, and when.

Which was innocent enough. The Bradshaw sat on the shelf in this room, and any of the staff could make a note of trains to certain destinations on a scrap of paper and slip it into his or her pocket.

But why were those train times important enough for a man to sneak into the larder in the middle of the night to search for them or leave them for someone else, and fight off Daniel when he was caught?

My heart beat faster and my fingertips tingled. I must speak to Daniel right away, never mind the tittle-tattle about me rushing to the stables to seek him.

"Excuse me, my lady," I began absently, closing the book and sliding it into my apron pocket. "Something I must see to."

I was so intent on rushing away to hunt up Daniel that I didn't notice Lady Cynthia, until she stepped in front of me to block my way out of the parlor.

I nearly ran into her. "I beg your pardon," I said, stepping back. "As I said, I must see to something, my lady."

Lady Cynthia did not move. I looked up into her face, and found anguish, determination, and a bleakness so vast I halted in surprise.

"No, Mrs. H.," Lady Cynthia said, almost sadly. "I cannot let you go. You need to give me the paper you found in the larder. *At once.*"

15

Lady Cynthia stood solidly before me, her hand out as though ready to wrestle me down if I tried to walk around her.

I remained still, my thoughts spinning. Last night Daniel had chased a man from here—or so we'd concluded. I'd decided then, from the way he'd pushed me, that it hadn't been a woman dressed as a man. I thought again about the person I'd glimpsed fleeing Daniel, the two of them dashing up the stairs outside, silhouetted by the gas lamps of Mount Street through the high windows.

No—that person had run like a man. Lady Cynthia, no matter what her garb, moved and gestured like a woman. It could not have been her down here last night.

"How did you know about the paper?" I asked her.

"Never you mind that." Lady Cynthia's voice went hard, but I heard the tremor in it. "Give it to me." She took a step toward me, crowding me back into the parlor.

Lady Cynthia was young and strong, but so was I. We were of an age, she and I, both of us healthy and hearty.

"What is it?" I persisted. "What is on the paper you do not want me to see? It is only railway times, is it not?" I gave her a challenging look.

Lady Cynthia's face went ashen, the lamplight barely brushing color into her cheeks. "It wasn't the girl's fault, Mrs. H. She was a dupe—a go-between. Not fair on her or her family."

"What girl?" I demanded. "You mean Sinead?"

Lady Cynthia swallowed. "Yes—that's what she called herself. She'd been with me and Em for ages, came with us to London because the poor creature thought she'd have a better chance attracting a husband. She found a man all right, a loathsome bastard. But I don't blame *her*. Give me the damned paper."

"I don't have it," I said truthfully. Daniel had taken the scrap away with him after I'd copied it. "If it wasn't you in the larder looking for it last night—who was it?"

Lady Cynthia opened her lips to speak, but the decided voice of Mrs. Bowen interrupted her. "*I* sent him."

Mrs. Bowen, who obviously had finished sending off Lady Rankin, halted in the doorway behind Lady Cynthia. The jet buttons on her bodice moved with her sharp breath, and her eyes held glittering rage.

The pair of them wished me to meekly bow my head, hand them the paper, and scuttle to my kitchen, asking no more questions. They certainly looked angry enough to shove me bodily back to my domain.

"Sent who?" I asked Mrs. Bowen, remaining where I was, and then I realized the answer. "Ah. He was your beau." I remembered Sara, the upstairs maid, telling me Mrs. Bowen was walking out with a gentleman. Apparently, this gentleman was not above performing a theft for her. Perhaps Mrs. Bowen had decided to return to her post because he'd failed to find the paper and she wanted to look for it herself.

"Sinead was a good girl, Mrs. Holloway," Mrs. Bowen said stiffly. "She became mixed up with an awful man who used her and endangered her. I at first thought that he must have killed her, but unfortunately he was out of London at the time."

"How do you know he was out of London?" I asked, my eyes narrowing.

"It was in the newspapers, wasn't it?" Mrs. Bowen said, and Lady Cynthia nodded, as though I ought to have known this. I hadn't looked at a paper in days, had only heard what news Mr. Davis had read out to me. "A railway line blown up in the north of England," Mrs. Bowen reminded me. "Sinead's young man was there, arrested as a suspect. As much as I desire to see him hanged for Sinead's death, I know that he was not guilty of the actual deed. But he killed her, as certainly as if he'd struck her down himself."

I recalled Mr. Davis reading from his newspaper the day after Sinead's death, telling me about the Fenians, dynamite, and railways. The papers had been full of such things for months—I had stopped reading the accounts altogether, as journalists are bound to wallow in the things that are the most upsetting.

"Good heavens, Mrs. Bowen," I said impatiently. "If you knew Sinead was mixed up with Fenians, why did you not tell the police? You might have prevented her death." I remembered her adamance that all Irishmen should be expelled from England—I'd wondered at her statement at the time, since Sinead and her mum had been Irish, but Mrs. Bowen must have been thinking of this young man and his cohorts.

Lady Cynthia answered for her. "And tell the world Sinead was a Fenian? Smear her reputation? Wasn't her fault she fell for a bad 'un. Least said, the better, I say."

"But this might be why she died," I argued. "One of her young man's friends might have feared she knew too much, crept in here, and killed her. Why is that piece of paper so important? It does have to do with railways, doesn't it? The next target? Good Lord, we ought to warn someone."

I started forward, but Lady Cynthia's outstretched hand stopped me. This time she actually touched me, her palm on my chest. "We don't know what the paper is about," she said. "Or even who Sinead was supposed to pass it to."

"How do you know about it at all? You seem to know much about Fenian plots." My accusing gaze took in the pair of them.

Mrs. Bowen shook her head. "We have no idea what it means. I found the paper when I went to the larder to pray by Sinead's body, just before the police came—it was in the pocket of her pinafore. I put it in my own pocket and took it away with me, in case it was something from her young man. When I examined the paper later, I realized a piece had been torn off, and the other piece might have been lost when she struggled, or when the killer dragged her body into the corner. I was at my boardinghouse by that time, and so I sent Mr. Greer—my beau, as you call him—here to look for it." Color flushed her face. "I gave him my key to the back door, and he waited until he thought you'd gone to bed. When you and that man McAdam nearly caught him, I rescinded my notice and returned. Lady Cynthia and I were going to turn the house upside down to search for the paper and destroy it. If you give it to us, we will finish and say no more about it."

"What did you do with the other half?" I asked, ignoring her last demand.

"I burned it." Mrs. Bowen regarded me defiantly.

"For heaven's sake, Mrs. Bowen, there might have been information on that paper that could save people's lives. You had no right to burn it."

Lady Cynthia looked shamefaced and lowered her hand from my chest. "We were trying to save Sinead, Mrs. H., if only her reputation. As Mrs. Bowen said, *she* wasn't to blame for her young man's villainy."

"*You* will be to blame if another railway station gets destroyed." I started forward, but the two ladies continued to block the door.

Much as I wished to, I couldn't simply shove Lady Cynthia aside. A servant putting her hands on a highborn lady would only land herself in the dock. However, I'd gleefully send Mrs. Bowen tumbling if I had to.

"Excuse me," I said to them. "If you let me out of this room, I will speak to a person who is *not* the police but who can warn the right people. No one needs to know Sinead had anything to do with it at all." At least, I believed Daniel could warn the right people. He seemed to know a good many persons of influence, which last year had freed me from Newgate and saved me the anguish of standing trial for murder.

Lady Cynthia, after a moment's hesitation, stood aside. Mrs. Bowen, on the other hand, refused to budge.

"What person?" she asked, her eyes hard.

"I'd rather keep that to myself. You will have to trust me."

Mrs. Bowen did not—I saw that in her fierce gaze and the fists that curled at her sides.

"Mrs. Bowen," I said, trying to remain calm. "I feel quite responsible for Sinead's death. She was working for *me* at the time, and I ought to have stayed with her that night and looked after her better. I will not tarnish her memory now by allowing people to believe she was the sort who could hurt others, or even condone such things. Her name will not come into it at all. I promise you that."

Once I finished my resolute speech, Lady Cynthia, her blue eyes softening, gave Mrs. Bowen a nod. "I trust her, Mrs. B."

"Well, I do not." Mrs. Bowen spoke only to Lady Cynthia, as though I no longer stood at her side. "I will let her go, my lady, if *you* accompany her. *You*, I trust. You are a good person, and you have the power to sack Mrs. Holloway straightaway if she puts a foot wrong."

"Really, Mrs. Bowen . . ." I began.

"Take Lady Cynthia with you," Mrs. Bowen said, switching her focus to me. "Or I promise that I will tie you up and drag you to the outskirts of London myself—*after* I destroy the paper you have—to prevent you speaking to anyone about this. I wish to stop the Fenians as much as you, but I will not have that poor girl or her mother paraded through the newspapers. God rest them both."

Lady Cynthia sent me a look of sympathy and resignation. "There you have it, Mrs. H. Take me to this person of yours." She patted Mrs. Bowen's arm. "Don't worry, Mrs. B. I'll make sure she does right by Sinead. You can depend upon it."

L ady Cynthia was somewhat puzzled when, after I fetched both my notebook and my coat, I took her through the darkness only as far as the mews, to Lord Rankin's own stables. The lad I startled upon hastening inside straightened up from tumbling grooming brushes into a wooden box, then went ramrod stiff when he saw Lady Cynthia. I bade him fetch Daniel, and the lad ran upstairs, relieved to be gone from us.

Daniel came unhurriedly down from above, putting on a genial expression when he saw Lady Cynthia with me. He stopped at the bottom of the stairs, pulled off his cap, and mashed it in his hands, evading Lady Cynthia's gaze even as he spoke to her.

"Somefink I do for you, me lady?" he asked.

"Never mind all that," I cut in. "This is important. Is there somewhere we can speak? Alone?"

Daniel's gaze sharpened as he took in my agitated state, but he did not drop his persona. "If you want a bit of a chin-wag, missus," he said to me in his South London voice, "house is best for it, I'd say."

Lady Cynthia shook her head. "Bugger that. Nowhere's private in that pile. Come on, you. I'll take you somewhere we can have that chin-wag. It's not far."

16

Lady Cynthia led us from the mews at a brisk pace and waved for a hansom cab, letting out a whistle as loud as any I'd heard Daniel produce. A hansom stopped quickly, the driver no doubt recognizing the eccentric Lady Cynthia, and we squashed into the hansom's seat.

Cynthia told the cabbie to take us north of Oxford Street, near the lavish Langham Hotel, and the cabbie set off, the horse moving at a smart trot.

We said little as we traveled through the dark but crowded streets, I crushed between Lady Cynthia on my right and Daniel on my left. Cynthia sent Daniel curious glances around me, but he studiously looked out to the lighted houses as we went, behaving as though he rarely had the luxury of riding in a conveyance. He was keeping determinedly to his man-of-all-work guise, I saw.

The hansom stopped at the door of a tall house in Duchess Street, and Lady Cynthia was on the ground before Daniel could descend and move around to assist her. He helped me down instead, while Cynthia marched to the door and pounded on it.

Cynthia's enthusiastic knock was answered by a maid in a starched apron and cap who pulled open the door, letting a square of light spill to the pavement, and peered at us in bewilderment.

"Only me," Lady Cynthia told her. "I know she's not here, but she won't mind." Cynthia waved for us to follow as she strode inside, the maid stepping hastily aside for her.

The maid gave a most disapproving look as first I then Daniel followed Lady Cynthia in and to the staircase at the rear of the hall. Daniel sent the maid a warm smile and a shrug as he went by.

The smile seemed to mollify the maid, though her face softened only for Daniel, not me. She must have been used to Lady Cynthia, because she only shook her head once Cynthia was running up the stairs, and disappeared into the back of the house.

I wasn't certain what to expect when Cynthia unlocked and opened the door to a high-ceilinged, well-furnished room on the first floor. Lady Cynthia quickly closed the thick velvet curtains over all the windows and then opened a squat stove whose pipe dove back into what used to be the fireplace. She crouched down and poked the glowing coals inside, encouraging the fire to flare high.

"Wish I could move in here with her," Cynthia said as she wielded the poker. "Old Rankin won't hear of it, of course. But this place is far cozier than that drafty mausoleum on Mount Street with open fires instead of stoves, don't you think?"

I had considered the Mount Street house to be up-to-date and plenty efficient, but I had to admit that this flat was warmer and more modern than the elegant house. The furniture was new, in the simpler style that had become the rage since the scan-

dalous artists who called themselves the Pre-Raphaelite Broth-
erhood had begun designing wallpaper and furniture and the
like. A paper of leafy motif decorated the walls, and the chairs
had clean, straight lines with no carving or fuss. The velvet
drapes were light green, and potted ferns had been placed
around the room to convey the idea that we sat in a lush conser-
vatory rather than a sitting room in the middle of London.

"Is this where Bobby lives?" I asked. "I beg your pardon,
my lady; I know no other name for her."

"Bobby don't mind," Cynthia said breezily, unfolding to
her feet. I had to admit that trousers let her move with far
more ease than would a frock. "She thinks we should all be
free of titles and classes. Good luck to her, I say. Her real name
is Lady Roberta Perry—Earl of Lockwood's her dad. She's not
here; she's off visiting her brother in Surrey, who just brought
another squalling aristocrat into the world. Well, his wife did,
but he goes on as though he did all the hard work himself. The
poor brat will be earl one day if he lives long enough. That's
why Bobby suggested a trip to Brighton, to recover her nerves
afterward." Cynthia moved to a table littered with notebooks
and papers and swept them together into a haphazard pile.
"We can talk here. The landlady ignores Bobby. And me."

Daniel still had no idea why I'd dragged him out of the stables and all the way to Marylebone, but he remained quiet, not
saying a word until he understood what role he was to play. Now
Cynthia plopped into a chair and put her elbows on the table.

"What's your game, Mrs. H.?" she asked. "And how can *he*
help?"

I took the Bradshaw and my notebook from my coat pockets, turned to the page in the notebook on which I'd copied
down the numbers and letters, and opened the Bradshaw
next to it. "There," I said, pushing both toward Daniel.

He stared at both books, mystified, before his attention was caught, and he leaned to study the numbers, hands coming to rest on the table. "Damnation," he said softly.

Cynthia's brows rose. "What's the matter?"

Daniel slowly sat down, never taking his eyes off the pages. He ran his finger along the column of numbers I'd copied into my notebook. "You're right, Kat. These figures could very well mean a train schedule, the train passing these stations at these specific times. Hmm." He bent closer, frowning.

I seated myself across from him. "It would help if we had the other half of the paper," I said. "But Mrs. Bowen destroyed it." I sent Lady Cynthia a disapproving look. "Did you see it?"

"No," Cynthia answered regretfully. "Mrs. B. only told me about it when she asked me to help her look for it, and to keep Sin—" She broke off and reddened, glancing at Daniel, whose attention was all for the notebook.

"It's all right," I said. "Daniel knows about Sinead. Or at least, most things. Am I correct?" I asked Daniel. "These are times for trains passing through stations? That Fenians are marking as potential for dynamiting?"

"Possibly." Daniel glanced up at me, his interest and worry evident. "Or that someone simply wishes to take to reach a destination. The trouble is, there's no way to tell what these times mean—which stations? Which trains? Which lines?"

"Well," I said in my no-nonsense way, "there's nothing for it but that we must look them up. Read over every single train schedule and find which ones the times correspond to."

Daniel nodded, undaunted. "If we each take a section and search for a match, it will go faster." He flipped the worn timetable book closed, studied its cover, and heaved a resigned sigh. "We'll need more Bradshaws."

Cynthia jumped to her feet. "I'll go. I'll pound on the door of every newsagents until they cough some up. Back in a tick." She ran out, more animated than I'd seen her.

Daniel gave me a doubtful look as the door banged behind her. "Why did you bring her into this?"

"I hadn't much choice." I told him about my encounter with Lady Cynthia and Mrs. Bowen, and the information Mrs. Bowen had imparted about Sinead.

Daniel listened with concern. "I will have to talk to Sinead's young man, if they haven't already strung him up for the railway incident. Mrs. Bowen is right—though he wasn't in London, his confederates might have killed her. They might be connected to the men I'm trying to catch through Lord Rankin, or they may not." He looked unhappy. "No matter what, I ought to have prevented her death."

"You couldn't have known," I said, trying to sound reassuring. "I blame myself." I let out a breath. "I suppose both of us will always feel remorse for not helping her. As for Lady Cynthia, she seemed fond of Sinead—she worked for Lady Cynthia's family in Hertfordshire." I shook my head. "And, I believe Lady Cynthia is lonely and in need of stimulation of the mind. She's wasted in that house, and she knows it."

Daniel listened with half his attention, his gaze straying back to the numbers. "If she's willing to help us unravel this mess, I'm happy to give her something to do." He sat back and ran a hand through his already rumpled hair. "I need to stop these bloody men, Kat."

Daniel's eyes held seriousness and a deep anger. The real Daniel was down there in that anger, the determination to find those who hurt others, punish them, rid the world of them. I remembered remarking upon the similar look in the eyes of Daniel's colleague, Mr. Thanos, before the man had been caught up in his fascination with the balance sheets.

"I met Mr. Thanos," I said. "In your rooms earlier today, when I stopped there to rest."

"Did you?" Daniel seemed in no way put out that I'd gone to his lodgings uninvited, nor surprised I'd met his friend there. "Yes, I told Thanos to fetch papers from my rooms. What did you think of him?"

"He has an odd name," I said. "But he's not foreign, I'd wager."

Daniel shook his head. "Elgin's grandfather was Greek. A banker in Constantinople. Elgin's grandfather fled that city during the Greek War of Independence, back in 1820-something, when the Ottomans started slaughtering anyone of Greek origin in Constantinople. When Britain sent troops to help Greece against the Ottomans, Elgin's grandfather decided to try his luck in London, as there was nothing for him in Greece itself. He'd lived in Constantinople too long and lost everything there. Once he reached *this* shore, Elgin's grandfather married an Englishwoman and settled down to raise his family as Britons."

I listened, intrigued. "Mr. Thanos seems a kindly sort."

Daniel gave a short laugh. "I will tell him you said so. He is unworldly, that is certain. Doesn't notice what color the sky is, but with numbers, he's a genius."

"How do you know him?" I'd observed from Mr. Thanos's pallor that he stayed indoors much of the time, probably with his head bent over a ledger. Daniel, on the other hand, never ceased moving. I could not imagine how the two had crossed paths.

"Met him at Cambridge," Daniel answered. "He took a first degree so easily it put his professors to shame. He'd ask them plenty of questions they couldn't answer. I wouldn't wonder if he finds the mathematical answer to the entire universe before he's forty."

"Cambridge." I opened the Bradshaw to the first page of

timetables, flattening the spine to make the book stay open. "You see? I knew you were a toff."

"Working-class men *do* go to university," Daniel answered, unruffled. "If they're extremely intelligent and have a benefactor, that is." He rose and moved to a desk across the room, opening its drawer and extracting paper, pens, and ink. He sat down again and began sorting the blank paper into three piles. "And I don't remember mentioning I actually studied there."

I sent him a severe look. "One day, Daniel McAdam, I will open up your head and find out all that is inside."

Daniel gave a mock shiver. "Shouldn't joke like that, Mrs. H., the way you wave that cleaver about." His voice softened. "I'll tell you one day, Kat, I swear it. We'll make an appointment."

"But not today," I said.

"Today—or tonight—we will find out what information Sinead was given by whom and why. Whether it is innocuous or the reason she was killed. Villains first, then we'll sort ourselves out. Yes?" Daniel stuck out his hand across the table.

I shook it. "Very well. Villains first. May God have mercy on them."

"That's the spirit." Daniel squeezed my hand, the warmth of it seeping into my bones.

He released me as Lady Cynthia banged back in, brandishing two brand-new yellow-covered Bradshaws. "Got 'em," she cried, triumphant. "Let's go to it."

I t was well past midnight when I turned the last page of my section of the timetable and sighed in defeat. Lady Cynthia threw down her pen at the same time, half-dried ink scattering from the pen nib to blotch her page.

"Damned if I found any matches." Cynthia hauled herself

to her feet, strolled to a long cabinet next to the window, and lifted a decanter. "Need a stiff whisky. How about you, McAdam? Mrs. H.?"

"No, thank you," I answered. Although I was not averse to spirits entirely, I was careful about imbibing them.

"Please," Daniel said without raising his head.

Lady Cynthia poured liquid, clinked glasses together, and moved back to the table, balancing glasses in her hands, the whisky decanter tucked under her arm. "Brought you amontillado, Mrs. H. Can't stand the stuff myself, but Bobby keeps it on hand for visitors." She plunked a small goblet in front of me that smelled strongly of sherry.

I didn't much like the taste of amontillado, but I sipped politely, admitting that its warmth took away my stiffness.

Daniel at last pushed aside his papers, took the cut-crystal glass of whisky Cynthia shoved at him, and upended the liquid into his mouth.

He let out a breath and clapped the empty glass to the table. "I conclude," he said, "that these numbers correspond to no stops at railway stations the length and breadth of England or Scotland."

"Bloody hell," Cynthia exclaimed in dismay. "We've done all this for nothing?"

"Not nothing," Daniel said. "Eliminating possibilities is always useful."

Daniel had dropped his working-class accent. Cynthia gazed at him in frustration mixed with perplexity, but as she opened her mouth to speak, there was a knock on the front door downstairs. A pounding, more like. Cynthia sprang up, but Daniel forestalled her and went down to answer it himself.

I was not very alarmed about who the visitor might be—earlier, while we'd worked, Daniel had gone down to the street, and I'd heard the younger tones of James floating up from the stairwell. Daniel now returned, followed by Mr. Thanos—whom he'd presumably sent James to fetch—followed by James himself.

"I told you to go home," Daniel was growling to his son as they entered.

"Naw," James said cheerfully. "More interesting here, innit?" He gave Lady Cynthia and me deferential nods. "Yer ladyship. Ma'am."

Mr. Thanos, in his neat suit, his black hair rumpled when he removed his hat, glanced at me in polite acknowledgment. When Lady Cynthia rose from her chair, he halted in astonishment, hat frozen in his hands, his mouth falling open.

"Good Lord." He looked her up and down with his very dark eyes as though he could not believe what he was seeing. "Forgive me, but are you a hermaphrodite?"

Lady Cynthia's brows climbed. "Cheek. What a thing to ask."

Mr. Thanos did not look abashed. "I meant no offense. I've never met a hermaphrodite, you see. That is—I don't *believe* I have. I might, you know, on a tram or at the British Museum, and never realized. It's not what one first says in those places, does one? Rather it's *Excuse me, may I take this seat?* or *The jewels of the Egyptian queen are in the room down this corridor.*"

Lady Cynthia listened in fascination, her lips parting.

"Don't terrify the poor lady, Thanos," Daniel admonished. "Sit down—I need your brain."

Mr. Thanos ignored him. "I do beg your pardon," he said to Lady Cynthia. "My manners are appalling, and McAdam's are worse—he never makes introductions. Mr. Elgin Thanos, at your service." He gave her a correct bow.

Lady Cynthia sent him a brief nod in return. "Cynthia Shires."

"Ah," Elgin said with interest. "The family of the Earls of Clifford. Son deceased, youngest daughter married to Lord Rankin, in whose house McAdam and Mrs. Holloway are making their home at present. You must be the eldest daughter, Lady Cynthia. Very pleased to make your acquaintance, my lady."

Cynthia listened in bewilderment that held no anger. "Charmed, I'm sure," she said when he'd finished. "And to answer your question, no, I am not a hermaphrodite."

"Oh." Elgin looked disappointed. "Pity. I would have liked to learn all about being a hermaphrodite from one who actually practiced such things. One shouldn't rely on hearsay."

"For God's sake, sit down," Daniel growled at him. "The British Empire will fall by the time you finish talking. Have a look at this."

"I do beg your pardon again, ladies," Elgin said, including me in his sweeping smile. He landed on a chair beside Daniel, removed his spectacles from his pocket, hooked them on, and studied the papers. "Is that whisky?" he asked, glancing at the decanter. "Is there another glass about?"

Cynthia herself went to the cabinet to fetch him one.

Daniel glared at James. "Go home."

"Don't think I will," James said easily. "Unless her ladyship don't want me about. Then I'll wait downstairs for ya."

Lady Cynthia seemed much entertained by us all. "Sit," she said to James, pointing to a chair on her way back to the table. "Don't get it dirty. Bobby's landlady is particular."

"No worries, yer ladyship." James dragged a straight-backed chair to the stove, plopping down and sticking his boots as close to the heat as possible. I noticed that the boots were whole and well-made, the stockings sticking out from under his trousers free of rents. James might enjoy roaming the streets, but Daniel at least made sure he had decent clothes to wear.

During the drama, I had turned once again to the Bradshaw, absently thumbing through it. Advertisements took up a part of the book—the Queen's Hotel had a page, extolling its many rooms and its proximity to sights in the City of London, proclaiming it fit for both gentlemen and families. There was plenty of information on hotels in London or on the coasts, as well as a few adverts for chemists selling creams for the skin after it had been subjected to the sun at these coastal hotels.

The main bulk of the book was devoted to the timetables, instructing every British subject as to when they could catch a train that would whisk them to Brighton, Cornwall, Scotland. Or Dover, where they could sail to France and catch other trains there—those routes were covered in Bradshaw's books on the Continent.

The sherry must have unstiffened my thoughts as well as my body, because as I gazed at the times copied out in my notebook, I had another idea.

"We have proved these don't correspond to *scheduled* stops," I said. "What about unscheduled ones?"

Lady Cynthia sat down, shoving an empty glass across the tabletop to Elgin and opening the whisky decanter. "How can anyone know when an unscheduled stop is to be," she asked, "if it's unscheduled?"

Elgin frowned as he poured whisky, but Daniel caught my eye, understanding.

"Mr. Davis likes to read out from the paper," I explained slowly. "He remarked on a story yesterday, that the Queen was traveling again. She goes on her own private train, does she not?" I touched my notebook. "Perhaps, just perhaps, these times mean when *her* train will be passing stations."

17

The entire room went silent, all eyes on me. I could not know whether my convictions were correct, as I only had a scrap of paper and a wild idea. But I felt it, deep down inside, just as I knew when a fish was off, even though it looked and smelled perfectly innocuous on the fishmonger's stall. I'd been to plays of the Bard, and remembered a verse chanted by of one of his witches: *By the pricking of my thumbs, something wicked this way comes . . .*

If I was right, the Fenians' target was not a random train station in Britain but the person of the Queen herself.

Elgin tossed back his whisky and clattered his glass to the table. "Oh, bloody hell," he said in a breathless voice. He wiped his mouth, his spectacles making his eyes look inhumanly large.

"Whew," James said from his chair by the stove. "If she's right, Dad—if they're going after Her Majesty—what a turnup."

Daniel said nothing. He gazed across the table at me, but

he wasn't truly seeing *me*, his friend Kat Holloway, the cook. He was envisioning something beyond me, beyond this room, the entire house.

He must be imagining, as I did, the train with the Queen aboard, chugging along at its slow pace. Then an explosion ripping through the cars, killing the monarch and the ladies and gentlemen who attended her.

The entire country would be in an uproar. To avenge her, the prime minister and the cabinet might decide to retaliate against the nation of Ireland itself, and people there—innocents doing nothing but trying to eke out their existence—would lose their lives or be rounded up and terrorized.

Queen Victoria's government couldn't be seen to let the Fenians win. The Fenians would then have to fight back using their secret plots, and more people would die.

"This cannot happen," I said.

It was an obvious thing to state, but I felt the words needed to be voiced.

"We must make certain it does not," Daniel said. "The Queen is unlikely to alter her plans—I know this—unless she has proof that the threat is real. Even then, her courtiers will have a hell of a time holding her back. She's a headstrong woman. Thanos—I need you to tell me what is in those ledgers. Discovering the Queen's route won't be easy, but perhaps I could—"

"I'll find *that* out," Lady Cynthia broke in.

We turned to her, Daniel the only one not startled. "You can speak to the Queen?" he asked. "Even she might not know the exact times her train will run, or choose to tell you even if she does."

"Perhaps not to the Queen herself, but I know plenty of her ladies-in-waiting, and their daughters," Cynthia said without worry. "They'll know when she's going and where, or at least an idea of when. They might not tell *you*, but they'd tell me."

Because she was one of them, I thought. The ladies wouldn't see the harm in letting such details slip to a friend they'd known all their lives.

"It is the middle of the night," I pointed out. "Would you be able to visit a palace this late?"

Cynthia grinned. "Won't need to. The ladies don't attend her all the time—they have weeks off to themselves. They'll be out at balls and operas and the theatre, like my sister, until dawn. If they don't already know what the Queen is up to, they can find out for me." Cynthia leapt to her feet and snatched up her coat and tall hat. "Stay as long as you like—Bobby's landlady is used to hearing gentlemen up here."

Elgin flushed. "Is she? Oh dear."

Cynthia's grin widened. "Smoking, swearing, and looking at naughty photographs. Bobby would shoot a man before she let him touch her. Ta-ta, my friends, I sally forth."

She strode out with a vibrant step and was gone.

"Good Lord," Elgin said as the door slammed behind her, and he let out a sharp breath. "I believe I'm in love."

Elgin and Daniel made no move to vacate the rooms and go home. James did depart a few minutes after Cynthia did, and Daniel walked down with him, but whether he convinced the boy to go home, I did not know, and Daniel did not say when he returned.

I was exhausted from my early morning, my anguished indecision over my friends' offer to adopt Grace, and then searching the Bradshaws for the answer to the code. But I would not leave. My mad idea that someone plotted to kill the

Queen took hold of me and would not loosen, and I could not make myself scuttle meekly home and to bed.

I did retire to the divan that stretched beneath one of the tall windows. I did not like to lie down in front of gentlemen, so I simply put my feet on an ottoman I'd dragged close and leaned against the cushions. I rested my eyes while Daniel and Elgin began discussing the figures Elgin had pored over in Daniel's rooms.

"A beautiful problem," Elgin said, sounding happy. "Very elegant—like unwrapping layer upon layer of paper to find a lovely gift inside. I ought to thank you for your generosity."

"You are welcome," Daniel said good-naturedly. "What does this gift I've given you have to tell us?"

Elgin's tone became businesslike. "That these friends of Lord Rankin's are uncommonly clever. They've swooped and dodged all over the place. An ordinary scan of the accounts is unlikely to spot the discrepancies, because even with a careful reading, there aren't any. But . . ."

I opened my eyes to see the two men bending their heads together over whatever Elgin had spread on the table. Both men were dark, but Daniel's hair had streaks of reddish brown, caught by the lamplight, whereas Elgin's hair was inky black. They murmured to each other, Elgin saying things like *credit notes*, *derivatives*, *bond swaps*, and *embezzlement*. The last word I at least understood.

"They set up a company," Elgin was saying. "Sold themselves plenty of credit notes to make their price go up on the market. Claimed to have *this* much in profits, *this* much in loss." He tapped his pen to the page. "But in truth"—he shuffled papers—"the loss is *this* much, the funds shunted in secret to the accounts here"—more shuffling—"in a private bank in France. I know this place is a private bank, in spite of its name, because I followed another fellow to the building in Paris that houses it a few years ago, and the bastard tried to kill me." Elgin pulled off his spectacles and rubbed his eyes. "Couldn't prove he did, because he escaped me, so nothing came of it. But that's where their gold is, mark my words."

Daniel pulled the papers toward him. "The only way this kind of fraud could go past Rankin after this much time is if he let it. How does the money return to this country? And to Ireland?"

"That is another beautiful part," Elgin said. "Paid out to investors, but only those invited to invest—like a private club. They are legitimate investments, so if these people are investigated, they've done nothing wrong. They aren't taking bribes or passing along money to fund anarchists—they're collecting on a well-paying scheme. They have several innocent gentlemen involved to make it all look highly respectable."

"Gentlemen like the Marquis of Chalminster," Daniel said. "I saw his name when I collected these papers to give you. But I'm certain his son is the true investor, using his father's name. Gives himself the sobriquet of Minty."

"Bleh," Elgin made a noise of disgust. "A little tick like that would."

Minty, the young man who'd beaten Daniel outside Euston Station, his friends joining with enthusiasm.

"It will all dry up, of course," Daniel said. "When I pass all this on, Minty will have to find a new hobby."

I had guessed Daniel knew more about Minty than he'd let on. He hadn't been surprised when he'd read Minty's name on the card. Again, I could not help wondering whether Daniel had deliberately provoked Minty in order to pick Minty's pocket, so he'd have an excuse to visit his father, the marquis. If Daniel was investigating a fraudulent scheme the marquis seemed to be a part of—especially one involving Fenians—Daniel's knowledge of that plus a threat to prosecute Minty for assaulting him might make the marquis bend to Daniel's wishes. If the marquis truly weren't a part of it, the man could punish his son, and perhaps Minty would tell all he knew about the fraud and the plots.

I started to ask Daniel whether that had been the case, but my tongue suddenly felt heavy in my mouth, and I could not move my lips.

I drifted into darkness, where my daughter laughed and spun away from me, straight toward a railway track that blossomed into flame as I watched. I tried to scream to Grace to run, to flee as fire engulfed us both, but I couldn't make a sound.

"K at."

I pried open my eyes sometime later to find myself surrounded by golden light, everything hazy. In that haze was Daniel, leaning to me, his voice low.

"Daniel." I don't know whether the word came out of my mouth or remained unspoken. I lifted my hand and rested it on his chest.

Daniel's face softened, and the shadows rendered his eyes a very dark blue. I didn't know which Daniel bent over me, the laborer or the gentleman. But in a dream, it didn't matter. We weren't really here, he and I, and I felt free to touch his face, feel the warmth of his unshaved jaw through my thin gloves. Daniel turned his head and pressed a kiss to my palm.

I was floating, and didn't notice the seat beneath me or the chill from the window at my back. We remained locked in this place of no time, where I could be Kat and he could be Daniel, nothing of the world intruding.

"Kat." His voice slid through my senses, loosening the tightness in my limbs.

Did love feel like this? I wondered. A quiet happiness, not the giddy, heart-pounding excitement that led to disaster?

My love for my daughter was still and deep, and ever so strong. It filled me in a way nothing else did. The silent satisfaction I experienced now as Daniel hovered over me, his lips on my glove, was similar, slipping into my life before I was aware enough to stop it.

"Kat," he whispered once more. "Time to wake up, love."

I was awake. I knew it as soon as he said the words. Daniel was standing over me in truth, holding my hand, pressing light kisses to it, his eyes telling me all.

I gasped and jumped, but one wild glance showed me that the room was empty. Elgin had gone, and Cynthia had not returned.

Daniel released me before I could yank my hand from his grasp. His expression held regret, though I wasn't certain what for.

I got my feet firmly under me and accepted his help to stand. I was stiff from my awkward position on the divan, but the stiffness wore away quickly as I shook out my skirts and put a hand to my hair.

"I am a mess," I announced as I moved to the nearest mirror. I did not look as unkempt as I feared, though I needed to unpin and recomb my hair. I'd feel better when I could wash my face as well.

"You're lovely," Daniel said behind me.

"Base flattery." I smoothed out my hair the best I could—it

would have to do until I reached home. "What is the time?" The windows were dark, but the early spring sun didn't rise until after six.

Daniel stepped behind me and rested his hands on my waist. I confess I rather enjoyed the firmness of his touch, but I turned and broke his hold. He didn't move away, which meant he stood far too close to me.

I drew a breath and made myself take a crisp tone. "You do understand why I am angry with you, do you not? Why I have been for . . ." I trailed off. I couldn't remember how long anymore.

"Months," Daniel finished for me. "Since you saw me that night in Oxford Street."

"Indeed." That had been the first time I'd seen him in a gentleman's suit, and what's more, he'd been handing a lovely woman into a posh coach. "I believe you are a good man, Daniel McAdam, but you are not to be trusted."

To my surprise, his face crumpled with amusement. "You have the measure of me, Kat. You and no other."

He at last moved from my side, seeming to understand that he made me uncomfortable, and twitched back a curtain. The gray light outlined his tall form, which no longer held the deferential stoop he adopted when he carried boxes and bags into lords' and ladies' houses.

"It's six, and will be sunrise soon," he said. "Stay here and rest. I'm certain they can do without you for a day."

"Six?" I gasped. I snatched my coat from the large hall tree near the door. "What sort of a cook would I be if I neglected to fix breakfast? I'd never find a position again." Only one thought kept me from dashing straight out the door. "You will tell me what you and Lady Cynthia and Mr. Thanos discover, won't you?" I tried not to sound too wistful, but without success.

Daniel's smile was as warm as Bobby's cozy stove. "I'll not leave you out, Kat, do not worry. I know you'd find me if I did try to leave you behind, no matter how diligently I hid."

I buttoned my coat with jerking movements. "Don't talk nonsense," I said, then opened the door and stalked from the room. Daniel didn't follow me, but his laughter did.

Mrs. Bowen pounced on me the moment I walked into the kitchen at the Mount Street house. Her eyes were red-rimmed and wisps of gray hair straggled from her usually neat bun.

"What has happened?" she demanded. "Where is Lady Cynthia? She hasn't come home."

I steered Mrs. Bowen into her empty parlor and shut the door. I felt fusty and wanted a wash and change of clothes, but there would be no time now.

Mrs. Bowen refused to sit down, no matter how much I entreated her. She was clearly upset, and worried I'd done something with Lady Cynthia, so I quickly told her what we had found with the timetables—which was nothing—and that Lady Cynthia had gone out to hunt up her chums.

I did not like to impart we thought the timetables had something to do with the Queen's travels. Mrs. Bowen had spoken out fiercely against Fenians, but she also had tried to suppress Sinead's ties to them and had destroyed possible evidence that might lead to them. I was becoming like Daniel, I realized, to my dismay. Watchful of everyone.

"And Sinead?" Mrs. Bowen asked me, her face pinched. "She will remain blameless, whatever this is about?"

"If she *is* blameless," I said. "But I agree with you—Sinead did not seem the sort to come up with wicked plots or wittingly participate in them. She likely had no idea what sort of information her beau was passing to her. If he did pass it to her."

This seemed to satisfy Mrs. Bowen somewhat—at least, she looked less anguished. I advised her to go to bed after reassuring her again that Lady Cynthia was fine and likely would soon be home. I was too tired and in no mood to stay and placate Mrs. Bowen further, so I left her sinking down into her chair in relief and made my way to the kitchen.

Had Sinead been given the timetable by her lover to deliver to another conspirator? Or had she been meant to deliver the paper from a conspirator to her young man? And why would either of them use a kitchen maid turned cook's assistant for communication?

Likely because few would suspect such an innocent-looking young woman of carrying terrible secrets, I surmised.

I stepped to the scullery and its sink and opened the tap, using the freezing water to wash my face and hands—it would have to do for now. My mind continued to spin as I scrubbed my face. If using Sinead to pass information was useful, then why kill the poor thing?

I might not be as good at sums as Mr. Thanos, but nothing was adding up to any satisfactory answer.

It is fairly easy to please an Englishman at breakfast, and so I quickly had plenty of boiled eggs, sausage, bacon, ham, and potatoes ready as well as a stack of muffins dripping with butter. I sent them up to the dining room for Lord Rankin to devour alone.

Later I'd prepare a tray for Lady Rankin, to be delivered whenever she finally rang for Sara to bring her breakfast. I reflected that I hadn't seen the woman since she'd interviewed me for the post, but she rarely left her chamber except to dine with the family and go out in the evenings.

Lady Cynthia was completely different from her sister, I mused as I checked that Mary had started the dough for a seed bread as I'd instructed, and then went to my table and mixed together flour and butter—three parts butter to four parts flour—plus a bit of sugar and cold water for a pastry crust. There were pears in the larder that needed to be eaten, and what better way than a pear tart with a lemon glaze and a sweet custard sauce?

I pegged Lady Cynthia as a "doer." She didn't like to sit and gossip or ride in coaches or idle at a theatre, like Lady Rankin. Lady Cynthia liked to be up and about, riding horses, driving a rig, traveling with her friend Bobby, or tearing about London helping Daniel and me discover things.

Lord Rankin struck me as a doer as well, rising early to go to his business in the City, not taking up the life of a gentleman of leisure. I again wondered at his choice of Lady Emily instead of Lady Cynthia. Had he picked Emily because he knew he could rule her with a firm hand?

Or perhaps he'd fallen in love, I thought, trying to give him the benefit of the doubt as I gathered my dough into a ball and put it into a bowl to rest. The heart makes the choice. One sister does not necessarily equal the other.

As I prepared to carry the bowl to the larder to let the dough chill, I spied Lord Rankin's boots through the high windows as he moved toward his carriage to head for the City. It was Friday—Davis told me Lord Rankin worked on Saturday as well, conceding to stay home only on the Lord's day. On Sunday, he worked upstairs in his study while his wife and Lady Cynthia attended church.

Once I cleaned up my mess from making the pastry and set Mary to peeling and stewing the pears, I climbed to my chamber at the top of the house and allowed myself the luxury of a sponge bath with hot water I'd convinced Paul to carry up for me. I combed out my long dark hair after I dried myself and glanced at the bed with regret. If I indulged in stretching out on the mattress, I'd likely fall asleep and then would have no time the rest of the day for anything but cookery. I braided my hair, dressed, and returned to the kitchen.

I donned a clean apron and started in again. The pears were finished—Mary had done well with the simple recipe—and I'd let them baste in their juices for a time.

As I turned to my notebook to decide what I would do for luncheon, Lady Cynthia walked into the kitchen, tipped me a wink, and motioned for me to follow her outside. Mr. Davis, already in the servants' hall filling his plate, saw this and raised his brows high, but said nothing, mercifully.

I was hungry, so I snatched up a stale roll from breakfast and quickly spread it with the potted meat I'd made yesterday morning, devouring it as I slid on my coat and followed Cynthia up the scullery stairs.

A cab was waiting to take us back to Bobby's flat—I had no time to argue before Cynthia pushed me in, and we were off. We arrived in a short time to find Mr. Thanos and Daniel already there, sitting at a table near the window.

"McAdam insists this is the best place to chat," Cynthia said, shutting the paneled door behind me. "Exciting," she said as she threw herself into a chair. "Like a council of war. Except we ladies are allowed to attend. As it should be."

18

As I took the upholstered seat Daniel held out for me at the table, I realized that they hadn't been obligated to invite me here. Lady Cynthia, Mr. Thanos, and Daniel could have discussed this problem on their own, leaving me to my kitchen. I was certain Daniel had insisted on fetching me, and I was grateful.

"I made a nuisance of myself last night to all my old friends," Lady Cynthia began as soon as we were seated. "I happen to be acquainted with most of the ladies who have been honored by Queen Vic—some are friends, some friends of friends. My mum was proposed once to be part of her court, because Papa was a war hero and highly thought of in some circles. But we were far too scandalous." Lady Cynthia chuckled. "Poor Mum would have been stifled as a lady-in-waiting. She has quite the temper, does our mum. She'd have been throwing dishes and screaming like a fishwife if she had to stay long in freezing Balmoral or in boring Osborne House."

Cynthia seemed quite pleased with her family's tempestuousness. I remembered Mr. Davis telling me that Lady Cynthia's brother had died by his own hand. I wondered how old Cynthia had been at the time and what that grief had done to her. At the moment, her eyes took on a fond look as she smiled about her mother.

"Anyway," Cynthia went on. "I have the interesting information that the Queen isn't going to Scotland as per usual—at least, not directly. She has decided to make her way north by going leisurely west, seeing a few sights she enjoyed with dear Albert. She'll be following the Great Western route in her special train, through Cornwall and to Wales, back to Bristol, and then north. Something of the sort. I wasn't handed an exact itinerary—this is what I pieced together around gossip about who is in love with whom and whose husband is walking out with whose wife." She laughed. "I could write a hell of a story today and sell it to one of the more salacious news sheets."

"Interesting," Elgin said, his dark gaze fixed on Cynthia. "That route changes gauges—I wonder how they manage this with her train? Or do they move her from one to another?"

"More to the point," Daniel broke in, "how do these times correspond to her route? If they do at all?"

"And how would we know?" I asked. "The Queen won't be stopping at the usual stations, will she? And other trains will have to get out of her way, will they not?"

"That is simple, good lady," Elgin said. He spread the copy he'd made of the numbers from my notebook and opened a Bradshaw. "If I know the route, and the approximate speed her train travels, it's a simple calculation to see if these times correspond to towns she'll pass through. Let me see . . ."

He hooked on his spectacles again, removed a pencil from a case in his pocket, and began to jot notes on the paper.

"She likes to travel slowly," Elgin murmured. "So let's say twenty-five miles per hour. That would put her . . ." He trailed off as he looked back and forth from the Bradshaw to the paper. His pencil danced, and we all watched as numbers poured out of his fingers.

Elgin wrote for a time, doing swift calculations that would have left me writing laboriously and whispering the answers as I found them. Elgin skipped steps, or he seemed to, and scribbled new numbers along the margins of his page.

"Hmm." His pencil slowed and then halted and dropped. He massaged his fingers and wrung them out.

Lady Cynthia leaned forward. "*Hmm*, what?"

Daniel made no move from his casual slouch in the chair he'd taken, but his eyes came alert. Of the three of us, I was the only one who sat primly upright.

Elgin tapped the original numbers. "These times having nothing to do with stations the Queen's train will pass on her journey." He sighed, dropped his hands to his lap, and looked morose.

I deflated. "Then maybe the numbers have nothing to do with trains at all."

Cynthia was peering narrowly at Elgin. "How do you know? Trains never go all at one pace. They slow down and speed up, climb hills, wait for other trains . . . Last journey I took home, the train's speed was all over the place."

"I took that into account, my dear lady," Elgin said. "You see?" He skimmed his fingertips down his calculations, which were pure gibberish to me.

"That is why he had to write the calculations out," Daniel

said in dry tones. "If the train went only one speed, he'd have been able to figure it all in his head."

Elgin nodded, looking not the least offended.

"We're back to nothing, then," I said, as gloomy as Elgin.

Daniel's eyes sparkled. "Not necessarily. Trains pass things other than stations." He turned to me, a smile spreading over his face. "How would you like to take a railway journey, Mrs. Holloway?"

I thought Daniel was absolutely mad, but at the same time, the idea of climbing aboard a train with him and speeding out of London for a while was enticing.

I had, once upon a time, traveled to Bath, when a woman I worked for moved her household there. She knew I didn't want to work outside London, so she'd agreed that once the staff was settled, I would return to Town and take another post. For that sojourn, I was mostly concerned with making certain crates, maids, and adventurous footmen didn't go astray, so I'd seen little of the countryside. The return journey had been at night, and I'd slept.

The thought of rushing away, leaving behind Lord Rankin, the place of Sinead's death, and my impending decision about my daughter was appealing.

The Queen, according to Lady Cynthia, was traveling this Sunday, when the fewest trains ran, so we hadn't much time to investigate. However, a cook doesn't suddenly run away on a brief holiday.

"I have my duties," I argued with Daniel once we'd returned to Lord Rankin's, making a brief stop at a greengrocers along the way so I'd have an excuse for my outing. We were alone in the kitchen, the staff upstairs cleaning, Mary and another maid washing up in the scullery. The rush of water and clatter of dishes ensured we would not be overheard if we spoke quietly.

"Lord Rankin will let you go without impediment," Daniel said. "I'll make certain of it."

"Hardly the point." After setting aside the asparagus and greens I'd purchased, I put on my apron and moved the dough for my seeded bread from its bowl to the table, rolled it in the spread of caraway and sesame seeds, cracked pepper, and coarse salt, divided it into two loaves, and popped them into pans for their final rise. "Cooking is a great deal of work, Mr. McAdam. I cannot leave the other staff to take it over. It isn't fair to them, and they wouldn't much know what to do anyway."

Daniel folded his arms and leaned against the table, not looking bothered in the slightest. "I will arrange for someone to come in and take your duties temporarily, a good enough cook that your reputation won't suffer. Will that do?"

Temporary staff can be two-edged swords—if they are unskilled, the household complains for months; if they are brilliant, the household might not want you back.

"Be that as it may," I went on, "surely it's more important for you to take a policeman or someone who works for the Queen on this mad journey."

Daniel only continued leaning against the table. He didn't scowl or frown, but I became aware as I watched him that Daniel McAdam was an uncommonly stubborn man. He used amiability rather than harsh words to get his way, but he had a strength of will that could push aside a mountain.

"A policeman or one of the Queen's equerries wouldn't thank me for leading them on a wild-goose chase," he said. "I want to be certain of our speculations before I alert the palace. They take a dim view of false alarms."

"And who are you to alert an entire palace?" I asked him as I set the loaf pans on their shelf over the stove and covered them with floured cloths.

Daniel only gave me his enigmatic look. "Not the *entire* palace, Kat. But I am alone in this. If I make a mess, it is entirely on my head. I prefer to have irrefutable evidence before I present my theories to the world."

"Elgin is helping you," I pointed out.

"Yes, as a friend; not in an official capacity. Elgin does me favors because he's interested in the problems I give him. I make certain no blame falls on him for my mistakes."

"But what on earth can *I* do?" I asked, bewildered. "I'm a cook—I don't know about railways and dynamite and the Fenians."

Daniel had left the table and now stood immediately in front of me. "Because you have a wisdom and kindness that sees me through the hardest days," he said in a low voice. "Because I'd like you to come."

I had difficulty drawing my next breath. Daniel was watching me as he had when I'd copied out the paper of numbers and he'd thought my attention safely elsewhere. Now he didn't care that I looked straight at him.

I wavered. I knew Daniel could make it easy for me to run away for a day, and truth to tell, I very much wanted to.

"You have flattery for every occasion," I said, trying to sound offhand.

"You may take it as flattery if you wish," Daniel replied without moving. "I would still like you to come."

"I suppose you will let me prepare things for the rest of today's meals?" I asked.

Daniel gave me a nod, his eyes showing triumph. He knew

he'd won. "Certainly. I will send messages, and we will catch the two o'clock from Paddington."

My eyes widened. It was already noon. "That's very little time."

"You'll do well. A cab will be waiting at the end of the mews at one o'clock." He flashed me a cocky grin, the good-natured deliveryman once more, and headed through the scullery to the back door before I could protest.

D aniel had procured first-class tickets for all of us. I generally dressed well when I traveled by train—no need to be slovenly when the entire world can observe one. Or, if not the *entire* world, then at least the travelers on a Friday afternoon at Paddington Station.

I liked my second-best dress, a rich brown broadcloth trimmed with black piping, and my hat with its matching black ribbon, but I felt a fool being helped aboard by the conductor among the ladies in their gowns created by high-fashion modistes and hats made by the best milliners in London. They rather stared at me, but we were all too well-bred to say anything.

I breathed a sigh of relief when the conductor ushered me into a large compartment with its seats facing each other and shut the door, leaving me in relative privacy.

I was alone for the moment. The hansom cab that had brought me here had been waiting at the end of the mews, as Daniel had promised, at one o'clock precisely, though Daniel hadn't been in it. The driver was Lewis, who'd driven us from Euston Station after Daniel's fracas there, and he'd greeted me cheerfully. Lewis let me off at the station and handed me a ticket he said Daniel had obtained for me, giving me barely enough time to find the correct carriage and get aboard before the train was due to depart.

I'd never been inside a first-class compartment. When I'd traveled with my previous employer to Bath, only her lady's maid went with her to her first-class seat while the rest of the servants rode together in third.

This compartment was certainly luxurious. So it should be for a fare that cost nearly four pounds, according to the Bradshaw, to go all the way to Cornwall. The walls were polished wood with an inlay of flowers and curling designs, and the seats were upholstered in softest velvet, with extra cushions to lounge against and footstools if one wished. Lush carpet covered the generous amount of floor between the forward- and rear-facing seats—we'd not sit with our knees squashed against one another's. The glass windows were etched with the same sort of curlicues as on the walls, and velvet curtains could be pulled across these windows and the door to the corridor if the occupants desired more seclusion.

I automatically plopped down onto a seat that would be facing forward when the train moved, as I always did when riding third class—a cook in third class was at the top of the hierarchy and so was entitled to a more comfortable seat than her assistants. But *here* I was at the bottom of the chain, so I rose again and reseated myself facing the rear.

The door onto the platform opened at that moment to admit Daniel and Mr. Thanos, a porter slamming it shut behind them. Mr. Thanos wore clothes no different from what I'd seen him in last night—indeed, I believe it was the same suit—but Daniel had once again dressed the part of a gentleman.

I was sorry, because I didn't feel as comfortable with him when he was in this guise. His hair had been tamed to lie flat, like Elgin's, and he wore a coat of finely woven fabric, dark with a thin gray stripe. A waistcoat of the same material buttoned nearly to his throat, and a cravat poked above that, its ends tucked neatly beneath the waistcoat. Daniel's trousers were slim but cut to flow over polished, well-made boots. He removed a tall hat as he entered, as did Elgin, Daniel placing his above one of the seats in the space made for such things.

"Mrs. Holloway," Daniel said, gesturing to the forward-facing seat I'd vacated as he removed his gloves. "Please."

When Daniel dressed like this his voice changed as well, taking on the smooth tones of an educated man, the edge of the London streets gone. He also was more polite, stiffly so. This Daniel was a stranger to me.

I drew my feet back under my skirt and clutched my reticule in my lap. "I am quite comfortable where I am, thank you."

Daniel remained with his hand out to indicate the other seat—where a lady should sit. I didn't budge.

Elgin settled the argument by dropping into the seat facing me. "Leave her alone, McAdam. Sit down. We're about to start."

Daniel finished stripping off his gloves and laying them next to his hat before he took the place next to Elgin, resigned, but I saw the glint in his eye that said he'd renew the argument as soon as he was able.

The train jolted and bumped, moving slowly out of the station. It backed out, as Paddington was the end of the line for this train, so I had a hollow victory—for the moment *my* seat was the forward-facing one.

"James is not with you?" I asked Daniel. As the young man seemed to lurk wherever Daniel was, I was surprised not to see him slide into the compartment after him, or perhaps haunting the corridor.

"Not at all," Daniel said, retaining his quiet politeness. "Oh, he wanted to come, but I explained that it was far too dangerous, and he should stay in my rooms in Southampton Street until I returned."

I raised my brows. "James agreed to that?"

"No." Daniel made a wry face, looking like his old self a moment. "We had a flaming row about it. In the end, I locked him in my bedchamber and gave the landlady the key. She'll see that he's fed."

Elgin gaped at him. "Good Lord, McAdam, you can't go about locking your son into your rooms. Anyway, won't he just go out the window?"

"I imagine he'll free himself before long," Daniel said, unworried. "But too late to follow me. Perhaps while he's busy thinking up ways to escape, he'll see sense and remain in London."

I wasn't so certain James would suddenly become obedient. He was quite resourceful—I would be interested to learn what he would do.

The conversation was interrupted when Lady Cynthia shoved open the door, bracing herself against the train's movement, her head turned as she bellowed down the corridor. "No, put the box in *that* compartment, man. Yes, that's the one."

She rolled her eyes in exasperation and then nearly fell into the compartment as the train went around a curve. Elgin surged to his feet to steady her, but he stumbled over Daniel in doing so. Daniel half rose to catch them both.

Lady Cynthia swung out of the men's reaches and landed on the seat beside me. "Sorry. Had to run for it—impossible in this gear."

She referred to what had all three of us staring at her. Lady Cynthia was wearing a gown, a white, high-necked affair, rather like the one I'd seen on Lady Rankin the first day I'd entered Lord Rankin's house. Lace edged her bodice's placket, the cuffs of the long sleeves, and the collar. The gown's underskirt bore three rows of ruffles, and the overskirt was gathered over a small bustle, which Lady Cynthia shoved out of the way as she settled herself.

"My damned sister decided she wouldn't let me go with you unless I wore a frock. She had Simms and Davis block my way to the front door, if you please. Was easier to give in. Bloody nuisance. For what possible reason should a woman lock a cage around her middle and strap a wad of padding to her bum?"

I understood her point. Ladies' gowns could be works of beauty, it was true, but not very practical.

Elgin listened to her shocking speech with his mouth slightly open. Daniel showed he didn't care one whit for what Lady Cynthia wore or said by opening a notebook he pulled from his pocket.

Cynthia studied Daniel across from her. "You clean up well, McAdam. Knew you weren't quite cricket. You the police?"

Daniel glanced up briefly. "Don't insult me, Lady C.," he said with a touch of impudence, then returned to his notebook.

Lady Cynthia looked to me for explanation, but I could only shrug. Elgin continued to gape at her, so Lady Cynthia gave up, sent Daniel another narrow look, then turned to watch out of the window as the train righted itself and went chugging off west.

We made our slow way through London, the wheels beneath us bumping along the points. This particular train did not stop in the smaller stations in London and would not pause until Slough. I knew this because I had looked it up, by way of my handy Bradshaw.

We didn't speak much until we pulled away from Slough then Maidenhead–the train would continue without a break now until Reading.

Lady Cynthia rose in a rustle of skirts. "Back in a tick," she said cheerfully.

Daniel began to politely get to his feet, but Elgin launched himself from the seat and managed to get around Daniel and wrench open the door into the corridor for her. Lady Cynthia sent him a surprised look but slipped away without a word. Elgin watched her go, his hand remaining on the door handle.

Daniel sat back down and winked at me. "Are we going to calculate the times?" he asked Elgin. "Or are we making a journey to the seaside for the health benefits?"

"Eh? Oh." Elgin closed the door, tripped back over Daniel's feet again, and landed heavily on his seat. "Right." He pulled out his pocket watch, but his gaze strayed to the windows to the corridor. "A damn fine-looking woman," he pronounced. "No matter what she wears."

I did not think it possible for Elgin to work out where the Queen's train would be at the times on the paper we'd found, as we couldn't be sure *our* train would ever keep to a steady speed, but he cheerfully said that was no bother. He would compensate.

"In his head," Daniel told me disparagingly as Elgin looked out the window, humming a tune in his throat. "I remember the day I explained to him that not everyone can carry on multiple calculations in his brain plus memorize several theorems at the same time as admiring art in the Louvre."

Elgin paid no attention. He was fully absorbed in the countryside flying past the window.

The only distraction for him was when Lady Cynthia threw open the door to stroll back inside, now dressed in her full suit of gentlemen's clothing.

"Much better," she said as she flopped down beside me. "A person can be comfortable in this." She demonstrated by stretching out her legs and crossing her booted ankles. "Your frocks are more sensible than most, Mrs. H., but Rankin would have even worse apoplexy if I wore servants' clothes. At least I have these made by a Bond Street tailor." She ran a hand down her jacket in admiration of an expert's work.

I took no offense, because I quite agreed with her.

Daniel gave Elgin, who again was staring at her, a sharp nudge. Elgin blinked, flushed, and returned to gazing out the window.

The weather was good, and as we left the metropolis far behind, I saw skies clear and blue, dotted with white clouds sailing over stretches of green gashed with the black of newly plowed fields. There was a reason London was called the Smoke—very apparent now that the black smudge of incessant coal fires had faded from the expanse of sky.

My daughter would love this. I could imagine holding her on my lap while I pointed out things we passed, pictured her delight watching the lambs following their mothers in the fields, their legs too long as they stumbled along.

My heart burned. I wanted this—wanted to be with Grace every second, with every breath. The rightness of it swelled in my chest.

We reached Swindon around five o'clock. I wished I had been able to pack some food for us, but Daniel had arranged this as well, it seemed. A porter brought us a basket stuffed with bread, fruit, cheese, cold meat, and wine, and we feasted. Daniel must have known where to procure the best provender, because the oranges were juicy, the hard cheese had a sharp bite, the meat was moist, the bread crusty but soft inside. Elgin stuffed food and drink absently into his mouth, and Daniel ate without comment, but Lady Cynthia robustly enjoyed every bite.

We passed Bath, the farthest extent of my travels, and then as the sky darkened, Bristol, where the train waited as new cars were coupled to ours and we changed tracks to head to the southwest. Next, Weston-super-Mare, Bridgwater, Taunton, Exeter. As the moon rose, we traveled along the edge of what Daniel told me was Dartmoor. The expanse of it stretched to the horizon, this treacherous moor the site of many dire tales, as well as a prison where men were sent to labor until they dropped of it.

I decided the moor didn't strike the terror into my heart it was supposed to—I found something rather appealing in the dark expanse, with rises of gray rock sharp in the moonlight. I would have to come here in daylight one day, and explore.

As we slowed much later to click into Plymouth, Elgin turned to us. He'd been silent much of the time, staring out of the window or checking the pocket watch in his hand. Daniel had occasionally studied his own watch, but I'd seen him shake his head, frowning. Cynthia had fallen asleep after Exeter, her face innocent as a babe's as she relaxed. Now she sat up, her fair hair mussed, looking around muzzily.

Elgin's expression was troubled as he regarded us, a somber light in his eyes.

"They're bridges," he announced.

19

The two simple words fell into silence. The four of us looked at one another as Elgin's statement sank in.

Bridges were vulnerable places on a train line, taking tracks across wide rivers or rolling over steep valleys as viaducts. A bridge failing and falling could be a horrific disaster, a tragedy for so many. Even with all the engineering marvels in the world and men who could work out how to build stronger and more stable structures, bridges still gave way, destroying trains, cargo, and people.

Fresh in the mind of every Briton was the catastrophe at Tay Bridge a little more than a year ago. The Tay, on the line that ran from Edinburgh to Dundee, had been the longest bridge in existence, before it had suddenly collapsed one night, taking a train and all its passengers down, down into the dark waters of the firth with it. The disaster and ensuing scandal had been the talk of newspapers and on everyone's lips for months, still was.

"Which bridges?" Daniel asked. We had rumbled over so many since London.

Elgin answered without hesitation. "Seven so far correspond to the times, or nearly, when the Queen's train will be passing over them. Maidenhead, Reading, Swindon, one outside Chippenham, over the Avon after Bristol, one a little north of Dartmoor, and finally . . ."

He trailed off. We'd left Plymouth, continuing our journey into Cornwall over the River Tamar. We all went quiet as we started over the bridge that led across the river to the town of Saltash—the famous bridge I'd seen in photographs and drawings, a triumph of engineering. Two crescents of iron ran from tower to tower, curving down to each other in the middle of the bridge. Two nearly identical crescents curved upward from the bottom of each span—a wave suspended forever in time.

The bridge had been here since I was a child, opened in an official ceremony by Albert, the Prince Consort. The man who'd designed the bridge went by the interesting name of Isambard Kingdom Brunel, which I always remembered, as it was such an unusual moniker.

We sat transfixed as the train rolled slowly over the bridge, the wheels clicking ponderously, the iron trusses appearing to bend down to us and then up again as we passed.

We rode in darkness, the lamps in our compartment not lighted—Elgin had waved off the conductor who'd tried to light them long ago, saying he could peer outside better without them. The headlight from our train and the flames from its firebox glinted on the great pile of iron and stone.

"Good heavens," I whispered.

"Firing this bridge with the Queen on top of it would be a grand statement," Cynthia said in a hushed voice. "The world would watch."

"How can we be certain it's *this* bridge?" I asked. "Mr. Thanos says other bridges are possible, and we don't know what was on the part of the paper Mrs. Bowen burned."

But I knew in my heart that Elgin and Lady Cynthia were right. This bridge had caught the imaginations of artists and tourists alike, and was portrayed on banners advertising seaside sojourns to the west coast of England as well as pictures depicting the might of British industry. The Royal Albert Bridge, or the Cornwall Railway Bridge at Saltash, straddled the border between Devon and Cornwall, serving as the entrance to the far western county. Our Queen's beloved prince had walked its length the day he'd opened it, declaring that it would connect Cornwall to the rest of the kingdom.

"We check them all," Daniel said grimly. "We cannot take a chance that while we're looking here, they're planning elsewhere."

"What can *we* do?" I asked, in some despair. It was difficult to banish that despair—England was vast, and at any time, anywhere, some vandal could be destroying people and things, unbeknownst to us, beyond our reach.

"We stop it," Daniel said. He turned on me a look of such fierceness that further words died on my lips. I'd never seen him look so before, and knew that what shone out of his eyes came from a place deep inside himself. His voice echoed in the small space of the compartment as he went on grimly. "We stop it, no matter what we have to do."

We left the train at Saltash. I watched the train chug on without us, disappearing into the darkness, making its way to Penzance. Here the line became the Cornwall Railway and would switch gauges as it went west and south, as Elgin had mentioned. Passengers would have to change trains at Truro, where the gauge changeover happened, but we would be sleeping here. We'd missed the last train up to London, so we would have to spend the night.

Fortunately, a small inn down the hill from the Saltash station had accommodation, and Daniel obtained three rooms, one each for me and Lady Cynthia, and one he would share with Elgin. Lady Cynthia had conceded to don her frock before we descended from the train, with me to help her with her lacings—so she wouldn't shock the natives, she said. I could see she was tired, however, and likely she didn't want to risk the inn turning us away. The folk of faraway Cornwall might not care that the oddly dressed female was Lady Cynthia, an earl's daughter from a fashionable address in London, and refuse to accommodate an eccentric.

Once we reached the inn, Daniel returned alone to the station to send off telegrams, leaving the rest of us to settle in, none of us much wanting to speak or to even gather for a meal.

The room I was given was luxurious, at least in my eyes, with a wide bed, a soft carpet, and windows that gave out to the curve of the river. The bridge loomed above the inn, a reminder of why we'd come.

The thing seemed so solid. The iron girders that curved down to the tracks were thick and substantial, the pillars that held it over the river vast. It would take some doing to destroy a bridge like that.

And yet in December of the year before last, the huge Tay Bridge had fallen, crumbling into the water. The blame for that tragedy was proved to be faulty bridge construction, not a deliberate act—speculation was that the bridge simply couldn't stand against the constant wind that blew through the firth. Still, it proved that even a mighty bridge like the Tay could fall.

The landlady, a woman called Mrs. Rigby, brought me a bit of bread and cheese on a tray, with tea to wash it down. The bread was stale, the cheese a bit leathery, but I ate it, knowing it would be some time before I saw my kitchen again. The tea, on the other hand, was quite nice, and I sipped it as I looked out of the window.

It was very late, and I was exhausted, but I did not yet want to lie down and sleep. I wondered if I waited for Daniel's return, and why that should be. He would no doubt come in and go to bed without speaking to me, and we'd reconvene in the morning.

Even so, I sat, sipping tea until the pot was empty. The occasional train clacked past on the bridge, freight cars carrying goods, and one passenger train, probably the last of the night, heading into Cornwall.

Otherwise there was quiet darkness, broken only by the trickle of the river and a white glow when the moon sailed from behind torn clouds.

That moonlight showed me a dark figure slipping out of the inn around one o'clock. At first I thought it a man—Daniel?—but I dismissed the idea immediately.

I rose, set my empty teacup aside, and took my coat from the wardrobe where the maid had hung it. I buttoned it as I quietly left my room and went down the stairs, not bothering with my hat.

The inn's front door was unlocked, and no one came to see what I might be doing as I opened it and crept into the night. The air outside was chill and damp, a rising wind sending clouds up the river from the nearby coast. I pulled my coat closer as I hurried down the tiny lane and out to the shingle that led under the bridge.

The figure ahead of me moved more quickly than I could, boots better for tramping along a riverbed than my city shoes. I stumbled over rocks, my ankles turning, but I managed to keep the person in sight.

I halted when my quarry did; then I watched the silhouette climb onto the base of one of the great pillars that held up the bridge. I moved forward slowly, not wanting to make my presence known, the mud muffling my footsteps.

When I reached the pillar, I saw a flame flare up above my head, making my nerves jump. The flame went out, and a small orange glow took its place, the lit end of a cigar.

"You shouldn't have followed me, Mrs. H."

Lady Cynthia stood above me on the pillar's massive base, leaning back against the tower of stone. A puff on a cigar followed, Lady Cynthia pressing her free hand against the stones to keep her balance.

"Come down from there," I said sternly. "Before you fall and hurt yourself."

Cynthia shrugged. "Who would care?" She let the cigar dangle at her side, the glow like a firefly, the acrid scent of smoke swallowed by the tang of the river and a smell of fish. "My sister would adore it if I cleared off and left her alone with Rankin. Rankin wants me in his house, but only so he can keep his eye on me and make sure I don't do anything too sensational. My parents don't want me underfoot—they wish I'*d* been the one to top myself, not my brother."

I opened my mouth to assure her she was wrong, but sadly, she likely had the right of it. From what I understood, her parents had nearly gone off their heads at the death of her brother, but they'd shoved Cynthia off on her sister and Lord Rankin without remorse.

"Of course we would care," I said stalwartly. "What about Bobby? She is your great friend, is she not?"

Cynthia groaned. "Bobby." She sank into a crouch, rubbing her forehead with a shaking hand. "Oh, Mrs. H., I'm afraid, so afraid, that Bobby was the one who killed Sinead."

20

I stared in astonishment. "Bobby—I mean, Lady Roberta? Why would you believe so? Why should she?"

"I don't know." Cynthia raised her head, her eyes bleak in the shadows. "That is why I wanted to go away to Brighton with her—I planned to put her to the question once we got there."

"A dangerous idea if you are right," I said, my heart beating faster. "But good heavens, what makes you think *she* killed Sinead? For what purpose?"

Cynthia heaved a long sigh. "Because Bobby was at the house that night. I slipped her in—with the help of Mrs. Bowen. Rankin, of course, hates Bobby, and I always want to put one over on him. Bobby and I shared a bottle of his best brandy, and she slept on the floor of my bedchamber—she thought it a great lark. I pushed her out in the wee hours, sent her down the back stairs through the servants' hall and the kitchen." Cynthia coughed, her voice growing hoarse in the chill. "What if Sinead saw her, perhaps threatened to report to

Rankin that she'd been there, demanded a price for her silence? Bobby isn't worried about what Rankin thinks of her, but she lives in fear that her father will cut her off if she takes her larks too far. As we told you, neither of us have a bean of our own. What if she grew angry at Sinead and . . ." Cynthia's fears shone in her eyes. "She might not have meant to, but Bobby is strong, and she's learned to fight like a man. She wants to *be* a man—never mind the impossibility of that."

I listened in growing astonishment. "If you are casting Sinead as a blackmailer, you are being fanciful. She seemed a sweet girl. Why should she threaten to tell Lord Rankin of your pranks?"

Cynthia shook her head. "You did not know Sinead long, Mrs. H. She could be quite friendly—and I know she's innocent of the sorts of terrible things her young man has been doing—but she knew things." Cynthia stubbed out the cigar, as though already tiring of it. The orange glow died, which made the pale moonlight seem all the colder. "I told you, Sinead lived with my family in Hertfordshire. She was one of the servants Em insisted on bringing with her into her marriage—Mrs. Bowen was the other. Mrs. B. was a sort of under-housekeeper in the Gothic mess my parents live in, and Em insisted she come down to London and work for her. But Sinead—one found oneself imparting secrets in front of her, because you'd forget she was in the room. Next thing you'd know, Sinead was using that knowledge to finagle little favors—time to walk out with her man, someone else to do an unpleasant chore like empty the chamber pots, a few pennies so she could buy ribbons in the village. Nothing she asked was very dire or expensive, so we always capitulated. Sinead never told what she knew—she was good at keeping secrets. But maybe Bobby didn't understand that, and panicked."

Cynthia looked miserable. If Bobby *had* been the culprit . . . Well, she'd likely be arrested for it. A person needs to be held accountable for the harm they do others, whether they meant to do the harm or not.

But I understood what her guilt would mean for Cynthia. Even if Lord Rankin decided to have the fact that Bobby killed Sinead hushed up—and he had the money and position to do such a thing—he would use the incident to make Cynthia's life even more unbearable than it already was. Lord Rankin was that sort of gentleman.

"It might not have been Lady Roberta at all," I pointed out; then I made an impatient noise. "Do come down from there. I am getting a crick in my neck talking to you like this."

Lady Cynthia slowly unfolded her legs and slid from the pillar, landing on her feet beside me. She overbalanced, and I caught her before she could slip and fall in the mud.

"Thank you," she said sincerely as I helped her to stand.

A mean-spirited young woman might have snapped at me, a servant, for growing too familiar, or boxed my ears for my impertinence at touching her, but Cynthia only gave me a look of pathetic gratitude.

She let out a breath that steamed in the damp air and turned to face the slowly flowing river. "Do you think it runs in families, Mrs. H.? Suicide?"

I regarded her with a twinge of worry. "I really have no idea. I shouldn't think so. It's not like the color of your eyes or shape of your nose."

"My brother was mad." Cynthia threw the half-smoked cigar into the river. "Spoiled rotten as well. He gambled, like my father, was up to his ears in debt even when he was in university. He traded on my father's name to get credit, but after a while even the most loyal creditors refused him. Then he came under the power of that oik, Piedmont. Piedmont had some kind of hold over my brother—I was too young to understand what."

I drew a sharp breath. "Piedmont? Does he go by the odd nickname of Minty?"

"That's the chap," Cynthia said. "I've always wanted to turn him upside down and shake him until he tells me what he did to my brother, why he had so much influence over him."

I wondered as well, very much. Things had been connecting in my head during our journey, and now thoughts danced and spun until they made me dizzy—Minty, the financiers Lord Rankin had been told to spy on, the death of Sinead, the Fenians, Cynthia's family.

I needed to speak to Daniel.

However, Lady Cynthia was still morose, and I did not want to simply run away and abandon her. "I do not believe it runs in families," I repeated. "Your brother might have had troubles you know nothing of. If this Minty *did* do something to upset your brother, you might be able to bring suit against him."

Lady Cynthia perked up a little at my words. The wind, which had been steadily increasing, ruffled her hair and mine. "Jove—I hadn't thought of that. I'll speak to a solicitor, dig up some dirt on the dreadful Minty." She did a little dance step on the muddy sand, slipped, and righted herself by putting a light hand on my shoulder. "You're cheering me up no end, Mrs. H."

"Good. Now let us get indoors. It's going to rain." Clouds had built as we'd spoken, and the wind held dampness.

"Right you are." Cynthia stuck her hands in her pockets, and we started for the inn. I wanted to move quickly, as the stiffening breeze began to slap at us, but Cynthia strolled without haste, seemingly oblivious of the weather.

"That Daniel is an odd duck," she observed. "What's he

about? If he can dress like a gent, why is he working as a drudge for Rankin?"

"I'm certain he has his reasons." My retort came out more sharply than I'd meant it to, but I had no answer to the question, and this irritated me.

"He *must* have something to do with the police," Cynthia said, not noticing my tone. "No other reason a man would become a menial if he didn't have to. Oh, no offense, Mrs. H. I don't think of you as a menial."

"Thank you," I said. A cook was *not* the equivalent of a scullery maid—my mother and then my mentor had taught me that.

My mother had been a charwoman, not even in the employ of a big house. She'd scrubbed her fingers to the bone to see that I had some schooling instead of going straight to the factories and then finagled me a position as a kitchen maid so I could apprentice to a skilled cook. I owed my present good fortune entirely to my mother and to the cook who'd given me such valuable training.

I shuddered to think I'd nearly tossed it all away when a duplicitous man had smiled at me. I was somewhat glad my mother had already passed by the time I'd been drawn into my false marriage, so she hadn't had to watch me ruin all she'd set up for me. My husband's departure and Grace's arrival had at last brought me to my senses.

Rain began coming down in fine needles, and our conversation had to cease. The wind increased—it would be a gale before morning. I hoped the weather would deter the anarchists, though true fanatics might either not be bothered or simply choose another venue for their crimes.

Cynthia gave me a breezy good night as we parted, she in much better spirits. If I'd done nothing else this evening, at least I'd cheered her.

I saw no light under the door of the room Daniel shared with Mr. Thanos. I'd not observed Daniel enter the inn while I'd been sitting up, nor had I spied him returning while Cynthia and I had been out by the bridge. I'd kept a close eye out, even there. I knew Mr. Thanos had already gone to bed, as he'd bade us a formal good night and shut himself into his room when we'd first arrived.

In my chamber once more, I resumed my seat at my window. I remained dressed but wrapped myself in a blanket to stave off the chill. Rain and mist blew along the river, obscuring the far shore and the lights of Plymouth. The bridge became a dark shadow in the night, but its presence could be felt—huge, iron, industrial. Indestructible.

A train rumbled by in the next hour, moving slowly over the bridge, its lanterns pinpoints of light in the rain. Once the train cleared the bridge and slowed into Saltash, I saw a man emerge from the shadows at the bottom of the hill and dart through the front door of the inn.

I untangled myself from my blanket, left my room, and went down to meet him.

Daniel paused at the bottom of the stairs to shake rain from his hatless hair. The inn was dark save for the light a lamp hanging outside the door cast through the transom.

I couldn't very well scold Daniel and say, *Where have you been?* I did not feel I had that right, and besides, I didn't want to wake those upstairs with my shrill demand. I settled for, "Did you send your telegrams?"

"Hours ago," Daniel answered. "Had a few replies already. I'll return to the station in the morning for any more."

"Oh." My fingers twitched on my skirt. "You've been in the telegraph office all this time?"

"Hmm?" Daniel slid his greatcoat off and wiped it down with his hand. "No, I've been chatting up the locals . . . in the local."

I noticed he was a bit unsteady on his feet. Also that he wore his working-man's clothes, his hair loose and plastered with rain.

"I need to speak to you," I said in a low voice, sending a furtive glance up the stairs.

Daniel caught my urgency, grasped my arm, and steered me into the empty parlor. He closed the door, towed me to the middle of the room, and lit a lamp on the table there. He'd known exactly where the lamp stood and where to find the box of matches to light it, which meant he'd thoroughly investigated this room already.

I quickly told him about my conversation with Cynthia under the bridge—the fact that Bobby had been in the house the night of Sinead's death and Cynthia's speculation that innocent Sinead had been a blackmailer. Daniel listened, interest in his dark eyes.

"We will have to question this Bobby," he said when I finished. "She might have killed Sinead in a moment of alarm, or she might have simply gone home and is completely innocent. I'd rather know before the police get hold of her—or the newspapers."

I agreed—journalists would make a meal of two women who liked to dress as gentlemen being together in the night, with a maid found dead in the morning.

When I told Daniel about Cynthia's speculations about young Lord Minty hounding her brother to his death, a grim light entered his eyes.

"If that is true, I will make him answer for it," Daniel said with finality. "Lady Cynthia's brother was half crazed, from what I hear, wild and brash, and fell in with a bad crowd. He caused much grief to that family. Does still."

"She worries she will turn out be much the same," I said, unhappy for her. "I think she'd do better if she could get away from her family altogether, Lord Rankin included. But she'd have to marry to do that, and I'd only feel comfortable if she married a decent man. Someone like Mr. Thanos, perhaps?" I let my inquiry linger.

Daniel's eyes widened. "Thanos?" He regarded me in amazement for a moment, then looked thoughtful, then shook his head. "I don't know. Thanos is a good-hearted chap, yes, but he barely lives in this world. Lady Cynthia would have to take him in hand, make certain he ate meals and put on matching shoes, that sort of thing."

I wasn't certain the idea was so far-fetched. Perhaps Cynthia would thrive with a man like Mr. Thanos to look after, a kind person who cherished her presence. It is always good to feel needed.

"What did you learn from the local men?" I asked, setting aside my matchmaking for now.

Daniel made a noise of exasperation. "That the fishermen of this village do not like outsiders. Including me. Even after standing a few rounds, which loosened tongues the slightest bit, I did not hear of any hordes of Fenians descending on the area or of anyone hanging about with an interest in the bridge. It's been rather quiet, the natives say. That might be true, or they might have closed ranks against me."

"Very likely they did," I said. "It ought to be *me* going about asking questions, you know. I wager I could find out a great deal, without having to buy a pint."

Daniel shook his head. "This is dangerous. Even aside

from the threat of Fenians, the fishermen around here are hardened and tough. I don't want you near them."

"Not *them*, ridiculous man. The servants. The cooks and maids and chars in these houses learn everything that goes on in a town and will tell another servant. Those in service know far more than any journalist or policeman is ever likely to, still more than the gentlemen who sit in Parliament all day and believe they run the empire."

Daniel's eyes danced. "Fair dues. But I had in mind that you'd return to London tomorrow morning with Thanos and Lady Cynthia."

He spoke firmly, but if he thought I'd meekly agree and rush off to bed, he was much mistaken. "Not a bit of it. You are neither my father nor brother, nor husband, not even a cousin, and I do not have to answer to you." I lifted my chin as he regarded me in surprise. "Being alone in the world has the one benefit of allowing me to decide for myself what I will and will not do. I'll remain here until I choose to return to London—and if I have to move from the very large room you procured for me to a broom closet near the kitchen and purchase my own third-class ticket back to Town, then so be it."

Daniel studied me with an expression that had gone flinty. "I've dealt with Fenians and men like them—they're unpredictable, violent, desperate. They've seen terrible things, and they're not averse to doing terrible things in return, even to women."

I took his point, but the dratted man was maddening me. "My dear Daniel, if I come across a Fenian with a store of dynamite, I do not plan to wrestle him to the ground. I will prudently send for the police—and you. I'm a sensible woman."

"I know," Daniel muttered. "That's what concerns me."

I ignored him. "Besides, I have not heard that *you* will join us on this morning journey to London. All the more reason I should stay. How would I face James if anything happened to you? How could I tell him I left you on your own when I should have been looking after you?"

Emotions chased themselves across Daniel's face—anger, resolve, guilt, irritation, and finally, resignation.

He let out a long breath. "Well, then," he said. "Let us hope the Queen is more reasonable than you and postpones her journey. Good night, Kat."

"Good night, Daniel."

We both stood still, neither wishing to give way first. I broke the impasse by sending him a faint smile and walking out of the room ahead of him, but I waited at the foot of the stairs to make certain he came out behind me.

He did, gesturing that I should precede him up the stairs. I made my way quietly upward, and Daniel came after me, his tread heavy. We parted at the top of the staircase, where I whispered another good night. Daniel pointedly waited until I'd entered my chamber and shut the door, but I opened it a crack again to watch until he went into the bedchamber he shared with Mr. Thanos.

I closed the door all the way and turned the key in the lock, but I returned to my chair to sit until I heard Daniel's boots hit the floor and a creak of a bedstead. Only then did I rise, don my nightclothes, and slide into bed.

The Queen was not reasonable—she refused to put off her trip to Cornwall, and would travel on Sunday as planned.

I knew this because I rose very early—not wanting Daniel to slip away somewhere—and watched him walk to the train station to collect the morning's telegrams. I could see the station at the top of the hill through the downstairs sitting room window, in spite of the continuing rain, and knew when Daniel went into the station and when he came out.

I sipped a cup of tea the landlady, Mrs. Rigby, brought me and chewed on an indifferent buttered muffin, but both were warm and welcome in the cold. As blustery as it was, however, I admitted it was nice to be out of London's smoke. One could breathe here, even if the air smelled of fish. I should like to bring Grace to stay in this cozy inn and show her the river, the hills, the bridge.

"Is this usual weather?" I asked Mrs. Rigby as she refilled my teapot from a steaming kettle, a towel wrapped around its handle.

"Aye." Mrs. Rigby poured the water as I held the teapot's lid out of the way, steam billowing pleasantly around us. "This time of year there's always much rain. We have a few fine days in the summer, and so many come through from London for the sea bathing then, you wouldn't believe it, dear. But in early spring, the weather's blustery. I hear it will be worse tonight, and a big storm coming in tomorrow."

Well, perhaps the weather would keep the Queen away if nothing else would.

But we could not count on that, so I began to chat to Mrs. Rigby, conversationally, not about much of anything. I learned that she and her husband had two daughters who'd married fishermen in Plymouth but who still came home to help when the inn was full.

I satisfied *her* curiosity by telling her I worked for Lady Cynthia—more or less true—and that Mr. Thanos was Cynthia's stepbrother—a complete fabrication, but I did not like to sully Lady Cynthia's reputation. I put it that Daniel was Mr. Thanos's friend, again the truth, though not all of it.

Mrs. Rigby seemed happy with my answers and at last bustled away to continue her work. I watched Daniel come down the road from the station and rose to meet him at the front door.

He did not look at all surprised to see me awake and dressed, and let me herd him back into the sitting room, where I closed the door and demanded he tell me all.

Daniel threw himself into a chair and scrubbed his hands through his hair, scraping it with the telegrams he clutched.

"Bloody woman won't listen to anyone," he growled. "She refuses to change a thing. My contacts say she'll leave London at ten o'clock this evening and travel overnight to reach the coast tomorrow morning. She'll be through here about six in the morning—the exact time Thanos calculated she'd be riding over that bridge."

"By 'bloody woman,' I take it you mean Her Majesty," I said, placing myself calmly in front of him. "I imagine those plotting against her will count on her stubbornness, unfortunately."

"She refuses to show that she is afraid of these people. *Won't cringe in cowardice*, were apparently her very words." Daniel raked his hair again, the papers crackling.

"I cannot blame her, you know," I told him. "It's best not to give way. If she does—even once—they will have won a victory. The anarchists will believe that all they have to do is threaten, and everyone will capitulate. And they'll be right."

"I know." Daniel lowered his hands and regarded me glumly. "Her Unyielding Majesty will expect the rest of us to take care of the problem so she won't be endangered." He heaved a sigh that came from the bottom of his boots. "I suppose that is what we are for."

I wondered very much whom he meant by *we*. He might

be speaking about British subjects in general, or perhaps he had some sort of direct connection to the Queen and her court, which would explain some of his secrecy and his ability to make gentlemen like Lord Rankin obey his commands. Not a satisfactory explanation, but I was not likely to get a better one soon.

"What will you do?" I asked.

Daniel let out another breath. "*I* will meet with the police here and comb every inch of space on and around that bridge." He pointed a blunt finger at me. "*You* will return to London with Lady Cynthia and Thanos."

"I believe we had this conversation last night." I lifted my teacup from the side table where I'd left it and took a sip. "Best you get at it. If I discover anything important, I will seek you out."

Daniel scowled, curling his fists and tensing like coiled spring. I half expected him to leap from the chair and carry me off over his shoulder up the hill to throw me onto a passing train.

He did nothing so dramatic. Daniel only shook his head, cast a despairing look out the window, and rose to his feet.

"I don't have time to fight you, Kat," he said as I took another calm sip of tea. "But you stay *away* from that bloody bridge. I don't care if the whole damn thing falls down, as long as *you* are nowhere near it."

His eyes were hard as he glared at me, though I knew he exaggerated. He did care if it fell down—he wanted to prevent the Queen and her entourage from coming to tragedy. His whole body quivered with it.

"*You* take care," I returned. "I have a bit more sense of caution than you do, Daniel, that is certain. I will be well."

Daniel continued to regard me in vexation; then he put his

hands on my shoulders and gave me a swift kiss on the lips before he released me and strode out of the room without another word.

I lifted my cup again, my hand shaking. "Daft man," I muttered as I tried to catch my breath. "He nearly spilled my tea."

21

Lady Cynthia did not want to obediently return to London and neither did Mr. Thanos. I heard the arguments as I slipped out to the kitchen, which had been built onto the back of the inn, to seek Mrs. Rigby. The kitchen had obviously once been a separate building and was now connected to the main house by a narrow, chilly passage.

I paused to listen before I went down this passage—Daniel was busy getting 'round Lady Cynthia by telling her she needed to take urgent messages to Lord Rankin and give that man further instruction. Lady Cynthia perked up at that.

"Chivvy Rankin?" she said, her voice ringing. "It would be my pleasure."

I heard her pound up the stairs again, leaving Daniel with Mr. Thanos. "I need *you* to keep an eye on her," Daniel said to Elgin. "Look after her—help her stand on Rankin until he stops that flow of money. What I do here only patches the gaps. The finances is where we'll truly hurt them."

"They'll only find another source, you know," Elgin warned.

"True, but Rankin can assist with that as well. He knows to whom they're likely to turn if Rankin becomes a wall. Also make a nuisance of yourself with Lord Chalminster. Put the fear of God into him—or at least the fear of me. I'll be home to deal with him and his son on Monday."

"Chalminster?" Elgin sounded thoughtful. "I see."

Daniel gave him a few more names of men to visit, then I heard Elgin retreat upstairs, his step buoyant.

I could not help feeling a bit of admiration—Daniel had turned both of them to his side with a few well-chosen sentences. But he'd not get around me, I decided, no matter how many times he tried to kiss me.

My lips tingled when I thought of the kiss, and I touched my fingers to them. Then I told myself not to be so silly and hastened the rest of the way to the kitchen. Daniel might suppose he held the world in the palm of his hand, but the kitchen was *my* demesne, and Daniel, no matter how many aristocrats he had influence over, would never rule there.

Mrs. Rigby welcomed my help, and the two of us set about making meat pies—beef and kidney as well as pork. I showed her how I used a combination of drippings and butter to make my pastry light and yet robust as well as a dribble of gravy inside the crust to make the entire pie moist and hot.

We also made custard pastries and bread rolls. I mixed up a batch of my brioche and showed Mrs. Rigby how to make little cake pans full of the sweet buttery bread, each topped with a small ball of dough.

All the while I kept my eyes and ears open. One wall in the kitchen had plentiful windows, unusual because most kitchens are enclosed and dark. But perhaps whoever had laid in the passage between house and kitchen had been forward-thinking enough to add windows.

Through them I could see most of the town and out to the river and the bridge. Not long after we began baking, I spied uniformed constables flowing down to the flat riverbank under the tall bridge, walking in a slow, careful way, heads down. More constables moved up the hill along the train tracks.

Mrs. Rigby saw my interest and peered out with me. "Quite a lot of policemen about, aren't there? Must be to do with Her Majesty coming through in the morning."

"Most like," I agreed, as though I had only passing curiosity. "Not a thing that happens often, I suppose."

Mrs. Rigby, her plump face red from the heat of the two ovens stoked high, returned to rolling out pastry. "You must see her all the time up in London."

I heard a mixture of wistfulness and disapproval in her voice. She'd already made clear she had no idea why anyone would live in the Smoke, but at the same time envied me my place there.

"No indeed," I answered. "The Queen keeps herself to herself when she's at her palace in London. She stays most often in Scotland these days, in any case."

"Well, a woman *ought* to stay indoors and not make a spectacle of herself," Mrs. Rigby said as she vigorously scrubbed her rolling pin over a large lump of dough. "Though it's different for a queen, I suppose."

We agreed, and continued our baking. Inwardly, my heart was thumping. The rain came down and the number of constables increased. Would they find a threat? Or frighten off the villains? The fact that Mrs. Rigby had not been surprised by the policemen and knew exactly when the Queen would be coming through meant the Queen's journey was not the secret she'd likely wanted it to be. The world watched her, and news spread.

Mrs. Rigby and I made extra rolls and cakes after we'd finished those for the guests, intended for Mrs. Coombe, her nearest neighbor, who was poorly, Mrs. Rigby said. Having eleven children was part of the reason of her decline, in Mrs. Rigby's opinion, and I could not disagree.

We piled the baked goods into baskets, covered them with cloth, and proceeded to take our treats next door.

I had been correct when I'd told Daniel that a cook or a maid could find out more things than a policeman. Mrs. Rigby's frail neighbor, Mrs. Coombe, had nothing to do but recline on a sofa in the front room while her daughters saw to her, bringing in the gossip of the village. The maid of the house mingled with them, gossiping as much as they did.

Mrs. Coombe and her daughters asked me many questions about London, and as I answered them, I asked questions in return about life in this edge of Cornwall. They were not entirely cut off from the world here, because just across the river was Plymouth, a port city with plenty of comings and goings, and the sea itself was not far away.

I learned much about Saltash—who lived where and who was related to whom, and even who was having it off with a chap across the river, rowing herself over in the dead of night. *I ask you*, Mrs. Coombe finished. Another neighbor came to call, bringing her maid and yet more tales.

They were delighted to have someone new to speak to, a person who didn't know all the local stories, and one who listened avidly. I imagined I'd been their best audience in a long while. Tourists stayed at Mrs. Rigby's inn, of course, but very few had any interest in the local inhabitants, according to her.

When Mrs. Coombe began to tire, Mrs. Rigby and I departed and strolled back to the inn. There, I bundled up some tea cakes and buns and walked out to look for Daniel.

The rain had lightened while I'd visited with Mrs. Coombe and her neighbors, but now it began to stream down, the wind rising to send it into me as I huddled in my coat and a big shawl.

I found Daniel at the railway station up the hill, standing in a snug, dry office with the signalman and several uniformed police. Daniel looked up quickly as I came in but did not admonish me. One of the police sergeants began to do it for him, but broke off when I displayed the baked goods in my basket. The constables crowded around in eagerness, and I decided that the poor things must not have eaten this well in a good while.

Daniel came to usher me out. He behaved as though he merely escorted a well-meaning woman away from men's business, but he led me to a tiny private room across the station's large passageway. The kettle on the small stove inside told me this was where the signalmen and ticket sellers brewed up their tea. Daniel shut the door, closing us into a stuffy chamber that smelled of tobacco, coffee, and burned tea leaves.

"Well," I said before Daniel could begin, "have you found any incendiary devices, or the men trying to lay them?"

"No." He looked frustrated. "Though we are still searching. That bridge has many nooks and crannies, not to mention the pillars beneath."

"Surely it would take a great lot of dynamite to even dent it," I said. "It is quite solid."

Daniel shook his head. "Bridges are all about balance. How much weight and tension can the trusses or beams take before they fail? If the correct section is knocked out, the entire thing can tumble down."

"As happened at the Tay Bridge," I said.

"Exactly." His tone was somber. "One weakness in the wrong place . . ." He rubbed his forehead. "Well, we can only continue to look. Thank you for the cakes. It was thoughtful of you."

"An excellent excuse to hunt you down," I corrected him. "I have been having a chat with our innkeepers' neighbors. They know everything that goes on in this village, as I said." I folded my hands, now empty of the basket, which the policemen and signalman had happily taken from me, and regarded Daniel with some satisfaction. "There is a house at the end of those that line the river. According to the biggest gossip in the village, Mrs. Coombe, the woman who lives in it was recently blessed by a visit from several members of her family, all big strapping young men. Nephews, Mrs. Coombe says, all Irish, all come for a visit. But not from Ireland. From America."

"Bloody hell," Daniel said softly.

The Fenian movement, from what I understood, had begun in America, in the eastern part of that nation, by Irishmen who had emigrated there. American Irish, it seemed, were happy to provide money and men to help in the efforts to remove Ireland from British rule.

I myself was appalled at some of the terrible things the Irish people had to endure in their country—dire poverty and downright starvation, landlords who beggared their tenants while living in luxury, harsh punishments for any perceived crime, the violence born of frustration that inflicted harm on innocent Irish inhabitants.

On the other hand, I certainly did not approve of people gathering in yet another country to make plans to hurt those in mine who were simply going about their day-to-day lives.

Their target this time might be the Queen, but there would be plenty of other people on the journey with her, including the working men who operated the train and this railway line and the women who attended the Queen, who were Lady Cynthia's friends. Not to mention anyone in the village who happened to be hurt by the disaster, and of course the police constables, most of whom couldn't be more than twenty, lads who were risking their lives to find explosive devices that might have been laid on the bridge.

"Where is this house?" Daniel asked me. His eyes were motionless, but I decided that the quiet fury in his voice was far more frightening than any shouting my husband had ever done.

"The end of the lane on the waterfront. As far as you can go before the road peters out."

Daniel moved his gaze to the window, through which was the train platform, the tops of trees, and the land sloping to the level ground by the river. I watched him withdraw, his thoughts turning inward, the affable Daniel vanishing. "Thank you, Kat," he said absently and started for the door.

"Daniel."

He turned back, but like an automaton—he wasn't seeing me anymore.

"They may simply be a woman's nephews visiting from America."

"I know." He gave me a nod but turned away, the shell of Daniel walking out of the room to become the commanding man who gave orders to half a police force.

I followed, but no one paid me any mind. As Daniel led the constables out of the station, I collected my empty basket, the cakes gone. They'd eaten every crumb.

I left the office at the same time a train came puffing across the bridge, slowing as it reached this side of the river and drew onto the station's platform. The wheels squealed mightily against the steel tracks as the brakeman worked to stop the train. The locomotive let out a bellow of steam followed by a long hiss as it settled in to take a rest—engines always seemed live things to me.

Idly, I watched the passengers disembark, not many on this rainy morning. Most on the train would be heading deeper into Cornwall and for the coast. It was my ambition one day to take my daughter all the way to Land's End. We'd stand at the very edge of England and imagine what was beyond it, out in the wide world.

Those who stepped off the train were locals, it appeared—women in plain gowns gathering children before scurrying off into the lanes, a man in a dark worsted suit who lifted his hand to the signalman and walked away, and a young man in brown wool who glanced furtively about.

The young man was the only one who looked out of place. He was very dirty, for one thing, his face grimy under his pulled-down cap. I walked across the platform and placed myself directly in front of him, holding my empty basket in front of me.

The lad didn't see me—he was so busy looking about—then he turned to take a step and let out a yelp as he nearly ran me down.

"James," I said severely as he scrambled to right himself. "Whatever are you doing here?"

As much as I wanted to follow Daniel and the constables to the cottage at the end of the lane, I had no intention of leading James into danger. Instead I latched my fingers around his wrist and pulled him from the station, intending to take him with me to the inn.

"I see you managed to escape from Daniel's rooms," I remarked as we walked.

"Oh aye, that was simple," James said without modesty. "I picked the lock, and his landlady has a good heart. She was shocked at his bad treatment of me. No, the hardest thing was finding out where he'd slunk off to."

"How *did* you find out?" I asked in curiosity. I couldn't imagine Daniel leaving a note with directions.

"Housekeeper at the posh digs where you work," James said, Daniel's sparkle in his eyes. "She's worried about her ladyship what dresses like a gent and told me she'd gone off to Cornwall with you. Stands to reason Dad was with you too. I've been out at every station in between looking for him. Had quite the journey."

Tenacious, that was James. I patted his arm. "Your diligence is commendable, but your father was right that it was very dangerous for you to come here. Anyway, this sounds like an expensive endeavor. Where did you get the money for the fare? Or did you stow away? Oh, James, tell me you have not been stowing away on every train from here to London."

James laughed, his exuberance undimmed. "Naw." Then he flushed. "Dad had some coins in his room, didn't he? I'll pay him back. I ain't no tea leaf."

Tea leaf. Thief. I remembered rhyming slang from my childhood. My mother had been very good at it.

"I doubt your father will begrudge you the money. However, I can't say he'll be kind to you for disobeying. He is only trying to keep you safe."

James's good humor fled. "Well, he never tries to keep himself safe, does he? I came to look after him. He'll get himself blown to bits or shot or stabbed, or some daft thing. We have to help him, Mrs. H."

I quite agreed. I also agreed with Daniel that the danger was too great for a boy, but I softened. "Truth to tell, I am glad to see you, James. I will indeed welcome your assistance to watch over Daniel. But I'm afraid what he's into is perilous in the extreme."

The wind slackened once more, the rain becoming a thin mist, which was damp but not as cold as it had been. Spring was trying to push its way in.

As we walked, I explained as much as I dared to James, emphasizing that Daniel was surrounded by policemen who would look out for him. The best thing we could do for Daniel at the moment, I told him, was to keep out of the way.

It was not easy for me to stay to this course, however. To distract myself, I showed James the bridge and said we were keeping an eye out for incendiary devices.

The lane from the railway station led down a sharp hill, curving through a narrow cut in a steep bank. The railroad tracks continued on the same level as the station above us, passing over the street on which we walked on a simple viaduct. As the lane went ever downward, the bridge rose higher, until finally it ran out over the river in the lofty structure that had caught the eye of the public.

A narrow road off to the left took us directly under the main part of the bridge, where we could admire the double pillars of gray stone that held up the tracks high above us. The timbers of the tracks looked alarmingly far overhead and, at the same time, so vulnerable.

"It's too big," James said. "No one will pull that lot down."

"They won't have to destroy the entire thing to cause damage," I said, my hand at my lips as I stared upward. "Even a small explosion could rip through the train cars, or derail the train coming into the station, or block up the tracks while anarchists attack. We must prepare for all events."

James sent me a narrow look. "Dad would never let you go up against anarchists. He's too fond of you. If you try, he'll lock you in somewhere like he did to me."

My face grew warm, but I held on to the words. *He's too fond of you.*

"Well, if an anarchist rushes past me, I won't sit idly by," I said. "I will find a stout stick and have at him while I shout for the police. Would your father expect me to simply move out of the way and let such a person flee? I'd trip him up if nothing else."

James burst out laughing. "That's the spirit, Mrs. H."

"I suppose I've lost all the other letters of my surname for good," I said in a mild tone. "Let us retreat to the inn for the moment and get some tea and bread inside you, my lad. *And* have you washed. You are absolutely filthy."

The sky was dark when Daniel finally returned to the inn. I knew he'd try to come in and go out again without bothering to speak to me, so I left my room, where I'd been watching out the window, and put myself in front of his chamber door. His tread on the stairs was heavy, and when he came into sight, he looked exhausted. Shadows traced his eyes, mud and grime smeared his clothes, and his hair was slick with the rain that had begun to come down again.

I knew Daniel was spent when, instead of dodging past me or turning around to avoid me, he only gave me a tired smile and said, "Ah, Kat."

"James has come," I said, getting the news over with quickly.

"He's in there—asleep." I pointed to Daniel's chamber door. Whether James was asleep was speculation, but I'd ordered him to rest himself.

Daniel's smile fled. "Damnation."

"You ought to have known he would follow you. But never mind about that now. What did you find? Please tell me before I burst."

Daniel looked me up and down, some of his composure returning. "You look well enough. Come here." He took my hand and guided me into my own chamber and shut the door.

It said much for my agitated state that I said nothing about the impropriety of this—I barely noticed. Guarding my reputation was not my most pressing concern at the moment.

"We found the house as you said, and I was welcomed inside," Daniel began. "The strapping nephews had been there all right, but they've gone. Back to America, said their aunt, smiling at us as though she'd pulled a great trick. The sergeant fetched the magistrate, and we searched the house. They'd cleared out almost everything, but too hastily. We found pieces of fuse and bits of the protective casing that wraps dynamite. But that was all. This was in a box that would have held a hundred sticks of the stuff."

Daniel sighed, the light of my single kerosene lamp glinting on his sodden hair. "That means they've already set the charges and scarpered. A hundred sticks, Kat. Waiting to go off, and we don't have any bloody idea where they are."

22

I'd never seen Daniel defeated. Always he'd look at the mess around him, see things others didn't, and happily rush off to solve the problem or conquer a villain.

Now he regarded me morosely, a deadness in his eyes I didn't like.

"We'll find it," I said, taking a step closer to him. Outside, the wind slapped a shutter against the house's wall, the storm rushing along the river to drench the town. "We'll keep looking until we do. This might be the wrong bridge, the wrong town."

Daniel didn't look any happier. "Constables and anyone the police can recruit are searching every bridge on Elgin's list and others along the line. So far, nothing. I've been at the railway station sending telegrams until I'm struggling to speak in complete sentences. There is no news, the Queen has already departed, and I can't find the culprits or prevent their crime."

I stepped closer to him and took his hands. They were trembling.

Alarmed, I looked up into his face. It was drained of color behind almost as much grime as had been on James's cheeks, and Daniel was swaying on his feet.

I realized he'd slept little and probably eaten next to nothing. I firmed my grip and tugged him toward the chair at my window. "Come and sit down. You need a rest."

Daniel shook his head like the stubborn man he was. "I'll rest when it's done, when we stop it."

"You can do nothing if you collapse in the middle of the river," I pointed out. "Take a rest and eat something. I learned long ago that I was no good to anyone if I didn't look after myself first."

Daniel gave me a dark glance, but he did at last sit down in the chair. I brought out a plate of scones I'd held back for him and poured another cup of tea from the pot Mrs. Rigby had given me before I'd settled in.

Daniel caught up a scone and downed it so hungrily I knew my speculation that he'd eaten very little today had been spot on. He took a long drink of tea then peered at me over the cup's rim with a bit of his old sparkle.

"You are good to me, Kat."

I shrugged. "Tea and scones are the best things for easing one's troubles, I've always believed. Have some lemon curd with the next one. I mixed it myself." Lemon, eggs, sugar, and butter came together magically to make the sweet sauce I loved. Mrs. Rigby bought her lemons from a grocer who obtained them from an estate near Truro that had an extensive hothouse.

"Not what I meant," Daniel said, his voice quiet.

His look made me uncomfortable, but fortunately, he said no more and drank his tea.

I pulled a straight-backed chair from the writing table to sit next to him at the window. "Now, then." I put my feet on a footstool to keep them from the cold floor and laid my hands in my lap. "Let us see if we can think about where to search next rather than blundering about in the dark. A bit of planning beforehand can be of much help."

I heard a noise, which I realized was Daniel snorting behind his teacup, but he lowered the cup and looked at me with a straight face. "I ought to have thought of that."

"Do not laugh at me, if you please." I scanned the slice of river I could see and then the lane that led up the hill to the station. The bridge was dark, though lanterns hung at its ends, and lights twinkled on the strand on both sides of the river, presumably the searching constables.

My gaze became riveted to the bridge. I remembered standing under one of its pillars with James, looking up to the underside of it high above.

"What if they put all those sticks of dynamite between the ties?" I asked. "We've been concentrating on how someone would make a bridge fall, but what if they simply destroyed the train? The bridge falling or not would be irrelevant then."

Daniel nodded slowly. "I would agree with you, except the constables have been all over the bridge, walking its length and looking for just such things. They've found no explosives on or under the bridge."

"Inside, then?" I mused. "Men could drill holes in the pillars, put the sticks into them, and seal them up again."

"No evidence of that either," Daniel said, sounding discouraged. "Would be difficult to detonate as well, without getting caught in the blast oneself. We'd find any long fuses they laid, and we haven't."

I twined my fingers together. "I have a feeling some of these fanatics wouldn't mind going up with their devices. Martyrs for their cause. Hmm. Let me think."

I saw Daniel's look of near despair as he lifted his teacup once more. The poor man truly was at his wits' end and on the edge of collapse, terrified he'd missed something that might mean the death of our Queen. Not only would it be tragic because a poor woman was dead, but it could mean the destruction of the nation.

Though Parliament and the cabinet did far more ruling than the monarch these days, the loss of our Queen would be a huge blow for her subjects and also signal that we couldn't keep even the highest in the land safe. Not only would the Fenian revolutionaries rejoice, but it would spark uprisings all over the empire, encouraging others to strike a blow against imperial Britain. There was no telling where that could end, including the downfall of the British Isles themselves.

Daniel broke open a scone, dribbling lemon curd on it, and took a bite. I wished again I'd had time to pack food from London, but I hadn't known we'd stay so long. Mrs. Rigby meant well, but she was an indifferent cook—her food was edible, but hardly the stuff of poetry. The potted meat I'd made a few days before we'd left would come in handy now, I decided, nice to spread on a bit of bread or roll.

That thought tapped another in my brain, and I sat up straight, drawing a quick breath.

Daniel glanced at me. He swallowed his scone, licking crumbs and lemon curd from his fingers. "What is it?"

"Could a person explode dynamite underwater?" I asked, trying to work through the idea in my head.

"If he found a way to keep it perfectly dry," Daniel answered. "Which would be difficult. We have been looking for things that could float explosives close to the bridge and have found nothing."

"But what if it were wrapped in oilskin and sealed with

something—when I want to keep meat dry in a jar and vermin out, I pour drippings on top of it, then let it harden somewhere cool, like a cellar or larder. When the drippings are solid, they form a cap. You can do the same thing with wax, as long as you protect the food below. I suppose you could seal a stick of dynamite into a bottle or jar, with the fuse protected with wax or some such. The fuse would take time to melt its way through the wax, so that the person who lit it could be well away, though perhaps it would have to burn quickly enough that it wouldn't be put out by water or the melted wax itself." I stopped, noticing Daniel staring at me hard in the gloom.

I shrugged. "It is only an idea. I don't know much about how explosives work."

Daniel sat up, his teacup in danger of falling from his hand. "If they buried them under the water, in the riverbed, at the pillars, they could simply blast through the stones, weakening the pillars themselves. Doesn't matter how many iron trusses are at the top then."

"That could be done?" I asked.

"It's done all the time, in mines, and in tunneling for railroads. It's why dynamite was invented—so men could lay charges in relative safety rather than messing about with black powder." He sat forward on the chair, his gaze leaving me to focus out of the window.

I rescued his teacup before tea could slosh to the floor. "Even so, I imagine you would have found the leavings of such things before now. And people in the village would have seen men going out in boats to bury the charges, or working under the pillars in the dry areas. As I say, it was only an idea."

Daniel sprang to his feet, his animation returning. "Fishermen run up and down this river all day, and a ferry boat still crosses it, in spite of the train. In the dark or mists, a larger boat could hide smaller ones—someone could build a fortress under the bridge like that and no one would notice until morning."

Indeed, the shadows beneath the bridge were thick and black, and the rain hid all but the lights above. Even those lights were beginning to smear to colored streaks on my windowpane. I set aside the teacup and rose to look out the window with him.

"If they dug deep," Daniel said, "and protected the charges as you suggest—even if some got too wet to detonate, enough would go off. They brought plenty of ammunition. Bloody hell."

He spun to me, caught me by the shoulders, and kissed me noisily on the mouth. "You are an amazing woman, Mrs. Holloway. Of all the great minds I have access to, *you* are the only one with any sense. You spark me. Thank you."

Another quick kiss—liberties I was allowing due to the anxiousness of the situation—and he was out the door, his step as exuberant as ever.

"Tea and scones," I said to the open door. "Nothing like them for settling the mind."

I put on my coat and gloves, snatching up a shawl for my head, and went downstairs and out. Daniel was not leaving me to drum my fingers and wait for him this time.

I could not be surprised when James joined me on the strand. He tried to be quiet about it, but I knew he was behind me—not because he made noise, but because I expected him.

The night had grown very cold, the wind blowing the storm higher. James stopped beside me, hunkering into a coat that was too big for him—one of Daniel's, I imagined.

"What's he doing?" James asked as we peered into the darkness.

The wind was high, muffling his speech. I stood on tiptoe to answer in his ear. "Looking for explosives in the river."

James shuddered and turned up the collar of his coat. "He'll be all right, won't he?"

I had no idea. I kept Daniel in sight for a time, while he shouted for the constables and other men to join him. Then they piled into a boat and rowed out into the water.

As the rain came down, the boat vanished into the mist and darkness. I could no longer see Daniel, and my heart beat with worry.

"He's clever," I said, to reassure myself as well as James. "He knows how to take care." When James turned a skeptical gaze on me, I shrugged. "He's lived this long," I amended.

We both fell anxiously silent.

The wind was strong and cold, so we retreated to the leeward side of the inn. I did not want to wait indoors—for some reason I thought things would go better if I remained outside. At least, I would feel less helpless.

"I wish I had a spyglass," I said after a time.

"Dad has some brilliant spyglasses," James said gloomily. "He took me out to the country once, away from the coal smoke, and showed me the stars through them. One had rings around it."

"That is a planet," I told him. "It's called Saturn." I thought about something Mr. Davis had read in the newspaper the other day. "He didn't show you the one that's supposed to be throwing off the orbit of Mercury, did he? A planet nearer to the sun?"

James shook his head, not looking very interested.

"There's no such thing," I said determinedly. "We have

eight planets, and that is all." I paused. "Perhaps your father would show me the stars someday."

I heard the wistfulness in my voice and hoped the rising wind disguised it from James.

"Wager he will. He likes you, Mrs. H. Ain't seen him like someone so much in a long time." James darted me a look of appeal, as though hoping I'd tell him that I liked his father in return. James had never had a family, not really. Perhaps he wished . . .

The turn of conversation was making me decidedly uneasy. "Mr. Rigby might have a spyglass. Or know someone who has, this being a fishermen's village so near to a port town. People must like to go to the harbor and watch for ships at sea to come in."

"Could be," James agreed.

I told James I would inquire, and I hurried back to the inn, but James came with me, perhaps worried he'd lose me as well if he let me out of his sight. I stepped into the inn, glad to get out of the cold, truth to tell, and hunted up Mrs. Rigby.

"A spyglass?" Mrs. Rigby asked in amazement. "What d'ye want one of them for on a night like this? You ought to stay in, you and the lad, before you catch your death."

"We will." I curbed my impatience. "When we know all is well."

"I'm guessing you want it to watch the constables climbing around to make sure the Queen comes through safely. Leave them to it, I say. Nothing you or I can do about it."

"I know." I could not think how to explain why I hated doing nothing, without sounding querulous, so I didn't bother. "Even so."

Mr. Rigby did not own a spyglass, but the elderly fisherman two doors down did. The man spent much time explaining to me how the device worked and then admonishing me to bring it back in one piece. At the last minute, he nearly didn't let me take it, declaring that women had no notion of how to work gadgets. James stepped in, however, assured him his father had taught him, and we took it away with us.

The problem with spyglasses is they need light upon which to focus. From what I understand, the light comes in through the lens and bounces off mirrors to the eye—that and you see everything upside down.

James and I returned to the leeward side of the inn and took turns training the glass to the middle of the river. At first, I could make out nothing, then gradually I discovered how to fix on the lights in the boats.

I saw men moving about in these boats, lanterns showing me flashes of one then another as the constables worked. The boats were surrounding the pillars in the middle of the river, the men leaning over, dragging sticks through the water, holding lanterns high.

I grew sick with fear. Any of the boats could stumble upon explosives and set them off accidentally. I couldn't tell which craft Daniel was in, but I knew he'd be at the forefront. Despite my reassurances to James, both James and I knew that Daniel could be reckless in his zeal.

However, nothing dire happened as we watched. Each minute brought relief, but also more worry because perhaps the *next* minute could mean catastrophe and disaster.

Eventually the boats spread out, fanning slowly through the river, which told me they'd found nothing yet. Perhaps our conclusions were completely wrong.

The church clock tolled through the night—midnight, one, two. James and I were driven inside by the cold, but we sat in the front room, neither of us willing to go up to our beds until this was over for good or ill. James nodded off in a chair, a faint snore issuing from his young mouth.

I remained rigidly at the window. I used the spyglass, better able to now that I could brace my elbows on the arms of the chair I sat in, though the window glass distorted things a bit.

By five, an hour before the Queen's train was due, I'd given up trying to see, and merely sat, waiting. James had in turn woken and paced and then sat and slept, and now he dozed again, slumped into his chair.

At half past five, the household began to stir. Mrs. Rigby and her two maids came downstairs to poke up fires and begin the day's cooking. I knew I ought to help with the cookery, but I could not bring myself to move.

"Good gracious, have you been here all night, Mrs. Holloway?" Mrs. Rigby asked as she trundled into the sitting room. "Everything will be fine, love. You'll see. Men just like to make a fuss."

As soon as the words left her mouth, I heard a shout rise from outside. It was answered by another shout and another—cries of alarm that turned to panic.

I could see nothing through the rain-streaked windows, and I was out of the room in an instant, running for the front door, barely remembering to snatch up my coat as I went.

I dragged on the coat as I dashed outside. Rain pelted down, making footing perilous, and wind whipped needle-like drops into my face. I ran for the river, and James came behind me.

On the water, lanterns were moving every which way, glowing through the rain and gleaming on the river's surface.

I heard yells of "Loose! Get it loose!" "Cut that rope *now*, damn you!" The last came from Daniel, his voice slicing over the others.

He was all right, I thought. He'd contain the situation, and they'd row in, damp, hungry, tired. All would be well.

The moment after this thought formed, my entire world lit up with a fire brighter than sunshine on a fine and fair day. The bridge glowed above us in silhouette, its reflection repeated on the ripples of water that boiled beneath it.

Pieces of wood and stone burst upward along with a sheet of water that erupted in a geyser, every drop glittering in the flames that shot high. A second later, a hot wind pushed at me, coming on top of a *boom* that shook my body and blasted the very air.

Shouts sounded as villagers rushed from their homes and from the inn, and fishermen who'd been going for their boats darted back from the water, cursing.

I stood in place, staring at the fire burning like a rope along the river, the light showing chunks of torn-apart boats floating on the surface. My body felt like ice, no blood flowing in my veins, while my throat dried and squeezed shut.

A body slammed past me, sending me staggering. "Dad!" James screamed and launched himself at the burning river.

23

James's dash for the water unstuck my feet. I ran after him, slipping and sliding on the rocks and mud and not caring a toss. My heart was beating again, pounding pain through me.

James ran right into the river. I couldn't catch him. He moved swiftly, and I struggled behind.

Another explosion rang high as we charged forward, hot shards of wood bursting from it to cut my face and singe my skin.

"Daniel!" I shouted. "Daniel!"

The river pulled at my boots. It was freezing, the leather of my shoes not meant to be plunged into flowing water. But I couldn't turn back, couldn't seek safety. Not until I knew.

Boats poured out of the fire, smoke, and rain, running for the shingle. Fishermen rushed into the river to help them, grabbing gunwales and hauling the craft up onto the strand. Constables and other men piled out of the boats, but none were Daniel.

My throat hurt from my screams, and my voice was broken, but I couldn't keep quiet. "What happened?" I yelled as the men climbed shakily to shore. "Where is Mr. McAdam?"

None would answer me. They were a quiet lot, round-eyed with horror—one constable staggered over the side of his boat and collapsed to the shingle. Another lifted him over his shoulder and carried him onward.

"Daniel," I whispered, no longer able to speak.

I could hear James ahead of me, his voice full of fear. "Dad! Dad!"

I started forward. Water poured into my boots, but I kept moving toward James's voice. My skirts were sodden, and tears trickled hotly down my cheeks.

Large chunks of debris tore by me, the water rushing with the great wave that had boiled out of its midst. In time, the waves would subside, and the natural flow of the river would carry the wreckage and stirred-up silt out to sea.

The glare of the explosions faded, but the dawn was reddened by fires that continued to burn. A few more boats slid up to the shore, but none of them held Daniel.

I wanted to sink down right there, never minding the chill water. I couldn't feel my feet, and I wasn't certain my legs would continue to hold me.

I knew in my heart that Daniel had gone to his death protecting a royal woman he'd likely never met, and a country that had consigned him to eking out his life on the streets as a child, that had consigned his son to the same fate before Daniel had found him.

The thought of never seeing Daniel's blue eyes twinkling with some secret, feeling the warmth of his smile, hearing the rumble of his voice, was an empty one. I wanted to be in my kitchen in London, rolling out my richly buttered pastry, scolding Daniel when he tramped in, pretending not to be charmed by him.

I wanted it so much I could feel the heat of the kitchen's stove, smell the butter and spices, feel the flour on my hands. I could hear his voice, low with laughter, Daniel making some quip as he stole whatever bit of sweet he'd managed to purloin from my table.

I snapped out of my daze. The warmth was the strange heat from the fires, but everything else was false, except for the voice.

I heard James shout, anguish in his cry, heard a rasp from beyond him. I sloshed forward, my skirts falling from my hands, the wet things twisting my legs and dragging me back.

Daniel came out of the smoke and mist, every bit of him drenched, his hair sodden with water, his face smeared with mud and soot. He cradled the body of a man over his shoulders, the man dead or alive, I could not say.

James splashed to them, reaching for Daniel, helping him. Daniel and James climbed from the water, Daniel hunched with his burden. They rose steadily from the wide shallows to where I waited yards from shore.

As they neared me, Daniel lifted his head and looked at me. His eyes were haunted but held a touch of triumph.

"What are you doing, Kat?" he asked, his voice cracking. "You know you are up to your knees, don't you?"

I tried to speak, but the only thing that came out was a hoarse, wheezing sound. Daniel sent me a tired smile and kept walking.

I woodenly turned around and fell into step with him and James, reaching up to steady the young man across Daniel's shoulders—who was alive. He was warm, breathing, and groaned when I touched him.

We reached the strand. Men and women swarmed us as Daniel set down the young man he carried. The lad proved to be a fisherman's son who'd volunteered to help look for the explosives, and his family surrounded him and took him away.

"He'll be all right," Daniel said, watching them go. He drew a ragged breath. "He was hit on the head when the boat went up, knocked into the water. I had a devil of a time finding him and fishing him out. Thought I'd lost him." He shook his head, a shiver of remembered fear moving through his body.

I had hold of Daniel's arm, and I couldn't seem to let it go. "Come inside. Get warm. And tell us *everything*."

"Not much to tell," Daniel said. We moved slowly toward the inn, he stumbling, but neither James nor I were much better on our feet. "We found the explosives, buried as you suggested, around the base of the pillars. They were in small barrels, sealed with tar and wax, buried well under the riverbed. We dug them out and floated them in boats, towing them far from the bridge. We were going to open them up and drown them when a man came out of nowhere at us, screaming, and lit the lot. Killed himself, the bloody fool. Might have killed others—I don't know yet."

"But you found it all." I rubbed Daniel's arm. His coat was sodden, his hair slick against his head. He'd freeze to death if we didn't quickly get him indoors.

"Yes." Daniel didn't sound as joyful as he could have. "But I have to wonder why they spread it so thin. All the sticks were accounted for, but divided up so that any one detonation would only make a small blast. Some of the barrels were far out in the river, nowhere near the bridge. They couldn't hope to topple it like that."

"But it certainly got our attention," I said. "Perhaps they only wanted to frighten the Queen away—to show what they *could* do—"

I halted off because Daniel was staring at me in horror.

At the same time, the cacophony of wind, rain, and voices was broken by the shrill note of a whistle, followed by the rumble of an engine. Sparks shot out from the top of the bridge as iron wheels met iron rails and a train turned to cross the Tamar from Plymouth to Saltash.

Daniel broke from me and began running, running, across the shore, around the inn, and up the lane toward the station. James, after one stunned moment, sprinted after him, and I came behind, lifting my soaked skirts, my feet squishing in my wet boots.

Daniel ran up the hill to where the tracks bridged the lane. He caught a branch of a tree growing close to the low end of the bridge, and used it to help pull himself up the steep bank to the top.

"James!" I shouted. "Run—tell the signalman to stop the train!"

James gaped at me but understood quickly. He dashed past me up the hill, tearing into the station.

The train came on. So did the three men who were hiding on top of the bridge over the lane, moving straight for Daniel. Daniel met them and they began fighting, the three large men surrounding and pummeling Daniel as the aristocratic lads had done in front of Euston Station in London.

I knew I'd never climb up the steep hill as Daniel had, so I ran on to the station and through it to the platform, hearing James yelling desperate commands at the signalman. I scrambled down from the low platform and ran along the track toward the bridge.

The men had piled rocks and other debris on the ties between the rails, I saw when I reached the spot where Daniel fought. Large stones, tree limbs, and boxes—of dynamite? My heart squeezed in fear.

Trains were heavy and powerful—one could easily sweep aside such things in the tracks, but a well-placed rock or tree branch could derail a train. Explosives would do terrible things if the train couldn't stop, and the men who'd been waiting alongside the train could do terrible things if it did. They would, if nothing else, break into the train and attack the Queen herself.

This train wasn't long, a locomotive pulling cars for the Queen and her entourage, and it chugged along fairly slowly. But it kept coming. I didn't know if the signalman had put out the flag for it to stop, and I couldn't turn to look without taking my eyes from Daniel and the men he fought.

At any moment, they would fling Daniel from the bridge, or they might all go over the side. Or, the train would hit the four of them, or any incendiary devices in the pile could go off.

It occurred to me dimly that an explosion or the train itself would hurt me as well, but all I could think was to stop the men from beating on Daniel and to get him well away.

The train's whistle sounded again. I heard the screech of wheels on rails as the train began to slow, the clanking of cars displaced by the change in speed.

The men were of good size and battering Daniel viciously. Daniel punched, kicked, spun, and elbowed, keeping the three at bay, if only barely. I realized as I watched that young Minty and his friends wouldn't have stood a chance if Daniel had fought them in truth.

Daniel spun in a crouch, bringing both arms hard into one man's middle. That man folded up, staggered, hit the low wall on the side of the bridge, and toppled over. He crashed through the trees and landed on the lane below, where he lay in a heap and moaned.

The remaining two men redoubled their efforts. Daniel fought harder as the train grew ever closer—despite it slowing, it would take some time to stop. Rain beat on my face and wind jerked at my skirts, bringing with it the smell of coal and, incongruously, the sulfurous odor of a match.

One man had broken away from Daniel, while the other still fought him. He ran to the heap of debris, and I saw a flare of flame in his cupped hands. He was going to light the pile.

I wasn't having *that*. I grabbed a stout branch that had been discarded on the track, and I ran at the man, raising my weapon high.

He never saw me. He reached to thrust his match into the debris at the same time my branch came down hard on his shoulder. The match spun away, dying in the wind as it fell to the wet ties.

The man whirled, snarled, and came at me. I drew back my weapon and smote him in the middle, a maneuver I'd learned on a day long ago, when a friend of my husband's had become far too ready with his hands. That day I'd had a rolling pin, and this early morning it was a branch, but the principle was the same.

The man grunted as he doubled over, but he was soon up again, his face so tight with his snarl it was like looking at a skull with skin stretched thinly over it.

I saw out of the corner of my eye that Daniel and the man he fought were struggling on the low wall at the edge of the bridge, the man pulling Daniel over onto the steep bank below us. I could not rush to make sure Daniel was all right, because the man I fought came at me once more.

I hit him again, this time in the face between those glaring eyes and drawn-back lips.

My attacker shouted and pawed at his face just as Daniel sprang back over the wall, the man he'd fought gone, and landed a blow on the side of my attacker's head with a balled-up fist. The man staggered, but as Daniel reached for him, the man twisted aside and sprinted away from us, straight toward the train.

The black bulk of engine came closer and closer, the round of its face, the glaring lamp above it, and the belching smoke-stack growing larger every second. The noise of the train drowned all other sound; the hiss of steam and shriek of the wheels filled my ears.

The man who'd attacked me ran right at the engine, and it hit him. Because the train had slowed, it only knocked him aside, but hard, and he tumbled rapidly over the wall of the bridge and vanished. If he screamed, I couldn't hear. The rum-ble of the wheels, the blast of the whistle, the roar of the engine suffused my body until nothing else existed.

The next thing I knew, something careened into me, wrapped me in tentacles, and yanked me from the tracks. It was Daniel, and in his arms I hit the side of the bridge, and then we were falling, down, down . . .

We halted abruptly on the nearly vertical grassy bank, Daniel having reached out to snag a thick branch of a tree with one arm. We hung there, face-to-face, the roar of the en-gine and clang of the bell moving by only a few feet above us.

I heard no crash, no explosion, just the metal wheels pro-testing as they slid on the rails, until the cars jolted again at the train's sudden lack of movement. Puffs of steam rolled upward, along with a billow of smoke, and constables swarmed from the station toward the train.

Daniel let go of the tree. We slithered down through mud and grass, he holding me and slowing our descent with his booted feet until we landed on solid earth beneath the bridge.

Cold wind blasted us through the cut in the hill, jerking at my skirts and tossing Daniel's wet hair. My legs were numb, and my knees buckled. But I didn't fall. Daniel had his arms around me and kept me on my feet.

He kissed me.

And such a kiss. Daniel pressed his hand to the back of my neck and pulled me up to him, his kiss hard and deep, the like of which I'd not had in a long, long time. Daniel's arms were shaking, even as solidly as he held me, even as soundly as he kissed my mouth.

When Daniel finally lifted his head, his breath was ragged, but so was mine, oxygen eluding me.

Daniel cupped my face with his torn, wet, and muddy glove. "Kat," he said, his voice the only thing I could hear. "What am I going to do with you?"

I stood toe-to-toe with him, speechless. For once in my life, not one thing came into my head to say.

James said it for me. "Bloody hell, Dad." He appeared out of the darkness, silhouetted by the glow of the lamplight from the station, the glare of the train's firebox, and the dawn light that touched the sky.

I tried to step away from Daniel, but his arm remained firmly around my waist. Because of this, when James launched himself at Daniel to grab him in a merciless embrace, he caught me in it too.

The breath went out of me entirely as I was squashed against Daniel and James both, Daniel's laughter in my ears like a soothing caress.

24

After the track was cleared of the detritus, which did contain two sticks of dynamite, the Queen's train rolled on
following its brief halt, clacking its way toward Penzance. The
engineer, worried and angry, gabbled with the police before
he climbed back into his aerie and nudged the train forward.

If the Queen had been awakened by the unscheduled stop,
I was not to know. She never appeared, nor did any of her
retinue.

I thought Daniel might accompany the train to make certain all was well for the rest of the journey, but he'd faded out
of sight as the police in uniforms began checking the train,
the tracks, and the station, and finally waved the train
through. The train was gone, and quiet descended on the village once more. The villagers themselves were shaken, but
tended to those hurt in the blast and then headed out to clean
up the debris in the river.

Dressed in dry clothes, James and I walked through the

village with Mrs. Rigby—I insisted on helping those in need, as shaken as I was. I knew that if I remained indoors, I'd only huddle in my bedchamber feeling sorry for myself.

I noticed as we moved along the shore carrying baskets of bread, James with blankets, that the cottage where the American nephews had visited was deserted. The villagers must know by now that the dynamite had come from there. The local constables would have let that slip, and the information would have flown to all ears. The villagers' own people had been hurt in the mad scheme, and they'd want justice. The woman must have decided to flee before she was driven out or arrested, if she hadn't been arrested and taken away already.

I did not see Daniel until James and I made our way back to the inn later that morning, both of us exhausted, though neither of us wanted to admit it. Daniel was there, seemingly out of nowhere—I hadn't seen him approach the inn as we walked back. He too was in dry clothes and informed us that we had just enough time to pack our things to catch the eleven thirty up to Town.

Dratted man. No mention of where he'd been or what he'd been up to, and he didn't linger to explain. He only slung his valise over his shoulder and left again for the station, where he'd purchase the tickets and meet us.

Mrs. Rigby was sorry to see me depart and insisted I take a basket heaped with bread, tea cakes, cold meat, and cheese so we wouldn't grow faint with hunger on our journey.

"You come and see us anytime, Mrs. Holloway," she said as she walked me outside. James was waiting for me, strolling along the river, looking up at the bridge that had taken so much of our attention. He was nearly as tall as his father now, their gait and stance so similar my heart missed a beat when I saw him.

Mrs. Rigby pulled me out of my contemplation as she handed me the basket. "You look after that Mr. McAdam now," she said. "I'd say he's a man what needs a lot of looking after. Mayhap when you return, it will be to take one room together?"

She gave me a coy look, and my cheeks grew warm. "I don't know about that, Mrs. Rigby," I said hastily as I took the basket from her.

"*I* know something about it." Mrs. Rigby's eyes glinted with amusement. "He's got fine manners, does Mr. McAdam, but he needs a bit of the softer life. Once he takes your excellent meals regular, he'll stop running around with policemen and stay home. You're a kind woman, Mrs. Holloway, and he's a good man. I know it."

Mrs. Rigby spoke as a woman who was long and happily married. I had been quite *un*happily married and knew the situation was a bit more complicated.

But I thanked her, shook her hand with affection, and trudged out to meet James. James gave me a grin, his spirits restored, and he took the heavy basket from me as we walked up the hill.

Daniel, dressed in his working-man's clothes, had procured third-class tickets this time, and while the compartment was nowhere near as comfortable and spacious as the first-class one, I breathed a sigh of relief as I sat down. The train was not very crowded this day, and we had the compartment to ourselves.

This time I took the forward-facing seat, with Daniel and James opposite me. I expected Daniel to fall asleep right away after being awake all night long—James kept nodding off—but Daniel only gazed out the window as we pulled out of the Saltash station.

The train crossed the bridge we'd spent so much time defending, the arcs of its iron beams soaring high and then bowing down as the small train snaked past them. Then we were on the other side, in Plymouth and Devonshire, the famous curved trusses falling behind us. The gale of the night had calmed, and now a gentle rain fell as the train took us into the countryside.

As I watched the bridge fade into the mist, the questions bubbling inside me came forth.

"How on earth did those men get all that debris onto the tracks without anyone noticing?" I asked Daniel. "I know you lot were rushing about the river looking for dynamite, but surely the signalman would have seen them creeping about near the station. He seemed a responsible gentleman, so he must have been at his post. The Queen's train was due any minute."

Daniel's eyes were tired as he turned to me, but I saw a gleam of triumph deep inside them. "The signalman was in on it," he said. "He was friends with the 'nephews' of the fisherman's wife and assisted them at every turn. He was arrested this morning. The fisherman's wife gave us the slip, but the police are hunting for her."

My mouth hung open as Daniel related the news about the signalman, but I closed it as my anger surged. "Drat the fellow. To think I gave him my best tea cakes."

James opened his eyes. "*I'll* eat your tea cakes, Mrs. H. I ain't no Fenian, I promise."

"No, but you are a bloody nuisance," Daniel growled at him. "I can't stop villains and their evil plots *and* keep you out of danger at the same time. Next time I tell you to stay in London, *stay* there."

James gave him a mutinous look. "Well, you don't have no call to go running about after villains at your age. You ought to stick to delivering goods and paying calls on Mrs. Holloway."

Daniel scowled, but I could see that James had been very badly frightened. I remembered his desperate cries for his father when he was terrified that Daniel had been killed. Daniel might believe James thought their connection casual, but James, I could see, had latched on to Daniel and wasn't about to let go. He'd been in need of a father, and then Daniel had appeared, not to stifle him, but to love him.

"I likely will, for a time," Daniel said, surprisingly compliant. "I wouldn't mind putting me plates up for a bit."

"Chuffed to hear it," James said, his frown in place.

"Where will you be putting up these plates?" I asked calmly. More rhyming slang: *Plates of meat—feet.*

"Yeah," James echoed. "Where?"

"Where I bloody well choose, lad," Daniel said in near shout. "I always tell you where I am, don't I?"

"Yeah," James said, deflating. That wasn't enough for him, I could tell. The poor lad longed for a home, a true family, though he might not admit it.

But perhaps people like us didn't have families, not in the way others did. We grubbed about doing our best, coming together when we could, enjoying the time in one another's company as something to treasure.

"You're welcome in my kitchen anytime, James," I said. "Your father, now . . . well . . ." I gave James a look of mock despair.

James laughed, as I had intended. "Cheers, Mrs. H. Don't be too soft on 'im." He unfolded his long body, steadying himself against the sway of the train, which had started trundling along at a good speed, and reached for the door to the corridor. "Just popping out for some air."

"No cigars," Daniel said sternly.

James looked crestfallen a moment, then brightened.

"Right you are, guv." He threw back the door in all exuberance, bounded into the corridor, and was gone.

"Bloody hell," Daniel said softly as he reached up and closed the door. "I forgot to say no pipes, cigarillos, cheroots . . ."

"Lecture him later," I said. "He is exhausted, and he was scared. As was I, of course."

"Yes, but you're not likely to hang off the end of the train smoking cheap tobacco. What am I to do with him, Kat?"

"What you've been doing," I said. "Be his dad. He admires you, but he's not going to worship you. Not at that age." I let out a breath, all of me suddenly craving to be back in the metropolis, in a lane near St. Paul's in particular. "My daughter will be his age in no time. Then she'll have no use for her old mum."

Daniel didn't answer for a time and only watched me, weariness lining his eyes. "Have you decided what to do?" he asked, his voice gentle. "About Grace?"

"I have." I glanced out the window at the rainy expanse of Dartmoor spreading to the horizon, so lovely, so empty, beckoning me to discover its secrets. "I will thank my friends for being generous and kind, but tell them Grace will remain my daughter. We've come this far together, she and I, and we'll continue."

"Good." The one word, spoken firmly, with Daniel's approving look, was all I needed. "I know a solicitor who can ensure Grace is permanently in your custody until she is of age, no matter who should appear and try to claim her. I assume your husband left no instructions for her upbringing, or any money for her care?"

"He left nothing but an old pair of boots," I said, ancient pain raising its head to see if I would acknowledge it. I didn't, and it subsided, dispersing to nothing. "Not even fit to be sold to the rag-and-bone man."

"Will you let me do this for you?" Daniel asked. "The solicitor I have in mind would do it as a favor to me, no expense."

My heart squeezed until it hurt. I had investigated my rights to Grace when a housekeeper I'd once worked with had mentioned that mothers could be separated from their children after the child was a certain age, especially if the father's family interfered. She was mine in her "tender years," but later, she could be taken if someone wanted her enough to fight for her.

If Grace was made my legal ward until she was twenty-one, then it would be much harder for anyone to claim her, or so I understood. I would have done such a thing long ago, but hiring solicitors cost money I didn't have, and I might have had to go to court, which would reveal to the world that she'd in truth been born out of wedlock. Such a thing might negate my custody of her altogether, because apparently women who bore illegitimate children had no natural maternal instinct. Absolute idiocy, but then, most law is written by men.

"Would it have to come out?" I asked in a small voice. "None but you and the Millburns know about Grace. I am not ashamed to be Grace's mother, but there is a matter of my employment. Few families want a brazen hussy as a cook."

Daniel's smile flashed. "Mrs. Holloway, I've never met a woman surer about right and wrong than you. My solicitor can do this without anyone in the world knowing but you and me."

I swallowed the lump that had wedged high in my throat. "Then please do." My answer began in a ringing tone then died to a whisper. "And thank you."

A fter all that had happened, I still was uncertain who had killed young Sinead or why. We didn't discuss it as we rolled the many miles back to London, but it was in my head.

Daniel seemed happy to assume she'd been murdered by the Fenians she'd been passing messages for, but I was not so certain.

One reason we did not discuss it was that by the time we reached Taunton, Daniel and James—restored to the compartment and smelling faintly of tobacco smoke—finally succumbed to fatigue. They'd partaken of most of Mrs. Rigby's basket, then they'd slept, each leaning against the walls on either side of the compartment like slumbering bookends.

My thoughts were running too feverishly for sleep, my mind spinning with the remembered terror of the explosions under the bridge, when I'd been convinced Daniel was gone forever, and then the fight on top of it.

The stunned moment when I'd stared down the locomotive, its iron face and blaring light coming straight at me, continued to play in my head. I could still hear the rumble of the engine, feel the hideous vibration of the ties under my feet, hear the loud clanging of the bell. The moment would be forever imprinted on my mind, would forever haunt my dreams.

My thoughts moved to the sensation of falling, and Daniel kissing me in a way he'd never kissed me before. He'd given me a lover's kiss, more intimate than anything I'd shared with my husband, even when I'd been in his bed.

I would have to think about that for a while.

Father and son didn't wake fully until we slowed to chug through the outskirts of London. They'd come alert from time to time when we stopped at stations along the way, but they'd take one look at the platform sign and sink back to oblivion. It was amusing to watch how they'd do it at almost exactly the same moment and in exactly the same fashion.

After Slough, they rubbed their eyes, stretched, blinked, and gradually regained their full senses.

It was late, the dark metropolis peppered with glows from gaslights on main roads, candles and kerosene lamps in windows, and fires here and there as men burned things outdoors to keep warm. Smoke crept over all, billowing from London's myriad chimneys.

"I am happy to be home," I said, peering out at the streets that rolled past us, the train sometimes lifting above them. "Why, when the country is quiet and green, the air much cleaner, does my heart beat with gladness when we rush through the mess that is London?"

"The Great Wen," Daniel said. James shot him a confused look, and Daniel shook his head. "I've heard it so called."

"Just means you're a Londoner, Mrs. H.," James said. "Like us. Country's pretty," he concluded. "But there ain't much to do there."

Whereas something new and different lurked around every corner of London, that was certain.

The train slowed mightily, the cars jerking against their couplings as we clanged our way into Paddington Station.

Daniel rose, obligingly lifting down my little bag and Mrs. Rigby's basket. "Shall I see you home, Mrs. Holloway?" he asked.

"No, indeed." I stood up and shook out my skirts. "I will be walking far down the corridor and exiting from a door at the end. If I'm seen climbing out of a compartment with you, Daniel McAdam, my reputation will surely be in tatters."

The next morning I descended to the kitchen after a night of fitful slumber and terrible dreams, and tied on my apron, longing for a normal day. This was Monday, my half day out, but Lady Rankin apparently had told Mrs. Bowen that because I'd just returned from an absence, I would have to forgo it.

Mrs. Bowen had already been up when I reached the kitchen this morning, and gave me the news. I was longing to go to Grace, but I'd have to grit my teeth and wait until Thursday. *That* full day would not be denied me, I vowed.

Mrs. Bowen did not ask me about my journey and what had happened—presumably Cynthia had told her the tale. She'd only said, "Is all well, Mrs. Holloway?"

I'd given her a reassuring nod. "It is indeed, Mrs. Bowen."

She'd nodded at me and gone above stairs, likely to marshal the forces to begin scouring every inch of the house, as they did every day.

I turned out dough Mary had left for me, tasting it before kneading in a bit more salt. She was doing well, was Mary, though she didn't yet have my experience. However, she was learning quickly.

As I divided the dough between pans and put them on the warm shelf to rise, I heard Mr. Davis trundle down the stairs. He stepped into the servants' hall to drop an armful of newspapers on the table, then came to the kitchen doorway, halted, and exclaimed in delight.

"Mrs. Holloway—I am so very, very happy to see you." He advanced, holding out his hands, but I didn't take them, mine being floury.

"Oh dear," I said in alarm as I wiped my fingers on a towel. "I hope your joy doesn't mean the temporary cook was so very awful."

"She weren't bad," Mr. Davis conceded. "Mrs. Curtis. But she didn't have your touch."

"Mrs. Curtis," I repeated. I called to mind a stern-faced, rather thin woman, who looked sour but was friendly in truth. "I know her a little. She is with my agency, but I've never sampled her cooking."

"All I can say is, I'm glad you have returned. Mrs. Curtis won't be here today—we received your telegram that you were on your way last night, and she went away after supper."

I hadn't sent a telegram. I assumed Daniel had when he'd purchased our tickets in the Saltash station.

Mr. Davis leaned against my table. "I was sorry to hear about your mum, Mrs. H. But I'm glad she's better."

My mum had passed away many years ago, but I nodded my thanks, going along with the story Daniel must have used to explain my absence.

I convinced Mr. Davis to cease leaning on my table, gave him a towel so he could wipe away the streak of flour he'd gotten on his trousers, and carried on with my cooking. I made a hearty breakfast for his lordship and Lady Cynthia of beefsteak, eggs, and a pork cheese—leftover roast pork and gravy that Mrs. Curtis had made, put into a mold with parsley, herbs, lemon peel, and nutmeg and served chilled. I saved a batch of this pork cheese for the staff, putting aside a lightly laden tray of bread and cold beef for Lady Rankin when she woke.

I saw nothing of Daniel, but I decided not to expect him to turn up. He might be with the police discussing what had happened in Saltash, or cleaning out stalls for Lord Rankin's head groom—possibly both these things and everything in between. Or he might be gone from Lord Rankin's house altogether, the trouble over. I wondered if he'd retain his rooms in Southampton Street near Covent Garden, or vanish from those as well.

Breakfast ended, and Mary and the scullery maid cleaned the pots and dishes. I scrubbed my wooden table, readying it for the meals I'd prepare during the rest of the day.

How restful it was to simply chop carrots, cut butter into flour for scones, muse upon which sauce I'd serve with the fish. None of these comestibles were liable to blow up, attack me with savage ferocity, or try to kill a man and boy I'd come to regard with fondness. We might have saved the monarch, even the empire, but I knew in my heart I'd send the empire to the devil as long as I never had to relive the moment I'd stood knee-deep in a cold river and believed I'd witnessed Daniel's fiery death.

During the lull in the middle of the day, after Lady Rankin's tray had gone up, the maids and footmen were upstairs cleaning, and Mr. Davis was in his pantry going over the wine, Lady Cynthia banged down the stairs and into the kitchen and threw herself into a chair at my table, just as she'd done the first day I'd worked here. She wore her gentleman's tailored suit and looked as haunted today as she had then.

"Hell," she growled.

"Everything all right, my lady?" I asked as I patted out dough to cut into scones.

"Don't go all prudish on me, Mrs. H. I feel wretched. Rankin was in a snit this morning because those financiers bankrolling the Fenians are being closely questioned, as is Lord Chalminster and his wretched son, Minty—I hope they throw Minty into a cell and let him rot. Rankin is upset because he's going to lose money. *Money.* That's all the bloody man thinks about."

I agreed with her, but I serenely cut scones and put them onto a flat baking pan. "You must admit, a bit of blunt is a good thing to have," I said.

"Ha." Lady Cynthia's pretty face puckered with a grimace. "There's a difference between being able to pay one's tailor's bill and becoming obsessed with numbers on a bank sheet. They don't even look real, do they? Just figures."

"And yet, those figures make the world go 'round," I said as I turned to set the pan in the oven. Nearly dying on a railway bridge had made me philosophical.

"And the worst is, I missed all the excitement." Lady Cynthia tilted the chair back on its legs so she could glance out the door into the servants' hall, then thumped forward, leaning to me over the table. "No one is about. Do tell, Mrs. H."

I wiped down my table then brought out my knife, carrots, and greens to prepare for the staff's afternoon meal. As I chopped, I related in a low voice all that had happened after she'd left Cornwall.

Cynthia lost her sour expression as she listened, and by the time I finished, her look turned admiring. "Good on you," she said with hearty approval. "That's the spirit. Will the Queen give you and Mr. McAdam medals? Mr. Thanos deserves one too. He figured out exactly where the target would be."

"I doubt it, somehow." I set aside my chopped carrots and began tearing lettuce for a salad. I'd keep it cool in the larder while I prepared the rest of the meal. "She likely won't know anything about us."

"Well, that would be a crime." Cynthia sat up straight and let out an unhappy breath. "Talking of crime, I cornered Bobby last night and asked her point-blank about Sinead."

I expected Cynthia to go on, but she fell silent, studying her fingers, which rested against the table's edge.

"Yes?" I prompted. I had my own ideas about Sinead's death, but I wanted to mull all possibilities.

"Bobby says she didn't do it." Cynthia heaved another sigh. "She's furious at me for believing she even could. I suppose she's right. I ought to have trusted her."

"Not at all," I said. "Lady Roberta was on the spot, and she would have had a good motive if Sinead did try to blackmail her about being covertly in the house. Lady Roberta might not have meant to kill Sinead, but was only trying to make her be quiet."

"Do you think Bobby's lying, then?" Cynthia asked me, dejected. "I'd swear she was telling the truth."

"I imagine she was. I was only thinking of possibilities." I wiped my knife clean and picked up a sharpening steel to run the knife along it for a moment. This is a different tool from a whetstone—the sharpening steel takes little nicks off the edges of the knife between uses and prevents it from going dull too quickly.

If Sinead liked to blackmail, I wondered if she'd done so to Lord Rankin as well. He with his proclivities for dabbling with the maids—she might have found him a mine of pocket money. If she had threatened to tell Lady Rankin of anything her husband had done to Sinead or any other of the maids, Lord Rankin would certainly have reason for wanting to silence her.

I continued to run my knife over the steel, absently, as I pondered. When I'd brought in the coffee my first night, when Rankin had asked for Sinead, what must he have thought? That Sinead had brought me in on her blackmailing scheme? That I was warning him we might go to his wife? The next morning, after Sinead had been found, he'd tried to have me dismissed. Because he feared I'd take over Sinead's blackmailing? Or because I'd realize he'd killed her?

"You're a dab hand with those knives, Mrs. H.," Cynthia said, sounding a bit envious.

I came to myself with a start. "Sharp knives do not slip and cut fingers," I said, trying to shake off my thoughts, which were going in the wrong direction, I was certain. "The cook who apprenticed me taught me how to be very cautious."

"Why didn't the killer use them, then?" Cynthia asked. "Instead of striking out with the bowl?"

"I keep them locked up. Far too dangerous to leave knives where anyone can snatch them up. The crime must have been committed in the heat of the moment. The killer didn't plan. Or didn't plan well."

"The Fenians?"

I laid my knife carefully on the table and sat down. "I have been thinking very hard about all this. If whoever killed Sinead was a Fenian—one, we assume, for whom she had been passing messages to and from her young man—why would he have left the paper with the times of the Queen's train on it? Surely he would have taken that, knowing it would reveal their plans."

"Hmm. Perhaps he didn't realize she had it."

"He would have searched Sinead to make sure she didn't have any messages at all on her. Then he would have searched the kitchen. And, most likely, if he meant to kill her, he'd have lured Sinead away from the house altogether. Why do it here and leave her in the larder?"

Cynthia looked thoughtful. "As you say, it was a crime in the heat of the moment. That's why Mrs. Bowen first thought that it was Sinead's young man."

"If her young man had been in London that night, I would have agreed with Mrs. Bowen most readily," I said. "Men have been known to lose their tempers and bash their wives or lovers on the head—too many, unfortunately. But we already know that Sinead's beau was in the north of England. Unless she had another lover?"

I sent Cynthia an inquiring look, but she shook her head.

"Sinead was devoted to the little tick," Cynthia said. "She was a romantic. But I take your point, Mrs. H. Why should a

Fenian come to the house at all? It would be too dangerous for him. Unless it was to make sure Sinead didn't tell Lord Rankin some important detail. Or perhaps he was onto the fact that Rankin was watching their financiers for foul dealings. But then, why wouldn't he try to off Rankin instead?" Cynthia sighed. "Pity he didn't. Sinead was a much kinder person."

"I thought you said she was a blackmailer," I pointed out.

"She was. A bit. She wasn't cruel or anything—she simply wanted to lessen her workload or put a few coins aside for her trousseau. As I said, the poor gel was a romantic."

"Tell me about her," I said, resting my elbows on the table. "She worked for your family before Lady Rankin married, you said."

"Yes, she came to London with us—Em wanted her. Mrs. Bowen too. As I said, Mrs. Bowen was an under-housekeeper, but she also acted as Em's lady's maid, and Em didn't want anyone looking after her house but good old Mrs. B. Then Rankin didn't want the expense of finding Em another lady's maid, so we make do with Sara. Sinead was a good worker but a bit too innocent, if you understand me. She thought God would protect her no matter what she did, because she wore a crucifix around her neck and lit candles in the church and said prayers to the Virgin."

I remembered the mark on Sinead's neck, which the coroner said meant she'd had a necklace there, wrenched away. I wondered why the killer had taken it.

"She was a scullery maid for your family?" I asked. "Why did your sister want to bring a scullery maid?"

Cynthia shrugged. "To look after her. Em grows fond of people. When she does, she feels responsible for them. Sinead rather adored Em, thought she looked like one of the Fair

Folk or some such. Em wanted people around her who made her feel special. She certainly wasn't going to get that from Rankin." Cynthia barked a laugh then became subdued. "Or me. I'm rather hard on Em, the poor kid."

It seemed to me that Cynthia had got the worst end of the bargain when Lady Rankin married, but I said nothing.

"I asked," I began slowly, "because I was wondering if someone Sinead had been blackmailing at your family home—your mother, father, another of the servants—became alarmed that Sinead would tell their secrets, came to London, and killed her. She'd have let someone like that into the kitchen without suspicion, knowing them so well. Sinead never raised the alarm or tried to scream, or even fight, which means she probably knew her killer. Knew him well. Or her." I had been fixated on a man having done this heinous thing, but the marble bowl had been heavy enough that a woman could have done much damage simply striking out.

"Oh." A flush spread across Cynthia's face. "I hadn't thought of that. I suppose . . ."

She trailed off, the terrible guilt in her eyes catching me off guard. *No*, I thought in dismay. *I have so come to like her . . .*

Before I could answer, another voice cut through the silence.

"You may cease speculating, Mrs. Holloway. I know exactly who killed Sinead. *I* did."

25

Mrs. Bowen stood on the threshold of the kitchen, her head up, so motionless that the keys on her belt were mute.

I remained seated as she stared back at me, her eyes glittering.

"Good Lord." Cynthia twisted out of her chair and came to her feet, her eyes wide in shock. "Mrs. B., how could you? What the devil did Sinead have on you that you would do such a thing?"

Cynthia's face was ashen, her equally pale hair and gray lips completing her colorlessness.

Mrs. Bowen flicked her gaze to Cynthia. "That is my business," she said stiffly. "My lady."

"But to *kill* her." Cynthia regarded her in horror. "If it was that bad, why not go to Em? Or come to me? Or Mrs. Holloway? We could have stepped in."

Mrs. Bowen shook her head. "No, you couldn't. I couldn't

take the chance she wouldn't give away my secrets to Mrs. Holloway. Sinead admired her."

I rose. I did not like that Mrs. Bowen tried to cast part of the guilt on *me*, if you please.

"But—" Cynthia began, but I held up my hand to silence her.

"She's lying, my lady," I said quietly. The defiance in Mrs. Bowen's eyes told me I was correct. "She didn't do anything to Sinead. She is shielding someone."

"Who?" Cynthia looked bewildered. "The only person Mrs. B. would try to protect is—" Her words choked off and she moaned, a sound of pure grief. "No." Her hand to her mouth to catch her sob, Cynthia bolted from the room.

I went after her. That is, I tried, but Mrs. Bowen reached out a strong hand and caught me by the wrist.

"Leave it," she snapped.

"I will not." I tried to jerk away, but Mrs. Bowen held me fast. "Sinead didn't deserve to die," I said, angry. "She was misguided, yes, but she was unworldly. An innocent. I could have brought her 'round."

"No, you could not have." Mrs. Bowen's fingers bit down. "You believe you hold the answer to everything, don't you? In this case, you do not."

This had gone far enough. Mrs. Bowen's grip was powerful, but I was quite fit myself. I yanked my wrist free and hastened out of the kitchen, past the servants' hall, and up the back stairs.

Mrs. Bowen came after me. "Stop!" she commanded.

I halted at the top of the stairs, before the door with green baize nailed to it, the barrier that shielded the genteel inhabitants upstairs from the noises of the kitchen and servants' hall below.

"What do you believe Cynthia will do?" I asked in a hard voice. "Do you not realize *she* will be in danger as well?"

Mrs. Bowen's expression turned to one of despair. "Go, then." She waved me onward. "There will be nothing you can do."

I intended to see about that.

I opened the door and plunged into a different world. I knew the back stairs would be full of maids and footmen going about their duties, so I took the front stairs in the elegant hall of the main house, empty at this time of day.

I didn't much like being upstairs in Mayfair houses—the halls were too quiet and too ornate, and belied the fact that it took an army of staff to keep it all clean. Silence reigned here, broken only by the quiet chime of a tall Chippendale case clock that must have marked time in this house for at least a hundred years.

Mrs. Bowen was on my heels. I lifted my skirts and ran up to the landing where I'd carried the tray of coffee to Lord Rankin on the first night of my employment. It seemed so very long ago now.

I took the door to the right of Lord Rankin's study and charged into Lady Rankin's boudoir.

Cynthia was already there. Lady Rankin—Emily—was seated at a writing table, her high-necked cream-colored gown as frothy and filmy as the one she'd worn the day I'd met her.

Facing her over the table was Cynthia, dressed in trousers, waistcoat, and frock coat, her feet in their heavy boots planted in a mannish style.

And yet, there was little difference between them. Both women were fair-haired, blue-eyed, and slender, both possessing the fragile air aristocrats could have—one that masked a hideous strength of will.

"Why did you do it, Em?" Cynthia was saying, her voice broken.

Lady Rankin blinked over the desk at her sister, then she

turned her head—slowly, as though she found the movement difficult—and regarded her cook and housekeeper standing breathlessly in the doorway of her private room.

"Mrs. Bowen?" she asked doubtfully, as though scarcely believing what she saw. "Please explain yourself."

Lady Rankin didn't look at me at all. Her gaze was for Mrs. Bowen, as though begging her to speak, to explain this strangeness.

Mrs. Bowen pushed me all the way inside the room and closed the door firmly behind us.

"My lady," she began, her voice taking on the tone of one not wishing to frighten a child. "I am afraid they know about Sinead."

Lady Rankin's brows came together in a puzzled frown. "Who?"

"Katie Doyle as she was properly, my lady. We called her Ellen. She liked the name Sinead." Mrs. Bowen drew a breath and, as Lady Rankin continued to regard her with the same bafflement, went on. "They know she threatened you. You should have come to me, my lady, as you always did before."

Lady Rankin's puzzlement left her, and hurt filled her light blue eyes. "You weren't here. I did look for you, but you weren't here."

I remembered the upstairs maid telling me that Mrs. Bowen had gone out the night of Sinead's death, to be with her beau, Mr. Greer. I'd berated myself for not staying downstairs longer with Sinead that night, but Mrs. Bowen had not been there at all. Mrs. Bowen had sent this same Mr. Greer into the house the next night to hunt for the torn part of the paper she'd found in Sinead's apron pocket.

Had Mrs. Bowen truly wanted to shield the fact that Sinead had been a go-between for members of the Fenians, or had she thought the paper meant something else? Something to do with Lady Rankin? When Daniel and I had discovered that it indeed was connected to the Fenians, Mrs. Bowen had retreated and not objected to us and Lady Cynthia pursuing the matter.

"It was something to do with your family," I said to Lady Rankin. I was guessing, but I was fairly certain I was correct. "Something it would never do for Lord Rankin to discover."

Lady Rankin at last acknowledged that I was in the room. "You are clever, Mrs. Holloway. I knew it as soon as I met you. And such a good cook."

She smiled a watery smile, but she couldn't melt my heart. Sinead had been on the verge of womanhood, poised to begin life, and that had been taken away from her. Yes, she'd made foolish mistakes, but those could have been corrected before it was too late. Lady Rankin hadn't given her the chance.

Cynthia broke in, anguished. "What was it, Em? What the devil did she know that was so important?"

Lady Rankin laid down her pen as though it had grown too heavy for her. "She knew about Papa. Poor, dear, feckless Papa."

"Oh." Lady Cynthia went gray. "Bloody hell." She drew a long breath. "But it doesn't matter anymore, does it? It's finished—it doesn't *matter*."

"It would matter to dear Charles," Lady Rankin said. *Charles* was Lord Rankin. "He sets such store by these things. And he hates deception. That's why he doesn't like you in men's clothing." Lady Rankin reached across the slim desk and ran a delicate finger over Cynthia's sleeve. "I find it droll, myself."

Mrs. Bowen broke in, her voice hard. "Say nothing more, my lady. I will take care of it. I will look after you, as I always do."

"No." Lady Rankin rose and drifted to the chaise longue near her bed. "No, I will explain. It will get into the papers—Charles won't like it, but I won't be here to see him grow angry. I'll be locked away, won't I? For killing Ellen? Then hanged."

She sank down on the chaise, looking woeful but not too worried. I realized as I watched her that, like Cynthia, she was playing a part. I'd thought the same about both of them the first day I'd met them. Lady Rankin was taking the role of delicate, pampered daughter of an aristocrat, spoiled and disinclined to do anything she did not want to. She'd continue playing this role for the magistrate, and then for the judge and jury, if she even reached the courtroom. She would play the scandal for all it was worth, I imagined.

Their parents had been wild in their youth, from what I'd heard of the Earl and Countess of Clifford, confirmed by Mr. Davis's gossip. So had their brother. Why should the daughters of the family be any different?

"She oughtn't have argued with me," Lady Rankin said. "I couldn't have her keep coming to me about it, could I?"

I imagined the scene, Lady Rankin gliding down the back stairs when everyone else was in bed to meet Sinead in the linen room, to give her—money? A gift? A promise? For her continued silence. I'd had the feeling that night that Sinead was lingering to meet someone, but I'd never dreamed it had been the lady of the house.

Perhaps Lady Rankin had tried to tell Sinead the gifts were finished, and Sinead had threatened to tell Lord Rankin what she knew. The heavy bowl of the mortar and pestle had been sitting on the table, near to hand. Easy for Lady Rankin to snatch up and swing, for Sinead to go down.

I could picture Lady Rankin then realizing she should try

to hide her crime and tucking the bowl into a dark corner of the dresser and pulling Sinead into the shadows. Sinead had not been a large girl. Lady Rankin—whom I suspected was not as fragile as she pretended to be—would likely have been able to manage it. She probably hadn't thought much beyond this half-hearted attempt—Sinead's death could easily be put down to a housebreaker or perhaps the violent young man she walked out with. Lady Rankin might have had no idea that the young man had been in jail in the north of England and so had an alibi. I wondered if Lady Rankin had taken the necklace that had been around Sinead's neck—something she had given Sinead herself? Or perhaps Mrs. Bowen had, in her anguish, wanting something to remember the girl and her mother by.

Mrs. Bowen, out for the evening with Mr. Greer, had not been able to stop the murder. She must have guessed right away that Lady Rankin had done it, the only person in the house with a motive to kill Sinead. No wonder Mrs. Bowen had shut herself away in her rooms the next morning, unable to face me, unable to face anyone, until she worked out how she felt about Lady Rankin's guilt and what to do. She'd gone on about Sinead's young man and about Fenians to throw me off the scent, perhaps. She'd distracted me from the truth just as had the villains focusing attention to the explosions on the bridge while they hid near the station and waited to murder the Queen.

"I am tired now, Bowen," Lady Rankin said as I stood in dazed silence. "Please bring me my tonic."

She addressed Mrs. Bowen as though she were still a lady's maid. Lady's maids were called by last name only—housekeepers and cooks were given the honorific of *Mrs.*

Lady Rankin lay back on the chaise as Mrs. Bowen obediently went to the bedside table. I heard the clink of glass on glass, the trickle of tonic from the bottle.

Lady Cynthia remained frozen by the desk, and I closed my fists as Mrs. Bowen handed Lady Rankin the tonic. "Now you drink that down," Mrs. Bowen said. "You'll have a nice sleep."

Lady Rankin took the glass. "Thank you," she whispered.

For one moment, stark fear entered her eyes, then she firmed her mouth in resolution, and lifted the glass to her lips.

"No!" I cried, coming out of my transfixed state, but too late. Lady Rankin gave me a faint smile as she poured the tonic into her mouth and swallowed it.

I started forward, but Mrs. Bowen put herself in front of me. "It will be all right, Mrs. Holloway. Take Lady Cynthia and go."

My body had gone so tight I could scarcely breathe. But I understood. I moved woodenly to Lady Cynthia and touched her arm.

Cynthia jumped as though I'd sent a spark through her. She stared at me then at her sister, and then she jerked from me and fled the room.

I followed her more slowly, turning back at the door. "I'm sorry," I said, more to Mrs. Bowen than Lady Rankin. "But it wasn't right."

Mrs. Bowen shot me a furious look. "This is *your* fault."

It was not, but my heart was heavy.

Lady Rankin seemed to have forgotten all about me. "You'll stay with me, won't you, Bowen?" she asked, gazing up at the older woman.

Mrs. Bowen lost her anger as she looked down at Lady Rankin, tenderness in her eyes. "Of course I will, dear. Don't you worry. I'm here now."

I turned away, my chest hollow, and closed the door.

I heard sobbing from behind a half-open door on the other end of the landing. I walked to it on quiet feet and peered inside to see Lady Cynthia sitting on a chair in a bedchamber, slumped forward, face in her hands. She wept, her back shaking.

I went to her and laid my hand on her shoulder. "I am sorry," I said, in a much gentler tone than I'd used for Mrs. Bowen. "Come downstairs with me. Don't stay up here alone."

Cynthia raised her head, her face mottled red and white and covered with tears. She swiped at her cheeks with the back of her hand. "Are you going to give me a tonic as well?" she asked, her voice barely a whisper.

"Not at all," I said. "I was thinking more along the lines of a strong bottle of wine. Mr. Davis left me a fine Burgundy for the sauces tonight, but I think he'll understand if we each take a fortifying glass of it."

L ady Cynthia poured out the wine in Mrs. Bowen's parlor, saying Rankin couldn't sack *her* for pilfering it. I accepted my glass gratefully, letting the thick-bodied wine settle my shakes while Cynthia explained why her sister had done what she'd done.

"Poor dear Papa, as Em calls him, is good at fraud." Lady Cynthia took a long sip of wine and lolled back in Mrs. Bowen's Belter chair. "Always has been. When he was younger, he'd coerce friends to invest in nonexistent ventures—things like that. Never made much at it, because he'd feel guilty and return most of the money, telling them the investment hadn't come to fruition. And then a grand scheme fell into his lap."

She drank deeply of the Burgundy and refilled her glass, while I took another sip. The wine was very good—all Lord

Rankin's were—which was why my sauces could be so rich and savory.

"The Earl of Clifford—the one before Papa—died," Cynthia went on. "So there was the earldom, with its cash, large house, land, title, and instant respectability, ripe for the taking. So Papa took it. Oh, he was an heir," she added as my eyes widened. "But not as far up in the succession as everyone thought. He doctored the family tree."

"Good Lord." I blinked, then frowned. "But how could he? Surely people would know who was who." The upper-class families I'd worked for had all had a clear and almost fanatic knowledge of their bloodlines.

Cynthia's words began to slur. "Not when the Shires family was scattered to the four winds. The previous earl had no sons. He had cousins, but they were distant—third, fourth, fifth. It was all written down somewhere, but no one bothered to look hard for the documents. The solicitors took the papers my father produced, which claimed he was a second cousin, as genuine. Truth was, he was a lot more distant than that— probably fourth or more in the line of succession. And so my father stole the earldom." She rested her head on the ornate carving on the chair's back. "No one knew except me, Em, Mrs. Bowen, and my mother and father, of course. I suppose Sinead got hold of the information and used it to finagle little presents and money out of my sister as she did. I'll wager Em wasn't bothered so much when we lived in Hertfordshire, but after she married Rankin, well . . ." Cynthia took a gulp of wine. "Em would pay to keep such a thing from Rankin, wouldn't she?"

"Surely it's not that easy to steal a title," I said. "These other cousins must have protested."

Cynthia shrugged. The shoulder of her jacket caught on a bit of carving on the chair's back and stayed there. "I believe Papa paid them, once he came into the money, which is one reason he went through the blunt so fast. One cousin was going to put up a stink, but then he took sick and died in an apoplectic fit. Stroke of luck, my father used to joke. Horrible of him. The others have died off as well, so Papa truly is the earl now."

"Lady Rankin would know that," I pointed out. "She had no more cause to worry."

"Oh, she would if Sinead told Rankin," Cynthia said. "Old Rankin would make Em's life hell—both because Papa was such a confidence trickster, and because Emily had hidden the story. Rankin would never have married Em if he'd tumbled to the truth, and Em knows it."

"I believe you." I sighed. Lord Rankin wasn't above double-dealing himself or chasing maids in his own household, but he strove to put forth a show of utmost respectability, especially in his marriage. A man trusted with other people's money had to live an impeccable life. If anyone discovered that Lady Emily's father shouldn't have been the Earl of Clifford, that fact would disgrace Lady Rankin and have her shunned, possibly Lord Rankin with her. The fragile-looking aristocrats were unforgiving.

"I imagine she was afraid Rankin would divorce her," Cynthia said. "Or that he'd put her away somewhere, like in an estate in the back of beyond, and not let her out. Em loves society. She'd waste away like that."

Indeed. The delicate Lady Rankin was not made to be a country woman in stout boots who hosted shooting parties and ran village fêtes.

I firmed my lips. "Even so, she should not have killed Sinead. It was a wicked, terrible thing to do."

"I know," Cynthia said glumly. She drained her glass of wine and reached for the bottle. "And she'll pay for it, I suppose. God, this is going to be awful."

"What will you do now?" I asked, softening my tone.

Cynthia drew back her hand before she touched the bottle, and set down her glass. "I don't know. Maybe go with Bobby to the seaside. But she wants . . ." She let out a breath. "What I don't want." She shook her head and looked miserable.

I understood. Mr. Thanos had asked Cynthia if she were a hermaphrodite, by which he meant a woman who prefers the company of women—in all respects. Cynthia had answered in the negative. Bobby, on the other hand, must have those proclivities, and wanted Lady Cynthia to share them. It was a trouble I'd had no experience with, but pain was pain, no matter what.

"Would you have an objection to marrying?" I asked her. "If the right gentleman proposed?"

Cynthia stared at me, and then barked a laugh. "Me, marry? What man would have me? And even if one did ask me, he'd have to take me as I am. I refuse to squeeze myself into a frock and act as though I haven't got an opinion in my head except what my husband decides for me. No man is worth that."

I understood. I wouldn't put up with a man who dictated what I should believe either.

When a woman marries, her husband becomes her lord and master. All very well if the gentleman in question is intelligent, reasonable, sweet tempered, well-mannered, and sensible—but it is a rare man, in my experience, who possesses all those qualities.

"Well," I said regretfully as I lifted my glass. "I suppose I'm out a place. My name will have to go back on the books."

"No reason for it to." Cynthia reached across the table and put her hand on my wrist. "Please stay with me awhile, Mrs. H. I'll see that Rankin pays you a proper wage and a bit extra besides."

Her pleading look was more than I could bear. I nodded, though I moved my hand to take another drink of wine, which made her fingers slip away. It would never do for the lady of the house—which was what Cynthia would become, if only temporarily—to be too friendly with the servants.

"I will remain," I said. "Until everything is settled."

Cynthia let out a breath of relief. "You're a peach, Mrs. H.," she said, and raised her glass to me. "Thank you."

Lady Rankin died in her sleep. The household was told this the next morning, relayed by Sara, who came flying downstairs in near hysterics, babbling that Mrs. Bowen had found her on the chaise, dead as a stone. Apparently, Lady Rankin had accidentally drunk too much of her tonic.

The staff gathered around, distressed and worried, both for Lady Cynthia and for themselves. A house without a mistress would break apart.

I knew exactly what had happened, and remained silent. I remembered Mrs. Bowen insisting Lady Rankin take the glass of tonic, and the flash of fear in Lady Rankin's eyes, followed by resignation. Mrs. Bowen had decided that her lady should not face the ignominy of arrest, trial, and conviction, then scandal, imprisonment, and death.

Possibly Lady Rankin would never have gone to trial—Lord Rankin had enough power, money, and connections to have the charges dismissed, and he might appeal to Daniel and whoever Daniel worked for to help. Or, if Lord Rankin couldn't completely keep his wife from being tried, at least he might be able to save her from the gallows. Mrs. Bowen must have believed she couldn't take that chance.

Lady Rankin had been aware of what Mrs. Bowen had done, I knew, and she'd chosen to drink the tonic, taking what she thought the simplest way out. Her brother had once decided the same thing.

The preparations for Lady Rankin's funeral took up the next few days, and I of course had to prepare the meals for those who'd return with Lord Rankin after Lady Rankin was placed into the tomb of the barons Rankin in Surrey.

At one point as Mary and I worked on the after-funeral repast, I caught Mr. Simms in the larder with his hand on a top shelf, helping himself to cheese tucked into a cool spot—he'd been cutting bits off the edges, all the way around, so it would look uniform if anyone checked it. I scolded him soundly, and he was so guilt stricken he emptied his pockets of fruit he'd taken—pieces from different boxes so too many wouldn't be missed. He also confessed it had been he who'd eaten the dinner I'd put aside for myself the night I'd slipped out to have a chat with Daniel. That mystery was solved, then. Bloody man.

I was prepared to tell Lord Rankin about Simms, but decided to spare Lord Rankin for the moment when I saw how ill and shaken he looked when he climbed down from the carriage upon his return from Surrey and entered the house. He was followed by the guests and family, including the Earl and Countess of Clifford, who had their heads bowed in grief. They looked nothing like a blackguard who'd stolen an earldom and the famous beauty who'd caught his eye. Now they were middle-aged, graying, and in debt, having lost two of their children in shocking circumstances.

Cynthia held Rankin's arm—she was dressed in a somber black gown and hat with a veil—and he leaned on her as they walked inside.

I had agreed to stay on through the funeral and until Lady Cynthia decided what to do. She did not want to go home to Hertfordshire with her family. Lord Rankin, in a curious fit of generosity, had told Cynthia she could remain in the Mount Street house as long as she liked, while he took a sabbatical at his estate in Surrey for a period of mourning. I was not certain what working directly for Lady Cynthia would be like, but I decided to remain where I was and see what happened.

Mrs. Bowen had gone. She'd helped lay out Lady Rankin, then she'd departed, telling me the coroner had released Sinead's body to her after the inquest—which had returned the verdict of death by misadventure by person or persons unknown. The blame was put down to a burglar she surprised, and the violent nature of life in the metropolis was condemned.

Mrs. Bowen would take care of Sinead's funeral, she'd told me in a firm voice. She was the only family Sinead had now.

I did not see Mrs. Bowen again, and where she'd gone, I was never to learn. Perhaps she'd marry her Mr. Greer, a man who'd agreed to search the larder of a Mayfair house in the middle of the night at her command. A devoted gentleman, indeed.

I knew Mrs. Bowen had killed Lady Rankin. She had committed murder as much as Lady Rankin had. But I said nothing. I knew why Mrs. Bowen had done it, and I hardly condoned her action even if I understood it, but proving the matter would be difficult. There was nothing to say Lady Rankin hadn't given herself a second dose of tonic sometime later in the day, which was what the coroner believed happened. He'd already given his verdict of accidental death, and so the record stood. I decided, after wrestling with my conscience, to keep my silence. The stark truth, at this point, helped no one.

The day after the funeral, I took my day out–Thursday was always mine, no matter what–and visited my daughter.

I'd already written to my friend Joanna, upon my return to London, and told her that I declined her and her husband's offer to adopt Grace. I thanked them for their kindness, as I'd told Daniel I would, but explained that I could not accept. Today, Joanna embraced me and told me she understood. I could see she was disappointed, but she was a good and kind soul, as was her husband.

Grace, who knew nothing of this, was chatty and happy, and we had our outing, this time a walk in Hyde Park followed by our treat of tea in a shop.

I left Grace again, holding her as I hugged her good-bye, letting her child's arms around my neck soothe me. I walked away from the Millburns' and trudged toward home, my eyes blurred with tears.

As I made my way along Ludgate Hill, a young man stepped abruptly out of the crowd and halted directly in front of me.

"James," I said with a gasp, and pressed my hand to my heart. "You *really* should not do that."

26

"Sorry, Mrs. H.," James said, though he didn't look one bit apologetic. "Only way I could think to stop you, you were walking so unswervingly. His nibs wants to see yer. In his digs."

"I suppose you mean your father, in his rooms on South-ampton Street," I said.

"That I do." James gave me his lopsided grin. "He said to put you into a cab so you wouldn't have to walk. He'll pay the fare at t'other end."

A hansom waited in the road for me, driven by Daniel's friend Lewis, other vehicles moving impatiently around it. I imagined Daniel had sent Lewis and his cab not only to save my feet but to prevent me from ignoring his summons.

Nothing for it. I headed for the hansom. James helped me in, but he did not climb up beside me.

"Aren't you coming with me?" I asked. I hadn't seen him in days, and I wanted to discover how he fared—I'd become quite fond of James.

"Naw." He shrugged. "I'm off to do a little of this, a little of that. Nothing bad, Mrs. H.," he added quickly. "Odd jobs. For pay."

I shook my head. "Mr. McAdam really ought to find a house where you two can live together. So you can keep an eye on each other."

James shrugged again, his young shoulders jerking up and down. "I don't know about that. If I lived with Dad, he'd be terribly underfoot, wouldn't he?"

I gave him a skeptical look, and he returned it with a serene, dark-eyed gaze. I supposed he and Daniel would work out between themselves what they would do. I also knew I had not mistaken the great love I'd seen in James for his father when he'd thought Daniel dead in the blast in Saltash.

James raised his arm to wave the cabbie on, and we jolted off. Not long later, I was admitted to the house in Southampton Street by Mrs. Williams, Daniel's landlady, who stood back discreetly and let me ascend the stairs to Daniel's rooms alone.

I found him in his sitting room, which had been dusted, swept, and polished until it glowed, a faint scent of wax lingering in the air. Daniel wore a neutral suit today—the only way I can describe it—a dark gray ensemble that was neither citified nor working-class. His hair hung in thick waves, the way I preferred it.

He came to greet me with correct politeness when I entered, and he led me to the small sofa. "How are you, Kat?" he asked as I seated myself.

"As well as can be expected," I answered. "And you?"

Daniel gave me a copy of James's tilt-mouthed grin and dropped into the plain chair he'd drawn near. "The same. Tea?"

He, or more likely Mrs. Williams, had brought in a low table filled with a tray, porcelain cups and saucers, a teapot, a mound of cakes, and two delicate plates. Daniel reached for the pot, but I waved him away and was mother—that is, I served the tea for both of us.

"Has the Queen summoned you yet?" I asked him as I poured out. "To give you a knighthood for saving her life?"

"No." Daniel looked amused as he accepted the cup I handed him. He waited until I had one ready for myself before taking a sip. "I doubt she'll ever know I was there."

I lost my constrained formality and gave him an indignant look. "That is hardly fair. Without your diligence, her train would have run smack into that dynamite, and she'd have either been blown to bits, or murdered by those men lying in wait."

"I know," Daniel said with irritating patience. "And *your* diligence too, Kat. And Thanos's. And Lady Cynthia, who found out for us where the Queen was going on her supposedly secret journey. But it doesn't matter. The Queen is safe—at least for now. She will praise the policemen at the scene and her brave engineer, and that will be that. I prefer it so."

I took another sip of tea and handed him a seedcake on one of the small plates.

"Because you wish to remain in the shadows," I said in sudden understanding. "So that the next villains will not know you are after them. They won't expect you."

"Exactly," Daniel said. He lifted the cake and took a large bite. "Mmph," he said as he chewed and swallowed. "These came from a bakery down the street. Never as good as yours."

"Do not ply me with flattery, Mr. McAdam." I nibbled a piece of cake and had to agree with him—my seedcakes were far richer, and I used more caraway. "Tell me why you asked to see me."

"To make certain you were well."

Daniel knew all about what happened to Lady Rankin—Mr. Davis had spied Daniel in the street before the funeral and gone out to relate the tale, though Daniel had not returned to the house with him. He'd resigned his post, Mr. Davis had said, shaking his head at Daniel's itinerancy. Whether Daniel had concluded that Lady Rankin had killed Sinead, or still believed a Fenian had done so, I did not know, and I did not want to speak of it now. When I felt better, we could discuss things.

However, I hadn't seen Daniel since we'd parted at Paddington Station, and he hadn't bothered to send word to me or tell me good-bye. He might have had a good reason why he could not—those he worked for might have kept him away—but I was not about to let him know I understood.

"I'll do," I said, lifting my teacup.

"And to explain," Daniel went on, "why I can't explain things." He regarded me openly, no more guile. "I would tell you my secrets, but they are not my secrets to tell. One day—I promise you." He reached for my hand, took the teacup from it and set it down, and then twined his fingers through mine. "One day."

"But not today," I said, echoing my words from the previous occasion.

Daniel's expression held hope. "Can you forgive me for that?"

"Probably not," I said. "Though it will depend on what the secret is when I learn it. What I do know, Daniel, is what *you* are. It doesn't matter whether you're a gent in a posh suit who can purchase first-class railway tickets on the spur of the moment, or a deliveryman who talks like a South London villain. I've seen *you*."

Daniel's dark brows went up. "I'm not certain I like that."

"You ought to. I've seen that you're a good man. You sacrifice much for the well-being of others. You're kind to your son—a lad you could have turned your back on, and no one would have condemned you for it. Except me, of course. No matter which guise you wear, that man is beneath it."

"Well." Daniel's voice turned soft, and he caressed the backs of my fingers. "Thank you, Mrs. Holloway."

His lips parted as though he would like to say something else, then he shook his head and closed his mouth again.

"What?" I asked. His hand on mine was making my heart beat erratically, and I wasn't comfortable with that. I did not draw away, however.

"I was thinking how fortunate I was to have met you," he said. "Remembering delivering a bushel of potatoes to Mrs. Pauling a year or so ago, tramping down into the kitchen to behold a cook with glossy dark hair turning a rather scornful expression on me—with eyes I could drown in."

I remembered the occasion well, how I'd stood numbly at the stove, holding a spoon in midair while hot fat dropped onto the slates at my feet. I'd had to scrub them hard later.

Daniel had smiled at me, and the world had changed.

"Do not be so silly," I said, easing my hand from his clasp. "You cannot drown in eyes."

Daniel sat back and took up his teacup but didn't drink. "You don't like poetry, then."

I did enjoy *this*, having tea with Daniel as though we belonged together, with nothing pressing at us, nothing taking us from the moment.

"Poetry has its place, I suppose," I said, as he seemed to be waiting for my response.

He shrugged. "Ah, well. I will search until I find something you *do* like."

"I doubt that will take long. I am easy to please. A comfortable chair, seedcake that is better than this, and good company. I can't ask for much more than that."

Daniel sent me a knowing look. "So you claim to be uncomplicated. But I know better. There are layers and layers of you—each time I peel one layer back, I find another more intriguing beneath it."

"What absolute rot," I said. Grace was right—*rot* was a perfectly good word.

Daniel shook his head, his laughter rumbling. "You'll be the death of me, Kat Holloway."

"Goodness, I hope not."

A vision flared through my head of the explosion on the river, of the blinding light in the darkness, James screaming for Daniel, as I could only stand mutely, fearing a loss that would tear me in two.

Daniel was beside me in the next moment, his arms around me, and I found myself drawing a long, burning breath, though I hadn't been aware I'd been holding it.

"Forgive me," he whispered. "I wouldn't blame you if you chucked me in, told me to go to the devil."

"No, indeed," I struggled to say. "I would never use words like that."

Daniel laughed softly as he kissed my hair. "I will weather what I have to if I can count you as my friend."

"Of course." I cleared my throat, finding it difficult to speak. "I will save tea and scones for whenever you waltz into my kitchen without so much as a by-your-leave."

"Will you make it seedcake?" His lips touched my hair again.

"You will take what I have on hand, you daft man."

"That's enough for me, Kat." Daniel tilted my head toward him and gave me a brief kiss on the lips. "That's plenty enough for me."

Author's Note

Thank you for reading!

I conceived of Kat Holloway, the young cook in Victorian London, so long ago now that I no longer remember my first inspiration for the stories (this was before my very first novel was published). I know that the no-nonsense Kat in command of her kitchen has been dancing around in my head for years, as well as the mysterious Daniel McAdam and his son, and various other characters in her saga.

The inspiration for finally putting Kat's story into readable form, however, was a broken water heater. This modern and conventional appliance flooded our house, with the result that we had to tear up all the old flooring and have new put down. This forced me to clear out closets that hadn't been emptied in a good long while, and there, in a box, I found a folder with the beginnings of a Kat Holloway mystery.

I'd had many books published since jotting down the few chapters, and I grew excited as I remembered Kat and my plans for her series. I transferred what I'd written of the story to my laptop, and then kept typing. That story turned into *A Soupçon of Poison*, which I published to introduce Kat to my readers.

The response was amazing—so many wrote to tell me how

much they enjoyed Kat Holloway and hoped to see more! I sat down and started working on a full-length novel, and the result is *Death Below Stairs*.

I very much enjoy writing about a cook and the world beneath London's elegant houses. My primary resource for Kat's kitchen and all she makes in it is *Mrs Beeton's Book of Household Management*, first published in 1861.

Isabella Beeton was a young Englishwoman who wrote articles on cookery and housekeeping for a magazine her husband edited and published—she was more or less a food blogger of her day. The *Book of Household Management* was a compendium of articles and magazine supplements she and her husband had put together, published into one volume.

The book was an instant bestseller and went on to become an enormous success, even after Isabella's tragic death in childbirth at the young age of twenty-eight. Edition after edition was published well into the twentieth century, and the book still continues to be printed.

In it, the Victorian housewife could learn everything she needed to know about the running of a household, the duties of various servants, where to find a good stove, and of course hundreds of recipes, many of which contain ingredients familiar today (e.g., a recipe for a pastry crust consists of flour, sugar, salt, butter, and cold water, and made the same way we would now: cutting or rubbing the butter into the flour, adding the small amount of sugar and salt and then the water until a ball of dough forms, before it is rolled out for the pie pan). We're less likely to reach for a recipe for jugged hare these days (though the ingredients are simple, aside from the hare: beef gravy, butter, onion, lemon, cloves, and black and cayenne peppers), but Mrs. Beeton's recipes for omelets, macaroni and cheese, and vanilla custard are ones we could walk into our kitchen and make today (though she advises boiling the macaroni for one and a half hours).

I look forward to continuing Kat's adventures both in sleuthing and cookery, with the next book already in the works. I hope you enjoy this new series!

Best wishes,
Jennifer Ashley

Keep reading for an excerpt of
Jennifer Ashley's next
Below Stairs Mystery . . .

SCANDAL
ABOVE STAIRS

Coming soon from
Berkley Prime Crime!

May 1881

The clatter of crockery on the flagstone floor broke my heart. I knew without turning that it was my platter of whole roast pig, the crowning glory of the vast meal I'd created for the supper party upstairs.

A less capable cook would have sunk down into wailing, or perhaps run out through the scullery and shrieking into the night. I had a better head on my shoulders than that, though I was not quite thirty years old. I snapped at the footmen who were scampering after the clove-studded onions rolling about the floor and the screaming scullery maid who'd been splashed with the juices in which the pig had been roasting.

"Leave it," I said curtly to the footmen. "I'll send up the fowl, and they'll have mutton to follow. Elsie, cease your shrieking and scrub those parsnips for me. A dice of them will have to do, but I must be quick."

I should be mortified to serve a joint of mutton with a scattering of parsnips at Lady Cynthia's aunt's supper party in the Mayfair house in which we lived. But I was too worn down from the work that had gone into this night, too exasperated by the incompetence of the staff to worry at the moment. If I got the sack—well, I needed a rest.

But first to finish this meal. I must pull myself together and get on with it. There was no use crying over spilled . . . pork.

My task was made more difficult by the fact that my kitchen assistant, Mary, whom I'd painstakingly trained all spring, had left a few days before to get married, if you please. I'd tried to tell the silly girl that looking after a husband was far more difficult than being in service. Husbands didn't pay wages, for one thing, and you never got any days out. Asking for extra pin money or an hour to oneself could send a husband into a towering rage and earn a wife a trip to the doctor, both to have her bruises seen to and so the doctor could assess whether there was something wrong with the woman's mind. A true wife was a sacrificing angel who asked nothing for herself.

I had taken time to explain this to Mary, but nothing had penetrated the haze of love into which she'd lapsed. Her young man seemed personable enough to me, at least upon first assessment. Some married couples rubbed along quite well, I'd heard, which definitely had not been the case for me.

I hadn't exactly given Mary my blessing, but I hadn't hindered her from going either. I was not as heartless as I made myself out to be. Lady Cynthia, at my behest, gave Mary a parting gift of a few guineas—or at least, Cynthia borrowed the sum from her uncle to give, as she hadn't a penny to her name.

However generous I'd been to Mary, her going left me

shorthanded. The agency had not yet sent a satisfactory replacement, and the other maids in the house had too many chores of their own to be of much help to me. We still had no housekeeper, as the last one, Mrs. Bowen, had retired in March after a bereavement.

Therefore, the butler, Mr. Davis, and I struggled to do the housekeeping duties as well as our own. So, of course, Mary chose this very time to waltz away and leave us.

None of the potential housekeepers Lady Cynthia's aunt had interviewed had taken the post, so many now that I feared the agencies would stop sending them altogether.

But I could not worry about that at present. At *this* moment, I had to save the feast.

I at last convinced the footmen to cease trying to put the roast-blackened pig back onto the platter, and to run up to the dining room to receive the two capons laden with carrots and greens the maids had lifted into the dumbwaiter. The maids cranked the lift upward while I got on with chopping the parsnips Elsie had scrubbed and thrusting them into already boiling water. A quarter of an hour in and they'd be soft enough to brown with onions and carrots and adorn the mutton. A sauce of mint and lemon would accompany it, and then the meal would finish with puddings.

Those at least I'd made well in advance, and they already waited upstairs on a sideboard—a raspberry tart with chocolate film on its crust, a lemon and blueberry custard, ices in bright fruit flavors, a platter of fine cheeses, a chocolate gâteau piled with cream, and a syllabub. Syllabub was a rather old-fashioned dish, but as it was full of sherry and brandy, I could not wonder that ladies and gentlemen of London still enjoyed it.

I was halfway through preparing the mutton, perspiration

dripping from my face and soaking my collar, when Mr. Davis himself appeared in the kitchen doorway.

Mr. Davis had been butler to Lady Cynthia's brother-in-law, Lord Rankin, for years, and could be haughty as you please above stairs. Below stairs, he dropped his toffy-nosed accent, sat about in his shirtsleeves, and gossiped like an old biddy, reading interesting bits out of his newspapers to me. This evening he was in his full butler's kit, his eyes wide with consternation, the hairpiece he wore to cover his thinning hair on top askew.

"*Mrs. Holloway.*" His horrified gaze took in the skinless pig on the floor in a spreading puddle of spiced sauce, and the two maids at the table chopping vegetables as though their lives depended upon it. One was the upstairs maid, Sara, whom I'd laid my hands on and dragged in to help when she'd been unfortunate enough to come down in search of something to eat.

"What the devil has happened?" he demanded. "I announced the pièce de résistance to Lord and Lady Fitzhugh and Lady Cynthia and all their guests—which include His Grace of Guildford and the Bishop of Dorset, I might add— and I uncover two chickens. The same as their Saturday lunch at home."

I did not bother to look up after one hasty and irritated glance at him. "It is perfectly obvious what happened. Your footmen are clumsy fools. And I'll thank you *not* to compare my *blanquettes de poulet à l'estragon* to a Saturday lunch. They will find them tender and declare the fowl the best they've had in years. Now, unless you wish to don an apron and peel carrots, you may leave my kitchen." When Davis only stood in the middle of the floor, his mouth open, I took up the paring knife that lay next to me. "At once, Mr. Davis."

I'd only intended to hand him the knife and tell him to get on with the carrots if he continued to stare at me, but Mr. Davis eyed the blade, closed his mouth, and scuttled away, nearly tripping over the mountain of pig in his haste.

How we finished the meal, I had no notion. Somehow the two maids and I had the vegetables peeled, chopped, sautéed, and seasoned, the mutton sauced and presented quite prettily, and everything hauled upstairs via the dumb-waiter.

The upstairs maid, Sara, who had at first resented mightily that I'd recruited her for kitchen duty, beamed as the last of the food went up, and impulsively hugged the scullery maid. Sara looked as though she wished to embrace *me*, but of course, I could not allow such a thing. I gave her shoulder a pat instead.

"I'll never doubt you again, Mrs. Holloway," Sara said. "You worked a miracle. Like a general, you are."

I abandoned the kitchen, letting the footmen clean up the remains of the roasted pig—which I knew they'd devour or rush it home to their families. If I wasn't in the room to see it go, I couldn't stop them, could I?

I had eaten little tonight but I crossed the passage to sink down in a chair in the servants' hall, thoroughly tired of food. I slumped back in my chair a moment until my shaking ceased, and then I drew my notebook from my apron pocket and began to jot my thoughts on the meal.

I did this most nights, especially after I'd prepared a large repast. The notes were for my own guidance or perhaps would be used to train my assistant, if I ever found another one.

Sara brought me a cup of tea, for which I thanked her warmly. She looked upon me with admiration—at last, after three months of employment in this house in Mount Street, she had found respect for me. Oh, she'd respected my firm-voiced orders, but she'd not really understood what it was I did. Sara put on airs because Lady Cynthia was training her to be a lady's maid, but perhaps tonight had cured her of some of her haughtiness.

I wrote in relative peace for a time—what had turned out well in the meal, and what needed more polish. I did my best to ignore the noises across the hall—I heard more broken dishes and made a note to ask for funds to replace them.

Mr. Davis found me there an hour later. I'd long ceased to write, my pen idle on the paper, my thoughts far from the meal and the noises around me.

Last week, on my day out, I'd gone to a lane near St. Paul's Churchyard to spend the time with my daughter. She'd grown an inch since I'd taken this post, I was certain of it. She was ten years old and becoming more of a young lady every time I saw her. One day, I vowed, I'd take what I'd saved of my wages, and Grace and I would live in a house together, taking care of each other.

My daughter and I always made a special outing when I visited her, and that day we'd joined the queues to look at the exhibits in the British Museum. While we'd stood waiting to enter the building, I'd sworn I'd seen the face of a man I knew. His name was Daniel McAdam, and I'd come to look upon him as a friend—a very close friend.

Of late, I had been revising that opinion. I'd seen much of him in the early spring, and then nothing at all in the last two months. I'd decided, as I'd lectured Mary about marriage, that I'd not make a fool of myself over a man—ever again. I'd put Daniel straight out of my head.

When I'd glimpsed a man in a suit, however, his dark hair barely tamed under a black bowler hat, every resolve fled. I'd found myself stepping out of the queue, craning to see him, nearly turning away to follow the man, blast it.

Only Grace's puzzled query—"Where are you going, Mum?"—had brought me to my senses.

Mr. Davis cleared his throat, and I jumped, opening my eyes. I seemed to have dozed off.

"Lady Cynthia wishes to see you," Mr. Davis announced, looking a bit too smug about that. "You're for it now, Mrs. H."

I gave him a prim stare. "I am quite busy, Mr. Davis. I must prepare for tomorrow."

A cook's work was never done. While the rest of the household sat back and patted their full stomachs, I would be in my kitchen starting dough for tomorrow's bread, making lists of ingredients I'd need for the next day's meals, and making sure the scullery maid had finished the washing up.

Mr. Davis's brows climbed. He'd shed his coat, and damp patches adorned his shirtsleeves beneath his arms. "You expect me to go upstairs and tell her ladyship you're too busy to speak to her?"

"She will understand," I said. I liked Lady Cynthia, for all her eccentricities, but at the moment, I did not wish to have a conversation with anyone at all.

Mr. Davis eyed me closely as though expecting me to change my mind, but I only turned a page of my notebook and pointedly took up my pen.

I heard Mr. Davis heave a great sigh, and then his footsteps receded. He stopped in his pantry—probably to fetch his coat—

then I heard him start up the stairs. He was gone, and blissful quiet descended.

The peace was shattered not long later by heels clicking sharply on the slate floor and an impatient rustle of taffeta. A breeze burst over me as a lady halted next to me and leaned her fists on my table in a very unladylike manner.

I jumped to my feet. The lady straightened up as I did so, a frown slanting her blond brows, her light blue eyes bearing agitation.

The lady had a fine-boned face and very fair hair, lovely if one enjoys the pale-skinned, aristocratic version of beauty. Her high-necked and long-sleeved gown was deep gray with black soutache braid for trim—she wore mourning for her sister, recently deceased.

I had not seen much of Lady Cynthia since Lord Rankin had retreated to his country estate to console himself, but he'd allowed Lady Cynthia to remain in his London house, as she had nowhere else to go. Her parents, the Earl and Countess of Clifford, lived in impoverished isolation in Hertfordshire, and Cynthia had no desire to return to them.

A lady could not live alone without scandal, however, so Cynthia's aunt and uncle—the respectable Mr. Neville Bywater, younger brother to Cynthia's mother, and his wife, Isobel, had moved into Lord Rankin's house to look after her. Her aunt was content to put her feet up here and enjoy the luxurious house in Mount Street while her husband went off to work in the City.

"It is important, Mrs. H." Lady Cynthia's anxiousness was clear. "Clementina's out of her head with worry."

I had no idea who Clementina was—I assumed one of Lady Cynthia's vast acquaintance.

I made a very contrite curtsy. "I beg your pardon, my lady. What has happened?"

"She was here tonight, very upset." Cynthia waved impatiently at the chairs. "Oh, do let us sit down. Davis, bring me tea to steady my nerves, there's a good chap."

Davis stuck his nose in the air at being ordered about like a footman, said a haughty, "Yes, my lady," and glided into the kitchen to shout to a maid to make a pot of tea and be quick about it.

"Clemmie's married to a baronet," Cynthia went on as soon as she and I sat down. "He is appallingly rich and has priceless artwork hanging on his walls. That is, he *did*—that artwork has started to go missing, whole pictures gone. Sir Evan Bloody Godfrey is blaming Clemmie."

I blinked as Sara scurried in with tea on a tray and set it carefully on the table. She curtsied, waited for any further instruction from Cynthia, then faded away when Cynthia dismissed her.

I reached for the teapot and poured out a steaming cup of fragrant tea for Lady Cynthia, then topped up my empty teacup. The scent of oolong came to me, my favorite. "Why should the baronet blame his wife?" I asked. "It seems a bizarre assumption to make."

"Because Clemmie is always up to her ears in debt. She plays cards—badly—and wagers too much. And she likes a flutter on the horses. As a result, creditors visit her husband. Before this, he's paid up like a lamb, but a few weeks ago said enough was enough. He forbade Clemmie to wager ever again, but of course, Clemmie couldn't help herself."

"Her husband believes she sold the paintings to pay the debts," I finished.

"Exactly, Mrs. H. But Clemmie swears it isn't true. She says she has no idea who she'd sell the paintings to, or how to go about finding a buyer, and I believe her. Clemmie is an innocent soul." Cynthia sighed, running her finger around the rim of her teacup. "She says there's been no sign of a break-in or burglary. The paintings were simply there in the evening, gone the next morning."

Interesting. The problem perked my exhausted brain. However, I did not allow myself to speculate too deeply. Simple explanations are usually the wisest ones—a person can complicate a straightforward situation with unnecessary dramatics, and end up in a complete mess.

"Perhaps an enterprising butler is having the paintings cleaned," I suggested. "I understand old paintings can acquire quite a bit of grime, especially in London."

Cynthia waved her long-fingered hand. "I thought of that, but Clemmie swears she's questioned the staff and none have touched them. They rather dote on her, so I'm sure they would tell if they knew anything."

"Hm." Either one of the servants was lying quite fervently, or someone was managing to creep into the baronet's house in the middle of the night and silently rob it. I tried to picture a man walking in, taking a painting from the wall, and walking out again with it under his arm, frame and all. No, he'd never manage such a thing. Houses in London had servants all over them at all hours of the day and night.

"You are intrigued," Cynthia said in triumph. "I see the sparkle in your eyes."

"I admit, it is odd," I answered with caution. Lady Cynthia was apt to throw herself into things rather recklessly. "Though I am certain there will be a clear explanation."

"Clemmie would be happy with *any* explanation. The silly cow is devastated her husband doesn't believe her, terrified he'll cut her off without a shilling. She wants to find the culprit and present him to the baronet on a platter."

"If she finds the culprit, she should summon the police," I said sternly. "Does she mean to catch the burglar herself, tie him up, and wait for her husband to come home?"

Cynthia snorted with laughter. "Sir Evan is a high-handed, dried-up stick, but I don't want him putting it about that Clemmie is stealing from him. The only reason he doesn't have her up before a magistrate is that he'd die of shame." Cynthia set down her teacup with a clatter and leaned to me. "Say you'll help, Mrs. H. I could bribe you with extra wages, but Rankin holds the purse strings and my aunt and uncle are parsimonious." She brightened. "But Clemmie would reward you. The baronet might embrace you and give you a heady remuneration if you found his precious paintings. He is oozing with wealth."

I was comfortable with my salary, as Lord Rankin, Cynthia's brother-in-law, paid what was fair for a cook of my abilities and experience. The thought of extra was always welcome—something to put by for my daughter—but that was not why I nodded in agreement. The puzzle did make me curious. Besides, looking for missing paintings seemed far less dangerous than hunting murderers or chasing Fenians.

Sometimes I can be a foolishly confident woman.

Cynthia fixed our date to meet with Clementina the day after tomorrow. Not *tomorrow*, I said firmly, as it was Thursday, my day out. No one, not even a wealthy baron with missing paintings—not the Queen herself—would sway me from taking my day.

Cynthia looked annoyed she'd have to wait, but she knew I was immovable. We'd go Friday after breakfast, she agreed, then she left me. She was going out, she said, giving me a dark look.

I smothered a sigh. She meant she would be donning gentleman's attire and meeting her lady friends who enjoyed dressing thus. They'd lark about and try to gain admission to gentlemen's clubs undetected. I worried when Cynthia did this, certain that one night her uncle would have to retrieve her from some filthy jail.

But she would not be dissuaded—I had tried to reason with her before. The look also meant I should see that the scullery door was kept unlocked for her and that her activities remained a secret from her aunt and uncle. They were amiable people but uncomfortable with Cynthia's wild streak.

Cynthia's mother and father—especially her father—had been wild in their day as well. Still were, from all accounts, though Cynthia's mother had become a near recluse after Cynthia's brother had shot himself years ago.

Mr. Bywater, Cynthia's uncle, seemed to have inherited everything staid in the family. He believed Cynthia should find a husband who would settle her down—his idea was that having a child or two would calm her even more. Mr. Bywater enjoyed inviting eligible young men to the house, hoping Cynthia would fall madly in love with one of them and accept his inevitable proposal.

Hence the supper party tonight, and Cynthia's rebellion of the moment.

I promised to aid in her deception, as usual, and we parted ways.

* * *

Cynthia returned safely to the house in the wee hours and crept off to bed. Or so Sara assured me in the morning. I fixed a full breakfast for the household, then put aside enough food for a luncheon for the staff and family. I would be back in time to make supper.

As I prepared the repast I'd leave behind, Mr. Davis, as usual, found the time to sit in his shirtsleeves at my table and read things out of the newspaper.

Today it was the French foray into the lands of the Bey of Tunis, because tribesmen there had been crossing into Algeria, a French colony, and pillaging as they saw fit. He was reading along through the details when on a sudden, he paused and looked up.

"By the bye, I saw that chap who worked here a few months ago—what was his name? Daniel—that was it. Daniel McAdam. In a pawnbrokers on the Strand, of all places. Looking as though he's running the place."

Photo by Silvio Portrait Design

Jennifer Ashley is the *New York Times* and *USA Today* bestselling author of the Below Stairs Mysteries; the Shifters Unbound paranormal romances, including *Red Wolf* and *Guardian's Mate*; and the Mackenzies historical romances, including *The Madness of Lord Ian Mackenzie* and *The Stolen Mackenzie Bride*. Winner of a Romance Writers of America RITA Award, she also writes as *USA Today* bestselling mystery author Ashley Gardner. She lives in the Southwest with her husband and cats, and spends most of her time in the wonderful worlds of her stories.

Find out more about the Below Stairs Mysteries at katholloway.com, and visit Jennifer on facebook.com/jenniferashleyallyson jamesashleygardner and twitter.com/JennAllyson.